The Woman at The Well

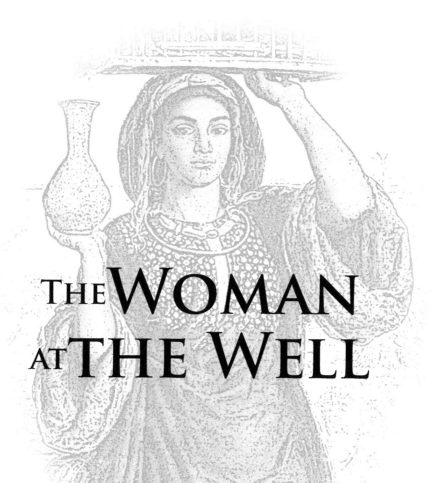

The WOMAN at THE WELL

Ann Chamberlin

Epigraph books
Rhinebeck, NY

The Woman at the Well Copyright © 2011 by Ann Chamberlin.

All rights reserved. No part of this book may be used or reproduced in any manner without written permission from the author except in critical articles and reviews. Contact the publisher for information.

Printed in the United States of America.
Book and cover design by Joe Tantillo.

Epigraph Books
22 East Market Street, Suite 304
Rhinebeck, New York 12572
www.epigraphPS.com
USA 845-876-4861

Hardcover: ISBN 978-1-9369400-9-7
Softcover: ISBN 978-1-9369401-0-3

Library of Congress Control Number: 2011932256

For LC
remembering Palmyra
in the PT Cruiser
and the ruins of Macedon

List of Characters

Main Characters in Order of Appearance *Note:* Asterisk indicates a real historical character.

Rayah	Twelve-year-old girl who lives in the house of the turpentine sellers in Tadmor (Palmyra), Syria
Abd Allah	Eunuch scribe employed by Khalid ibn al-Walid to write his dictated memoirs in Homs, Syria, near the end of Khalid's life
Sitt Umm Ali	Rayah's neighbor and instructor in Quranic studies
Adilah	Rayah's favorite "Aunt" in the family of turpentine sellers
Sitt Sameh*	Rayah's mother, a strange woman of the desert who lives in refuge in the house of the turpentine sellers
Khalid ibn al-Walid (or al-Wahid) abu Sulayman*	Called "The Conqueror," the Prophet Muhammad's* most famous general, conqueror of both Iraq and Syria. A member of the Quraysh tribe, he was famous for never having lost a battle, whether fighting for the Prophet or against him.
Bint Zura	Sitt Sameh's mother and Rayah's grandmother, actually named Amat al-Uzza.
Omar ibn al-Khuttab*	Second khalifah (successor) to the Prophet Muhammad* and a distant cousin to Khalid.
Zura	Bint Zura's father, a member of the Taghlib tribe converted to Christianity and husband to Umm Taghlib
Umm Taghlib	Bint Zura's mother, a kahinah (witch or priestess) of Taghlibi origin who found refuge among the Tamim. She is Sitt Sameh's grandmother and Rayah's great-grandmother.
Umm Mutammim	Khalid's milk mother, birth mother to his two milk brothers, Mutammim and Malik of the Tamimi tribe.
Mutammim ibn Nuwaira*	The elder of Khalid's milk brothers, a famous poet who was blinded in childhood.
Malik ibn Nuwaira*	The younger of Khalid's milk brothers, sharif (leader) of the Banu Tamim.
al-Harith ibn Suwaid*	A herdsman working for Mutammim and Malik ibn Nuwaira, and a companion of Khalid in childhood and youth.

Ghusoon	A young woman who is Rayah's friend, driven to madness by being forced to marry against her will.
Jaffar	A young man of Tadmor, nephew of Sitt Umm Ali.
Abu Ragheb	Bint Zura's uncle, her father's brother of the Taghlibi tribe.
az-Zuharah	The white camel, named for the evening star, a Goddess.
Hanzala ibn Thalaba*	Sharif of the Idjl clan of the Banu Bakr ibn Wa'il, who led the Arabs at the battle of Dhu Qar. For this story Hanzala's character is melded with that of Hani ibn Qabisa*, to whom King an-Numan* left his armor and women in trust before the battle.
Antar ibn Shaddad*	The chivalrous hero of a famous Arabic epic poem, he was the son of an African slave and her Arab tribal master.

Terms Used in Arabic Names

Abd (feminine, Amat)	"Servant, slave," used in pre-Islamic times in front of the names of any divinity to which a child might be dedicated; used in Islam in front of any of the ninety-nine names of God as popular given names.
Abu	"Father of"
Al	"The"; in front of certain consonants, the *l* changes to that consonant (as in az-Zuharah)
Ammi	"My auntie," my mother's sister, a term of respect and endearment for older women
Baba	Arabic for Papa
Banu	"Sons of," used to indicate desert tribes by reference to their distant ancestor
Bint	"Daughter of"
Ibn	"Son of," used to form patronymic last names to this day. Actually pronounced "Bin" when in the middle of a name, the spelling has been standardized here to avoid confusion.
Umm	"Mother of"
Ummi	"My mother"

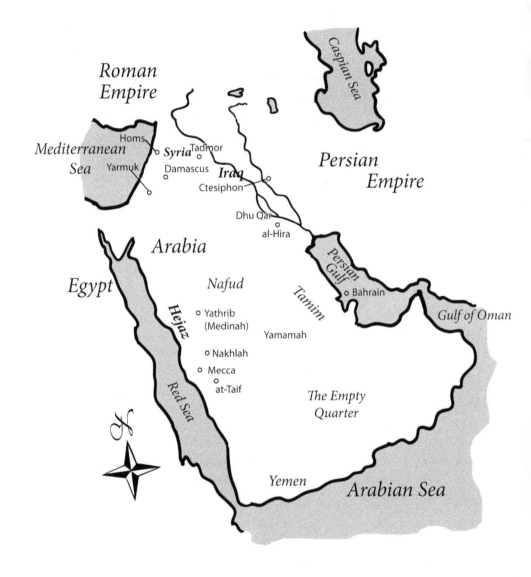

THE MIDDLE EAST IN THE TIME OF MUHAMMAD

AUTHOR'S NOTE

Can I be assured that my faults will not devolve upon the scores of teachers, family members, friends, librarians, and publishing people who have allowed my consuming passion to become theirs, if only for an hour? Hoping this is the case, and that my need to acknowledge them outweighs other considerations, here is a list of the most outstanding: Linda Cook, Jeri Smith, Francesca Koomen, all the women of the Wasatch Mountain Fiction Writers—some of whom had to struggle with this for a thousand pages before it began to grow on them; Alexis Warlock, Teddi Kachi, Solmaz Kamuran, Karen Porcher, Curt Setzer, Ernö Steinmetz, Ralph and Ute Chamberlin, my mother, my sons; Drs. Leonard Chiarelli, Laurence Loeb, and Peter von Sievers; Marian Florence, Rod Daynes, Giles Florence, John Keahey, Connie Disney, and members of Xenobia writers' group. Natalia Aponte, Linn Prentis, Christine Cohen, Vaughne Hansen, Virginia Kidd of blessed memory. Paul Cohen, Maura Shaw, Joe Tantillo. All of the wonderful people I met in Syria. And of course, as always, the woman whose face veiled behind coins and shells in the Sinai desert first set me on this journey.

Those people I may have overlooked know who they are and know that I couldn't have done it without them. Thanks to one and all.

This is a historical novel. I have invented things, lots of things, the biggest one being Khalid's relationship to the woman called Sitt Sameh in this volume. No, I know of no tradition that says he was her father. But he did exist, fighting both for and against Muhammad at the dawn of Islam in the seventh century AD. And so, by God, did she.

On the other hand, I did do my best to accurately research. This novel was the product of a burning desire to answer, for myself, "What were the people in the time of the Prophet, blessed be he, thinking, doing, feeling?" So many things, even most things, are supported by one hadith, tradition, or another. This is not to say that the traditions don't contradict themselves; they do. This is not even to say I actually believe that the tradition I have chosen to follow is, in every case, the most accurate one. It was the one that best suited the story.

One final note: The land between the Tigris and Euphrates has always been called "Iraq" in the Arabic language since before Muhammad's time. It means "The fertile or deep-rooted land." This is not an anachronism.

1

> "Call upon your God to bring forth fountains of living waters, like unto the gardens of Syria."
> —an appeal of the Arabs to the Prophet Muhammad, peace be upon him

Tadmor (Palmyra), Syria, in the twenty-second year of the Hijra, 643 of the Christian era

Shrill shouts came from the inner courtyard behind Rayah. With a sigh, the twelve-year-old orphan daughter of the house of the turpentine sellers turned back under the silver hand with the blue eye in its center that protected the door to her harem. She would not be going out to study the Holy Quran this day either; with that stranger still sitting there, she couldn't even get past the gate.

In the heat of the summer afternoon, the young wives and cousins were taking basins of water from the fountain. Sloshing them across the mosaic floor cooled it down to make napping easier. Today, one misplaced slosh and the chore had become a wild water fight. The chickens had fled to the alcove for shelter, and the cock crowed with excitement.

Cousin Demiella, her damp skirts clinging to her big-boned limbs, held the spigot against all comers. But small, quick Auntie Adilah was organizing the younger ones for a final assault. With a trilling warcry of her own, Rayah ran in, hoping to forget both the mysterious stranger blocking the gate and her Quranic studies as she sided with the underdogs. She and little Bushra took the left flank, coming up from behind, around the jasmine vine, with damp rags to flip as weapons.

They waited in a cloud of jasmine fragrance until Demiella had spent her basin on those coming from the right, then charged. But Demiella had armed herself with two basins, one filling while she swung the other, and she was ready for them with deadly aim. The spring-cold wave stole Rayah's breath. In front of her, Bushra gave a high-pitched shriek choked with giggles and tried to turn away.

Rayah watched what happened next with the odd torpor of a hawk lifting from its perch. Bushra's little bare foot, turning, reaching for purchase, found only a pool of water. Rayah stretched out an arm to catch her cousin but slowly, too slowly. The little girl slipped, hung airbound, then landed hard. Her head hit first, and Rayah heard a sound like an overripe melon dropping to the floor.

For one dreadful moment, everyone in the courtyard was as limp as the little victim, unable to move, their shrieks lingering over them like the souls of unplaced jinn. Then, horror exploded in half a dozen different, desperate acts all around the little girl, who remained unnaturally white and still. Rayah's act was to kneel beside her cousin. She felt for life in the neck and couldn't find it. The puddle of water was already growing pink, Bushra's small face even paler in contrast.

Demiella jumped down from the fountain's coping and came to kneel, too. "She's dead." Her voice was thin with hopeless guilt.

For her part, when she found the repeated call of Bushra's name had no effect, Rayah began a chant of "Ya Latif, ya Latif, O Sensitive One," over and over. This was one of the Ninety-Nine Names of God that Sitt Umm Ali had taught her students, the Name best to call on in times of hopelessness.

Auntie Adilah had run for Bushra's mother and the other older women, resting in the shade of their arbor, but they had already heard the courtyard's change of sound, the loud silence of death.

Bushra's mother set up an inhuman wail as she flew across the court, threatening to slip as her daughter had done. Grownups reached for Rayah, to pull her out of the way. But she had her hand beneath the little girl's head where, under the fine, dark hair, she felt the spot soft as a damp loofah.

"Ya Latif, ya Latif," she sobbed and prepared to move away when she felt the strangest sensation under her fingers. Actually, it came through her fingers, centered upon the holy Name of God. Energy twitched, and the pieces of skull, like bits of broken eggshell beneath the skin, began to shift back into place.

Glued to her little cousin with blood, Rayah didn't dare remove her hand, even though she trembled from head to foot. Her teeth chattered, and she had to repeat the prayer with her jaw clenched. The water dripping from her hair and clothes might have been thrown on her in mid-winter. Her eyes, her eyes were the worst. She squeezed them closed against needles of pain.

The pieces of skull swam, then locked, fused together like hot wax, smoothed. The tingling energy, the miracle, stopped.

What was happening? Rayah gasped with fear. What unearthly power was this? It couldn't be her doing—she just a child herself. She tried to pull away.

And Bushra moved with a choking whimper.

"Ah God, ah God, she's alive," the child's mother cried and caught the little body up in her arms to carry her to the best cushions under the arbor.

"Sitt Sameh will know what to do, God willing. Has somebody gone for Sitt Sameh?" Demiella asked, trying to brush away tears with a corner of her already damp sleeve.

But Sitt Sameh didn't need to be fetched. She must have heard the silence of death, too, and stood on the stairs that ran down into the courtyard from the roof and her aerie. Her brow bunched around the blue-black tattoos of a desert tribe etched in the skin there, the ring in her nose held still. She stood just at the shadowy bend, Rayah noticed, where the cousins always said dark jinn hid.

Rayah looked away, but not before she felt that uncomfortable cool blue gaze—seeming blind and yet all-seeing both at once. The eyes rested, not where little Bushra had been borne, but on Rayah herself.

2

> In the Name of God, the Merciful, the Compassionate.
> Praise belongs to God, the Lord of all Being,
> the All-Merciful, the All-Compassionate,
>   the Lord of the Day of Doom.
> You only do we serve; to You alone do we pray for succor.
>   Guide us in the straight path,
> the path of those whom You have blessed,
> not those against whom You are wrathful,
>   nor of those who are astray.
>   —First Surah of the Holy Quran

The strange man had been waiting at the gate for three days. That's where Rayah had been, before the shouts of play had drawn her back to the inner courtyard. Tiptoeing down one sharp bend and twisting her head around the next, she had just been able to glimpse him.

She had had to leave the protection of the silver hand with the blue eye that hung above the harem. Now, in spite of these signs, evil had come in. Little Bushra lay—by the mercy of God—not quite dead under the arbor in the inner courtyard. Beside the jasmine vine, out of the grownups' way, Rayah looked down at her own hand. There were no red marks, nothing she could see. But the unearthly fire still burned as it had beneath her little cousin's skull.

Had the evil come back into the harem with her? To destroy the happy glee of her family? But she had gone to look at the stranger because he was keeping her from going to read the Quran. That desire was good, was it not?

A left hand formed the silver talisman over the door, held up against sinister magic that might seek to invade, and in its center was an eye of lapis lazuli. Sitt Umm Ali, bright red hair bent over the Holy Quran she taught, gave the symbol the name of Fatima, the daughter of the Prophet—blessings on him and on her. Sitt Umm Ali loved to describe how the venerable lady had been stirring halwah when her husband brought home a second wife. In her distress, Fatima had dropped the spoon and stirred with her hand instead, never mindful of the burn.

"May God grant you girls similar patience," Sitt Umm Ali told her students. Not, as had been Rayah's first thought, "May God grant you more sense."

"More patience," Rayah repeated to herself, trying to make the lesson sink in.

Sitt Umm Ali was a well-fed woman of older years who hennaed her hair—"As the Prophet did his beard, blessed be he"—and always smelled of that earthy herb.

But Rayah had also heard the hand called after Maryam, mother of the Prophet Isa, peace be upon him. Even, in lower voices, the hand of all the Goddesses—

And the eye, the baleful, black dot within a white circle within a pool of unnatural blue that stared down unblinking upon her— In olden times, a blue-eyed female demon with hair of snakes had stood sentry before such doors. One look into her eyes would turn the invader to stone. Then the day had come when one invader had turned that woman's weapon—a mirror—against her. Or veils had come. Veils or mirrors, one or the other, to tame women's eyes.

These were tales of long ago, of the time of Ignorance. With Islam, by the grace of God, superstition was suppressed. But Rayah could still sense the power in the unnatural emblem, power not quite held at bay.

"In the Name of God, the Compassionate, the Merciful . . ."

Squeezing her eyes shut, Rayah prayed for her little cousin. But all she saw against her closed eyelids was the glimpse she had stolen, out of the harem, down the passageway to the gate.

At the very end of the long, unlit hall echoing with tile, half the great wooden door stood open to the alley for air. The outer gate's bars, a warning made of old Indian spear shafts, striped the light. There the stranger's shadow shifted like the fringe of vine arcing over his head as he sat drinking endless cups of licorice water. Sometimes Rayah could see the wink of an emerald in his left ear.

Even Zabbai the gatekeeper's famous patience strained, no match for the lingering stranger, who divulged nothing but his mission: "To speak with the woman called Sitt Sameh." From time to time Zabbai helped his old bones up off his worn cushion with his staff. He left the stranger and hobbled into the narrow alleyway. With the same staff, he carefully, tenderly, got under the single longest tendril of narrow-leafed hamisa vine. He lifted it over the rough cord running from the turpentine sellers' wall to the one across the way. In the oasis of the house in Tadmor, no scrap of green was wasted, and each received Zabbai's personal attention. Thus he could escape the unnerving presence of the stranger, even if for just a moment.

Had the stranger been a proper man, he wouldn't have had to sit there. He would have taken the door immediately to his right after stepping in from the street. In the majlis, fragrant with terebinth resin clinging to the men's clothes from their work, on the cooler east side of the house, the stranger could have sat in the place of honor. He could have talked with the men of the family, Rayah's grandfather, uncles, and cousins, instead of wasting his time with Zabbai. If he'd been a proper man, he'd have taken "No" for his answer and gone away instead of enduring that in-between place where no one could rest.

If he'd been a proper man, he'd have known better even than to ask to speak to a woman. And as for speaking to Sitt Sameh— No comfort there.

Although at some point desert sand and wind had ravaged the woman's face so it was hard to tell her age, Sitt Sameh was no doubt old enough to be a mother, if not a grandmother. Yet she was neither. In fact, the oldest women in the harem conspired not to mention Sitt Sameh when the men were about, or even to women who weren't well known to them. Rayah read fear in the hunch of shoulders, the tugs at veils. In a household crammed with cousins, brothers, sisters, aunts, and uncles, Sitt Sameh's relationship to anyone in the family was vague at best. Rayah couldn't imagine why anyone would want to speak to the lone female. Sitt Sameh lacked any of the family connections that other women spent all their lives constructing as bastions of their power, reasons strangers might come to consult them.

Two women in Rayah's life took the name of honor Sitt: "Lady." These were Sitt Umm Ali, her teacher, who also had the honor of being called after her eldest son, "Mother of Ali." She even claimed the honor of pronouncing the word in the Arabic manner, "Umm," instead of in the older Syriac dialect, as "Am."

And Sitt Sameh.

Sitt Sameh, however, had no son. Her own name lay open to the world, unprotected by male relatives. That strange accent, the desert tattoos, those wild blue eyes.

The way Rayah felt those eyes on her—

Although the curious Sitt Sameh did live under the turpentine sellers' roof with the rest of the family, she almost never left her own space. Rayah knew that sometimes Sitt Sameh took trusted women into her small half-tent room, bare of furniture, on the third floor. Women with hopelessly sick children. Women who'd misplaced their mother-in-law's favorite bangle and needed a seer's eyes to find it quickly. Women who knew they were losing the love of their husbands, facing a second wife, or—worse—divorce. These were the most pathetic of God's creatures, cast-off women for whom the new, strong revelation of Islam could not spare patience, Rayah thought. Sitt Sameh herself never left her aerie, never ate with the family, never joined in when there was baking or a big feast to prepare. And as for speaking to a man ...

To be sure, for a woman in strict seclusion Sitt Sameh did get a lot of men calling for her. Well, two that Rayah knew of. That was a lot—more than any normal woman could have and keep her honor intact. But Sitt Sameh did have her modesty. Surely this man with the emerald in his ear would have no more luck than the first. Oh, that one must have been here a year ago or so. That older man had fumed and raged, in the majlis and out.

"A man should be able to see his own child!" He'd shouted so it echoed down the hall and into the harem.

Who was his child? Rayah knew the father of everyone in the house. Except, of course, her own, who had died before she was born. And Sitt Sameh's. Sitt Sameh had no real relations.

"And don't you know who I am?" that loud, pushy stranger had raged on. "For the fear of God, I am Khalid the Conqueror of Iraq and Syria for the glory of God and of His Prophet."

"To have claim to the Conqueror's blood would be something," Rayah remembered Auntie Adilah musing at the time, looking sideways up the stairs. "Think of the stream of visitors to the harem every day, if it were as he says."

"It's madness, of course," Cousin Demiella had replied. Then, avoiding the use even of Sitt Sameh's name, she had looked up the empty stairs as well. "*Her* religion is too dubious to own such an exalted relationship to Khalid the Conqueror. By God, she hasn't even made the Confession of Faith."

"Maybe she doesn't say the Shahada because she …"

Then Adilah had seen Rayah listening and smiled, perhaps just a little too broadly. "No one in this harem doesn't know her own father."

"Indeed, everyone can recite fathers' fathers back to the beginning of time." Demiella, too, joined the conspiracy.

Adilah is my aunt. In her mind Rayah recited the story she'd been told to be certain she, too, was included in Demiella's assertion. Adilah's brother who died, whom she misses so terribly, was my father. He brought me here to his sister's harem for safety. Their father is the old man who sits in the place of honor in the majlis, although he sometimes can't remember his own name. His brothers sired the rest of the turpentine workers. After that, my lineage must be the same as the rest of the family.

Why was it that just when a girl got old enough to understand grown-up talk, they began not to let you listen?

Auntie Adilah did not answer Rayah's unspoken question but her own. "The explanation is, of course, that that horribly rough man outside, for all his evoking of God, can't truly be the Conqueror."

"Or if he is, no wonder Khalifah Omar, God guide him and lengthen his days, has removed the man from command," Demiella concluded. "The Faithful must not be misled."

The wild stranger's madness, in any case, had been to no avail. Two prayer times had passed with him threatening to tear the house down stone by stone. Then he'd stormed off, leaving the gate resounding with his slam.

The second man out there now had more patience. This was the third day, and no one among the women had heard more than the whispers of a high voice slipping down the tile in the hall. Rayah didn't doubt, however, that this time, too, Sitt Sameh's "No" would, in the end, meet with the same result.

As long as Zabbai continued to fill the stranger's cup with licorice water, as long as the man wouldn't move, either away from the gate or into the majlis where he belonged, hospitality must reign. That was the problem. Rayah was too old to play with the younger cousins in the alley any more, where she might overhear some scraps of information, and she could not pass the man to go out the front gate.

And although not so very old, not yet twenty, her usual escort Cousin Kefa refused to take her out past the stranger. Kefa meant "Stone"—he had been named for the Prophet Isa's apostle before the family had submitted to Islam. He had not changed his name at conversion as others did, but he was careful of her honor and, stonelike, refused Rayah now. She could have taken the usual women's route, over the roofs, but that seemed an undignified way to approach the Holy Quran. And so, she could not go to Sitt Umm Ali.

Sitt Umm Ali was teaching Rayah the new language of desert Arabic, the language in which God had so recently spoken the most perfect of His revelations, the Holy Quran. Rayah knew no greater pleasure and now, for the stubbornness of one stranger and one peculiar old woman, it was denied her.

And now little Bushra lay so injured.

Rayah prayed under the jasmine vine, facing Mecca, facing south. Hunched and fearful in the house where she'd been born, she waited for news of her little cousin. Waited for what it might mean that her hand had done this. It was too frightening. She didn't want this power of life and death. She was too young. She held her hand with the other as if it pained her and stared at it. Every third or fourth pulse beat, she almost wished she could cut her foreign hand from her.

She'd watched the women streaming in and out of the arbor, carrying hot water, herbs, and clean linen, and she knew enough to stay out of the way. Finally, some of the women left to prepare supper and, with the crowd somewhat thinned, Rayah and the others could look in on her. They saw Bushra sitting up, well propped with pillows, her head swathed in a white turban, sipping a cool fruit drink.

Rayah rubbed the fingers of her right hand, seeing if she could reinvigorate the strange energy she had felt tingling in the fingertips. Seeing if she could erase the memory. She could do neither.

"I think she's going to be all right, thanks be to God," Auntie Adilah told Rayah and the other waiting youngsters. What would have been happy cheers subsided as she added, "But Sitt Sameh says Bushra must stay quiet for at least two days, so you children must help her by being just like little mice. Promise?"

Rayah and her cousins nodded solemnly.

On Auntie Adilah's heels, Sitt Sameh stepped out of the arbor and into the slanting light of evening. She stretched her back and gave a sigh. Rayah looked away, but knew the moment the blue eyes found her. Instead of climbing her stairs, the older woman stepped down the two into the courtyard and around the fountain. Rayah hunched further as the desert-bare feet came toward her. One set of Sitt Sameh's toes wiped back and forth across the very spot where Bushra had slipped. The pink puddle had almost completely dried in the passing time, but still the boney foot worked at it.

The floor was made of thousands of little bits of embedded stone. They'd been whitewashed and plastered over in the interest of Muslim piety and avoidance of images. But once upon a time, the different-colored stones had made a brilliant mosaic. Rayah had not seen the pattern in her lifetime, of course, but her family had lived in the same house for twenty-five generations, and memories lingered on the tongues of the oldest.

And sometimes, between plaster jobs, shadows of the floor's former glory appeared. The spot where everyone stepped coming down the stairs faded first. A bird in flight lay captured there. The luxurious curve of a woman's naked buttock wrapped around the base of the fountain. And here, where Sitt Sameh wiped her foot, the tendrils of some sweet vine twined, such as might very well trip up the unwary had it been real.

"Let me mop that up, Sitt," Auntie Adilah said, coming with a cloth. She felt guilty for her childish part in the mishap. "We don't want anyone else slipping."

Sitt Sameh looked up from the floor then, straight into Rayah's eyes. She knew, the girl realized, what had happened here better than Rayah did herself.

"Is that stranger still at the door?" Sitt Sameh asked, never taking the iron blue clamp of those eyes from Rayah.

"He was, last time I checked," Auntie Adilah replied. "He has the patience of a stone. Don't worry, Sitt, we'll see him fed. And encourage him to move on."

"I'd like this one to take the meal to him." Although pointing could cause the evil eye and so Sitt Sameh did not do it, Rayah still felt as if she'd been cursed. "Bring him up to me when he is done, child. I will see him now. Tell him to bring his scrolls and baggage as well."

"Are you certain, Sitt?" Auntie Adilah pursued. "A man? In your room? And Rayah. Why, she's almost grown, almost marriageable. Shouldn't we send someone younger? Or better, a boy?"

"Forget your scruples," Sitt Sameh said as she turned back to the stairs. "The man's a eunuch." She said this even though Rayah was quite certain Sitt Sameh herself had never turned that sharp blue gaze of hers down the hall to the gate and the man waiting there.

3

> **In the Name of God, the Compassionate, the Merciful.**
> **Recite in the Name of the Lord Who created—**
> **Created man from Clots of Blood—**
> **Recite! For your Lord is the Most Beneficent,**
> **Who taught the use of the pen;**
> **Taught man that which he knows not.**
>   **—The Holy Quran, Surah 96:15**

Dictated in the garden of Khalid ibn al-Walīd Abu Sulayman the Conqueror in Homs, Syria, one year earlier

T*oday by the well I, Khalid ibn al-Walīd abu Sulayman, saw a woman with her child. She set my mind to remembering . . .*

"A woman, master?"

My scribe twirls his writing reed between his fingers. Would scratching that word "woman" set his parchment on fire?

Not a bad use for parchment, starting fires.

The vanity of an emerald winks in his left ear. His unnatural beardlessness makes a whole man such as myself sick. I narrow my eyes. He blanches before the blade of my stare.

Do I tell him I won't hurt him? No, I won't surrender that scrap. Confess what I am really thinking? I am thinking I don't belong here. He does, but I—I have no place in this garden, in Homs, in Syria.

But who has more right than you, master? I can almost hear him say in that unnerving voice of his. That voice like drawing fingernails over slate.

Indeed. Who has more right to Homs than the Conqueror of Homs? Who has more right than the Sword of God?

But no right to a daughter.

Shame, I can almost hear my scribe's squeaky boy's voice say. I say it for him. "Shame that I do not begin with the first time I saw the Prophet."

"Blessed be he." The scribe rocks against his parchment, wrinkling it in his eagerness. "All historians from this day forward must do so."

"Certainly I remember the time my father pointed Muhammad out to me. He said something to this effect—"

I see the pen poised. I repeat my father's words.

"Muhammad the son of the late Abd Allah of the clan of the sons of Hashim."

The pen begins to scratch.

"Muhammad's orphanhood one can forgive him. That was divine Hubal's will."

I close my eyes. I remember ambushes at oases. I timed them for best effect—just as the quarry let their skins into the well. Just as they began to relax—

For a daughter, however, such timing does not work.

I am driven to my father's words once more.

"But his dreaminess! That Muhammad married for love, you know, a woman twice his age who is too old, even, to give him anything but daughters and stillborn sons. And for mad devotion, he will take no second. He will leave the world as if he'd never passed through it at all."

The pen stops scratching. I keep my eyes closed but don't stop speaking. I hear my father's voice in my own.

"'True, Khadijah is wealthy, left so by her father and two previous husbands.'" I hear no pen, still I repeat. "'She needed someone to manage the wealth for her and to run her trade caravans—someone other than her thief of a cousin. But she goes and marries for love! He is a dreamer, that Muhammad, and she's little better.'"

I open my eyes, prod the fellow with their keen edge. "No, friend, I have not forgotten this lesson in proper young Arab behavior by my father's pointing out a bad example. Nor have I forgotten when Muhammad began to preach, nor when I was converted, nor any of the other great standing stones that mark the desert of my life in his shadow."

Only today, so near the end of that life, I think about the shifting sands beneath the stones instead—

The boy doesn't flinch. At least, not from me. Has he heard my thoughts? "The khalifah—" he says.

"Ah, you would begin with Abu Bakr, that father of a camel?" I am still in my fury. "Abu Bakr, khalifah, successor of the Prophet, blessed be he." I let the titles roll over my tongue like a sandstorm. What good is a man's fury against a sandstorm? "Abu Bakr made it a project of his to collect all the words Muhammad ever spoke under inspiration. This collection, the Holy Quran, was first taken down on scraps of wood or bone, whatever was handy. And Abu Bakr wanted to have it written up in an orderly fashion so that none of the Faithful might remain ignorant."

The scribe nods. The gem in his ear wags eagerly.

I sigh and drop my voice. "And so contentions might cease. The bloody battle of Yamamah, where so many Companions fell—I, Khalid ibn al-Walīd, the Sword of God, was leader of the Muslims there; I refused to be defeated—"

The fellow has crossed out all he's done so far. He begins again, scribbling furiously.

The Battle of Yamamah, where I lost forever the right to a daughter—and a granddaughter after her— But I don't tell him that. Not yet. Instead—

That Battle of Yamamah first set the concern in Abu Bakr's heart. He was finally inspired to action when a difference of two words in the recitation of two preachers led to bloodshed and a feud which has yet to be healed.

I say nothing more for a while. The scribe feels obliged to prompt, "Omar, the great son of al-Khuttab, successor to Abu Bakr and to the Prophet, blessed be he—he has also called for all who remember God's Messenger, who lived and spoke with him, to surrender their reminiscence up to someone who writes."

"The khalifah—Omar—is a man," I reply. "He is, in fact, my cousin. Nothing more."

"The great, wise Omar, may God preserve him, hopes the younger generations may know all that can be gathered before the grave and Paradise steal it."

Younger generations. I think of how, after months of inquiry, I discovered where she might be, my daughter, our daughter. All that the present world still holds of my woman by the well. I followed the rumors to al-Hira. Fitting, that the story should end where it began. But no— History has become a line now, not a circle. A line beginning when the Prophet fled Mecca and ending—God knows where. With Judgment Day.

"She's in Basrah, in Iraq," somebody else said. "She submitted to Islam there, al-hamdulillah, before dying and being buried among the Believers." So I went to Basrah.

I should have known better. She might have died, like her mother. Like anyone. But submitted—? Never, not to Islam, not to anything.

Not to me.

I followed the rumors along the caravan route. I came to Tadmor, to the reeking house of turpentine sellers. I sensed what I could neither see nor hear. This was the place. I heard children playing in a courtyard beyond the walls. The cooling splash of a fountain—

I got no further than the men's majlis. She would not see me.

"A man should be able to see his own child!" I shouted. "And don't you know who I am? The Conqueror. The Conqueror of Syria. Your conqueror."

The voices in the courtyard fell silent, hiding. Could I force them to play? I could go no farther without breaking rules I myself have set.

My scribe would know my daughter's name if I said it aloud. Any Muslim would. He would know the sound of "S" to begin the name, to write it. But his hand would tremble, his eyes grow wide. He would make signs against the evil eye. So I keep my tongue between my teeth. A man doesn't speak of Those Behind him, of his women, his harem, neither for pride nor for shame. For the moment, I cradle the treasure carefully within my heart.

"Where there are men," I say to him instead, "there is dogma, and where there is dogma, there is blood. Would you write this history in blood?"

My eyes flash open again. The boy grows pale at what he sees there. Deliberately I reach across the space between us. I take the reed from his immobile hand. With great slowness, I bring it to my nose. I sniff at the pointed, stained end of the tool. The boy showed me how he makes his ink: a poisonous mixture of resin, soot, wine dregs, and cuttlefish spume.

I smell the resin, remember the turpentine sellers' house.

Am I a man to let this bane run through my veins instead of blood?

I hold the point over the spot where my veins throb exposed and vulnerable in my left wrist.

"The Prophet, blessed be he, mistrusted the pen." The scribe's unnatural voice raises the hair at the back of my neck.

I nod. "Its power to pass on truth is quite outweighed by its ability to spread lies."

I don't tell him, but he knows. I, too, mistrust the pen. "Surrender to the pen?" I, the Sword of God, surrender to a flimsy bit of reed? I, who never surrendered to any army, neither the Persians nor the Romans nor, worse, the rebellious desert tribes? Until this day, I rejected every approach by pen-wielding men, begging the honor.

"Who am I," I ask, "the Sword of God, to slash this net of dogma they are weaving, slash it with the clean blade of my words?"

I move the pen from my wrist. I hold it now, poised between us. I apply slow, even pressure. The reed snaps.

"Write it."

A flurry of choosing new parchment and pen, then all is silent in the garden.

The purl of the fountain—

Today by the well I saw a woman and her child.

Yes, back to the woman. This time you will write it.

4

> **Men stand up for women on account of the qualities with which God has gifted the one above the other, and on account of the outlay they make from their substance for them. Virtuous women are obedient, careful, during the husband's absence, because God has been careful of them.**
> **—The Holy Quran, Surah 4:38**

It was a male child I saw with the woman at the well today. The only way I could tell that, however, was by the blue beads stitched upon his orange-flowered bonnet to keep away covetous and evil eyes. In all other respects—in his dress and his full, dark, curly hair—he bore the mark of care bordering on silliness that women bestow on their children; childless women spend it on themselves. He was only one or two years old, this little lad, and it would be some time yet before he could stamp his foot and insist, "Mother, don't fuss," and get his way.

There was a deep, intuitive, and unfathomable wisdom in this little fellow's pure, dark, unprotesting eyes. I found myself hoping, hope against hope, that he might grow up and never lose that genius to the hard and unimaginative necessity of putting bread in his mouth. I saw the same hope in the hands of his mother—the way she held him to scrub his face with the corner of her veil—and heard in the way she prattled his name.

But his mother's hands also told me that there was very little chance he would escape this, the way of all the world. She was young—I suspect he was her first-born—but her hands were already old, bulging with work-knotted veins and tendons. A thin gold ring—polished not on purpose but as a result of scrubbing clothes and her little son's face—glared out of place there.

She saw me watching her and swept a corner of her veil up so her hands, too, were hidden. She couldn't see more of my face than I had ever glimpsed of hers—and from the start she was veiled too piously for me to guess any features. All I had to go on was the hint of her knees through the damp black cloth clinging to them.

My daughter. I wanted her to be my daughter, the child my grandson. How would I know if she had been?

The eyes. I would know the blue eyes.

These eyes were brown.

Swathed and encumbered as this woman was, she somehow managed to grasp the child to her and balance her jug on her head at the same time. She did it all with a nonchalance, feigned, but which would fool most onlookers.

Still, she reminded me of another.

Or perhaps it was only all women with their supreme agility in handling veils, skirts, jugs, children all at once that came to mind.

She, of course, knew who I was. The red turban gives me away to any soul in Homs—perhaps to any soul in all the world. Even three-year-olds who were not yet conceived when I stood outside Homs' gates—even they tie scraps of red around their heads and play at "Sulayman's Papa" in the streets. They demand obeisance from their playmate-subjects; they march past them in glory with a grand turn at the corner beyond which their mothers have strictly forbidden them to wander.

I will tell you the story of this red cloth. It has to do with women, too, as everything else suddenly seems to. But in proper order. Until then, I will leave you in awe of my turban like all the rest.

All the rest, they bow to it. And sometimes they come and take the loose corners of it and kiss them or cause their babies or their old, blind, lame, deaf, palsied to do likewise. This is for the sake of the lock of the Prophet's hair I wear twisted up in its folds.

At least, that is how the reverence started, after an ignominious beginning, as you shall see. But I feel that not a little of this reverence has filtered down through the folds to me now. They come and kiss that red when their troubles can be helped by a human hand as well as by the divine: Their brother is imprisoned and I must intercede. Or they want a letter of introduction here or there so their business may go on apace and their wives grow fat.

Nowadays I wear my red turban out of habit. Or perhaps out of pride. Even now I am too cursed proud to give up the illusion of what I was. Admit to the world that there is hardly an old, withered shadow left?

I wonder if she, this woman at the well, will let her son dress up in a miniature red turban. She was dressed as a Believer, but that means little here in Syria where only whores and the very poor went unveiled even before we came. Somehow, though, I got the impression that if her little man should think to tie red about his curls combed with such tender, hopeful love, she would slap it from his head—once she had made certain there were no spies around.

I think she thought I eyed her one thin scrap of gold as if I wished to add it to my coffers. Is this, then, the honor I have finally won for myself? I, the Sword of God, the warrior even the Prophet, blessed be he, could not stand against? After all these years, all my exploits and victories, a poor woman can only think I covet her wire-thin bit of gold—that is it?

"Write it," I snap.

"But master," my scribe hums. "The Prophet—"

And it occurs to me that this scribbler, this boy, for all his display of deference, may not really be afraid of me. There is a reason I picked him from among the others sitting on their low stools in the marketplace. I imagined he, of all of them, would not hesitate—would not fear—to begin this tale with the word "woman." So the worst has already been done to him? This boy doesn't even fear death any more? Or did I mistake him?

I call him "boy" for all that he sits on the same side of fifty that I do. He was, you will understand, pruned at twelve or thirteen to always be that age. The Romans do that sort of thing sometimes, to get bathhouse attendants they can trust with their women. Or scribes who won't be tempted, in some passion of the night, to pass on secrets they have scribbled at all day.

I wanted a scribe who might climb harem walls I have been denied. Who might find children where I may not.

I had hoped my old age would find this fellow the last of a dying breed, dying because the ways of the desert would shy from doing the propagating for them. The desert, blowing pure and clean into the decadent luxury of Syria— The desert where men are men and women—

But in this, as in so many other things, I was wrong. New generations have been conquered by the luxurious tastes we ourselves conquered with our simplicity.

When I saw her, that woman and her child by the well today, all the memories swelled within me like dried beans soaked in water overnight. And I had to hurry, as a tired old man with nothing left to win or lose and with his old wounds bothering him hurries. Once I would have called that pace a "leisurely stroll" and had no patience for it.

I had to hurry into the market to find a scribe with his inks and parchments and haul them here to my garden.

"God bless you for it," the boy interjects himself at this point. Will he say so by the time we're finished?

Before we began this lazy afternoon, my scribe pleaded that I roll up my sleeves so he could see my scars. And I humored him with a good long look. Yes, indeed, on neither arms nor legs nor chest do I wear a span's breadth of flesh unmarked by my foes.

I show it, my body, as I might show a bit of cloth worn to shreds. I own it, but I don't feel attachment anymore.

I assure the boy that every man who drew my blood paid for it. That's what he hopes to hear. He hopes we two will spend weeks of long afternoons here in my cool gardens while I recount all my deeds of war. He has the lively interest of one who finds a pen an insignificant weapon compared to the sword. The sword he was denied by a cruel cut at age twelve as surely as he was denied the exploits of love.

"If that's the sort of story you want," I tell him, "go find a reciter of the tales of the hero Antar. Or a poet of the Days of the Arabs. This will not be like them."

My scribe doesn't leave. He doesn't dare.

There are those who will condemn me for this course. Omar, Khalifah Omar, to name one. He has condemned me for so many things. His displeasure doesn't matter any longer.

I order, "Continue writing."

Al-Walid was my father. May he be eased in hell is all I can pray for him. He never confessed to the Faith. He was preeminent among all the sons of Makhzum, which was the clan preeminent in all

Mecca, among all the Quraysh. They called him al-Wahīd, the Unique One. What particular feat of his youth gained him the appellation, this play on his given name, I'm not sure. There were too many feats held up for emulation. Al-Walīd was one of six sons of his father, al-Mughira, who was the son of Abd Allah (a more illustrious man than the Prophet's sire) who was the son of Omar, that great hero for whom the present khalīfah, my cousin, was named.

But I don't want this to be a recitation of my genealogy, either. Another two names and I'll join the line of the Prophet himself. And that line any ten-year-old can crow back through prophets, patriarchs, and valiant men of war all the way to Adam, the father of all men. This is where I am expected to begin my tale.

I shall refrain from that habit of so many years.

My father, al-Wahīd, was unique to me—simply because he was my father. Even the Prophet, blessed be he, whose father died five months before his birth, claimed only a single sire, the single son of a single sire. It is when one adds the mother—or the mothers—that the chanted catechism, as the Christians would call it, becomes a story.

How curious! Seeing a mother and her child by the well set it in my heart to tell my tale today. More Christian, this taking of inspiration from a maternal icon. Not what one expects from the Sword of God. But where there are men and men only, there is purity: pure history, pure religion. There is pure dogma. Let one woman loose upon the scene, veil her or not as you will, and there begins the story. The myth, the innuendo. The doubt.

I, Khalid ibn al-Walīd, have grown old. Or not old—Muhammad lived fifteen years longer than the one or at most two years that I expect to see—so much as I have grown weary. I am weary of fighting. When one's whole life has been a war, what is left when that is gone?

Too, I am weary of the Prophet. Oh, no, I do not mean to say I no longer believe in him or in his message of One God.

For saying that, I could be put to death with no ceremony.

"Believe any man who calls himself a prophet."

I was told this once by someone who, if she had told me I could pass through fire unharmed, I would have believed.

Muhammad ibn Abd Allah (blessings on him) was a fine man, not given to telling untruths about what he had seen or heard. He was gentler and more forgiving than I often wished him to be. On the battlefield, I longed for a younger, more fiery leader. A better horseman, at least. Though he loved horses, by God, the son of Abd Allah was a disgrace in the saddle!

But then, of course, had Muhammad been a man with those skills, there would have been no place in the world for me.

As for matters of the spirit, I am not the best judge. But it always seemed to me we could have done no better, in the spirit. Not in a mortal. Not in a man. I am still convinced, pious Omar or no pious Omar, that we never shall.

God forbid that I should want to slight the Prophet whom I am blessed to have called my friend and my kinsman as well as my leader. I am not really angry that history should have condemned me to live in his great shadow, either. Being a man of the desert, I appreciate a shadow. But, by God, I've grown weary of this fawning, ignorant, two-faced praise of him.

At any rate, I mean in my tale to turn from the Prophet and speak of the Prophetess.

If I do well in this, as my heart tells me I do, let the praises go to God, Who is All-Knowing.

If I do wrong and am to suffer for it, then—let God be praised then, too, for He is Most-Merciful.

5

> Many a night, like sea waves, rolled
> me up in sorrow to test me: "Night," I
> said as it began to rise, stretch its
> loose limbs and recede, "go on, unveil
> the morning, your twin harbinger of
> loneliness to me—O night, your stars
> stand still as if tethered to the
> peaks of Yathbuli with ropes of flax!"
> —the Qasidah of Imru'l-Qays

"If I do wrong and am to suffer for it, then—let God be praised then, too, for He is Most-Merciful."

When the eunuch finished reading these words, Rayah said "Amen" without thinking about it, as Sitt Umm Ali had taught her to do. This in spite of the fact that these were the first truly pious thoughts she'd heard among so much that was strange and disturbing.

The emerald in the eunuch's left ear winked in the light of the oil lamp he'd pulled close to the first page of his thick stack of parchments. Abd Allah of Homs, as he had introduced himself. Servant of God. The name of a new convert. So many Abd Allahs these days that most of them continued with names from the Time of Ignorance, Christian or Jewish names, just to reduce confusion.

The eunuch's crisp, blindingly white linen tunic was heavily bordered at neck, hem, and wrists with thick bands of green, yellow, red, and purple wool. Did Rayah catch the glint of gold there, too? Coptic work, no doubt. But its neatness didn't change the tumble into which her world had been thrown since she'd carried his supper to him on a tray. In fact, it added to the chaos. And she'd agreed to follow Sitt Sameh's instructions to fetch the man because she hoped this would see the stranger off sooner. She hoped he'd be gone tomorrow, allowing her to go to Sitt Umm Ali and catch up on the studies she'd missed. That power she felt in her right hand—she must have imagined it.

"Peace to you and yours, Brother," Rayah had said at the gate, keeping her head down and the veil almost up to her eyes as she set the tray before him.

"And to you, peace and my humblest thanks, Little Blue Eyes," he'd replied.

She had almost dropped the tray. Jerking her head up in horror, she saw by his smile he meant no insult. He read her reaction immediately and began to apologize for something, although he clearly had no notion what.

Before he'd found words, Rayah had fled. She'd missed her own supper, hiding under the jasmine vine until Auntie Adilah found her. "Sitt Sameh is calling for you," Auntie scolded. "You didn't report to her on what the stranger had to say. She asked you to."

There was no escape. Rayah had to climb the steps. Never had she felt the jinn so ready to reach out and grab her in the shadows where the staircase turned. Reciting prayers didn't seem to hinder them, and she took the second flight at a run.

"So what did the stranger say?" Sitt Sameh asked.

Rayah had been unable to meet those dreadful eyes. But were they her eyes, too? "Nothing."

"Nothing at all? He is so rude he did not even offer thanks?"

"He said thanks. And wished us peace."

But there is no peace with him, Rayah thought, not a scrap. No peace with these blue eyes, either.

"So why could you not come at once to tell me so?"

Rayah's trembling suddenly would not let her be silent any longer. "I don't have blue eyes." She screamed so the whole night must hear her.

"So that's it." Sitt Sameh nodded.

"I don't, I don't."

She managed to be not quite so loud this time, but the sobs gave her so little control. For even as she spoke her firm denial, she remembered all the times she'd rejected the notion niggling her mind for years. A glance in a pool of water—the tint there was only the water, she'd tell herself, or the reflection of the sky. The way the family kept the shiny surfaces of pots from her, the reaction of women who came to visit for the first time, quickly hushed with whispers.

Until the man at the gate had spoken with impartial, even kind honesty. Which Sitt Sameh layered now with unflinching sternness.

"Your cousin Demiella has a mirror, I think. Go ask to borrow it."

When Rayah repeated, "I don't," and tried to refuse, Sitt Sameh insisted. "Go on."

Rayah scuffed her feet all the way down the stairs. Maybe Demiella had no such thing. Demiella did, however, and handed it over without a word, at such an angle that most other women would have at least stolen a glance. Rayah closed her eyes tight and pulled the shiny surface to her breast, carrying the thing that way even more slowly back up the stairs.

"Give it here," Sitt Sameh ordered.

Rayah held the disk tighter until the Sitt worked it out of her arms with force. Then she held it before Rayah's face. Rayah kept her eyes closed until Sitt Sameh forcibly lifted her chin and said, "Look."

The light wasn't very good. Demiella would have taken the mirror out to the sunny corner of the courtyard for her careful scrutinies. But there was no doubt. Blue eyes.

Rayah couldn't believe it. She wouldn't believe it. The same blue eyes—as Sitt Sameh had. The same face, in fact.

Evil. Evil eyes. Eyes with power. Eyes that consorted with jinn.

And yet, hadn't she known it? Since she was a child, hadn't she known she was different? That people looked at her strangely? That the women were more careful about her going into the alley than any of the other girls? That Sitt Umm Ali had murmured a prayer the first time Rayah had come to learn her *alef-ba*. Sitt Umm Ali had even said she didn't know if such a one could be taught to read the holy words of God.

That a miracle like the healing of little Bushra this afternoon had not taken her completely by surprise. The stabbing in her eyes when it had happened. Rayah squeezed her eyes shut now.

"Why should a daughter not have her mother's eyes?" Sitt Sameh murmured. "Her mother's skill at healing."

Never had Rayah heard this woman so tender. She even tried to put an arm around her. Rayah jerked the affection away. She hit out at the mirror and sent it flying with a crash. "You are not my mother! Both of my parents, Umm Rayah and Abd al-Wali, are dead."

Sitt Sameh bent and picked up the mirror. She carefully rubbed the bronze surface with her sleeve. A woman who kept no mirror herself, she looked deeply into it now, knowing the face she saw there. "I am—I have the honor to be—Umm Rayah."

"Oh yes? And Abd al-Wali?"

"You do know that women sometimes give their children the father's name al-Walīd—not al-Wali—when really they don't know the father."

"But al-Wali means the Unique One, praises to Him. It is one of the Holy Names."

"And Abd al-Walīd—a general name for all converts, like Abd Allah? Among other things, it means 'father of the child.' A good name when the father is not known. Or must be kept a secret. Don't you think?"

"No." Rayah began to sob uncontrollably.

"I didn't think I'd be very good at this," Sitt Sameh admitted. "That's why I put it off so long. You're old enough now, I thought. And when I saw you with your little cousin this afternoon—"

"But why did you start the lie in the first place? If this *is* the truth you tell me now, which I doubt." Rayah couldn't believe she was speaking to one of her elders like this.

The tattooed hands opened as if in place of words. Then the woman found a word—one answer. "Fear."

"Fear? Fear of what?" Manners still escaped Rayah.

"Fear for my life. But especially for yours. When you were so young and helpless. Even last year, when that old man came to the door, I felt the fear all over again, stronger than ever."

A sound of scoffing came from Rayah's throat, but then she swallowed it. Her good behavior was returning, al-hamdulillah. Or was it because she in truth had very little experience of the world? Is that what manners were for, after all—to keep her humble? But how could she ever gain experience if she never did anything but what was expected of her?

Sitt Sameh nodded. The blue eyes seemed to comprehend everything that had been running through Rayah's mind. "Well, no doubt our visitor will shed light on this, perhaps in a way more to your liking, my dear daughter. For that is what you are, daughter. Please—go and ask him to come up."

Rayah refused to move. In truth, she couldn't. Sobs made her knees weak.

To Rayah's surprise, Sitt Sameh, so accustomed to sending others on errands for anything she wanted, did not force her. Sitt Sameh went herself instead, until she found one of the young male cousins and sent him to bring the eunuch.

"And he'll bring some supper up for you as well," she said upon her return. "I think you didn't have any tonight?"

Rayah had been quite certain she couldn't eat, that she would never have stomach again. But the eunuch had come, been made comfortable, and spoken a number of things to Sitt Sameh as if they were old friends, things Rayah didn't understand. They spoke, to Rayah's chagrin, in the language of the desert, the holy language she was trying so hard to learn. She'd always known Sitt Sameh spoke with an accent but she'd never guessed it was *that* accent. At one point, the older woman had even seemed to recite some verses for the visitor, verses that had the flavor of the Holy Quran, something about night, but not a verse Rayah knew. Only now did she realize how far she had yet to study as she tried to keep up with their chatter—and failed.

Then Sitt Sameh had invited their guest to begin reading from his parchments, translating to Syriac for Rayah's benefit. Against her will, Rayah had found herself listening. She had learned to recite the Holy Quran and more, to associate what she recited with scratches on the parchment. What she could decipher of the words spread across Abd Allah's knees did coincide with what she knew. But then she stopped trying to catch him in a lie, this man who'd told her from the first what everyone all her life had kept hidden from her.

And while she listened, she ate. First, just an olive. Then two, because it was bad luck to leave just one pit on a plate. Then, to her surprise—she finished up the tray.

"So, Rayah, my dear." Sitt Sameh's voice came from the dark of the room when the eunuch's voice gave out, and he begged to be finished with reading for the day.

Sitt Sameh served him a refreshing fruit drink but spoke to Rayah. "Do you know who this Khalid ibn al-Walid is who writes to us, and thereby speaks, in a way, from such a distance?"

"He is the Conqueror of Syria," Rayah replied. "The great general of the Holy Prophet Muhammad, precious blessings on him. Abu Sulayman, who never knew defeat in the name of Islam."

"Known for his red turban?"

"Yes."

"Something like this?"

Sitt Sameh fingered a filthy rag the stranger had brought. It might once have been red. It lay before her on her rug with two other articles he'd brought on the back of his mule along with his bundle of leather-bound parchments all the way from Homs. He'd laid them all before her as part of his introduction and no doubt described each in words of the desert Rayah had not understood.

One of the items was a very fine sword. Had any of the men in the family known of it, it never would have made its way into the harem at all. For her part, Sitt Sameh avoided touching, even looking, at the blade, encased in a sheath of fine leather worked with jewels, worth a fortune. Rayah thought she seemed to regard the weapon in the way she might regard goods gotten through wicked means, certainly used for wicked purposes.

Rayah couldn't say what the third object was at all. It seemed to be a wooden framework covered with cloth and black ostrich feathers, but the object had seen such ill use, she couldn't fathom its purpose or even its original shape. The scraps of cloth were torn, the wood and feathers snapped. Sitt Sameh didn't touch this either, but here her attitude was one of deep reverence.

So they were back to the scrap of cloth. "I suppose it might once have been a turban," Rayah replied.

"Do you not think he honors us to write to us and send a messenger in this way?"

"Yes. But I do not understand why."

"All these years, for your safety, I kept your lineage hidden. As these tales unfold, I hope you will come to understand why. This family of turpentine sellers gave us sanctuary. When you were small, they knew enough not to set shiny copper bowls or anything before your face. In ignorance you might have given yourself the evil eye. They kept our past a secret—better, perhaps, than I begged them to. It was their lives and honor at stake as well. Then, last year, the secret came out. Somehow, he found his way here, the Conqueror. And I would not see him. But now—"

Her speech was interrupted then by the supernal cry of the muezzin that cleared the sky of thoughts of anything but God. Presently, the rhythmic wooden beat of the Christian sematron chimed in, for though there were more of the older faith still in Tadmor, it had to give place to the call of its conquerors.

"Mecca?" the stranger asked, rising to his feet.

He didn't ask the Sitt, but Rayah herself. She was proud to know the qiblah, the holy direction, from any place in her house: in the sky beneath the Two Friends stars in the Water Goat's tail at this time of year. She showed the stranger the direction of Mecca and thought, for a moment, that at least the silent skies didn't care what color her eyes were.

They went to separate corners of the terrace for their devotions, bending and kneeling beneath drying herbs and laundry. Sitt Sameh, not a convert, stood at the mudbrick edge of the roof between them and recited something different. In Arabic, she invoked the evening star.

When the guest had rolled up his rug and reclaimed his slippers, he went to stand with Sitt

Sameh. Rayah stood further back, in the shadows, suddenly tired and overwhelmed, wondering if she could be excused.

Sitt Sameh was not looking toward the holy cities, south and west, but more directly toward where a rosy gold still marked the sun's setting. "From Homs you say you come, sir?" she asked Abd Allah.

"If it please you, Sitt."

"It seems to have pleased the Conqueror to settle there."

"I would not say I recognized pleasure, or even contentment in him. Simply, Homs is where he found himself when God ruled that his life neared its close."

"Homs, the site of Queen Zaynab's downfall. Where the Roman enemy captured the great queen of the Arabs in the river. They called her Zenobia in their corrupt tongue and shackled her neck, wrists, and ankles with iron chains in mockery of the jewelry she'd once worn. And here you are in Tadmor, the site of the glories of her ancient kingdom, returning now to the desert sand."

"Yes, Sitt. Where your doorkeeper, Zabbai, still bears her name, I think."

"And others of us are obliged to maintain our true names in secret—because of the Conqueror of our day." Her voice held deep bitterness. "It would be just like him, to gloat over a fallen Arab woman with his last breath."

"Can you not think my master appreciated the parallel, his conquest of the Romans the glorious conclusion to what Queen Zaynab began?"

For a moment, in silence, Sitt Sameh studied the darker line the rooftops made against the thick-laid stars glinting to life over Tadmor. Out to the darkening desert beyond.

"Here, where the story began, the glorious Days of the Arabs. Here where it will end. And those of us who are her direct descendants—"

"Are you, Sitt, indeed? Descendant of Zaynab, the great spirit of her people?"

"They say she had eyes black 'beyond the usual wont, teeth as white as pearls from the Persian Gulf.' Only her eyes weren't black, of course. That is said by men who didn't dare meet her gaze. Her eyes were blue.

"As were those of Zarqa of Yamamah where, no doubt, the Conqueror's story will wend by and by. And those of Robab who led her tribe, the Riyan, against tyranny in her sacred litter. This is not to mention the four blue-eyed women in our direct line, my grandmother Umm Taghlib, my mother Bint Zura, myself, my daughter—"

Rayah could no longer keep biting her tongue to silence. "Blue eyes? Like yours, Sitt? Like—like mine?"

Sitt Sameh met her gaze, blue eye to blue eye, but did not answer the question. Some of the aunties had come up to the terrace and begun to take the bedding down from the lines to put their children to sleep. Avoiding their curious glances, Sitt Sameh led her guest back to her small chamber at the side. Rayah, wide awake again, followed them.

Once seated on her rugs and having offered both Abd Allah and Rayah more fruit drink, she said, "The Rum, the Romans, think it strange and unnatural that a woman ride into the battle at the head of her people." Her fingers reached out to the gifts the eunuch had brought. This time the tattooed hands found the broken knot of wood, white gauze, and feathers to which Rayah could give no name. Sitt Sameh touched it gently.

"To us, to the old ways," she said, "there is nothing strange about it at all, if she be the daughter of her mother, if she has blue eyes, and—and if she rides in the holy qubbah. But first the Romans, in the time of Zaynab, and then our own men who ought to have been our protectors—both chose to set us aside. They did this to the sacred litter."

She let the broken heap drop as if it had suddenly become good only to add to the fire. She sighed.

The eunuch said, "Khalid ibn al-Walid the Conqueror thought only for the best. When—if you let me read the whole of this to you, you will see."

"Khalid the Conqueror—" She gave an exasperated wave with her hand.

She turned suddenly, harshly, to Rayah, making her heart jump, making her choke on her drink. What she said made Rayah's heart race even faster.

"He is your grandfather, child. My father." Again she sighed and looked away. "So you see, it was not such a lie when I let you believe al-Wali was your father's name. It is your great-grandfather's name, my Rayah. And what reciter of genealogies does not skip a generation or two for convenience?"

"But my father?" The girl found it no easier to get her mouth around those words than her mind.

"I didn't give you a falsehood there, either. He is dead, died before you were born."

"But his name?"

"As the Conqueror says. Sometimes it is better just to know mothers' names."

"His name," Rayah insisted, feeling a return of tears.

"Well, perhaps we should wait and see how the Conqueror wishes to tell it. Don't they say, winners write the history? And since the coming of Islam by Khalid's conquering hand, what other history shall there be?"

6

> In the daytime you have continual employ,
> But verily, at the oncoming of night are
> devout impressions strongest, and words
> most collected.
> —The Holy Quran, Surah 57:3–4

The Prophet (blessed be he) used to recite this verse to us about the night. Now, in the evening of my years, I confess how true those words are. They were also true in my youth, before I ever heard Muhammad speak. Even then, if I allowed it, there would come into every day filled with boasting activity and vain hopes, a time of quiet and tenderness. It was at the oncoming of just such an evening long ago that I first met a woman at a well.

"A woman at a well?" my scribe repeats.

I return to that image as the herdsman drives his flocks, as the traveler marks out his desert journey—from well to well.

"Jews and Christians," my scribe speaks cautiously, "tell a tale of how the son of Ibrahim found his wife, by the will of God to be the mother of the Faithful, fetching water at the well."

"Yes, and how she quenched the thirst of his travel-worn camels and his own parched tongue."

He sees I know the story, that I do not find it heresy, that there is nothing to fear. He warms to the matter. "The mother of that son of Ibrahim, so say the People of the Book, she had just been gathered to her mothers. The maiden at the well comforted him much in that sorrow."

"I would like to believe that tale of Isma'il come of age, as I hope to share in the flowing wells of Paradise. I would like to believe that every great man is led by the Merciful One to the refreshment of his soul at just such a well at a time he feels his greatness to be waning."

"May God will it so," the eunuch says.

This morning in Homs I saw a woman at the well and was revived with purpose. So then, long ago on an evening in al-Hira, the Encampment, a whole burning desert away, I first saw another woman.

My scribe asks, "You had been to al-Hira even before you conquered it, with the favor of God, for Islam?"

"I could have conquered it blindfolded."

I rub at the sting in my eyes. Even temporarily blinded as I am, I find my nostrils clogged with ghostly smells: burning, blood, like jinn-views on the hot horizon.

I pause for control, then say: "It was sacred in those days."

"Sacred?"

"The sons of Tamim, Taghlib, Bakr, and Iyad all made pilgrimage there."

"But what of Mecca?"

"Mecca was for the Quraysh and a few minor tribes of the western desert who were their allies, no more."

"That was in the Time of Ignorance, of course."

"The time we used to call the Days of the Arabs. Write."

The air of al-Hira was thick with generations, numbered by some back to Adam, the first to fall to his knees when he contemplated heaven and earth in that spot. A pair of great and ancient pillars called the Besmeared Ones marked the place.

"Similar in meaning to what Mecca marks with the great cubic House?" he asks. "The Holy Ka'ba, center of all our pious yearning?"

I nod.

Had you seen those pillars in the Days of Ignorance—

—before I made the Muslims tear them down—

—you would have known the bleating of rams, the flash of knives, the spurt of blood. You would have known the savor of sacrifice, the stoning of evil spirits, and the slow circuits of the faithful, treading on one another's heels, praying in a frenzy.

He asks, "Such as in Mecca today?"

"Even so," I say.

Deep, sweet, ever-flowing wells and springs and canals pocked the ancient settlement in those days.

Although sands flow through it now. There never were enough springs to wash the jinn smell from my nose.

The earth was so fertile. I imagined that if I left my hand lying upon that earth for any length of time, the hand itself would sprout and blossom like any slip of cane. Such things are magic to desert men.

Al-Hira, the site of the spring pilgrimage, was like a string of turquoise worn by a well-dowered woman. Each well was a bead with all the surrounding green it could support. And for every well, al-Hira boasted twenty women come to fetch water, to wash clothes, to gossip. And, by God, al-Hira was as famous for its beautiful women as it was for its wells and its politics.

They say the three—politics, wells, and women—are braided fast in one strong and knotty strand. It's true, by God, and nowhere more than in al-Hira. I saw many fine ankles trimmed with silver and the drag of many fine veils across my path—ah!

I sigh. "No wonder we Arabs came to that pilgrimage in the holy month."

But what does a eunuch know of such things?

"Dhu'l Hijjah?" he asks.

"I mean the holy month bridled to the sun, not the moon. Go on. Write it."

How years were told before Muhammad, blessed be he, cut holy days loose from anything to do with seasons of harvest and sowing. This was before that, at the rise of the Follower. That star in the eye of the bull follows just at the end of the rainy season, graced by the maidens in Pleiades, when the bull carries the sun in his horns. This season the Magi call Nowruz, giving one another plates of sprouted wheat. The Jews celebrate by eating unleavened bread and by painting the lintels of their houses with hyssop dipped in lambs' blood.

Among the Arabs, who let the Goddesses al-Uzza, Manat, and bounteous Allat share heaven with God in those days, the rains had just ended. The peace of green pastures spread into every tent. No man raised his arm against his neighbor but was happy to be alive in the springtime moon. The settled lands teemed with new-harvested barley and spring wheat, the desert with newborn herds to exchange one for the other. The divine grew expansive in the Arab's heart. He went on pilgrimage to holy places and mingled with kinsman, stranger, friend, and foe alike in the adjoining markets.

How poetically I can speak of things that no longer exist. I rub hand on hand—those hands responsible for the town's destruction—as if that can release the vanished world to life once more.

In spite of the ancient pillars in al-Hira and the Jews and Magi gathered in their own places, it was the new ones, the Christians, who dominated the scene. They came like clouds of locusts from their caves in the desert, for it was a holy time for them, too. And if there were twenty women to a well, there were at least ten Christian monks, begging, praying, arguing their eye-of-needle dogmas. There were more possibilities for madness among these men, I decided, than among all the women combined.

Toward evening I came upon one particular half-mad hermit dominating the largest well with his preaching. Zura, they called him. He had drawn a fair-sized crowd.

Something about such holy men lured those of us who lived in the desert. Even Muhammad (blessed be he) conferred with monks living like animals in the caves near Busra.

Such holy men denied their bodies food for forty days on end. To Arabs on the march, there was much to admire in such austere control. And, too, the lamps of the hermits helped many a lost traveler find his way through the desert night to water and warmth.

Here were men, you see, who had known the comforts of houses and gardens. Men who, of their own soul's light, saw what freedom and spiritual strength the rigors of the desert held. No matter his words, this hermit's very being confirmed what we men of the tribes felt in our hearts.

This hermit represented all such things to the crowd he drew. Even I could not help but pause and listen. He was like some desert-drifted stump of wood, wind-whittled to the most fragile scrap that still held body and soul together. Some Great Hand, it seemed, had bled him dry from his hair, like a shock of summer-dusted camel grass, to his feet, twisted like the talons of a hawk on her prey. The sun-blackened color of his skin said that he usually wore nothing at all, but for this occasion he wore a goat skin, fresh-killed and swarming with flies, about his loins. The nakedness of his sunken belly and lice-picked ribs seemed a greater obscenity than anything he hid.

And he prophesied. I did not hear him speak more than ten words all together, but these have refused to leave me all these years. I hear his voice today in the stillness of this garden, as it has come to me at other times to stir feelings of fate and monument about my life.

"You shall behold the coming salvation of the Arabs," he said, his voice thin, hollow, seeming not his own and yet as well-balanced as a spear throw.

He said it again, louder and, so I thought, directly to me. "You shall behold the coming salvation of the Arabs."

I know. I know this is a trick of such showmen, but I was not the only one who got the feeling that those words were meant especially for me. As he spoke, the madman pointed a long thin arm, a long thin hand, a long thin finger, directly at my heart. Folk in front of me turned to stare as if I were to be the very instrument of this salvation, not just a passive beholder.

I defended myself with a laugh—for I had no other shield against this onslaught—and turned away.

"The coming salvation of the Arabs." My scribe rereads what we have written so far today and pauses to muse in awe. "The Nazarene hermit knew, then," he says, "of the coming of the Holy Prophet?"

I smile and sigh a little. A hoopoe hops about in the gravel very near us, his golden crest a crown. Our stillness makes him bold, the king of all he surveys.

"Perhaps," I say. "I have, yes, told this story on other occasions, always indicating that such was the case. And yet…"

"Yet what?" the scribe demands. "Surely there can be no doubt in the Prophet." His voice and sharp gestures have frightened the bird away.

"Yet listen to the story of the well," I say, "the evening by the well of al-Hira…"

"The coming salvation of the Arabs" rang in my ears and burned on my cheeks. I turned from the madman's bony finger and, in the same fate-tumbling, confusing instant, saw her.

Now Zura the hermit could have suddenly died and been buried for all the notice I gave his harangue.

She was among those staring at me because of the hermit's pointing.

I didn't know her. I was eighteen years old, by the grace of God. She was simply the most beautiful creature I had ever seen. In fact, I'd got no more glimpse of her, of her flesh, of any part of her that might show beauty, than a flash of sun-touched, drop-of-honey cheek.

And the eyes. I'd never seen anything like them. They were blue. As blue as the sky after a winter rain.

This woman, this girl (she was perhaps fourteen years old) wore no full veil, but only the loose cloth over her hair of one neither married nor promised. Yet when she saw me turning to look at her, she herself turned away in modesty already mature.

After a day of the settlers' female vanities, this girl was like a breath of fresh desert air. She wore the plain bluish black of an Arab's daughter. Anemones and asphodel made a festive crown about her head. The bands of cowrie shell that usually frame the faces of women of the northern tribes she had tossed over her shoulders so they would not obscure her vision. They hung down her back like bright stars in the dull black night of her veil and dress. Beneath her ragged hem, silver anklets hung loose from delicately formed ankles. The hem itself wore a span of dust from brushing against thistles or being trod upon in a free and careless clamber up a hillside to rescue a goat.

Beside her, a girlfriend bent to catch her giggles. The friend shared most outward appearance with her, but I hardly noticed the other as the one with blue eyes took her friend's elbow and walked her away.

Did the curious fate of our meeting at the bony hands of a God-touched man of the desert make me half mad, too?

And did my heart fool me, or was her interest in me more than that of the idly curious? With a dip of her head, she seemed to take this fortune-telling personally, as the manifest will of Heaven toward her. I was reminded of the way Maryam, sister of Harun, demanded answers of the Angel Jabra'il when he told her she would bear a holy son. The Holy Quran tells how, beneath the palm tree, a streamlet sprang from her feet. Her eye was refreshed.

And the Christians, who call this ancient holy woman Mary, have recorded her words, "Be it done to me according to Your will."

"What happened then? I mean, in your youth."

For a moment, I'm annoyed at this fellow I've let into my life. He calls me back to this old body of aches when in my mind I was there, young, light, wings on my feet—

"Then…?"

Then the girl and her friend walked off, swinging their hips playfully into one another and swishing great fans of palm fronds over their shoulders. They were, or so I thought, Christians, and among their shells and beads they wore tiny crosses of bronze. I followed them—or, rather, her, for I was hardly aware of her companion—until they melted into a group of others with palms. They were singing, I remember, and, as darkness fell, lamps were lit. The throng grew, milled, pressed, passed, thinned, as it performed its rites. God knows what those rites meant. Pagan that I was, I certainly did not. The palm branches would have told me, if I had known then as I know now, that they were celebrating the victorious entry of the son of Maryam into Jerusalem. But I had mind and eyes for one thing only.

No matter how many waves of people, dust, or shadow passed between us, I always found her again. Had she been the only one in the crowd to carry a lamp, had she headed the procession herself, she could not have impressed me more. Her presence was like the wind in a desert storm: I could not walk or face any direction other than the way it was blowing. At the same time, a man must avoid staring or even glancing at another's woman. I had plenty of practice at this skill. I could examine and comment to the driver on an animal's knees while a woman—a mere shadow to my eyes and no more than a breath of air—used those self-same camel's knees to clamber up into her litter. Afterward

I could not tell you whether the foot she had stepped with was bare or sandaled, clean, dusty, or henna-painted. Now I found it impossible to hide my interest. Had one of the girl's kinsmen been present, I might have had to fight for my life. As it was, I very nearly came to blows with men who had nothing to do with my attraction except that they got in the way, and I stumbled against them or trod upon their robes.

The girl was not ignorant of my presence. Sometimes she slipped here or there in the crowd to try to lose me. She did not do so out of fear, as many another girl would have done. Nor was it a childish game of run-and-seek she was playing to tease me. It seemed she was testing me. Just as a sharif taking on mercenaries for a great campaign may test their skill, their endurance, or their faithfulness, with demands beyond the ordinary.

Once I lost her in the crowd for such a long time I came near to bursting. At last I found her gaze, peering over someone else's shoulder directly at my heart. Her eyes fluttered down and away like timid doves the moment I got too close.

The eyes seemed to speak to me. They asked me something like this: "O Stranger? Can you feel it, O Stranger? Can you feel what I have been unable to share with anyone else since my world began? Can I trust you, then, for all that you are a stranger and not of my people, to side with me because of this?"

"By my life and by the Gods of my fathers, yes," I tried to communicate back to her.

Who can say if my answer satisfied her? The next instant she turned and disappeared with the mass of others behind great brass-studded portals. I could not follow her there. A cry rang out in a jarring, foreign voice: "For the initiate alone! All others depart!" I could not claim to be an initiate. It hurt to see how many others were admitted to join her within.

She was gone. I sank where I was upon the steps of the sandstone church. And I breathed the gusts of the evening desert as they came into the settled oasis.

By God, how much simpler things would have been had I never turned to see her in the crowd! I had not asked to see her. Yet heaven had decreed otherwise. Now I felt I must have her.

I would own her. Be her lord, her husband. I could think of no other way to gain her for myself. No better solution to my continued dissatisfaction than that I should marry this girl and make her a woman. How I proposed to do this, since I had learned neither her name nor her father's, nor even that of her tribe, I did not stop to ask myself. It did not seem an important part of the logic.

I roused from my reveries when night's chill brought renewed tension to my tired limbs. I stood, shook myself, yawned, and stretched as if waking from sleep. The church doors were still barred and shut against the uninitiated. Since I did not know whether they would remain so for another hour or the entire week, I decided to return with my puzzle to my own tent.

As I did so, a trace of divine breath lifted my headdress back from my shoulders, gently exposing the lovelocks underneath.

7

> Roast flesh, the glow of fiery wine,
> to speed on camel fleet and sure . . .
> White women statue-like that trail
> rich robes of price with golden hem,
> Wealth, easy lot, no dread of ill,
> to hear the oud's complaining string—
> These are life's joys. For man is set
> the prey of time, and time is change.
> —Sulmi ibn Rabiah of Dabbah,
> two generations before the Prophet

"So that is how he says he met my mother." Sitt Sameh nodded as the eunuch paused and took a sip of lemon water. "It does make a pretty story, does it not?"

That morning, Abd Allah the eunuch of Homs had begun reading his parchment before it would have been polite of Rayah to go to the Quranic teacher's house. So she had stayed in Sitt Sameh's room to hear him. Rayah had to admit she loved the idea of passion roused at first sight by the hand of a desert hermit almost, God forgive her, as much as she loved the revelations of the Prophet.

Suddenly, however, Auntie Adilah showed a frantic woman into Sitt Sameh's room. The whimpering child the woman bore in her arms had just fallen into the breakfast fire. The red, white, and black burns on the little round face condemned the child to grow up with the sort of deformity for which no bridegroom would pay brideprice. If she lived.

Sitt Sameh set to work at once, making the child comfortable with poppy juice, then beginning to concoct a healing salve. Rayah decided it would be a good time to go to Sitt Umm Ali. Quietly, she got up from Sitt Sameh's desert-style rug to creep toward the door.

"Rayah." Sitt Sameh's voice stopped her. "I'd like you to help me with this. Come. Lay your hands with me on this balm."

Obediently, Rayah made her way around the weeping mother and the prone child. But what she saw on the other side of Sitt Sameh made her stop. She wanted to turn and flee.

Sitt Sameh had thrown aside the cushions and rugs she kept piled against this wall. Jars and pouches of her medicines stood revealed, releasing their dark, musty odors to the room. Among them also stood three figurines of wood, each about the height of a man's hand. Legs, waist, arms, faces were only vaguely carved, the V of their sex rather more so, pendant breasts most of all. Their purpose could not have been more clear: satanic idols that the Prophet, blessed be he, had condemned in no uncertain terms.

Rayah shied as if a serpent slipped across her path.

"Oh, never mind the Ladies," Sitt Sameh told her. "The power is in you, child, in your hands and in your eyes. It isn't in them."

Still Rayah could think only of flight, although her legs refused to move.

"Say a prayer if you like. The power of words on your tongue—have you discovered that yet? Say any prayer you like, and I will recite one of mine with you."

Sitt Sameh began a poem of the desert, loping at a camel's gait. Rayah understood a few words, "fire", "God." Or rather—and it made her blood run cold—"Daughter of God." Rayah had to pray then, just to counteract the evil. The first verse of the Quran came to her, a very short Surah, easy to memorize. Sitt Umm Ali said it was good for all purposes if you sent your heart after the words. So Rayah recited: "In the Name of God, the Compassionate, the Merciful."

"And hands on the bowl of salve." Sitt Sameh didn't wait for Rayah to set her hands on the bowl at her own pace. She caught them up and placed them under hers on the curve of rough earthenware.

"Praise be to God, Lord of the world," Rayah prayed furiously.

"Hold the child's hands," Sitt Sameh said when their two prayers were over. "Gently, now. Try to comfort her. This will sting, and I can't have her thrashing. That would make it worse."

The poor little girl. Compassion overcame Rayah's fear of blasphemy. She did as she was told, and the little one did calm somewhat. Of course, that might have been the poppy juice finally taking effect. But it made Rayah feel she couldn't leave, even as her courage grew. She was doing good. Only when the mother gathered up her sleeping daughter to carry her home, did Rayah prepare to follow her out into the world.

"I will carry the rest of the salve home for you," she said, "and more poppy juice." And go to Sitt Umm Ali on the way back, she added to herself.

But Sitt Sameh called again for one of the boys to take on that task instead.

When mother and child were gone, Sitt Sameh moved to cover her idols once more and then stopped with the old, faded rug still in her hands. "No. First I will tell you the story of the Ladies. Part of it."

She must have sensed Rayah balking, backing toward the door. Sitt Sameh said, more to Abd Allah who'd slipped in the room quietly as the patient left than to the girl she called her daughter, "It has to do with my mother's first appearance. And it is not her first appearance as the object of Khalid Abu Sulayman's desire, as this kind visitor read to us this morning. It is her birth into this world."

Now, whenever talk in the harem turned to birthing and babies, Rayah always drew near to listen. So, in spite of her best intentions, she found her legs crossing under her on the rug once more as Sitt Sameh took up the tale.

"It was in the Valley of Nakhlah." Sitt Sameh addressed the eunuch, "Do you know it?"

"Not far from Mecca," Abd Allah replied, "although God has never willed that I come there." Then there was something uneasy and full of wistful knowledge at the same time as he said, "The Conqueror mentioned it often."

Rayah didn't know Nakhlah, but if it were near the birthplace of the holy Prophet, blessed be he, it must be good to learn about.

"The sons of Taghlib—for that was the tribe of both my mother's parents—made their encampment there for the night on their way to Mecca to trade in the pilgrimage moon."

"So the holy month was celebrated before the coming of the Messenger, blessed be he, just as my master said?"

"A month of peace, yes, as tribes from all over Arabia traveled—either to al-Hira, as the Conqueror told us he did—or to Mecca, as my grandmother's people were doing that year."

"For pilgrimage?"

"Yes, for pilgrimage. But also for trade. I cannot say where the one began and the other ended. The peace of Dhu'l Hijjah enabled tribes to travel even through the lands of their hereditary enemies without fear of blood feud."

Rayah interrupted. "Were your grandparents Muslims?"

"No. Muhammad had yet to receive his first revelation."

"Precious blessings on him," Rayah supplied reflexively. She should not have asked such an ignorant question. Sitt Umm Ali would be angry that she had forgotten the dates she had taught her. But the Faith of Islam seemed to have existed forever, in Rayah's mind. Sitt Sameh didn't seem at all disturbed by her question. "My grandfather Zura, however, had recently become a man of the Book, a Christian."

"Zura. Wasn't that the name of the hermit—?" Abd Allah commenced a shuffle through his pile of thin sheets. "I'm sure I wrote that name."

Sitt Sameh would not wait for the slowness of parchment. "You might say Christianity was the best he could do in those days, when Muhammad was but an impoverished orphan without much hope for his future."

"Blessings on him," Rayah repeated.

"Perhaps even your Sitt Umm Ali would agree that that was the best a man could do, to follow Isa ibn Maryam, the Christian's prophet. With the Romans all Christian, it seemed the way of most power, in any case. Muhammad himself would say that."

"Precious blessings on him. But your grandmother?"

"She clung rather to the ways of her mothers, which had holy words, poetry, power of their own."

A demonic power, Rayah thought. But then she remembered and had to ask. "Did she—did she have blue eyes, this grandmother?"

"She did, and into her charge had been placed the qubbah, the sacred, white-gauzed litter of the sons of Taghlib."

Sitt Sameh had packed the gifts Abd Allah had brought—the red turban, the sword, the wreck of bent wood, cloth, and feathers—neatly away the previous evening. They had a place under the rug and pillows. She dropped the rug aside now and brought the broken jumble forward. Rayah could see that it might once have been a women's camel litter—part of it. For though the frameworks of bent wood were made for lightness, they still had to be large enough for a woman to ride within, often with small children.

Sitt Sameh went on. "My grandmother, may the cool rains fall on her grave, had ridden in the holy qubbah, leading her people to victory, many times in her day. When the virgin daughter of a sharif rode thus, within the white gauze, bare-breasted, trilling the battlecry, every son of Taghlib would rather die than let the litter fall into enemy hands. So they fought more bravely than demons, like a sandstorm over the plain.

"Then, in Nakhlah, she was big with her first child, and so the three Goddesses, Allat, Manat, and al-Uzza, rode under the waving feathers and sheer curtains alone."

Sitt Sameh caressed her three idols with a glance, then continued: "Zura, my grandfather, with his new religion of the Nazarene, cared hardly more for such things than you do, my daughter. I suppose he might have been content to put blue robes on one of them and call her the Mother of God. Like this, however—naked—they were an insult and always a bone of contention between him and his wife.

"'Get rid of them,' he'd say. 'And replace them with the only thing that's sacred, a copy of my holy Book. How shall God bless us when such abomination rides before us?'

"'How shall They bless us if They do not?' she'd reply. 'How shall I come to my time and bring forth a healthy son for you if I don't have the Goddesses who were the support of my mothers before me? Set your Book—which I cannot read and need a man to interpret for me—set it within the sacred space along with the Ladies if you will. But this is my first child. What man can be there to interpret for me when the time comes? I must have something I myself can read, strong-wombed, full-breasted Mothers. I have no hope but to trust in how my mothers before me faced the same challenge.'

"So he promised her she could keep the Ladies until she was delivered. But that night, in Nakhlah, he broke that promise."

"He took the idols from her after giving a promise?" Rayah asked.

Sitt Sameh nodded.

"But why?" To Rayah's surprise, she felt herself pitying the woman, idols and all, as she approached the mystery of motherhood. Rayah herself would know her Quran when that uncertain time came to her.

"Because her time was almost come, and he didn't want pagan poison on his son? Because he thought he'd made more binding promises to Isa ibn Maryam? Who can tell about such things? My grandmother went to the qubbah that night, where it had been unloaded and its camel set free. She went to make her evening devotion, to pray for a safe delivery. She found the images gone. In their place was nothing but a book of the Gospel.

"'Who wants to know?' her husband demanded when she went to him to ask where they were.

"'How can the sons and daughters of Taghlib survive without their spirit, to go before them to the good grass and sweet wells? How shall Taghlib's daughters bear new sons without the help of the three wise Ladies? How can you have destroyed the very spirit of your own people?'

"She wept so bitterly, rolling on the ground before him, tearing her veil and getting her hair all filled with sand, that finally he took pity on her, at least enough to say, 'Calm yourself, mother of my son, if Isa ibn Maryam will it. I haven't destroyed your precious idols.'

"Before relief could completely overcome her, he went on: 'I merely buried them, here in Nakhlah, about the shrine, where old demons belong. And you need not ask me where, for I have already forgotten the places. Women, take her away and see her calm before she does damage to the seed of Taghlib, to a future servant of Isa of Nazareth.'

"My grandmother—may the gentle rain calm her owl-soul now—could not be calmed then. And because it was already dark, the moon of pilgrimage only in his thin first quarter, she took brands from the fire to see by. She went digging in every place within the precincts of the shrine, searching for the buried Goddesses. She dug with her bare hands, crawling here, there, like a dog, with her big belly.

"At first she made no headway and seemed a mere madwoman in her search. But then, as the night wore on, she began to pray. She prayed to the Lady of the Valley, praising Her sweet wells and the greenness of Her trees. When men set hidden things in women, the Goddess teaches them how to bring them forth to new life. My grandmother sang the spirit songs of the holy qubbah. And the Goddesses began, very faintly, to answer her. She found Manat some time near the middle of the night, with the moon lying low on the jagged horizon of the Buqum lava beds. After moonset, she heard al-Uzza under a clump of dry acacia. And then, immediately after, Allat, the eldest, almost leapt out of the sacred soil and into her hands, reborn.

"Sand caked the tracks of tears on her face, but tears of relief and joy carved wadis through it as my grandmother crawled back to the qubbah's curtains. With whispered prayers of thanksgiving and for forgiveness, she replaced the figures on their blood-red cushions. Suddenly overcome with exhaustion herself, aching in every joint, she collapsed against the framework, unable to return to her tent and her husband's side.

"Then, through her exhaustion, she heard a voice calling her: 'Come in, child. Come in and sleep.'

"And so she did what she hadn't done since she was a maid. She crept among the qubbah's sacred cushions herself to rest. Holy Manat gave a kick, and the Gospel tumbled out into Nakhlah's sand."

8

**Our children in our midst: What else
but our hearts are they, walking on the ground?**
—Hittan ibn al-Mu'alla of Tayyi

Sitt Sameh plucked a tuft of goat hair and fed it with calloused fingers into her spindle as she continued her story.

"The herdsman charged with setting the holy qubbah of Taghlib upon its camel had slept roughly. Come morning and the breaking of camp, the litter defied his old back. He called a younger man to come and help him. Together they got the oddly heavy burden loaded, but they didn't dare to peek inside the curtains to see what the weight was. The spirit of their ancestors might well grow heavier at whim. Who knew what dangers on the track ahead might call for extra divine weight? And the little moan they heard from inside—certainly the tribe of the jinn may moan whenever they wish. Men should not be too inquisitive about such things.

"My grandmother, Umm Taghlib—may she sleep now in peace under cooling rains—that morning, she awoke with a sharp pain low in her belly. She awoke to find the Banu Taghlib already underway, herself in the forbidden litter. Another pain came sharply, before she could think what to do.

"Another came, another. The baby. It was coming. Grandmother parted the curtain and tried to get the camel to stop. She didn't have the strength. The beast was unused to doing anything but following the tail in front of it. The camel had been harnessed without driving reins; Grandmother had no goad and just leaning forward brought on such pain.

"Grandmother tried to wave to women in other litters before and behind her, but the warm drowse of the move was upon them. She tried to shout, calling their names. No one heard. Should she try the men? If she did, her husband would hear of it and discover the Goddesses' return. Discover the holy qubbah full, not of a virgin but of the very opposite: his wife about to give birth to his heir.

"He would find his Gospel gone.

"They were moving up along a wadi, on a ridge where gravelly ground made the camel slope uncomfortably. A strong pinch suddenly sent water gushing from her. It soaked all the cushions beneath her, through all the sacred layers. The camel bellowed with pleasure, as if they had come to an oasis and there was water to spare, water to sprinkle on camel's backs. No one noticed, although a few other animals bellowed back, jealous.

"A woman in childbirth should have something between her teeth to bite on through the pains, Grandmother knew. Because al-Uzza had already been soaked with her fluid and they were part of each other anyway, the woman put the Goddess's head between her teeth. Look, you can still see the teeth marks. Allat went in one hand, Manat in the other.

"The sun throbbed down, trying to split through the arching wood frame over Grandmother's head like the jealous barren woman that heavenly orb is. Or like the baby, through the tent flaps of life.

"The swaying reminded Grandmother of the days when she had ridden within the curtains of the qubbah in triumph. Taghlib's bravest and finest, including her husband who had been so handsome then, had stood beside her in the fiercest battle. The clash and screams of combat roared in her pounding head once more, only now they pushed all the way down to the part of her that was most divine. The bellows of war camels, their lurching, their kicks, ran through her body one after another, then together. They came, she realized, all from her. Around the plug of divine acacia wood in her mouth, she tried to give the high trill of encouragement: 'Ya, Banu Taghlib, *yellah*!'

"In the end, however, the daughters of Taghlib abandoned her. The sons did as well. She alone felt the enemy's spears piercing, she alone caught the slash of their swords. She alone screamed and writhed with the death throes of her people when all but the triple Daughters of God deserted her.

"And then, with a cry that tore al-Uzza from her mouth, the sons of Taghlib rode into Mecca's holy precinct. Just at that place where the pilgrims rejoice to see the end of all their longing, hardship, and suffering, where with one tongue they cry out 'Here I am, O God, here I am,' the smallest of the children of Taghlib joined her first cry to those of all her ancestors.

"Grandmother saw just how sharp would be the disappointment of Zura, her husband. She saw that the child was perfectly formed, but not the son for whom he'd prayed to Isa ibn Maryam so fervently. She looked into the bright eyes, blinking at the world's sudden light. She saw that they were blue, of the color unlikely to darken over time.

"And in the sacred space of the qubbah, Grandmother loved her tiny, blue-eyed daughter as she'd never loved anything before."

Rayah looked at Sitt Sameh, this desert woman who claimed to be her mother. Had the baby's blue eyes somehow come down through the generations to Rayah herself? She wanted to know how.

Sitt Sameh resumed her story with a hoarse whispered wail.

"'For the love of Manat—no.' My grandmother pleaded to her husband. 'To please you, I call on Maryam Umm Isa to intercede. You would kill our daughter? I will do anything'

"The birth had been discovered upon the tribe's arrival in Mecca, its unnatural location and the gender of its fruit. And the loss of the Gospel as well.

"'Of course I will not kill her.' Zura's voice was as hard and sharp as black obsidian. 'I've been baptized in Isa's name. It's only the heathen demons you cling to who allow fathers to bury ill-formed children alive.'

"Grandmother dared to hope. 'I call her Amat al-Uzza, al-Uzza's handmaid.'

"'Bint Zura, Zura's daughter, is all you need to know of her until she comes to the hands of the priest.'

"Grandmother bowed her head, complying, but knowing all the same she could call her daughter whatever she wanted when the two of them were alone in the harem together.

"'To you, it will not matter,' Zura went on, cutting like obsidian now, 'for I divorce you. For what you have done, to lose God's holy Gospel, may you never come to my bed again.'

"Grandmother swallowed. That was not the worst that could happen. 'You must still allow me to nurse the child. Until she is weaned, at least. To do otherwise would be no better than to bury her alive, for she will die without a mother.'

"'My brother's sickly son died in the night. His wife will wet-nurse the child for me.'

"Still not the very worst. Umm Taghlib might still see her daughter, playing among the couching camels from time to time, from afar. Leave her presents, of honeycomb, of tasseled little dresses.

"Then Zura concluded: 'For what you have done to Taghlib's holy qubbah, you are banished from our people forever. You are a witch, a kahinah. Any man among us who sees you will be duty-bound to kill you upon sight, from this moment forward.'

"Grandmother wanted to explain about how what she had done was right, for the Goddess had called her. Birthing wasn't dirty but sacred, and sacred had this one been, among the sacred cushions. This child had been born in the litter she would grow to ride in as the virgin and lead the sons of Taghlib in their hour of darkest need.

"But Zura scooped up the Daughters of God, their wood stained with blood and fluid, and threw them after her. Grandmother was abandoned, tribeless, childless.

"At least she was abandoned in Mecca, in a city known to show mercy to its pilgrims. Had she been abandoned in the desert, camel-less without a water skin, as many were, she would have died. Now, however, when she bent, crushed with sobs over the ache of her full breasts, she knew Zura had been as cruel as he knew how: He had condemned her to live without her child."

"My grandmother was not the first woman ever to be abandoned by a tribe. Nor even the first in that spot. The holy well of Zamzam marked the place where Hajar Umm Isma'il had been left to die by her own husband, Ibrahim, because of a first wife's jealousy. She'd been left long ago, when there was nothing in the spot but the holy Ka'ba. At least Hajar had kept her son. At least Hajar had been left with the love of God, for when she had been unable to bear the thirsty cries of Isma'il any more, she had run from place to place. She'd run, distracted, calling on the name of God. Or on the Goddess, others say.

"'Dig, O daughter,' a voice had come to her.

"And when she had scratched in the barren sand, pure water sprang forth. From Hajar's well, pilgrims drink to this day.

"Like Hajar before her, Grandmother ran from hill to hill, to Zamzam. Grandmother drank of the holy water. She ran some more, pushing aside the crowds of pilgrims, crying on her daughter's name and on the Goddesses who'd been her midwives. If it hadn't been in Mecca's holy precinct, during the holy month, no doubt a son of Taghlib would have ended her misery, because of how she shamed his people.

"Unlike Hajar, Grandmother could not regain her child. Unlike Hajar, her husband did not come to restore her. Unlike Hajar, she was left with only the Goddesses she bundled in a blanket like a baby to fill her arms. Would a great people come of her child, as they had of Hajar? She would never know.

"But when she left Zamzam, having lived on nothing but well water for many days, everyone she met saw the hand of divinity upon her at once. Her hair had gone completely white, her face wrinkled like a woman of a great many more years. She walked, carrying her bundle, through the streets of the town where dogs barked at her. Every once in a while, women had pity and gave her something to eat.

"As she walked, she talked to herself. What did she say? Prayers, poems? No one could hear distinctly enough.

"But during that very Dhu'l Hijjah another tribe of the desert, the sons of Tamim, also came on pilgrimage. Besides their visits to the Ka'ba and Zamzam well, besides their bartering in the markets, the women of Tamim went, as daughters of Taghlib did, from house to house among the wealthy merchants of Mecca. Any with milk in her breasts would call to see if a merchant had a son he wished to foster to the desert. The milk mother would receive rich gifts from the father as long as the son lived with her—from the son, too, who would revere her all his life. Also, important bonds would be forged between the families; the merchants could pass through tribal lands with impunity as long as the ties held good.

"So it happened that Grandmother came upon some women of Tamim paying a call on the house of al-Wahīd Abu Khalid of Mecca, sons and milk sons in tow. The house of al-Wahīd Abu Khalid was one of the new square ones with lattice brought from Yemen in the windows. Before a lattice, at the women's entrance to this house, Grandmother caught one of the Tamimi women, Umm Mutammim, roughly by the arm.

"'Do not take that son of al-Wahīd to your breast,' she warned her, and these were a prophet's tones. 'By Manat, if you do, you'll rue the day. You will be as unhappy as am I, who will never see my child again.'

'Alas, good woman,' Umm Mutammim replied. 'Khalid ibn al-Walīd of the tribe of the

Quraysh has been at my fosterage for three years or four. I cannot now give up the relationship, for he is like my own sons to me. Surely you can understand that, you who have lost a child.'

"'Woe to the sons of Tamim, woe to Mutammim your son. The breast you give Ibn al-Wahīd to suck—you will cut it from you rather than live to see another deed of his dread doing.'

"An appalling silence fell upon the daughters of Tamim; they touched the amulets at their throats. By the echo of silence in the wind afterward, they knew they heard true words. Umm Mutammim's hand wandered protectively to the dark head at her skirts: little Khalid ibn al-Walīd. Grandmother sidled away from the large-eyed boy as if she'd seen a scorpion, but Umm Mutammim couldn't give him up.

"'Nevertheless, come with us, O lost woman, if you will,' said Umm Mutammim. 'Come join our tribe if you have none of your own. I know you cannot help but be a blessing to us, saving us from future ill. Who knows? Perhaps you may even save my dear foster son from this ill you foresee, if the Gods will.'

"And that was how my grandmother came to live among the Tamim, the ancient enemies of the tribe of her birth, in their dirah in the northern desert. Ever after she went by no other name than Umm Taghlib, for the tribe that had cast her childless from them for being an evil kahinah."

Sitt Sameh fell silent. The eunuch scribe ruffled through his parchments. Did he mean to write down this story as well? How dare he set it in the same form as the Holy Quran, even as the tale of Khalid the Conqueror?

Then Rayah saw he did not dare. "My master had me write something of his childhood with his foster family among the Tamim," Abd Allah said. "Will you allow me, Sitt, to read it?"

Still fingering the broken bits of the litter, Sitt Sameh nodded her agreement.

9

> Is this one of Umm Awfa's relics, now
> mute, by the sandy hills of ad-Daraji . . .?
> A hearth where she once lived . . . that seems
> like crisscrossed tattoos upon a wrist . . .
> Here I stood after
> twenty years, barely distinguishing it:
> … black stones in a hole where the cauldron was
>   slung, and
> a trench like an old well partly raised.
> So when I knew the hearth, I said, "Good
> morning to you, home: may you fare well."
> —the Qasidah of Zuhayr ibn Abi Sulma,
> contemporary of the Prophet

Ghru-grug.

I now live in Homs; my slaves buy cheese and yogurt ready-made. Still, over the rooftops, I hear that the local dairyman's daughters have begun to churn.

To my scribe, the sound is no more than the rustle of a breeze through the palm fronds. "Have you, master, no memory of the world before love struck you as a youth?" Does he laugh at me, this creature who lost the means to love before he could?

Yes, I remember. He won't like it. He would name the sound silence and relegate it to the harem. But I hear churning and I remember.

Ghru-grug, ghru-grug. A heartbeat. My own. At least I assume it is mine in an infantile haze that claims everything as its own.

Ghru-grug, ghru-grug. I cannot stop it. But then, I cannot stop my heart. I would not want to. It is the sound of God breathing life into dust.

I was asleep and now I am awake. There were wonderful dreams, and now there is only life. I keep my eyes closed a little while longer against the day's limitations.

Ghru-grug, ghru-grug. The breath of a God, the heartbeat of the world? Perhaps, in the language of the poet. It is the sound that began every day of my childhood. I might well have thought it was the sound that rouses the sun itself.

Ghru-grug is the sound of the churning. The milk left to settle overnight is now slung back and forth in an old goatskin to make curds for breakfast. When my will to thwart sleep finally gave out last night, Mother was still awake, tending the fire with crumbs of camel dung and snatches of song. Now she is awake again (or still), humming about her first task of the day.

I call her "Mother" but as I have suggested, where the father is unique, there may be many mothers. Umm Mutammim is my milk mother. My eyes are still shut, feigning sleep, but I know her breasts are as full and pendulous as the goatskin she swings from the tent poles. I can see those breasts, white where her bodice slit hangs loose as she sits and swings the churn. Outside the tent, seen through another slit between black fabric, dawn is pouring a thick white milk over all the desert hills. The sandy hills of ad-Dahna, no doubt. The flocks are roused. They trip about their pen—makeshift, of brush and dried thorn, to keep the foxes out—with full udders, chiming the hour to rise with their bleats.

This is my very first memory of the world. It is a milk memory, a woman's memory, a memory of life. It is a memory that teaches one first to remember.

"My poor little foreign, motherless babe," Umm Mutammim's eyes seem to say to me.

"Tell me this Umm Mutammim's lineage," my scribe insists. "I must write that down".

"Very well."

Umm Mutammim, my milk mother and mother of my personality and manners, was a woman of noble lineage. Nuwaira, sharif of the clan of the Banu Yarbu of the tribe of Tamim, had married her for her fabled beauty.

As long as I was, I thought in those early days, Mother would be. Though campsites, good and bad seasons, watering holes, everything else in the world convulsed with change, she and I were constants.

"But what of your real mother?" my scribe demands. "The mother who bore you? Or does honor keep you from naming her so publicly?"

True. A man shouldn't bandy the names of his women about. He'll create women who bandy their persons about. And my birth mother, my scribe thinks, must bring me closer to Muhammad.

But honor? No, for me, now, I wouldn't call it honor.

I have said I will speak more of mothers in this work than is usually the custom and so, with the help of the All-Knowing, I hope to do. Yet of the womb in which my father formed me, with the help and by the grace of the All-Powerful from a tiny clot of blood, I find but little to say. My milk mother was always more important. More—more real.

But genealogies go through the blood mother when they go through ink. Very well, what there is to say, let me pause to say it.

She was al-Walid's destined bride from the day they were born, his first cousin, his father's brother Umaiya ibn Abd Allah's daughter, she whom he could claim before all other suitors.

Her girlhood name was Lababa. All the time I knew her, however, I was the source of her name. She was called Umm Khalid, the mother of Khalid, and nothing else. She got her status and power from me, a promising and first-born son, but gave me little beyond a body in return. As often happens with women whose positions are as secure as mountains, when their men may as well cut their own throats as divorce them, she was pampered beyond wit. The one thing I can say I admired her for was her incredible skill at finding vanity to spend my father's fortune on. And then, by God, to find indispensable use for it. Such were the harems of Mecca in those days.

In Homs today.

Such women owe more to men than ever Umm Mutammim did.

"How did you come to be reared in the desert?"

It was a common practice. Arabs who lived in towns for the wealth and comfort of the trading life gave their sons out into the great womb that makes powerful men of sniveling infants—the desert. It was best, the reasoning went, to be raised far from the corrupt and unwholesome airs of crumbling clay such as Mecca held (and still does). Men like my father used their influence to purchase the best of both worlds for their sons. At least they hoped so.

The Prophet himself, on whom may God smile, knew a similar boyhood.

"Through compassion, I understand, for he was an orphan before he was born."

"He went to the Sa'adi clan of the Hawazin tribe, though I would not be surprised if other Arabs step up, as true memory fails, to claim the privilege."

My scribe's pen flies. He is writing more than I am speaking. I was afraid of that.

"What is it you write with that flimsy reed?" I demand.

"We have come at last to the Prophet, blessings on him. I would write down all that happened to him while a child among the Sa'adi. Angels visited him there and placed a new heart of pure fire within his breast. His presence in camp brought sudden prosperity—twins to the herds, rich milk to their udders."

"There are no tales of wonder from my boyhood in the desert such as they tell of Muhammad."

"Muhammad's presence did not bring the Sa'adi these benefits, as they say?"

"By God, I see no harm in their getting fat on their dreams. I will not say it is not true. I have witnessed greater miracles in my day. But don't you get fat on it, you who'll never raise any child. That is not what I'm paying you to write, man."

I don't free him from my gaze until he sets the old parchment aside. He'll scrape it off and reuse it later. For now, a new one—

The sons of Yarbu of Tamim, where I was sent, was a clan of vastly more consequence than the Sa'adi, and dreams and miracles were not for them. They were wont to take what increase they would from their weaker neighbors and never mind waiting on the mercy of heaven or the chance richness of the lambing season. They certainly had no need of me for their prosperity.

And yet, I can boast that the great sharif Nuwaira laid his war-mare's bridle and his curved dagger in my cradle swinging beneath the tent poles, like the butter skin. This he did for good omen, to make me what I am today.

I can remember a time of tumble-play about Umm Mutammim's feet and nestling sleep beside her curd-making, before I'd even ever heard of Umm Khalid or al-Wahīd or Mecca. Then all humanity seemed as united as Mother and me.

My first discovery of human variety within this whole unsettled me. Some of my little playmates—my milk sisters, the herdsman's daughters—were more like my milk mother than I was. They learned to weave and spin and churn and would always stay in the harem while I was destined to be a man, like Sharif Nuwaira. I was given to understand that this difference could be a source of pride for me. But when sorrows or darkness fell, I still found the comfort of my milk mother's bosom beyond the thrust of my pride.

Then I learned that two of the children, while they were boys like me and shared my masculine fate, were more particularly my milk mother's sons. They were the fruit of Nuwaira's loins and the true blood-bearers of the tent. Umm Mutammim is not to be blamed for the pain this revelation caused me. She shared her breasts and affections among us with perfect fairness, a love that was even beyond the subdividing that the word "fairness" implies.

But one evening the sharif grew expansive, and in this mood he seemed stingier than his woman ever was. He gave his true sons presents: a camel to Mutammim the first-born and a dagger to Malik the younger. He gave me equal rides on the gentle old mare, but nothing permanent.

"You are no son of Tamim," Mutammim explained.

His words were like a blow. I loved the sons of Tamim; their ancient poems of heroism weaned me. There could be no finer blood in all the world. For all the sweet Tamimi milk in me, their blood was not my blood? I might as well bleed water when I fell and scraped a knee.

Malik, who was very close to my own age, knew how to be particularly vicious. "You are no son of Tamim," he nearly sang the repetition of his brother's words. "You are one who dwells in town."

"Town? What's a town?" I asked, stupid with hurt.

"A place where men are less than men. They live like animals. They burrow in holes made of dirt. They stifle for air. They never move their tents. They live year after year in their own mess. No Tamimi live in towns. We are free men."

Mutammim tried to be kinder. Hard, cold facts are sometimes the kindest thing one can give. "The town is called Mecca. It is far away," he said. "Your people are the Quraysh."

"I don't know any place called Mecca," I insisted.

"Bad pastures there," Malik said. "Not worth the visit."

"I don't know any Quraysh."

"Your father paid us to raise you," Mutammim said.

"As if a little gold could buy blood," said Malik scornfully.

"How do you know all this? I never heard of such a thing."

"Well, you are a simpleton then," Malik shrugged. "Obviously not a Tamimi."

I scrambled to my feet and charged at him. Then I halted. Suddenly I could not think of shedding *blood so superior. So I screamed with shame and fury and flung myself to the ground until the grief made my mind black. Mother came and took me in her arms. She gave me more affection than her own sons and lied to me until she made me strong enough to take the truth.*

A fourth member of our boys' play circle was named al-Harith, and he was the son of Suwaid, Nuwaira's head herdsman. Active and exciting as the profession of herdsman may seem to a little boy, the great sharif's example soon taught me that the noble never work for another man. I grappled this fact to my mind with all I had. I did have something in common with the true sons of my milk mother after all, something al-Harith with his lineage could not share. It suddenly became fiercely important to me to exaggerate this division every chance I got.

Opportunities for picking at these scabs did not fail. Umm al-Harith spent each day with Umm Mutammim. Not only is there always plenty of work a herdsman's wife can lend a hand to in the tent of a sharif's wife, but the women were the best of friends, class meaning little between them.

So one day, not the first, we children got underfoot.

"Outside," Umm Mutammim ordered, lightly whipping us from the tent with a length of veil.

And so we found ourselves away from all calming and equalizing supervision. Away from women.

Outside, we played at slinging flat stones toward the tent pegs at fifteen paces. Mutammim hit, Malik hit. I always hit. Al-Harith, never.

"You are a herdsman's son," we taunted. "The wolves will come and eat you when you stand herdsman, with an arm like that."

I don't remember anything peculiar about the way al-Harith ran away crying on that particular day. Nor do I remember what my milk brothers and I played at on our own until suppertime.

But only too well do I remember when the herdsman's tent gave out alarm, with pale faces and fought-against tears. Their slender hope of a first-born son was missing from camp, and it was after dark.

Throughout the night I sought the evasion of sleep that a four-year-old is allowed. But how disturbed that luxury was! I was only too aware of the search parties growing larger and better armed and mounted. At last, Sharif Nuwaira himself rose from the comfort of his fire. He buckled on the sword of his forebears, took a torch, and rode off into the darkness on his mare.

Seeing the great earnestness of the search (wondering if I, even being the son of a noble man, should ever be worthy of such concern), I began to cry. I cried softly and into the rug at first, then louder and louder until I was gratified by being heard.

"What is it, O strange son of mine?" Umm Mutammim took me by the shoulders. That was when I cried loudest of all.

I wakened my two milk brothers. The story came out.

Nothing we three confessed could help the search, for we had not even noticed the direction our playmate had run. But Umm Mutammim listened closely to what we said. She let the air go silent for a few very oppressive moments while she thought. Then she produced an elegant speech as only the daughter of the desert can.

"Did you not see how the sharif your father, sharif of all the sons of Yarbu, arose himself just now

and went to look for his herdsman's son? You boast of your noble birth, but there is one thing you have yet to learn. Without this knowledge, you are anything but noble. A truly great man, a man like Nuwaira ibn Yarbu, is marked by the charity and compassion he holds toward his dependents. He is never harsh or despotic in his nobility. Your father and I prayed for noble sons so they could bless the world with these virtues. As for you, O Khalid ibn al-Walid, I did not share my breast with you so you could later spew out evil with that mouth."

Then she said something I didn't understand at the time. Yet it was so striking, I could not forget it. Something about a kahinah telling her she would some day cut off her breast in regret for having fostered me.

"That day may be this day, if the Gods will. Truly, I feel as she prophesied. But I do hope the sharif my master and I shall never have cause to doubt our high hopes again. If we do, it would have been better had you all been born girls and been buried at birth."

Women's tears and fears support true nobility, just as poles make the shelter of a tent from limp and formless fabric.

"It is never good for nightfall to find you alone and lost in the desert," Umm Mutammim continued her speech. "If it is not good for you, O noble sons of noble fathers, how much more dreadful is it for the weak and unprotected? Have I not taught you the law of desert hospitality? Al-Uzza is my witness that I have tried. Any wayfarer is the guest of heaven, even if he be the man who killed your own blood brother. Death is so close to us—always. Just beyond the light at the heart of the harem, who can say what dangers lie? Enemies less predictable, more hostile, and less personal than your greatest blood feud. Beings of fire have great enmity against those of us created from dust. Against them, all men are brothers. You would not turn a stranger from the center pole where the charms and amulets of power hang. If it is thus a shame to turn away a stranger from the comfort and safety of your tent, how much more shameful is it to send away a friend and a supporter?"

Now my tears knew no limits. Malik spoke in wide-eyed dread of the wolves that "Even now may be cracking poor al-Harith's bones for the marrow." Dread is quite akin to thrill in a four-year-old.

"Wolves and lions are only the most substantial of dangers in the desert. Umm Mutammim quickly silenced her younger son. She made a magic sign to ward off evil and touched a charm on the pole above her head.

None of us dared to speak the name of this danger but we all thought: "The jinn."

10

**We created man of dried clay, of dark loam molded;
And the jinn We created before, of subtle fire.
—The Holy Quran, Surah 15:26-27**

Of all the things in the Conqueror's parchment, Rayah noticed, Sitt Sameh picked up on the sandy hills he'd likened to his milk mother's breasts. Sitt Sameh took up her spinning and her own tale among such hills.

A day's ride on good mounts through the cliffs at Buwaib Pass, the winter sun at your back, will bring you to the wells of ar-Rumah. Here you must fill even the water skins that leak and offer the camels as much as they can drink three times, for ar-Rumah lies just at the southern end of the Dahna Sands.

The Dahna are bands of grit, burnt brick in color, threading their way across the desert like the roots of ancient trees, days' travel in every direction. Where sand appears between the grit, you can pick out numerous tracks in the desolate place, but do not follow them. No rain, no stream, no nesting ostrich or herding gazelle erases the signs of desperate attempts to take this way north.

Only those with a trusted guide from the Banu Tamim should even consider it. You must have good relations with all the man's kin if you hope to escape robbery or being led astray until death releases you. And you must be sure the Banu Tamim are in the good graces of the jinn. The jinn are the real masters here and swirl the footsteps of men to their own uncanny wills.

For all its dangers, the ad-Dahna is a more secure route northward than the one that heads from the wells of Dumat al-Jandal. Only one force has crossed that way in human memory, and Khalid ibn al-Walid led that one, moving like lightning to take the sluggish Romans at Yarmuk. No doubt the Conqueror will tell of that feat in time.

Suffice it here to say that the wells of ar-Rumah are the first the Banu Tamim claim on the border of their hereditary lands. They are good wells, the water sweet with only a tang of iron, a cluster of five deep-dug holes, each revetted neatly with stone. But because the Dahna Sands lie between them and the tribe's main dirah, the Tamim cannot guard this treasure of theirs as carefully as they like.

Sitt Sameh's grandmother—she who traveled with the Tamim now and was called Umm Taghlib—knew her former tribe's habit of ignoring the Tamimi claim and professing the wells as their own. At least, they dared to do so when there were no Banu Tamim about. And so dread filled Umm Taghlib when she saw the vultures' patient circling, etching wells of their own in the blue sky above ar-Rumah. The moon, though still veiled like a shy virgin, had passed out of the month of peace and into Safar, the month of emptying, when blood flows again.

Three scouts had been sent half a day ahead of the larger party with women and children returning from Mecca. Now the three scouts lay dead where they'd taken a hopeless stand to defend the wells against a much larger party. Their camels and weapons were stolen, their bodies stripped. The vultures already had their eyes.

"But who has done this deed?" Nuwaira ibn Yarbu, sharif of the Banu Tamim, mourned the loss of his kinsmen. "We must take revenge, but how can we say where to take it? The cowards have broken the fletches off their arrows and reclaimed their lances. We cannot tell whose marks were here."

"Yes, we can, O sharif," Umm Taghlib said. Unlike the rest of the women, she had not remained with the kneeling camels at some distance, keening at the news brought to them but not coming to see themselves. For Umm Taghlib had recognized the distinctive indentation of a camel that had been made to kneel in the same place not long before.

Under the shadow of his heavy brows, Nuwaira looked curiously at the kahinah, the madwoman his wife had insisted on bringing with them from Mecca. "Speak on, woman."

"Banu Taghlib," she spat. "More, I can give you the name of the man who threw the spear that felled Abu Essam there."

"Are you certain?" asked the sharif.

"Perhaps he didn't actually throw the spear, but his was the hand that reclaimed it. Zura." Like a horned asp, she spat more venom and gave the name no honorific. "There, I see the couching place of a camel I know well. She is calm and steady and bears the goatskin cradle of my daughter upon her back, swinging as she moves."

When Nuwaira still doubted, she went on. "You think I do not know the footprint of my own husband, when he walks out from my bed to relieve himself? That is he, flat-footed, broad at the toes from much scouting over the sand, with a crooked left toe where a camel stepped on it once and broke it. I'd know that print anywhere."

Nuwaira nodded his satisfaction and gave orders to his men. They would draw water for the women and animals, see them safely settled at the well and the dead men properly honored beneath their cairns. But they would stay no longer than that before riding after the enemy, pursuing north into ad-Dahna. "The blood of at least three Banu Taghlib must slake the thirst of our fallen kinsmen now."

"Yes, and let one of them be Zura," Umm Taghlib said, "the father of my child."

Then, as the first camel skins came sloshing out of the wells, dark, heavy, slick with their sweet burden, the kahinah cried: "Stop, O sons of Tamim."

For in the running slosh of water along the rounded sides, she had seen a horror. She saw her child. That was not so strange. Amat al-Uzza was everywhere before her eyes, her name in a whimper ever on her tongue as the milk knotted unspent in her breasts. But beside the baby, laid to rest on the sand, she saw in vision a pit growing as Zura dug with a camel's shoulder blade. Never mind the oath he'd made by Isa ibn Maryam. The desert's necessity brought other Gods even to the baptized. A tribe with blood on their hands had to move faster than a cradle could rock. Zura was going to bury his own flesh and blood, let her choke to death with sand. The hyneas would come when he was gone to dig the tiny, perfect body up.

"No one drink." Umm Taghlib spoke with the eery calm of the sandstorm's center.

"What is it?" Nuwaira demanded, anxious to be about his revenge. "Don't tell me the sons of dogs have poisoned ar-Rumah as well."

"Not so, but let me cast a spell first on every drop of water that has been drunk from these eyes-of-heaven under this moon."

"It will not affect the water permanently?"

"No. Once I have released the Lords of this Place to go after those with their water in them, ar-Rumah will run sweeter than ever. Abu Assam and his fallen companions it will not harm, for they are already dead. And my daughter it will not harm, either, since she is but an infant who drinks only mother's milk."

The thought of his quarry slowed by bellyache and the need to kneel his camel frequently gratified Nuwaira. "If it please the Gods, I will cut the dog down as he squats behind a boulder in ad-Dahna," he said. Then he sat with his men in their thirst, in wondering silence and the shade of their camels, to watch the kahinah perform.

First she unpacked her three Goddesses and set them in a glowering circle around the clearest of Zura's footprints, mid-point among the wells. Then she took off her veil, ungirdled her waist, and tied seven knots in the cord, from one end to the other. Upon each knot, she blew seven times, saying the name of Zura and evoking the jinn with each breath.

Encircling the footprint and Goddesses with the coil of her knotted girdle, she scooped up sand and let it run through her fingers with her eyes closed. She reopened her eyes and studied how it had fallen: "Hills, a plain, a wide dune's ridge." Then, with three quick stabs, she stuck a branch of camel thorn into the hollow of the print, muttering her dark words over all.

Some of the drawn water she sprinkled over the footprint with a branch of thorn; the rest she sprinkled back whence it had come, a share to each of the five wells. Into each cool hollow, she murmured her words. The sounds of lizards and scorpions hiding in the crevices came back up to her and, in the echoes, the hushed whispers of the jinn.

Some of the sons of Tamim moved their camels and themselves back to the women then, to be further out of harm's way. From a safe distance, they watched the kahinah begin to revolve around her figurines, and in that circuit, in a tight whirl of her own. So she circled, wider and wider, out toward the wells. The sons of Tamim saw the puffs of dust grow out of her bare heels. They watched the puffs grow together and, on a silent gust of wind, begin to spin on their own. A dust devil, chariot of the jinn.

The kahinah dropped to the ground, exhausted, her mind dizzy. But the cloud now had a life of its own. After a moment's hesitation, twirling in place, it began to move, past the wells, past sand, picking up speed, on toward the north and the first burnt-brick ridge of ad-Dahna.

The Spirits of Smokeless Fire, old as the day of creation, loosed of the wells they called home, spun out through the parched and arid world that formed them. Across ad-Dahna they whirled.

Zura of the Banu Taghlib, ankles drawn up on the neck of his bull camel, still carrying Tamimi spears as a trophy, heard them. He had just been thinking how clever he was to take a different track over these ridges, for the Tamimi cowards would never dare to follow him. People warned he would be lost, but he wasn't lost yet. All a man had to do was keep sunrise on his right hand, sunset on the left in order to keep going north.

Then he heard them. He strained to listen, ignoring the sound of his people who had started to moan as the bellyache hit them. Over the moans he listened, over the deafening silence of the gritty red ridges, through the humming deceit of distance.

He looked around. Four or five horizons shimmered pink before him. He tried to avoid the baffling sight, pulling up on the loose tail of his turban, down on the crown, to meet just at his eyes. All but one of the many distant, hazy lines—he couldn't tell which—were the abode of the Nameless Tribe.

He heard it again, over the protests of the camels on which his people rode. The whisper of one sand grain upon another rang in the silence, leaving him lonelier than the high cry of a kite. Like the bottom of a well. He should have remembered to recite some verses as he rode, putting words on the rock of camel gait, to remind himself he was human after all. There were words from the Gospel, "Our Father Who—" But Zura had never been a man of many words.

Then he saw it, the golden whirl almost beyond sight in its speed. He tried to turn his camel from its path but too late. It passed directly under the belly of his beast, who snorted in fear and skittered to one side, sensing the menace. Zura slid his legs from their rest, crossed upon the shaggy neck, to either side of the saddle for better balance.

Then he felt the Fire Spirits, like bits of cutting glass spinning up his leg.

The sons of Taghlib discovered him as they picked up the pieces, after their bellies settled, after the sons of Tamim had ridden down on them and then gone. The Banu Tamim, extracting their due revenge, blood for blood, had of course not bothered with recapturing a baby girl. Such a burden on a tribe's resources was best left with the father's tribe; they did not fight for a mother's wishes, after all.

The vengeance seekers had passed over this man as well. For what was the honor in killing one who had lost his wits? Who howled and hiccuped with hilarity like a hyena at the hollow waste? A man who sat gnawing on his own flesh, naked under the sun?

"The Spirits of Fire have exacted their own sort of vengeance," the sons of Taghlib muttered among themselves. "One mind for another, Zura's madness for the maddening grief he caused the kahinah."

And no one even whispered of burying little Bint Zura after that.

11

> I betake me for refuge to the Lord of the Daybreak
> Against the mischiefs of His creation;
> Against the mischief of the night when it overtaketh me;
> And against the mischief of weird women who blow on knots;
> And against the mischief of the envier when he envieth.
> —The Holy Quran, Surah 113

"A person could take this matter to her." Umm Mutammim, my milk mother, said that night when al-Harith, the herdsman's son, was missing in the desert. She spoke in a whisper that told me she hoped we children had all cried ourselves to sleep in our tumble among the cushions and rugs of the women's section. So naturally, I pricked up my ears and forced myself to stay awake to hear more.

"Ask her to intercede with the—you know—the Spirits of Fire?" Umm al-Harith didn't risk evoking the jinn by saying their name. She also did not say who "she" was. "Oh, no. I wouldn't dare."

"The life of your son is at stake this night."

Umm al-Harith wept helplessly. "His life is in al-Uzza's hands."

Umm Mutammim embraced her friend. "And my sons, without any sense of nobility, are to blame."

My milk mother did not let the fire die down and bank it as she usually did at night when the weather was not very cold. She kept it going and the tent flaps open upon it so a little lost boy might see it and follow it home. If he could still see. If he could still walk.

Everything a woman's hands could do to make a neat, provident household, Umm Mutammim had done. Extra quilts, rugs, clothes, cooking utensils, and her camel litter stood stacked against the rear curtain and that dividing her from the men's section. Supplies of dates and flour and herbs and roasted locusts hung from the tent poles in sacks she herself had woven with bright patterns. Among her children, a pair of orphaned kid goats also rested. A nest of dried brush in the cool night air cradled full water skins, carefully mended so they would not weep. More brush and a heap of camel dung stood ready to feed the fire. The tent was a bastion of order against the desert's chaos and hostility, and the firelight bathed all of this in a warm, cozy glow.

But Umm al-Harith, who had abandoned her own tent and hearth for the night, could not be comforted.

"They might well call her Umm Tamim instead of Umm Taghlib," my milk mother said, trying to explain her position. And that was the first time I heard the name that the herdsman's wife seemed as loathe to say as the name of the jinn, for I had been too young to remember the spell on the wells of ar-Rumah.

Umm al-Harith kept from screaming only by wringing her hands. And she kept glancing furtively, not at the comfort and providence all around her, but at the main pole, the center pole. From day to day, with every shift of campsite, my milk mother renewed her tent's center pole with charms: the ankle bones of hares, a wide-eyed fox's skull, her own menstrual rags, filthy things to disgust the jinn and keep them away. She stood up from the fire and touched them now, as Umm al-Harith seemed to long to do, if only her knees would hold her. Umm Mutammim stared out into the desert night.

To the stranger, the desert seems to be a great and lifeless void. The most vile acts, they imagine, when committed in or upon the desert have no repercussions, for who is there to see or to care? But one who learns of the desert from a mother's knee knows differently. The desert is peopled indeed, and it is a population, eroded by the harshness of the land, that maintains far less mercy than that which lives beside a sweet-flowing river.

Umm Mutammim pursued her argument. "As a midwife, Umm Taghlib has the skill of bringing forth just what is called for."

The herdsman's wife continued to wring her hands. "—Many sons—?" She choked on the word. Then she said, "She cannot be easy to find."

My milk mother disagreed. "Although we rarely see her, she shadows us. Whenever a young man rides into Nuwaira's camp, asking for the midwife in a frenzy, you must have seen: he gets waved out into the desert again. 'Ride on in the direction of the sun going down,' he is told. 'There you will find Umm Taghlib whom you seek.' And though it's been months and many changes of encampment since any of us has seen her, there indeed the kahinah will always be found."

"You are certain she follows Nuwaira our protector like his shadow at dawn?"

"She hovers only at the very edge of the influence of my son's father, just where his arrow could save her from an enemy raid if necessary."

"But never too close to interrupt her intercourse with marauders—of a different sort?"

"With the Lords of the open desert," my milk mother said for her. Even she wouldn't say the word "jinn."

"What?" I couldn't help but betray my wakefulness now. "Who's Umm Taghlib? She's a kahinah?"

"A midwife, my Khalid." Umm Mutammim brought her gentle, calming ways over to my side now. "A kahinah, a priestess, a seer, a blower-on-knots."

"A kahinah," I said firmly. No, it was not comforting to have things called by other than their proper names.

Sometime later, when again they thought we were asleep, Umm Mutammim made another attempt to calm her friend's shifting. "Umm Taghlib has given us ample proof of her powers."

"Praise al-Uzza, it may be true."

"Of course, I should go to her."

"Would you, mistress? Would you go for my son?"

"Because my sons are to blame" remained unsaid. Perhaps, even, "One foster son in particular."

"The moment dawn comes," she did say aloud.

Umm al-Harith stole another hopeful glance out to the dark night where, somewhere, her son lay. "Such power can be evil as well as good."

"True," Umm Mutammim admitted, and she laid a hand on what she thought was my sleeping side.

"Was it for being a kahinah that she was forced to flee her home tribe, the sons of Taghlib?"

"So they say."

"And forced to leave her infant daughter there."

"Yes, may the Gods keep us from a similar fate."

"And she turned Zura their sharif into a mad beast?"

"That is also true."

"Usually it is only men who face banishment from their tribes." Umm al-Harith considered. "Stoning us where we stand is the punishment for women, may the stars and the mid-month moon shield us."

"Umm Taghlib's crime was more akin to a man's rebellion than a woman's." The firelight set stern creases across the tattoos on my milk mother's forehead. "All Zura's people have turned to that new religion. They were washed in water as is their rite."

"He must have some power, this God, if his followers can afford to waste water for washing like that."

Umm Mutammim said: "Separating a child from her mother is only what one expects of the Banu Taghlib."

"No honor," the herdsman's wife agreed.

"So," my milk mother said, "Umm Taghlib, al-Uzza shield her, spends much time working spells, black ones against Zura and his sons, white ones to recall her daughter to her. Hearing the call of her tribe in thunder."

"Your good husband and our master Nuwaira must rejoice to have such power on his side against his ancient enemies the Taghlib."

"But as yet, she's seen little effect. Our two tribes are at the same delicately balanced odds as they were when I was a girl."

"You think, then, she can do nothing for me?"

"The Night Ones, those uncanny spirits, must be all and always in her debt. And shall be more so, come morning."

"You would do that? You will go for her, Umm Mutammim? Evoke her power? For me?"

"And for your son."

I heard a scrambling across the rugs. I couldn't imagine what it was and feared to turn and look, *lest they realize I was still awake. Then I understood that Umm al-Harith had crawled across the distance between them in order to kiss my milk mother's hands.*

"I didn't know where to turn when al-Harith did not come home at dark," she said. "I was too afraid."

"There is one thing I must ask you," Umm Mutammim said, her gaze outside the tent to the blackness behind the fire. Her unease was palpable.

"Of course. Anything."

"I would take my children with me."

"Umm Mutammim, do you think that's wise? To the kahinah? Surely you can leave them with me, as you've done before."

The thought remained unspoken between the women, but I realize now that my milk mother must have been worried about the evil eye. Jealousy could be very potent in a woman so helpless with grief for her own missing son. To say this is what Umm Mutammim feared, however, could twist the eye to a sharper, more dangerous point.

"Well, I cannot take all three," Umm Mutammim decided. "I have hands for only two, and it must be the two youngest."

"Yes, I see."

"What I ask of you, Umm al-Harith, is that you will keep an eye on my Mutammim while I am gone."

A trick of the firelight caused a shadow to pass over my milk mother as she thought over what she'd just said. It must have been her use of the word "eye." Yes, envy was liable to taint the glance of a woman who had lost a son, bringing evil upon the good things of others.

Umm Mutammim did not show more concern about the matter than this, for her eldest son was still awake, too, and betrayed it by crying out, "But I want to see the kahinah, too."

"Indeed you do not," his mother told him.

Indeed I did not. "I will stay home," I offered. "Take Mutammim to see the kahinah."

"No. Mutammim will stay," my milk mother said definitely. "He is the oldest, why, almost a man. He can take care of Umm al-Harith, even, as his father the sharif would do if he did not have to be out searching the desert for al-Harith."

Umm al-Harith smiled pleasantly at Mutammim, although it was a strain. Having turned toward her now, I saw how the firelight lit up the streaks of tears down her cheeks. She wiped at them with the corner of her veil. Then she spoke to the boy in a tone higher than usual; my flesh crawled. "Yes, Mutammim. You see how nervous I am. I will need a man around the tent."

This mollified my milk brother, but I saw there was still something uneasy about the herdsman's wife. It was as if she knew the possibilities of evil in her eyes, too, even under the tent's charms, and struggled against them.

Come the white desert morning, Umm Mutammim took Malik by one hand and me, protesting

and dragging, by the other. She left camp and crossed the desert valley going westward, following the path made by our dawn-extended shadows. After a very long way, she brought us to a lone tent made of a single width of fabric, held up by no more than the usual tent pole snapped in two.

Umm Mutammim called a greeting. There was no answer. This convinced me that no one really lived such a tiny, withdrawn sort of life. Surely this was a single strip of cloth blown away from some greater tent, I thought, caught on dry twigs.

But my milk mother knew better. Striding a few steps beyond the tent, she faced a mountainside and called the same greeting again. A rich response of echoes rolled over us. Then those echoes rolled off into the sky and became the sound of distant thunder.

"A good omen," my milk mother said, and she called up the mountainside again.

I fought a childish impatience with the barrenness of the mountain wall. Then I heard the magic purl of water, and I knew that somewhere in that mass of rock a fountain trickled forth. This spring was short-lived, fading back into the rocks from whence it had come before it ever reached the valley floor. But it was there and it was running, not stagnant.

Then a shadow flew down the rock face like some great bird passing overhead. It flew again, lower this time, then lower again. With every drop, a sick feeling in my stomach made it seem as if I myself were flying.

And then, when I thought I should die before this mystery, a final plummet brought it to the valley floor. The oldest being I had ever seen—or she seemed that way because of the shocking white of her hair. I suppose now she wasn't over thirty. She looked like a dusty stone herself and pushed down off the lowest rock of the pile with both hands. The jump was nearly as far as she was tall, and a waterskin burdened her besides. "Old woman" was incongruous with the ease and airiness of her descent.

Umm Mutammim went forward to the crone at once and took the burden from her back with reverence. The skin was very old and, in spite of numerous mendings, leaked on my milk mother's dress. The other woman wore nothing but rags, rags on rags, tatters until it was impossible to tell one layer from the next. And yet here was Umm Mutammim, the sharif's head wife, carrying her water for her and letting it soak her dress. This was a curious old woman indeed.

"These are my sons," my milk mother explained and asked the woman to bless us, which she did with hands like dripping silk upon our foreheads. "Sons," my milk mother said with some ferocity at the rudeness of our stares, "this is Umm Taghlib."

"Are you really Umm Taghlib?" Malik blurted out with awe. "The Mother of the Taghlib? Of the entire tribe?"

"The Banu Taghlib are our enemies," I said, claiming Tamimi blood with that.

My milk mother told us to hush and mind our manners.

In the midst of their wrinkles, the woman's eyes narrowed to slits on me.. "And isn't this the son of al-Wahid of Mecca?"

"Yes, lady."

"The one I told you would cause you such grief?"

Umm Mutammim hung her head. "Yes, lady."

Umm Taghlib gave a hum of disapproval. "So it begins."

Before I could find out what was beginning or what Umm Mutammim, to whose skirt I clung, meant to do about it, another rumble of distant thunder rolled across the desert.

"Ah," the old woman cried. She held her ears as if the sound pained her. "It is the sound of my tribeswomen, of my little daughter, calling for me. My daughter. Ah. And I want to go to her—but I may not. Ah!"

Another roll brought her to her knees in the dust, her head covered with her arms.

"Don't be afraid, Umm Taghlib," I said, hoping to redeem myself with this politeness. "It is a good omen. A man drives his herds toward thunder when he hears it, for he knows the grass grows green there."

"Hush," my milk mother said.

"But I'm only saying what you've said yourself—"

"Hush." And she went to the stricken woman, throwing her skirts over her to cover the huddled, trembling form. Then, between crashes, she helped her back to her dwelling.

The signs of Umm Taghlib's work—her magical battle against Zura and the sons of her native tribe—cramped her tiny tent. I wondered how she had room to lie down within as well. The charms at her tent pole included no rags—she had to wear them all—but there were bones that looked human. And tufts of crushed and dusty ostrich feathers, which came, I later learned, from a woman's litter. Soft gazelle skins full of herbs and bones, glittering amulets, magic stones winked at my milk brother and me through a fog of incense thick enough to make us sneeze.

"Don't pry," Umm Mutammim hissed sharply at us.

The distant rain clouds passed on to the north—a bad omen counteracting the good of their appearance. My milk mother made us squat beside her, Malik to one side and me to the other.

The older woman did not seem to hear us, talking to herself. "My daughter. And the son of this Meccan, perhaps?" No one guessed what that meant, except that her mind was turned by the loss of her child.

Now Umm Mutammim presented the old woman with a sack of rare Euphrates rice and a skin of curds. "Pray, Umm Taghlib," she said. "Forget your private grief just long enough to spy into the depths of another's." She explained al-Harith's disappearance.

With a grunt, Umm Taghlib consented to attempt the task, but not until she'd fixed me once more with that wrinkled glare. "Don't raise that one," the glare said.

Malik and I sucked our fingers to keep from asking questions to which even adults never learn the answers. We blinked against the sun, peering into the rag of shadow where Umm Taghlib squatted. I had not distinguished the ashes of a tiny fire from the yellow-gray of the desert floor itself until she stirred it to life. She fed it with the merest pinch of dung, crumpled between ash-desert-dung-colored fingers, calloused like horn, the nails cracked and yellow.

What I saw and understood, as the old woman's fingers plied sacred sand and salt and seer stones, was nothing to what I felt. I felt hollowed, opened, light, like a sheep's bladder inflated for a ball, thin and transparent, close to bursting.

The old woman hummed as she studied the lay of charms before her. Then she said, "We must take gifts to the jinn."

I shivered. "How do we do that?"

"Hush," Umm Mutammim said.

We swiveled on our heels to watch as Umm Taghlib left the shadow of her tent. She paced, toes curved high, over a stretch of sandy dirt, here, there. From time to time she shot a glance back toward her tent to consult her mounds of seeing salt and rice. She held her right hand straight before her, in it, by the knobby end, a sharpened human leg bone, point down. At length, a patch of soil seemed to suit her. She circled it with splayed feet. Then, in one movement, she stabbed it with her bone and squatted. In a moment, we heard the hiss of her urine.

She gestured us over and commanded each of us to wet the spot as well. I found it difficult to perform with everyone watching. But in the end, after Umm Taghlib had chanted over me, I did. As soon as I had, the kahinah plunged her hand into the mud. She worked quickly before the sun, near its zenith, dried the sharp-smelling lump. Under those hands, magically to my eyes, the head and neck, then humped back and knobby legs of a tiny camel took shape.

"Oh," I cried and clapped my hands. It looked like it might come to shaggy brown life any moment.

"Hush," Umm Mutammim said. "This is not a toy."

From her waist, Umm Taghlib withdrew a thin, black camel-hair cord. Muttering curses all the while, she tied seven knots in the cord, one by one, blowing on each three times as she made it. This she draped around the little figure so as to make tiny panniers on its back.

Carefully, she carried the figure to the fall of rock on the mountain behind her tent. Here in a shadowed niche, she set the clay.

"Now," she said. "The gifts. What will you send the tribe of the jinn in trade for this missing boy?"

Umm Mutammim offered more Euphrates rice. "Food from the mouths of my children," she said.

Umm Taghlib set the grains within the tiny panniers.

"A feather from the sacred litter I rode as a girl, the power of the Banu Taghlib." Umm Taghlib made her own offering, cursing her native tribe's power as she set the small tuft on the camel's back, too.

Malik found a date pit and offered it as an emblem of all the dates he would eat that year. I knew this was his favorite food.

Observing all of this, the spirit within me had continued to swell. My heart and stomach ached as if from hunger, and unmanly tears came to my eyes.

The two women watched my struggle. Waiting for my gift. "Well, son of al-Wahīd?" Making it more difficult.

After great turmoil, I tore a scrap of fine cloth from my right sleeve. Meccan city cloth, brought to our tents by my father on his once-a-year visit. "The strength of my right arm," I offered, striving for grown-up words, "For the return of al-Harith."

Umm Mutammim's gasp made the offered sacrifice worthwhile. That made me realize I truly could lose the use of my arm. I even began to feel a numbness in it. I whimpered. But I didn't dare pull the offer back.

Indeed, Umm Taghlib grunted as if to say, "Yes, let that one make such a deep sacrifice. It will do the world good."

Then the kahinah began to pace again, little squalls of dust rising from the springy tension in her feet. She consulted the heaps in her tent, the way the dying incense smoke curled, the residue of dung ash in the fire.

"There's another boy involved, isn't there?" she asked.

"Yes. My older son, Mutammim, the Gods shield him. I left him in my own harem."

Umm Taghlib nodded. "Offer something for Mutammim, too."

Umm Mutammim couldn't think of anything for a moment. "More curd—?" she suggested, then looked at me, at the scrap of cloth stuck in the panniers, and rejected that.

"Here's a stone," Malik said. "It could be the lands of the Banu Tamim."

"The lands of the Banu Tamim are not Mutammim's to give," his mother said.

"Even though he will be sharif when he grows up?"

"The Gods willing, even then. The land belongs to all the sons of our ancestor, with the favor of the Gods. Mutammim cannot offer them to the Spirits of Fire."

"Here's another stone," Malik said. "It looks like my brother's eye."

So it did, round and shiny and black, about eye-big.

My milk mother cried out at the sight. "No. Not his eye—"

"It is good," the old kahinah said and, with a struggle, Umm Mutammim held her peace.

We set Mutammim's eye in the panniers to be carried to the jinn.

"Give her the reins to race against the fastest ostrich," Umm Taghlib chanted, and other words to send the little clay legs on their way.

We went back to the kahinah's scrap of tent to drink boiled water, to eat curd and rice, and to wait.

By midafternoon, new storm clouds were gathering. The shadows ran on the ground like jinn. Then they covered the sun altogether as it lowered westward, swallowing shadow and casting all the world in uniform gray.

"We will see if the Fire Ones have been here," Umm Taghlib said.

We went with her back to the rock. Though gusts blew, twitching the black feather and stirring the scrap of my sleeve, every offering sat still in the panniers.

"The camel has far to go," Umm Taghlib explained, "striding across the hills of ad-Dahna to the abode of the Lords of this Place."

So we went back to the tent and waited some more. Umm Taghlib moved her heaps of salt and rice, lit more incense. Umm Mutammim stopped her son and me from scuffling. I slept, waking to the first glorious spatters of rain on the desiccated land. Tiny puffs of dust rose up around each fat, warm drop. Each left a tiny crater where it fell. A hundred scents driven dormant by dryness suddenly blossomed in layers in the air: wet earth, wet acacia, wet thorn and shrub, wet dung, wet bodies, wet wool overhead.

Malik turned up his face to the blessing, curled out his tongue to taste the drops. I did the same. When my milk brother lowered his face to laugh at me, with me, for sheer pleasure, tracks of rain ran clean through the everyday grime on his face. They must have been doing the same on me.

One drop ran down my neck. The drops were colder than body heat, and it sent a shiver down my spine.

"Maybe the Lords have come now," Umm Taghlib said.

We went to see. The figure had melted to a mound of mud and cord and rice grains that still held the form of a camel kneeling to rest after its long dream run. My cloth remained, heavy with slurry and rain. Malik's date pit . . . Even Umm Taghlib's feather stood upright, firmly planted in the sodden soil, at which the old kahinah muttered dark curses. I don't doubt that she had expected that to blow away first, and with it the power of her enemy Zura of the Banu Taghlib. She cried out loud with disappointment to see that it had not.

Then my milk mother gave a shriek that might have brought more stones tumbling down the mountainside upon us. "Mutammim's eye! The eye of my own eye."

We looked around. We dug through the melted camel, thinking a rock might sink to the bottom of all the heap. We looked further afield, where it might have rolled. We even looked in the crevices between the rocks. Umm Mutammim shoved our smaller hands down deep to feel—jabbing them on other rocks until they bled and we wept. But the rock like an eye we never found.

"The Lords of the Place have accepted the trade," Umm Taghlib said, her voice heavy as rain.

A flash of lighting made her face ashen. The following clap of thunder sent her scurrying back to her tent.

"The voice of the Lords," she said when we caught up with her.

She squatted before her heaps on the gazelle skin. Drops of rain blowing their way into her tent had changed the patterns in ways she understood. Umm Mutammim didn't bother to squat with my milk brother and me to try and read the message, too. She paced now, out in the rain, looking desperately over the empty desert to where, unseen, her elder son sat alone.

"The Fire Spirits have spoken," Umm Taghlib said, trying to assure her guest that there was nothing to be done about it now. "They have accepted the trade, the life of little al-Harith for Mutammim's eye."

Umm Mutammim shrieked at the heavens, and they thundered back.

"Ah, a little boy." Umm Taghlib swept her palm in circles just above the mounds on the gazelle skin. She spoke quickly, as if to get it all out before the crash of thunder rumbled away, taking the utterance with it. "Soft straight hair. Gentle eyes."

Umm Mutammim gave another sob at that word.

"Yes, I see him," Umm Taghlib said. Al-Harith was plainer to her than I was, standing right there in the doorway of her tent. That al-Harith should be found worthy of Umm Taghlib's attention when I was not—!

And I couldn't help but feel it was because, just as everyone had turned to run back to the tent, I had snatched my scrap of cloth back from the mound of melting clay. Might not the greedy and unpredictable jinn come back for more? I wouldn't let the jinn take the strength of my right arm. I was going to be a warrior when I grew up, as mighty as any son of Tamim, and I couldn't do that without a good arm. The life of a herdsman's son was not worth that to me.

The stolen fabric stretched with wet, allowing me to tie it around my arm, clumsily, but above the lower end of my sleeve, where no one could see. I wore it until it dropped off of its own. It may be that the jinn entered that arm of mine, from that day on. God knows best.

The directions Umm Taghlib gave my milk mother from her seer stones were faultless, as if al-Harith had stopped in her tent in the night to ask his way. Yet, from the route by which the men returned after finding him following Umm Mutammim's report, I knew Suwaid's son had never been near Umm Taghlib's scrap of tent. They found him fallen down a chasm, badly scraped and wounded, especially about the hips and belly. But some few weeks in his mother's arms would heal him.

When my milk mother brought Malik and me over to Umm al-Harith's tent to pay that first call to the sick, she made me carry some sweet dates and wild honey as a gift. I didn't want to go at all for shame, for the band of fabric around my right arm. But Umm Mutammim insisted that I learn to be a great man and that a great man is always open-handed. She did this even when the infection in Mutammim's eyes must already have been worrying her.

I had no choice but to go at last, and I thrust the gifts inside the tent flap without looking. When Umm al-Harith asked me to come in with a cheerful smile, I burst into tears. Umm al-Harith brushed her own tears aside, took her little son's hand, sending the flies up into the heat in a heavy, lazy cloud, and nodded.

"Thank you for your help, too, Ibn al-Walid."

The herdsman's wife offered me a seat by al-Harith's wounded side, plastered with camel grease and healing herbs. I could not look into his thin, forgiving, long-suffering face. I wept and wept as if I were the one who'd been injured. But I didn't take off the knot around my arm.

I have never had courage like that.

12

O God, I seek refuge with You from the punishment of hellfire and from the punishment of the grave and from the trials of the living and dying and from the evil of the false messiah.

> —a prayer of the Prophet, blessed be he, used daily by Believers

Rayah hurried down the stairs from Sitt Sameh's room and grabbed her veil from its peg in the corner of the courtyard.

"Where is my cousin Kefa?" she asked Auntie Adilah, who sat placidly grinding grain.

"He thought you weren't going to the mosque today, that you'd finally grown up and would stay home on the holy day like the rest of the women," Adilah replied.

"I was just upstairs listening—" There was no time to explain. Struggling with her veil, Rayah scurried to the light at the end of the passage, hoping she still had time to catch up to her cousin.

Reeking of their profession, all the male turpentine sellers went together to the baths early every Friday. They took clean clothes to change into. To newly washed and combed hair and beards, they liberally applied oil sweet with cedar and frankincense. Still, even with her eyes closed, she could pick out which section of the masjid the men of her house had chosen for their devotions that week. The Friday fragrance barely covered their workday smell of turpentine manufacture.

Cousin Kefa, however, was assigned to see to family honor. He was supposed to detour from the baths and stop by the house to escort Rayah, the only female of the family who regularly attended the jummah. Each Friday he dutifully waited for her, chewing on his bit of woody desert root to freshen his breath for the assembly, as the Prophet, blessed be he, recommended.

But today Kefa must have had friends of his own to meet, the up-and-coming young men of Tadmor. He had finally spat out his siwak and given up on her.

"I'll catch up to him," she promised Zabbai, who tried to stop her at the gate just as, from afar, she heard the first cry of the muezzin, "God is most great."

She brushed by the gatekeeper. Zabbai's father and grandfather had held the post before him; perhaps one of them had had the ferocity the post required. Zabbai, kind soul, hadn't the heart to stop her.

Sitt Umm Ali told a story about the present khalifah, Omar ibn al-Khattab in distant Medinah. He had said to his favorite wife, Atika, "You know, I would like to prevent you from attending Friday prayers." Now, there was a man with a true gatekeeper's personality.

"But the Prophet, blessings on him, prevents you from preventing me." Rayah could imagine Atika's sly smile, eyes down, as she replied to her husband. "For did he not command: 'Do not keep God's female slaves from going to His mosques'? I am only the obedient female slave of the Merciful One." Omar's wife could continue to smile, controlling her husband who controlled the armies conquering half the world.

"I am only the obedient female slave of the Merciful One," Rayah said aloud.

Perhaps that stern gatekeeper ancestor of Zabbai's had lived in the time of Queen Zaynab, Zenobia of the blue eyes, who fought the Romans. Perhaps the first Zabbai had earned his name serving her.

Hearing how far along the call to prayer had progressed by that time, Rayah began to run, in spite of the fact that God's Apostle had also said, "Never run to the assembly, but move with solemn dignity."

She had to give up that pace once she came out of the twists of alleyways and into the open of the great Roman colonnade. Men ambling late to prayers could see her, and women shouldn't run for any reason, particularly not for prayers. She reached the corner where the men of her family had had their turpentine stall longer than the twenty-five generations they had had the house. In recent years, they had built out into the colonnade like others: Islam encouraged more privacy.

Here she caught sight of Kefa. She might even have yelled for him, if yelling were permitted for believing women on their way to jummah. But he was almost at the great monumental arch and, with his long legs, would surely reach the mosque before she had closed half the distance.

Perhaps she should go back. Part of her, an uncomfortably large part, wanted to go back. She was going to miss some of what the eunuch would read to Sitt Sameh of the Conqueror's history. But waiting to hear the end of the deeds of the jinn in the desert was what had made her late in the first place.

Even as she'd scrambled to her feet to leave, Rayah had had to ask, "But the Conqueror's milk brother, Mutammim ibn Nuwaira of the tribe of Tamim? What happened to his eyes?"

"Ah, that's all written down in the next section," the eunuch had said, turning to his parchment.

Something very close to panic had clutched Rayah's heart when she'd seen all those closely formed words in their neat rows. They lured her when she ought to be reciting the holy, the one true revelation. "Can't you just tell me, ustadh? In a few short words before I go?"

And he'd said, "The jinn took them, of course. The very moment the three of them returned to Umm Mutammim's tent, she saw the yellow crust in her son's eyes, the flies feeding there.

She tried everything. She spat in his eyes, she wiped them with her veil, she painted their rims with kohl made from the fire's ashes. She even poured camel urine over them. To no avail. He became blind and could never become the sharif of the tribe as birth had granted him. That fell to his younger brother Malik instead."

"Mashallah," Rayah had exclaimed, protecting herself against the evil effects of too much wonder with the all-powerful Name of God.

Now worry about these people, pagans most of them, dead and gone to hellfire, kept creeping into her mind rather than worry for her own soul. She found her feet skittering over the uneven ground. Her haste was not so much to reach the mosque, she feared, but to have prayers over and to hurry home again. She thought of Sitt Umm Ali, of God and His Prophet, and tried to steady her mind there.

Ancient Tadmor spread its ruins around her. Rayah tried to keep her eyes on the rise ahead, where the mosque stood. But the building's exterior reminded her that before it had been converted to the revelation of Muhammad, blessings on him, it had been a Christian church. And before that, a pagan temple.

Tadmor, Palmyra, the City of Palms. Plenty of trees still greened the desert east and south of her along the usually dry wadi and what seeped, warm and sulphuric, from Afqa Spring. But here, in the old city, all the palms seemed changed to stone by some malicious spell, the terebinths to heaps of sand. Topped by fronds of stone, a thousand towering columns in long, stately rows held up only the baked blue of the sky.

The long colonnade led off to the desert behind her until the two lines of columns ran together in the hazy, yellow distance. She passed the nested, rising arcs of the theatre where only sand declaimed in whispers. Her people sought refuge among the ruins of the old city, the skirts of the city of the defeated woman, ancient Queen Zaynab. Her people patched aquaducts, stretched tenting over crumbled roofs, rolled away stones from ruins to buttress a crumbling wall or to use as querns. Many old quarters were deserted, save for lizards. And nightly, from the roof of her home, Rayah could hear foxes yipping in front of their dens, the hooting of owls.

She remembered the stories of how the city had been built by King Sulayman—with a twist of the ring on his finger that brought jinn rising out of the earth. For surely mere mortals could never have set up such stones, one upon another. Jinn rising to do the bidding of the one who summoned them—

Maybe they weren't owls calling at night at all.

"I seek refuge with the perfect words of God," she recited, quickly turning her back on the sight.

> "From the evil He created,
> and from the evil that descends from the sky
> and from the evil that rises in it."

But even as she turned, a pair of dust devils twisted past each other down the colonnade. Jinn. The word sent a shiver down the sweat swimming on her spine.

13

Only the night and my mare know me.
—Arab saying

In due time, my childhood was over and my true father called me back to Mecca. At first, he doubted the return on his investment in me, for the world to which he introduced me was as confusing and frightening as if I had just been born. What homesickness I felt for the openness of the desert and my foster family! No wonder my milk brothers taunted me. The people whose blood I shared were strangers.

I caught the smallpox almost immediately upon my arrival in Mecca.

My milk mother blamed my sickness on the close and unwholesome city air. "Houses are stuck to the ground and one must live forever in one's own filth, never moving on and letting the wind blow the place clean again."

"The desert," my womb mother said instead. In my fever it seemed her moist, painted lips dripped raw blood. "It's a wonder he survived that primitive place at all."

My father blamed it on the Africans. Bad health and bad prices were always their fault in his eyes.

For my part, I am inclined to believe that I wished the fever and boils upon myself, so miserable was I away from Umm Mutammim and the milk brothers I loved. I was taken from the desert in the best time of year, too, in spring when the rains set a transparent green haze over every brown mound of earth.

But the God who cured me of the disease, leaving me only pockmarked for life, saw to it that I found consolation among the noblest of animals.

My father specialized in this merchandise that carried itself from market to market, the swift and sturdy war horse bred in the Arabian desert. Neither Rome nor Persia ever had enough of such mounts. As long as their perpetual state of war required cavalry, my father could supply one empire and then, when the first would not pay top price, the other.

These beautiful creatures were so valuable to us that we called them not by their names but by poetical titles of honor, as one does the Merciful One. Drinkers of the Wind. Or Those Kept Close By, for it was the custom to stake one's war mare closer to the tents than any other beast, even among the guy ropes. Foals might be brought within the tent itself. A man would feed his horse on freshly churned curd or buttermilk, letting his children starve before he'd neglect his horse. The Prophet himself, blessings on him, was known to wipe the sweat from his horse's face with his own cloak after a desert run.

Alongside this business, my father had charge of Mecca's cavalry, such as it was: a score of war mares he kept tethered to mud-brick mangers because there was so little pasture away from the high desert. Their health disintegrated under such conditions but could be quickly revived with proper feed and exercise. For no matter what he sold to the empires, my father always kept the best stock for himself.

Between the winter caravan to Yemen and the summer caravan north to cooler climes, the men of Mecca devoted themselves to active pursuits: hunting in the hills beyond Mount Arafat, with the hawk on the wrist in the freshness of spring mornings. And races, of camels and, of course—horses.

And that first year after my return to Mecca, or maybe the second, my father had a wonderful mare. She was a sorrel, or rather, since we have so many different words for our horses, of the coloring we called sorrel-over-black. She had three white feet and a blaze on her nose so long that "It drinks with her." That nose went from broad at the eyes to narrow at the nostrils—the better to keep out sand—and every bone in that face could be clearly seen. Neck and tail she held in proud arcs, and she ran—she ran like the very south wind we say God made the mother of all horses.

That year, my father had had her covered by Nuwaira's stallion among the Tamim. Had the mare's own perfections not made her dear to me, this would have, for here was a connection to the tents of my milk family. There is an old saying that a noble man need not be ashamed to work with his hands in order to serve three beings: his father, his guest, and his horse. I had taken this saying to heart and loved to carry the barley mash to Jirwet every day and see that the area around her manger was clean. Then I would take her out of the city for a morning's ride to stretch her legs.

I was in charge of hanging her neck with the necessary charms: bent nails that clanged together, red wool tassels and, following my milk mother's magic, a fox skull. She learned to respond to my commands, just my voice to "Go on" and "Hold, Jirwet, hold, girl." And I learned how to vault myself onto her back like warriors do with their spears. I didn't have a spear yet; I used a long, plain stick instead. But when the day came that I did have a spear, both Jirwet and I would be ready.

This was long before the Prophet's final sermon sanctified Mount Arafat. The dun-colored plain around that featureless swelling of soil was nonetheless our place of assembly, where every man came to stand before the Gods, from the sun's zenith to its going down.

And the distance around the mount counted as one lap for the races.

That spring, Jirwet had grown so barrel-bellied that I had to ride her with my knees bent up like one rides a camel. My father knew not to schedule her for races, even in the single-lap heat, not in her condition. But we brought her out to the mount that day, just for the air, and I was to keep her on the side.

As I walked her to and fro, trying to catch a glimpse, over the heads of the crowd, of the horses that were racing, my cousin Omar came up to me. Omar was not too much older than my eight or nine years. I was small for my age, as I have been all my life, and that made me his target. I can see him now, plump and pasty-faced like barley gruel with more city living than I had seen.

"Why won't your father run this mare of his?" Omar asked, sneering.

"Because of her state," I said, more stoutly than I felt. "He doesn't want to lose the foal."

"Or is he just a coward?"

"My father's not a coward."

We'd all stuck flowers in our turbans for luck at the festivities, and Omar's was basil, white spires of bloom on the fragrant green leaves like little minarets. I wanted to tear that headdress from him and throttle him with it. I didn't do it then because he was so much bigger than I was. Hating myself for the cowardice only made me hate Omar more.

"Your father won't fight Rome and Persia. He's a coward," Omar taunted me. He must have read my feelings in my face and wanted to rub it in. Not only was I a coward, my father was.

"He is not," I said, angry tears stinging my eyes.

"This mare can't be so great if he's afraid to race her."

Omar was circling Jirwet, critically eyeing her every part as if he knew horses, judged them every day. He picked up a hoof, then roughly threw it down as if disgusted. He yanked open her lips to consider her teeth, pulled at her nostrils.

Jirwet snorted her displeasure at this treatment, and I winced. "He's not afraid," I said. "Wise, not afraid."

"Well, I for one am tired of going up and down, carrying goods for Rome and Persia. I'm tired of being a beast of burden." He must have been reciting things he'd heard his father say, for he himself had yet to travel with a caravan. I knew that for a fact.

"A man takes good care of his beasts of burden. They are his livelihood. He feeds his horse before he feeds himself, which you'd know if you knew enough about horses to even ride one."

I shifted my stance to stand between Jirwet's flank and my cousin.

"She ought to be raced."

Omar gave me a shove. Jirwet stood solidly behind me as he jarred me into her, a testimony to her good breeding.

"Not by you," I said, trying to keep the tremble I felt from my voice. "She's too good for you."

From his waistband, Omar drew a short whip of knotted black leather. Fear lashed me, not for myself but for the horse. The whip curled back. Again I stepped between Jirwet and my cousin, dropping the reins as I did. Jirwet stood perfectly still, but I cried out as I crumpled to the ground. Pain seared across my shoulders.

Omar scrambled into the saddle over my head and pulled on the reins. So I ignored the pain. I struggled up and sprang after him, trying to catch the halter. "She runs better without whipping," I yelled.

But Omar only laughed and whipped her sides with his heels to send her spiraling out into the wide empty plain toward the other riders.

I ran to my father, pulled on the skirt of his robe, trying to get his attention. "Father, Omar has a whip. Jirwet shouldn't be whipped, not in her condition."

But he and the rest of the men were laying their final bets and intent on how the field lined up for the starting signal. He didn't hear me.

The horses were off with great shouts. Jirwet sprang ahead of the rest as if stung by a scorpion. There was a scramble to replace bets as the field changed thus. The men around my father were already congratulating him. He chewed his lower lip at what he saw, but as long as the congratulations kept up, he decided not to act on it.

I knew what I had to do. Gathering up my robe, I set off around the hill, heading to the left, the opposite direction of the dust that rose over the tearing herd of horses.

It didn't take long for the racers to make their circuit and come into my view again. By then, I was winded, my lungs burning with the hot, arid air. I staggered to a halt far enough up the hillside, I hoped, that I would be out of their thundering way. But then what was I to do? I couldn't stop them. They would make the circuit, and I would have run for nothing.

Jirwet was in the lead, but a white mare owned by Abu Sufyan pressed her close. Omar had kept Jirwet well to the inside, near enough to the start of Arafat's slope that I feared the horse might stumble on the rising ground. Abu Sufyan's mare rode hard and fast on her outside flank, jostling her toward the danger.

And the black whip curled over Omar's head.

Renewed fury gave me no choice. My feet found a level stone in the hillside and balanced themselves on it. My weight shifted back, preparing to fling forward.

Jirwet's eyes passed me, wild and wide with fear and pain, begging for help. Omar's eyes in his pasty face were small and cruel under his twist of turban and the clumps of basil. He was intent on the path ahead and back on Abu Sufyan's mare. By the time I saw either pair of eyes, however, I was already airborne.

I flew, I thought, as if the jinn carried me. And the strong right arm I had promised the Fire Ones caught with inhuman strength.

I caught saddle horn and cantle, as I'd often done before, although never at such a speed and never with Omar's knee in the way.

That knee rammed my nose bruised and bloody. My sweaty hands slipped on hot, smooth wood. The saddle itself slipped on Jirwet's back. I could smell the fear strong on her. My grip on the rear cantle shook loose after two paces. I grabbed the back of Omar's robe instead and hung on.

"Calm, Jirwet. Fine, Jirwet. Jirwet, hold." I tried to shout the familiar orders, but they came between clenched teeth and were anything but calm themselves. The ears twitched, nevertheless, and I felt her pace begin to slow. I couldn't see Abu Sufyan's mare. I couldn't see much of anything—when I dared to open my eyes—but the weave of Omar's robes. Stress tore through my arms and rib cage. I quickly closed my eyes again. But by the dust I was eating, I knew we'd been bypassed.

A string of curses rained down from Omar somewhere above me. The roar in my ears was too loud to hear any details.

"Jirwet, hold."

The whip cracked down, first on my shoulders, then on Jirwet's flank. Torn between my familiar verbal commands and the whip's compulsion, the horse screamed and sprang raggedly forward. Her landing jarred my hand off the horn. I knew I was going to fall then. But, by Hubal, I would bring

Omar with me.

Both of my hands had him now. Against his struggle to stay in the saddle, I willed myself toward the ground.

Every joint in my body jarred as we hit. Fortunately, Omar's soft body was beneath mine as we were dragged together over Arafat's stone and dust. He still had hold of the reins and wouldn't let go. Our combined weight bore Jirwet's breast to the ground, back legs skittering. The scream she gave now made me hope all the pain I felt would shortly kill me.

The horses that had been trailing caught up. Now it wasn't so good to be on top. I protected my head by burying it into the stink under Omar's arm. But several hooves, even shying, landed heavily on my limbs.

Jirwet broke the reins and rolled to her feet, leaving the frayed ends in Omar's limp hand. Once free, she didn't run off, but came around to stand between my prone body and the oncoming herd so they would turn sooner—or so she would take the blows instead.

A quiet came, ringing in my ears. The dust settled, leaving Jirwet a light dun color and Omar and me coughing and spitting too much to go at each other's throats. Then the men were upon us. "What is this? What is the meaning of this? What has your evil jinni of a son done to mine? What have you done to my horse?"

I tried to explain. Omar had his own louder, higher-pitched tale to tell of my treacherous jealousy. But by then the whip nicks had begun to bleed through, frothing Jirwet's flanks a muddy, pink, and sweaty mess.

"See?" I heard my father say. "My son has only done his best to keep his beloved mare from harm."

Omar and I were picked up and brushed off and found to have nothing worse than scrapes and bruises.

"So you won't mind giving up your lost bet so much, Abu Khalid," someone jested.

My father was still not jesting. Even after such time to rest, Jirwet continued to blow hard, her sides heaving in and out, her eyes dull with concentration.

"By Hubal," my father cried. He went to her, hoping not to find what his face soon told me he did find. "She's going to lose her foal, three months too early." He turned on Omar's father. "Your brat has cost me this foal, sired by the best of Tamim."

Other men stepped in to keep the two men from causing each other more damage than their sons had done. Had they not, I'm certain, they would have started a blood feud that might have put even Muhammad's coming in the shade.

"Calm, Abu Khalid," men told my father—as if he were a horse.

Men led my uncle out of sight and my uncle led Omar. Omar's punishment, as long as it was private, did not seem sufficient to me. But that would have to wait for another time. Right now, Jirwet was suffering.

"There are means to stop an early labor, if it is the Gods' will," someone told my father. "Women know them. Let someone ride for women, Abu Khalid."

Women again.

So it was that they erected a tent there on the plain of Arafat. And I stood all that afternoon cradling Jirwet's head and speaking low, kind words to her while a trio of black-swathed women worked at the other end. I know they sewed up the horse's womb with her own tail hair, for men may do the same if they must drive their pregnant mares or she-camels far in the desert. My father had not done this earlier—he cursed himself soundly—only because he'd never meant Jirwet to run at Arafat.

I know they sewed Jirwet up because I was the one who took out the neat, small stitches later. I know they washed the horse down with precious water and treated her lacerations with tar and camel dung. But whatever else they did, wafting the smell of incense and other herbs toward me and Jirwet's flaring nostrils, I am ignorant of to this day. All I saw was the mare's eyes and the flash of an occasional white hand out of the heavy black veiling at her tail end.

Finally, one of the women whispered something to my father, and the three went away, one black mote in the eye of the dusty Plain of Arafat.

"You'll be fine now," I promised Jirwet. Was I lying to her?

Then I heard the whisper of steel as my father unsheathed his sword. I flinched so at the sound that Jirwet herself snorted with surprise. He strode toward me, the naked blade he had of his father and his father's father poised at my heart. I saw my own death and truly didn't care. I also saw the horse's death, and that I couldn't bear. I turned to face him, putting her neck protectively behind me.

"Here." He thrust the sword at me—hilt first. The sword of my fathers, passed down to me, if only for the moment. "The women tell me what must happen now is that a boy—someone who has not yet had his teeth sharpened and his manhood cut—must stand over Jirwet's tail all night. He must stand holding up a raised sword, lending his strength to her. Should he let the sword droop, should he doze off—especially if the sword touches the ground—things will go very ill for her and her foal. I think, Khalid, you are the boy for this task. What do you think, my son?"

I took the sword.

All that long, lonely night I struggled there beneath Arafat even as the mare struggled. Her flesh became mine. But it was more than her flesh. The sword, which had seemed light enough when my father handed it to me, grew heavier and heavier. At the dawn of time, I remembered, a brave ancestor stole the blade from giants. Not long into the night I knew it had come from giants indeed. What had always seemed—well, as no more than a reed pen in my father's hand—ground slowly to the weight of all the generations of my fathers upon my shoulders.

Together mare and sword and I stood against wolf and fox. I stood while the jinn came at me like the night wind, trying jealously to steal the fruit of her womb.

I stood while my feet ached. I shuffled from one to the other, then planted them, numb as stone, then shuffled again. The process repeated itself in my arms. Jinn came for my right arm, cutting it with glass. I switched the blade from hand to hand. I tried both hands. I switched when the pain reached my wrist. Then when it reached my elbow. Then my shoulder. Finally it arced fire from shoulder to shoulder across my chest. I set my teeth and stood.

I stood while the pain rose, then peaked and turned to numbness again. I stood and chanted the long verse of the names of the three hundred and sixty Gods of the Ka'ba that every child learned:

> "By Allat and al-Uzza
> And Manat, the third beside.
> Verily they are the most exalted females
> Whose intercession is to be sought.
> May Wadd keep you and bless you.
> By Him to whom the melodies of mankind rise,
> And round al-Uqaysir men sing his praise and glory.
> May my witness be God and the white quartz God of Tabalah..."

I stood and chanted until my voice was hoarse, until one verse blurred into another, until one God was the next and all were One. I stood until Jirwet was a God, the opening I guarded was God, and I was she and opening and God as well.

I stood while stars reeled. I stood as first light came, then proved to be only a lightness in my head. It came again. And again.

And then true light came to Arafat Plain. Beneath my still-raised arms I saw that Jirwet's sides were rising and falling easily. The stitches beneath her tail had ceased to strain. My father caught me up, sobbing, against his chest.

And finally, finally the arm holding the sword dropped. My father caught up the blade and resheathed it.

"That sword of my fathers will come to you, my son," he said. "By Hubal, I swear it."

Its weight continued to ring through every muscle as if my body and it were forged into one steely being. But my father knew he had return, at last, on his investment.

Several months later, in due time, my own dagger removed the stitches and Jirwet's filly was born. My father gave her to me—my own mare, Sadha. I rode her and then her daughter, also called Jirwet, throughout all my campaigns. The great-great-granddaughter of that night is in my stables in Homs now—but I'll never ride her again.

I am, in a way, ashamed even to visit her. As I am to visit my own daughter.

14

**I seek refuge with the perfect words of God
from the evil He created,
and from the evil that descends from the sky
and from the evil that rises in it.**
      **—a prayer for protection given by the Prophet,
blessed be he**

As Rayah recited protective words, watching fearfully behind her, a third figure appeared among the ruins of Tadmor, twirling with the other two, the dust demons. This one had more substance than the others, more threat. Rayah remembered the prayer gathering at the mosque, to which she'd set out with stiff bravery. Now it appeared as a sanctuary of safety. She all but turned on her heels and ran toward that haven, male-choked, but at least made of human flesh and blood.

Then she saw the third figure in the ruins was no demon but a girl like herself. This girl was spiraling out of Tadmor and toward the open desert. Swallowing her fear, Rayah left the path to the mosque and stepped out into the deserted place.

"Ya, sister," she called. "Hello. Peace to you."

The girl gave no answer, nor any sign that she had heard. With quick steps, Rayah closed the distance. She could hear the other singing, high tuneless notes like the blowing of the wind at the approach of a storm. Her eyes half closed, the girl twirled her head, shoulders, hips, shuffling in a little sort of dance.

Rayah reached out and caught a loose sleeve. The girl stopped, her eyes flying open with fright.

"It's all right. I won't hurt you," Rayah gentled. Then she spoke the girl's name, "Ghusoon," for after a moment she recognized her. Ghusoon used to come to Sitt Umm Ali to learn to recite. Rayah recalled that Ghusoon hadn't been in a few months, much longer than she herself had missed since the coming of the eunuch to their gates. And how that time had changed Ghusoon. She'd been quiet, mature, pretty. Now she had the look of a frightened rabbit.

Ghusoon seemed to relax at her touch. "Are you my mother?" She peered earnestly into

Rayah's face. Rayah wanted to laugh. Her mother? If anything, Ghusoon was a little older than she was. She was also unveiled, her waist ungirdled, her hair falling unheeded from its coiled dark braids. Rayah touched the placement of her own careful covering and broke the news as kindly as she could. "No. I'm Rayah. Remember? From Sitt Umm Ali's class?"

"You have blue eyes," the girl said in wonder, not fear.

"Yes. So does my mother." That was the first time Rayah had claimed Sitt Sameh, and she wasn't certain she would do the same in other, more complicated circumstances.

"Mashallah, you're so lucky."

To have blue eyes? Again Rayah wanted to laugh.

"You have a mother," the girl went on to explain.

"Don't you?"

"Of course I do. Everyone has a mother. But mine is—mine is—she's out in the desert."

"A daughter of one of the tribes?"

"She's waiting for me, calling for me." And the tone in the girl's voice was such hollow helplessness that Rayah stopped stifling laughter and felt ready to weep.

"What name does she call you, sister?" she asked instead.

"Ghusoon." A bright smile lit the haunted eyes at the thought. "My mother calls me Ghusoon. A budding branch."

"And your father?"

The eyes went suddenly dark and opaque. Before Rayah could probe further, numerous voices called out "Ghusoon, Ghusoon," behind her. "Ghusoon, for shame."

A family of strange men surrounded them. They pulled the girl from Rayah and shoved her out of the way.

"I just wanted to see if she needed any help," Rayah tried to tell them, but she was talking to their backs as they hurried her aquaintance away. Strange men made Rayah uncomfortable, anyway, and made her think of her own menfolk, of Cousin Kefa who would get angry if he knew she'd gone out without him.

So speaking not another word, she hurried her steps in the other direction, away from the ruins to the mosque and to Friday prayers. Up an incline that made her sweat in the sun, she reached the flattened top, the dust of something even older.

Upon their conquering arrival, the Muslims had found the edifice, a large, tripartite Christian basilica. They'd let the followers of Isa ibn Maryam remove their icons, incense, holy books, and vessels to the two or three smaller churches in town, and claimed the place for themselves. They'd raised a bastion along the outer wall, simple dried brick incongruous against the polished, immortal stone. Inside, a pulpit and qiblah arch sat awkwardly facing toward Mecca, despite the building's former orientation set more nearly to the rising and setting sun.

Rayah ran up a set of broad stairs, to the court and door set under the portico in the center of the long wall. She stepped to the rear of a sea of bodies, bending and turning their backs or at least their sides to the original cant of the walls around them. "Make your rows straight when you pray," God's Messenger, blessings on him, had said. "Bring them near each other and stand shoulder to shoulder. For by the One in Whose hand the soul of Muhammad is, I see shayatan, devils, coming in through gaps in the row like small black sheep." Did Rayah see such small black sheep? Or were they merely patches left in her eyes from the brilliance of the sun? Patches that had come there because she had walked without Cousin Kefa? Because she had stopped to speak with the girl dancing with the jinn?

The whoosh of several hundred bodies sinking and rising together, the hum of their voices, combined in an effort to sweep aside more ancient whispers, the patches of dark. They only half-succeeded in their housecleaning: too many years lingered, like the layers of whitewash on her family's floor through which ghosts still flitted.

Rayah hastily caught up and completed her salah among the women, closing her eyes tight and saying the name of God many times to send the vision away. It worked. Afterward, she sat on her heels, caught her breath, and tried to attend to the sermon. She hadn't been in time to take her usual place with Sitt Umm Ali and her other students in the first female row. So Rayah was obliged to concentrate over the tumble of toddlers about her and the gossip of their mothers to either side.

She could barely see the pulpit at the other end of the hall. The men raised quantities of dust in spite of rugs and flapping pigeons overhead. The close-packed heat loosed clashing Friday perfumes. The coughing and shifting of so many Believers weighed heavily on the brain. The gist she gathered from the diminutive, distant imam was this:

"One day of assembly, Abu Sa'id al-Khudri, personally known to me, found himself praying directly behind the Apostle of God, blessings and peace on him. He noticed to his surprise that the Prophet seemed confused in the recitation. A shaytan, Iblis, one of the mightiest of the jinn, had come from the hills and wadis with a brand of fire, meaning to thrust it in the face of God's Holy Messenger. The Prophet had to struggle against the burn until he felt the demon's cold spittle on his face and hands, and so was unable to follow the words he himself had revealed.

"Had it not been for the prayer of Abu Sa'id, whom I know personally and who saw the struggle when others did not, the Evil One might, God forbid, have succeeded. And if only the brother kneeling next to him had also joined his prayer with equal fervor in the same direction, Iblis might have been chained then and there to a pillar in the house of assembly. The Great Enemy, to be a plaything for the children of al-Medinah until the Judgment Day."

Instead, the moral was, shaytan, the adversary, was loose in all the world. "And whoever is not for the revealed word of God as given to Muhammad, bless him, is a clear foe to God, his Prophet and men, and deserves the sword first, then hellfire. Praises to God, amen."

As the sermon ended, Rayah got up and made her way to where Sitt Umm Ali sat. Rayah joined four or five girls and young women, her best friends, in a half-circle with leaves of the holy book in their center on a low wooden stand. They had closed over Ghusoon's place, she noticed, without comment. Rayah wanted to tell them she had seen Ghusoon, to ask if anybody knew a remedy for what was keeping her away. But they had closed over Rayah's place as well, so she asked nothing as they shifted to let her in.

Together the students recited the verses their teacher pointed out to them, written on a palm frond, a bolster to the imam's teaching of the day. They picked out the letters slowly:

> It is revealed that
> A company of jinn gave ear. Afterward they said:
> "We have heard a wonderful Quran,
> guiding to righteousness.
> We believe in it
> and we will not associate anyone
> with our Lord."

"Any questions?" Sitt Umm Ali asked, and then she smiled at her pupils' solid, wordless acceptance of the plain revealed word of God.

After a moment, however, Rayah could not help herself. "So to believe in the tribe of those created from the desert wind is a part of the Faith?"

"Praise be to God, those who deny the existence of the jinn deny the Quran." Sitt Umm Ali was a woman with a stone's solidity, the very model of the verse "He created mankind from dry clay." Rayah felt her teacher's eyes narrowing on the doubter.

Rayah wasn't a doubter, not at all. She just had to know. Because of what she had seen out among the ruins. Because of what awaited her at home. "Is it then as important as to know that there is no God but God? Or that Muhammad is His Messenger?"

"No, but it is the very next step. Those who deny the jinn and the Quran, God curse them, deny that there exists a world beyond the material. Only an ignorant person or an unbeliever would deny this, may God change their minds."

"So, if God were to make our eyes lighter, or the jinn of heavier substance, we could see them?"

"Yes," said Sitt Umm Ali shortly.

"And people who see them now—?"

"God hardly ever wills that."

"But people did have dealings with the jinn before the revelation of the glorious Quran."

"God was from the beginning, praise Him. He created the jinn not long after."

"Some people hear—or heard them. See them, feel them."

"Poets, mostly. Kahinahs, witches, I seek refuge from them, and for you, O my students."

"Sometimes regular mortals?" Rayah had to press, not letting Sitt Umm Ali lose her attention to the rest.

"Who were not on their guard because they didn't know how, in the Time of Ignorance."

"This verse we just read." Rayah looked down, more to escape the anger cracking her teacher's stony demeanor, but she used the excuse to sound out some of the letters as well: "'We believe in it.' That's the jinn speaking? So the jinn can be converted just like humans?"

"Praise God, yes." Sitt Umm Ali's words were perfectly phrased but warning.

"So jinn might be good *or* bad?"

"Blessings and peace be upon Muhammad, God's Messenger."

"How is one to know?" Rayah tried with mixed success to squelch her own impatience.

"How do you know a Muslim in this life?"

"He prays, he fasts, he gives charity."

"So you may know a believing jinni, if you ever meet one." Sitt Umm Ali sounded as if she thought that highly unlikely. "Ask him to recite the declaration of belief."

"But I know men who do so and who are yet evil."

"God blister your tongue for saying such things about any in the community of Believers."

Rayah did finally manage to hold her tongue. Or rather, she ran it around the inside of her mouth, fearing that she did in fact feel a blister growing.

After a brief pause, Sitt Umm Ali asked: "Do you know what the word shaytan means?"

"Shaytan, one of the jinn. One of the most powerful." Another of the students, Dhuha, gave this answer, quoting heavily from the day's sermon. Dhuha seemed eager to prove her worth over Rayah who, usually the best, was clearly stumbling today.

"Literally, shaytan means adversary," Sitt Umm Ali said. "Poets of the Time of Ignorance welcomed shayatan into their lives. Adversity, they said in their delusion, made them strong, gave more power to their words. Now we are wiser and know, as the imam said today, that anything not for the word of God is against it and must be destroyed."

And when she said that final word, the narrowness in Sitt Umm Ali's dry-clay eyes told Rayah what the woman was really looking at. *All she sees is that my eyes are blue. Or their absence of true, human weight. Even a veil cannot conceal them from the world. Are they all she has ever seen?*

15

Provide for your journey; but the best provision is the fear of God: fear Me, then, O men of understanding! It shall be no sin in you if you seek the bounty of your Lord.
—The Holy Quran, Surah 2:197

Racing passed the springtime. Then, as the pastures withered, the men of the Quraysh watched the sky for the rising of the bright star called al-Shira. This announced that the time of the summer caravan to Syria was upon us.

When that took place, Father planted his lance in the center of the spacious public square that encircled the Holy Ka'ba. Black wool fringed with sacred red leather, our clan's colors, fluttered from the top of my father's lance. It might have been indistinguishable, to a stranger, from all the fluttering offerings, gold-fringed poets' flags and camel-skull-upon-a-post idols that stood before the Great Black House and its three hundred and sixty gods.

"Every Meccan knows what the flag of your ancestor al-Mughira means," the slave I finally dared to ask told me, that first year back from the desert.

For all my success with the mare, or perhaps because of it, my father was still my father. I didn't dare betray ignorance to him.

The slave Nuri was huge and black and had no nose. His size and features were foreboding, but his usual silence invited my attention—he was like a cool, silent shadow in the midday glare of the desert.

One of my ancestors first planted his lance in the holy precincts to win heavenly favor for his expedition. By my father's day, heaven and fate had merged more closely with the fortunes of the marketplace. In the Meccan mind, they were like a dark and light thread seen in the hours before dawn on a day of fasting—we could not tell which was which.

Every Meccan seemed to understand the flag's meaning, for its appearance created a bustle of preparations all around me. Even Nuri was bustling, carrying saddles to the carpenter for repairs, tents to the tentmakers to have worn panels replaced.

After I'd chased him a while longer, Nuri relented on his silence a little more. "My uncle," by which inoffensive title he meant his master, "your father leads the caravan. But there is not a man, woman, or child of all the Quraysh who does not invest something in it and hope for the gain."

So I tagged around after Nuri as he went about his labors and saw how, in the wind-swept streets of Mecca, the haggling for principle had begun in earnest. I saw a man sell a pair of old sandals to another for an outrageous price. Then the buyer immediately turned around and sold the footwear back to the same man for a reasonable, even paltry sum.

"Allat protect us, the man is a raving fool!" I could not help but exclaim.

"Not so," Nuri said with his noseless twang. "The second man now has the money he needs to outfit a camel or two. His partner has given him a loan, with no need to collect interest. They will share the profits." Then, in a very quiet voice, he said, "I was bought with the proceeds of the sale of a saddlebag."

Other men were not even bothered with such a flimsy camouflage for their usury when the returns could well be over a hundred percent. It has been said that we Meccans were bankers by religion. Muhammad's pure Arab abhorrence of this propagation of sterile gold has done little to change things when the caravans gather.

When the necessary funds had been collected, the camels—all strong males—were brought in from the wilderness. Merchants drove the beasts—their own, rented, or plundered—through streets sweet with the fragrance of new-tanned skins, the resinous smell of qaraz pods, bundles of woolen cloaks, all in heaps as tall as I was. Smaller but more valuable heaps, mere handfuls, of our most valuable commodity from the nearby mines—gold—filled squares of silk in the sunlight.

The camels came to kneel around my father's fluttering banner. Here the drivers shoved cushions under the saddle frames this way and that and laid burdens on the thick blankets from Haleb that felt like the nap of Nuri's hair. The loads would not come off until they arrived in Syria, and they must not chafe. Drivers prodded the animals to their feet and let them down again until the fine balance was found between Indian cotton, Arabian leather, Sabaean spices, Persian pearls, and what the humps could in reality carry.

Then the travelers were chosen: this slave had grown too fat, yet this one was too inexperienced, although his lighter weight would allow for another casket of myrrh. How to choose between them?

Then the wives came, leaving the cool of their harems to mingle in the excitement of the caravan-ready square, weeping one moment, dancing, singing, piercing the air with their sharp trills the next. They loaded their men with half-finished garments and sacks of dates or good warm bread that could not possibly be taken along. And the children were everywhere, listening with wide eyes to the tales of faraway places, rifling the packs for sweets, mock-raiding and caravaning over the mounds of goods. It was a joyous, bustling, raggle-taggle time, the fits and starts of getting a caravan underway.

After that first year, in quiet times, before the caravan began to gather, Nuri was my best friend in Mecca. He regaled me with fantastic tales about how he had come to lose his nose and get that patch of gray-white scar in its place.

"A lion," Nuri said, lapsing into a prattle that suited the time of his memories better than the formal Arabic he had since learned. "Great lion, big as three men. Took my nose. I make him give it back. Kill him dead—so! No weapon. Bare hands." (And the great black hands he opened and closed at this point were indeed awesome.) "But—phew!—lion's teeth make nose no good."

"Princess," he told me next time. "Beautiful lady take my nose as brideprice, O my young uncle. She my wife. Most happy man."

My cousin Omar taunted me for my attachment to a slave and told me the truth. "He lost his nose to the slavers for being insubordinate." (Omar liked to show off with big words.) "And it didn't cure him. He sits around telling you tales to avoid having to work."

I didn't mind the truth. Nuri was still the only one I trusted.

Nuri was the one who, when I was ten, brought me word in the stables. Omar was bragging around the Ka'ba that he was man enough to go with the caravan that year. This helped me steel my jealousy to present calm in public when next I had to face him. It also made me long for my milk family again and to find a means by which I might escape Mecca and return to them at last.

When I was ten, I made my first deal for the summer caravan. I trusted Nuri enough to bribe him. I gave him a golden chain to add to the cache with which he hoped to buy his freedom some day.

"Keep me hidden in your saddlebag until the caravan is too far from Mecca for Father to send me back to my womb mother in disgrace," was the favor I asked in return. Perhaps then, I thought secretly, Father would let me go all the way to the pastures of the Tamim with him.

The black slave and I put off the actual packing as long as we dared. Father let it be known he would depart for the north on the eighth night of the month. That was the most favorable time because the moon, whom we worshipped as a merry and vigorous youth, lit the cool hours of the night. No raiders could come upon the caravan without a chance to prepare a defense. The eighth day, however, was a matter of debate. The eyes of an anxious boy and a keen slave might see the first slip of a new moon and start counting a night or even two before the glassy-eyed old man who took oracle from the moon god. Father would listen to the blind wisdom of age before he would trust his own eyes.

Even oracle-led, the caravan's departure was bound to be an erratic event. The only clear way to pinpoint it was by the instant when anticipation finally got the better of my father. He would then toss away his usual calm, controlled exterior. With a whoop and a holler, he would leap into his saddle and tear his banner out of the dust while his camel came to its feet with a bellow. In a moment, they would be out of town, the camel galloping with its neck and tail held horizontal, waving like flash-flood waters over the desert.

This instant never failed to catch my father's men by surprise, in the midst of repacking or bidding farewell to their families. For a day or more they would struggle on after him, driving before them the pack animals left behind in my father's eagerness.

But Nuri and I could not count on a day's grace to catch up with the main body of the caravan. My father would expect his slave to be not a lance's throw behind him from the start, so I had to be bundled up and ready to go any time within a two- or three-day period.

Nuri's bag was not the spacious pouch I remembered from days when my milk mother would balance her riding camel with Malik on one side and me on the other. Though men are allowed the vanity of longer tassels, women's bags are actually larger. The harems have more utensils and trinkets, after all, and can take slower marches from camp to camp.

More seriously, I had grown in the years since I'd left the desert. I was still short for my age and thin, but it was a breathless, cramping squeeze nonetheless. The dusty red wool weave was worn in places; I was grateful for the air. But Nuri said I had to cover even those spots with my headdress or my cloak. Something too suspiciously like a knee could be seen straining at the weakness.

"Hush, my young uncle," Nuri warned. "Baba coming." And then there was no more time to search for the nonexistent position of comfort.

Over the ringing in my ears from the cramp, I heard my father exclaim, "What, Nuri? No more room? I can't have given you more qaraz than would fill just one of your bags. Whatever have you got in the other?"

"Nothing, my uncle."

"By Hubal, Nuri! Your mother must have been the queen of asses. Must I help you with such an easy thing as packing saddlebags?"

"No, my uncle. Do not weary yourself. I'll do it."

Nuri's ruse was transparent, and I closed my eyes for the surrender. But then there was a pause and, incredibly, I heard my father's footsteps as he walked away. Days of intense, choking heat seemed to pass. Then Nuri hushed me again, and my father returned.

In spite of the warning, I shrieked with surprise as a shock of pain hit my back side. The sound of whacking was all that covered it. Several more good whacks from my father's camel goad punctuated the scolding the slave got. "We have the cooking bags to come, Nuri. They are leather, they fold, but they still need room. And utensils. Squeeze your things a little tighter. Whack them so! And so! We cannot leave without those bags."

I bit my lip until the blood came, refusing to let a childish sob defeat me.

When I had endured this beating, too, without discovery, I was certain the plot would work. But then came a sound I could not endure. It was the pretentious voice of my cousin Omar.

"Oh, no," I heard him say, a snatch of conversation dropped as it were in passing. "Khalid, my mother's uncle's son, not he. It will be years before he is allowed to join the caravan. He is, after all, but a child. And young for his age as well. The merchant's life here in Mecca does not agree with him. He is always talking to slaves and not tending to business. So how could he like Syria? No, I have heard it from his own lips. He says he would rather be herding camels in the desert. By Hubal, a camel only duplicates herself once every two years. A single gold piece will make fifty in one quick trip to Gaza. Poor Khalid! Gold pieces soon outgrow the number of his fingers, so he is too simple to have anything to do with them."

"Bite your tongue, O son of an ant hill!" I heard myself curse. "Or I'll come and tear it out by the roots."

I tumbled from my hiding place. The mid-morning light and dust were blinding. My cramped legs refused to stand upright. The dark mountains that bound the valley of Mecca with eternal rock whirled about me like meteors. It was several moments before I could fix my eyes on my cousin.

Even now Omar is a good head taller than I am, but then, when I was ten and he thirteen, there were two heads between us. He was big. He had already begun to compete in the annual wrestling matches at the fair of Ukaz, for which he would become famous. He stood with his legs apart, firm on the ground. My sudden appearance did not take him aback in the slightest. He was ready and waiting for me. And he remembered the horse race.

I hunched my shoulders and charged. The next moment I was flat on my back with the wind knocked out of me. Hubal blacken that dog's face! I thought, unable to say it aloud. And blacken my own for being a fool. I had forgotten that Omar was left-handed. He had flipped me with that sinister weapon as easily as a woman flips baking bread.

My breath came back to me in two fresh gulps. My vision cleared. I thanked heaven quickly, easy enough since the Ka'ba and its Gods were not far away. The peace of the place should have prevailed, but incense and dust raised by worshippers stuffed my head instead. Being flattened like that, though I would not have chosen it, was the best remedy I could have taken to get over the effects of half a day in Nuri's saddlebag. And it fed my fury.

Omar's face stood suddenly between me and the incense-streaked sky. The hollowness behind his robes told me his leg had gone back for a kick. Moving faster than he could see, I jumped up and went in. I went in low, grabbing that left hand and hauling it with me. Because I caught him on only one leg, he staggered back. I'd left my own feet, so we both depended on his one. It wasn't enough. We plowed backwards, into the very pole holding aloft the sacred camel's skull. Here we landed hard, among the stones at its base. Something snapped in my hands like so much dry thistle. I feared at first that the snap was the old God's pole.

Suddenly I was loose and free. A wail of pain came up from my cousin—I had broken his leg.

I stood back as they carried Omar off to a bone-setter. It was only then that I realized all Mecca had been there, all the pious "Neighbors of God." Rather than curse me for disturbing the Gods' peace, they stood now laughing in a ring around me. They offered congratulations. They collected their bets: I had been the long shot and made somebody rich.

Certainly the Gods had helped me.

Or—I looked down at the right hand that had done the deed and remembered gifts on a tiny clay camel for only the second time since my return to Mecca—the jinn.

Young men fight. Only God knows why. The same reason older men have for it, I suppose—their burning anger at something, anything. Only at ten, it is not yet given the cover of a battlecry or the dignity of a bit of dogma.

Young men break their legs, too. Young men heal, faster and cleaner than I shall ever heal for having slept wrong night before last.

But young men do not forgive. My father paid Omar's father well for the damage done, but I must endure Omar's malice against me until my grave.

My father was there in the crowd of fight-happy, caravan-ready Meccans. He was sitting, not standing, in the shade of the far wall, quietly chewing qat. The wad in his cheek hardly gave the rest of his face space on which to display his emotions. He was not exulting, or even broadly smiling. But I could tell. He had known I was in that saddlebag all along! He had set Omar to pick that fight, just to see what I would do.

"Come here, my son." He patted a spot on the rug next to him.

With hot tears blinding my eyes, I hung my head and turned away.

"Nuri, bring the boy here to me."

I tried to fight off the big black hands with their pinkish palms. They, too, had made a mockery of me. But the fight was gone. I found myself gently but firmly set before my father, who took four or five thoughtful chews before he spoke.

"So," he said finally. "You think you are old enough to travel with the caravan this year?"

"I want to go back to the sons of Tamim in the desert," I muttered.

"You think you are old enough, and yet you want to go back to your milk mother. Something is not quite right."

I had no answer to that.

My father tried to get me to sit again, and finally I did, however unwillingly. He offered me a branch of wilted qat leaves. I had wanted to go with the caravan; I had wanted to prove myself a man. Yet when this step toward manhood was offered me, I hung my head and refused. What sort of man took his status on another's terms, even those of his father?

My father nodded quietly, then spoke with deliberation.

"The Romans see us out of Damascus with half-closed eyes and the Persians look the other way when we ride into their well-watered land. They shake their heads at our caravans and think us madmen and fools to set out into the trackless desert. And they think us magicians or jinn when we return, Manat willing, loaded with luxuries from the province of their enemies. They reach into their overstuffed wallets to pay fortunes for what we offer.

"They pay us," my father went on, "we who build our routes not with finely polished stone, but with living blocks of flesh-and-blood genealogies.

"I was going to take Omar with me on this journey," he said. "Omar is my niece's son, and I meant to leave him with Sharif Nuwaira and the sons of Tamim to assure their good graces while we pass through their lands this year."

"Omar stay with the Tamim!" I exclaimed, my first words since I had joined my father on the rug. "By Hubal, that ass's son doesn't know the first thing about the people of Yarbu."

"Indeed," my father nodded. "But what else am I to do? They are a proud people, those Arabs of Tamim. They demand some sort of hostage before they will grant us trading rights. See now: Hubal has willed by your strong right arm that Omar lies at home with his mother and his broken leg. How am I ever to trade freely through the Tamimi lands? Without passing through their lands, I cannot get to Persia or to Bahrain beyond. It would be nice if I could leave someone there who knows those Arabs well, who understands their ways and could let me know all the secrets of their desert. But I must be realistic. Where is such a person to come from?"

"Me! Me!" I cried. "I could go and stay with them."

"You?" My father looked truly startled. "You only want to hide in Umm Mutammim's harem. You are my son, but you are still only a child."

"No!" I collapsed to the rug beside my sire and snatched up his bunch of wilting leaves. I stuffed qat in my mouth, wincing at the bitter taste. I chewed. "Let me go, O my father. I will be the best merchant's son you ever sent to the Tamim."

My father raised his great, heavy eyebrows. He munched on the great knob of qat in his cheek and pretended to think. Now I realize that his decision had been made long before he even set Omar up to taunt me. Then I sat by in impatient silence.

Finally my father spat out the brilliant green wad and got to his feet, straightening out the Persian silk of his cloak. "Very well, very well," he said as if more surprised at his decision than I was. "Hubal willing, you shall come with me. Oh, and Nuri—"

My co-conspirator stopped in his burst of joy at my success. His part would not be overlooked after all, and he answered dubiously, "Yes, my uncle?" He seemed ready to fall on his knees and beg for the kind mercy of only a beating.

"Nuri, what did my son give you for the use of your saddlebag?"

"Me, uncle?"

"Yes, you, Nuri. That was your saddlebag, was it not?"

Nuri gave a weak, noncommittal shrug.

"Nuri, I hope you are not such a fool that you let him get away with that for nothing."

Sadly Nuri drew the gold chain out of his robe and held it out toward my father.

"And here," my father said, bending his head toward the slave to remove an even heavier chain from his own neck. "Here is my fee. The two together should be enough. Go to the slave market and buy yourself a wife of the new shipment just come over from Abyssinia this week. That one with the hips like well-stuffed camel bags. Yes, I think you know the one I mean—I saw you looking at her."

Now Nuri fell to his knees in earnest, blubbering thanks and kisses all over my father's hands and feet.

"Go on," my father said. "The caravan leaves tomorrow. Give the girl one night of wedded bliss at least before we depart."

I learned Mecca's ways well. By the time I was eighteen, I had chief responsibility for the purchase of the animals from the markets by the wells of al-Hira.

I rejoiced to return to my milk family whenever business allowed, yet I learned not to mind when business kept me away. No more does one care for the stones of a Roman road, momentary supports on *a journey but quickly passed over and put behind. Nonetheless, I never forgot that the Tamim were men, not stones. And they were Arabs, true men of the desert, the proudest men God ever created.*

Once chiseled, stone remains as the mason's eye first leveled it. Not so human flesh. A son of Mecca had to be always ready to clear his roads with his sword.

16

> I . . . patched up the leather bucket and kneaded the flour, but I was not proficient in baking the bread, so my female neighbors of al-Ansar used to bake bread for me, and they were sincere women.
> —**Asma, daughter of the first khalifah, Abu Bakr**

"By the Merciful One, Rayah, why is my brother Kefa so angry?" Little Bushra stood wide-eyed at the arbor opening.

Rayah pulled off her sweat-damp veil and drank long from the ladle beside the courtyard fountain. "Never you mind him," she gasped. Then she plunged her hot face and hands in completely.

"Rayah, what did you do?"

Rayah surfaced and mopped up the trickles with the corner of her discarded black fabric. If only the unpleasantness of that walk home from the mosque under the lashes of Kefa's tongue were so easy to wipe away. "He's a young man. He just doesn't know anything else to do with himself when he feels out of control but get angry. And since God controls all, men's control is just a mirage in the first place. Let Kefa stay with the men out there. We don't want him disturbing your peace here in the harem."

"But you." Rayah tossed her veil in the direction of the hooks at the entry and strode toward her little cousin. "What are you doing out of bed? You know you're supposed to keep quiet a few more days. For your head."

Bushra gingerly touched the white cloth swaddling her brow. "But they're all making bread," she protested, nodding toward the chatter and laughter coming from the kitchen. The sounds along with the smoke of hot-burning camel dung and the delicious fragrance of baking twisted around the courtyard jasmine vine. "No one will come and sit with me."

Rayah understood. Bread-baking was such a communal pleasure that no one liked to miss it. Gossip and flour flew as ten or more hands reached for the neat balls of kneaded dough made from fresh-ground wheat. They rolled and patted the cakes flat. Then, on a round leather cushion, they handed them to the one whose job it was to bend deep into the pit and slap the dough onto the hot clay sides. Usually this task went to the one who was most pregnant at the time, so today that would be Auntie Johara. The bending and heat would be harder on her, of course, but her condition assured that the flat loaves would swell and round properly, with crisp brown burnt spots on their bellies. Many years of such toil—many pregnancies—toughened a woman's hands so she could do it all, even pull out the fresh hot loaves without aid of a stick.

Rayah's hands had far to go yet. And she still had to recover from the harried walk from the mosque.

"I'll sit with you," she said and, gathering her young cousin in her arms, carried her to her bed.

On the way, over the white bandage, Rayah spared a glance toward the stairs at the top of which lay Sitt Sameh's room. Cousin Lutfi, Kefa's younger brother, had come to him upon their return and whispered to him something about their friend Jaffar being in the house. That had stopped the tirade against her as Kefa had hurried happily toward the majlis, saying, "Mashallah, I wondered when he wasn't at prayers."

"But he's not there," she'd barely heard Lutfi murmur. He was trying not to let her overhear, so she strained all the more.

"Where is he then?"

"Up in Sitt Sameh's. They say he might never be a man." Their words fell even lower but were well padded with pious prayers to God; she'd distinctly heard the word "Die."

Well, she meant not to enter Sitt Sameh's room again. If it were true—how could it be?—that a strange young man was there, all the more reason. Sitting in that room had made her late for prayers. It had made her see strange visions in the ruins, besides making Sitt Umm Ali scowl at her and Cousin Kefa yell. She wouldn't go back.

"Uh, you're getting to be a big girl," Rayah said as she set Bushra down and plumped up the pillows behind the mending head.

Bushra giggled proudly. Rayah's fingers twitched as they remembered the broken pieces of skull fusing in the blood under them. She was glad to see Bushra well enough now to offer her something else to think about.

"Sing me a song," the little girl said.

"Oh, you don't want that." Rayah laughed.

"Yes, I do. Auntie Adilah always sings me songs."

"Auntie Adilah has a good voice. I do not."

"Is that because you're so pious?"

Rayah blushed, remembering Kefa on the way home. "Your brother wouldn't say so. Just the opposite."

"So we'll leave Kefa out with the men."

Hearing her own words parroted back made Rayah determine to watch her tongue around children in the future.

"Sing me the one about the donkey who eats the beans," Bushra ordered.

"But I would sound more like the donkey if I did. Besides, I don't know the words."

"Yes, you do. It goes 'ee-ah, ee-ah' at the end."

"I'm sorry. No song. Unless you'd like me to chant the Quran." And Rayah began: "Bismillah 'r-Rahmani 'r-Rahim . . ."

"No, stop," Bushra begged. "It's not fun. How about a poem?"

"The Quran is something like a poem. A divine poem, in the perfect language of God."

"Sitt Samah recited me some poems."

"Did she?" Rayah was surprised at how important this seemed. "What about?"

"The desert," Bushra said, wrinkling her nose. "And Gods."

"There is no God but God," Rayah stated firmly. But she couldn't fend off a stab of jealousy. If Sitt Sameh was her mother, as she said, why had she never recited this poetry to her?

"In Sitt Sameh's poetry there is. At least, she said there was. I don't know. Her poems are like the Quran."

"No. How can something divine be like something earthly?"

"Sitt Sameh's poems are in Arabic, like the Quran. I don't understand either of them."

Rayah smiled with some relief. "I see. Well, would a story do?"

"Good." Bushra folded her hands expectantly over her flat chest and waited for the tale to begin.

For some reason, Rayah wanted very much to tell the tale of Ghusoon, the young woman she'd met wandering with the dust devils among the ruins that midday. But that story had no ending yet. She told instead a tale her day's adventures had reminded her of: the tale of Amr ibn Luhayy and how idolatry came to the once pure Ka'ba built by Ibrahim in Mecca.

"Ibn Luhayy was a proud and brave man whose caravans ran between Syria and Mecca so that he became rich."

"What did he trade?" Bushra asked with her usual practicality.

Rayah thought of the tales of that other Meccan, Khalid the Sword of God. She'd made her decision in the mosque; she wasn't going back up to sit in Sitt Sameh's room. And, since that was true it wouldn't matter if what she'd heard up there went into her description of Amr's caravans—just a little.

"He traded horses," she decided.

"What? Not rare silks and spices?" Bushra sounded very disappointed.

"Oh, yes, those, too. Anyway, he became so rich and so well known for his hospitality that he became custodian of the holy shrine, the Ka'ba. And because of this, and because it was the Time of Ignorance, a jinni came to him to serve as his messenger between this world and the next."

"Was it a wicked jinni or a good one?"

"Listen and see. The next time Ibn Luhayy caravanned to trade, the jinni came with him, riding on the rump of his camel. 'Depart for Tihamah at once,' the jinni said, 'for good luck and fortune await you if you do not delay.'"

"It sounds like a good jinni," Bushra declared.

"Listen and see. The Fire Spirit led him to the shores of Jiddah and there, bathed by the waters of the Red Sea, Ibn Luhayy found many great idols half-buried in the sand.

"We have nothing like this in Mecca, he thought.

"And the jinni heard his thought and rubbed his hands with glee. 'Yes, you must dig them out,' he said, 'and take them back with you, a treasure greater than anything you may get in Syria.'

"So that is what Ibn Luhayy did. And that is why there were idols at the Ka'ba when God's Apostle arose, idols where there never were since the time of Ibrahim, blessings on him. And God's Apostle, God grant him all honors, had to cast the idols down to return Mecca to its original purity."

"So Muhammad was angry at the idols."

"That's right."

"Just like Kefa was angry with you today."

"Well, something like. Only I did nothing very wrong."

"Not like idols?"

"No, not at all."

"My brother yelled very much. He made my head ache."

"Mine, too. I'm sorry your head ached. Is it better now?"

"If you give me that cool lemon juice, it will be."

Rayah laughed and got the drink. She got some for herself as well and sat on the edge of the bed, feeling the leather straps beneath the wool-stuffed mattress while Bushra chatted on, clearly free from pain.

"That young man who went up to Sitt Sameh's room today..."

So Lutfi was right, Rayah thought. Jaffar is up there. But that's not what she said. "You mean Abd Allah? He's not so very young."

"No, not the eunuch. I know the eunuch. He helped carry the young man up."

"A young man? Surely not, Bushra dear. Sitt Sameh is very careful about such things. She wouldn't let a young man in her room."

"Well, this one she did," Bushra said definitely. "And his mother as well. I guess because maybe he won't live to be a young man after all. That's what Auntie Adilah said. He's very sick."

"He must be."

Now Rayah remembered when last she had heard Jaffar's name. There had been celebration in Sitt Umm Ali's house because her nephew had come to his circumcision. He had chosen to become a man, even though, the gossip ran, "the bride's family still refuses him." Rayah stroked the palm of her right hand. She had healed Bushra. But she could never do the same for Jaffar. Touch a strange young man?

Besides she'd promised herself she wouldn't go up to the third floor again for anything, at least not until another Friday had passed and she'd had a chance to prove herself to Sitt Umm

Ali. Rayah couldn't get any more information out of her little cousin anyway, since Auntie Adilah came in from the baking then. Adilah had flour in her hair and all down the embroidered front of her dress, her face flushed from the heat of the fire.

"Oh, good, Rayah," she said. "You're here, keeping her occupied. It's time to change that bandage, though, as Sitt Sameh said. The clean bandages are up on the roof drying. I'll just run up and bring them down."

"It's all right, Auntie. Why don't you sit down in this cool with Bushra and take a breath? I'll go and get the bandages."

Rayah hardly admitted to herself that the drying lines were just outside Sitt Sameh's door.

As she reached for the drying bandages on the line, Rayah could hear that the eunuch Abd Allah was once again reading the Conqueror's words. Because he recited the praises of Mecca to which, one day, God willing, she hoped to go on pilgrimage, she broke her vow.

She did not shut her ears and hurry away.

"Ah, Mecca. The valley was once called Bekka, on account of its narrowness. Naked mountains surround it on all sides; the valley is without brook, river, or any running water, without trees, plants, or any vegetation save camel thorn. Nothing to recommend it since the beginning of time but the House of God. At that spot, out of that clay, God created Adam and gave him the breath of life. Over that spot, the beneficent Provider gathered clouds to shade Ibrahim and his chosen son as they built.

"The House of which even Jews and Christians sing in their psalm that begins 'How amiable are Thy tabernacles, O Lord of hosts . . . Blessed is the man whose strength is in Thee . . ., who passing through the valley of Baca made it a well; the rain also filleth the pools . . .

"'My soul longeth, yea, even fainteth for the courts of the Lord: my heart and my flesh crieth out for the living God . . . For a day in Thy courts is better than a thousand.'"

More words from the Jews and Christians declaring how they, like the rest of creation, long for the Navel of the World. Rayah stood with her hand on the clothesline, on the very linen Bushra needed, and didn't move.

"No, nothing to recommend the narrow valley but the House, the well, the fact that it lay halfway between Syria and the spices of Yemen—

"And the fact that men had settled there who knew how to wrest advantage from little. Fierce men with teeth like sharks, the Quraysh. As the psalmist prophesied, seeing the birth of Muhammad before it happened: 'They go from strength to strength.'"

Abd Allah said, "Then the Conqueror Abu Sulayman had me write: 'I, too, was born in the narrow valley, and by the time I'd seen sixteen winters, I was ready to claim that strength. I was ready to step into my birthright.' Even this verse is applicable: 'I had rather be a doorkeeper in the House of my God than to dwell in . . . tents.'"

Rayah stared at the wall of Sitt Sameh's room, the battered black wool tenting rising above ancient clay. Here at the southeast corner, the vertical wall showed the effects of the khamsin winds that blew every year. The curtains of dust they raised reached to the third floor of any house, reached the heavens. Over many, many summers, the airborne bits of glass-like sand, so many tiny arrowheads, had whittled away the plaster. They left the courses of brick outlined, every seam of mortar growing hollower season by season. Rayah could see the bits of burnt straw in the fabric of the clay, the handprints of her ancestors who had slapped on the mix of sand-colored dung and let it dry.

And Abd Allah read and Rayah listened. The words of the Conqueror described the rituals he had undergone to become a man of the Quraysh. She felt pity for the young Jaffar hearing of this hero's bravery, when Jaffar's own rite of masculinity had gone so badly. And what did the eunuch feel about what he himself had endured in its opposite? Sitt Sameh continued to practice her black magic to counter the ill that had been done to the young man. And Rayah fled back to the ground floor with Bushra's bandages, shaken with fearful understanding of the horrors of being male.

17

"I had a daughter I loved very much. One day, I told her mother to dress her because I was taking her to her uncle. The poor mother knew what this meant, but she could only obey and weep . . . The infant rejoiced at the news of going to the uncle. I took her near the well, told her to look down. While she was looking . . . , I kicked her into it. As she rolled down, she cried, 'Baba, baba.'"
When I recounted this story, the Prophet . . . sobbed as if he had lost one of his nearest kinsfolk.
—a hadith of Sunan ad-Darimi

A season came in Mecca when the men of my blood gathered to initiate new members. Today, some—cowards, the effeminate of the old rotten empires—prefer the quick circumcision done on younger boys to bring them into the submission of Islam. We sons of the Sharks did not become full tribesmen until on the verge of marriage. Maybe one is better able to endure pain at a higher age, but the procedure is also much more dangerous on a man already sprouting his first beard.

I was young enough. I could have waited until the next cool season came. Even within this most male of ordeals, however, there was a woman, as at every turning.

Just come to her first uncleanliness, she was a young cousin of mine, which is to say, she was also cousin to Omar ibn al-Khuttab. A man may claim his cousin to wife without question, and yet, when there are other cousins, negotiations must be delicate.

At the time, I swore my choice had nothing to do with the young woman, whose name I won't even bother to give, but with the rivalry between Omar and me that hadn't healed with his leg. Should he become a man first, he would have her. If we underwent the ordeal together, the prize would go to the better man. I chose to go early, then, to prove I had what it takes to be a full son of the Sharks.

Our tribe is the Quraysh, which means simply "the association." By poetical extension, however, it may also be the diminutive of kirsh, "Shark," and no one loved poetical extension more than we Arabs in the Days of Ignorance. And to prove the name, a man, when he began to sprout his beard, would file his front teeth—two, or four for the particularly brave—to the sharp points of our namesake.

In rites that went on for a week or more, our short, ragged crest of boy's hair was shorn. Later it would grow into the full twisted lovelocks adults wear, and the beard never to be shorn except in shame. Then, peering into the shiny front of shields, we filed our teeth to their vicious points, digging into the tender, soft insides, as many as we dared.

"As you now sharpen your reeds." I grin at my scribe to show him the four filed teeth of Khalid ibn al-Walīd, only one of which has broken off in recent years.

Finally came the morning of frenzied dancing—naked, save for a dagger that wagged through the air so dangerously close to exposed ribs. Then came a squeal of flutes and a rattle of drums, a great shout of our war cry, "Teeth of the great House."

Omar stepped forward first, but I saw the leg I had snapped like a tamarisk branch tremble beneath him. I shoved him aside and ran forward with a yell, as if at the enemy. With both feet, I sprang to position in front of the circumciser, who was armed with an array of new-chipped flint knives. So I stood, hips and manhood thrust forward, hands clasped behind as blood-soaked old fingers pulled long the foreskin of a child—and cut it away forever.

It happened before my father could step up from behind to catch my elbows and sustain them. I stood alone.

Some men fainted right where they were. Such was Omar. The circumciser merely shifted a foot or two away to meet the next youth. The groans of these others rang in my ears; we weren't supposed to scream, but some did. My head was already light from the dancing, the lack of food and water, my skin slick with sweat, my whole body heaving with heavy gasps. My vision went red.

But the women were watching, trilling high trills and deciding, by my endurance, whether I was worth marrying.

I leapt from the knife with a roar of triumph. I went on, not to a soothing pack of warm camel dung as others did, but to hold my dripping parts over the hottest section of a green wood fire, further to flaunt my mettle. I stood, a man. I had proven myself the bravest son of the Quraysh.

And still I stood with the blood, like women's, running down the inside of my thighs—and yelled again in triumph.

My scribe grows pale at this. Only now do I realize that he endured a similar procedure that made him not a man but the furthest thing from it. I consider how a matter of knuckles' length makes all the difference.

Ah, youth, before we knew how the circumciser's knife could slip, the cut poison . . .

So I became a man.

As a man, I oversaw the training and care of our clan's war horses that winter of my eighteenth year in Mecca. And I married. The cousin my circumcision had won me, Umm Sulayman—I saw her with child again. Then I took a second wife. And a third.

The second gave little problem. She, too, mothered a son before I rejoined the caravan the following winter. I have all but forgotten her. I remember her only by her son—and because of the third wife. Whenever it crept up in conversation, as it did with meddlesome, undignified frequency, the term "my third wife" itself presupposed a second.

By all signs that one can weigh and test before the marriage night, my third wife was a splendid match. By the will of God, however, she had great difficulty conceiving.

The nights I spent with her, all my desire gone because we were obliged to lie with clunking fertility amulets under the pillows! Some days I mistook her for Umm Sulayman from a distance because she had borrowed the elder wife's veil in hopes that some of her fertility might be as easily borrowed. The money she spent on fortune-telling smith's wives and exorcists and magicians and potions and charms and sacrifices! The journeys to standing stones abroad—!

I have the impression her concern started up the very week of our marriage. Perhaps she had made attempts to conceive beforehand. God knows I paid the full price of a virgin, and I was no first-time bridegroom to be easily duped by a little squealing and partridge blood. Maybe it only seems like her magic began so soon. I certainly endured it three years longer than necessary.

Finally, I resolved to send her back to her father. Oh, I valued the alliance. I even liked the girl. She was a personable soul, attempting with ears and mind what she could not do with her other parts. I simply loathed the approach of evening when hers was the only womb in my courts as yet unfilled. I knew I would have to beat my way through the billows of smoke pouring from her doorway from some incense or camel placenta or foul-smelling herb she burned.

Then she was bundling her things to leave. Or rather, her slaves were packing for her, for she had neither the strength nor the will to do more than sit quietly on a bale. Her skirt was torn, there was dust in her hair. Perhaps the slaves had performed these tokens of grief for her as well, for her hands lay helpless, palms up in her lap; she was past tears.

I can see it now, of course. Her barrenness made her womanhood like a eunuch's manhood, the most important part missing. If all the henna and kohl and tattooing and jewelry and seclusion in the harem and knowledge of housekeeping, sewing, and cooking were not enough to make a woman of her, then what, by God, was she? Her mind had remained blank in answer to that riddle.

That emptiness reflected in her face. It drew me to her when I chanced to pass her door, as a man is drawn to contemplate the mystery of sunless nighttime. I waved the slaves away and there, in the empty, echoing room, without benefit of amulet or charm, I had compassion on her. I loved in a self-destructive sort of way. I loved an unremarkable spot in the desert, a spot neither sand nor rock, neither windswept nor still. A spot I might have passed over, only to think that the sway of the saddle must have momentarily lulled me to sleep through a place of doubted existence.

I left her when she slept in that big, empty room and, come morning, she was so much her former desperate self that I did not hesitate to have her out the door. Within three months, however, she was back in the court. Within nine, a child was born of my moment of compassion on emptiness.

The child was a girl, my first daughter.

It's true. As the generous Quran says: "For when the birth of a daughter is announced to any one of them, dark shadows settle on his face, and he is sad. He hides himself from the people because of the ill tidings."

I did all of that hiding and sulking. Muhammad never told us not to do such things. He himself had but a single child, a daughter, blessings on her, come to adulthood; he knew what such grief was like. Perhaps this was the Hand of the Almighty, teaching the Seal of the Prophets His great compassion. In our language, the word for compassion comes from the same root as the womb's emptiness.

I went further, however, on to the next verse. I asked myself, "Shall I keep the girl, which is not so much a child as a thing? Or—or shall I bury it in the dust?"

The vigorous practices of the desert kept the tribes lean and ready to fight. A man couldn't waste food on a daughter when he had the mouths of young warriors to fill. And what young warrior does not fight harder, knowing the prize may be one of the too-few women to go around?

The decision faced me late one afternoon. Shadows shifted long through the intricate patterns pierced in the plaster windows. I sat alone against many cushions and watched the pattern of light intermingle with the patterns woven on the rugs. The pink soles, black feet of a slave woman shuffled across those patterns. She sank to her knees before me. Avoiding my gaze, not daring a word, she presented the bundle to me. The mother hadn't come herself, for shame. But she had loaded the bundle with so many amulets and spells...

"Covetous spirits really don't care about baby girls at all," I informed the slave coolly. "They only search out the boys."

"Yes, master," the woman said.

Her black cheeks shone with tears. The bundle trembled in her outstretched arms. I remembered this was old Nuri's wife. She knew it was within my rights, my duty almost, to take the bundle out to the desert and return alone.

If I buried that girl-child, we would all be spared a lot of useless fuss.

Then I remembered the echoing emptiness of the child's conception.

The amulets were against me. Or for me. A wordless message to remember the emptiness. To have compassion.

What does it mean for every woman alive to know that when she was small and helpless she was held thus before her father, and he had power of life and death over her? What does it mean that she lives? What does it mean when she thinks of her sisters who did not?

So I took the infant in my arms and gave her a name.

"Which was? Master?" My scribe probes my silence like the toothache. "For the genealogy."

"Which shall remain unspoken," I insist.

The child outgrew her birthing ugliness. She thrived, plump and pretty and dauntless with spoiling and mother love. Then, I easily admit, she gave me more pleasure than all my sons. I would retire to the harem on an evening to have her perch on my knee, chattering nonsense like some exotic bird. I enjoyed undoing her little braids, ruffling up the hair to its full curl and thickness. Then, clapping, I would provoke her to dance or sing. Rightly convinced of her own charm, she never hesitated unless she was simply worn out. Then she would fall asleep within the cradle made by my crossed legs.

For the mother, my third wife, this attention to her child recompensed any amount of neglect to herself. Even for the fact that I never visited her room more than five times again and never gave her another child.

"Master, please. Not so fast. My pen cannot keep up with you. After the cradle—?"
"No. No more than that."
"But I didn't get it all."
"What you have is enough. More than enough."
"Shall I read it back to you?"
"If you do, I'll cut your throat."

He laughs nervously. He thinks I'm joking. I draw my dagger. I am not.

The dagger trembles. It drops from my hand to the softness of the garden soil.

I cry to the overstuffed garden. "By God, the tyranny of the pen!" The birds fly from their roost in the tamarisk tree. "You would dare to throw all that back on me. Serve a dog up his own vomit?"

My scribe, too, flees.

The next day, with more composure, we continue. I hope he has torn up that last. I told him to. But how do I know? I hate my own weakness in the face of words.

By virtue of all the same things with which she gave pleasure, my daughter also had the power to hurt. When old enough, she turned all my favoring to an inflated self-opinion, a pampered self-will. This, her mother was either unwilling or unable to cure, and I was not home to take action myself on the scandalous rumors that all Mecca knew.

Never mind what the Prophet said against the practice. It would have been better to follow my first inspiration. Yes, let the infant girl cry out against me before the throne of God on the last day: "For what crime am I, innocent, punished with death?"

Better that than to come home from yet another long trip to Syria to that same sun-streaked afternoon room. To have that same pretty child dragged before me a woman grown. And to see the rounded—cancer—deforming the belly of her gown, the unwedded shame which all her mother's amulets and incense had been unable to abort from her.

Then, then I had to drag that girl beyond the city's refuge of stones. Before, as an infant, I could have carried her, concealed her from the neighbors' scorn. Before, she wouldn't have given the years of delight to turn like a blade in my heart.

Then I had to throw her to the ground, to the hollow already dug. I screamed to keep her pleading from my ears. Then I had to raise the blade, plunge and turn, revenge for what she had done to me.

The fruit of that womb, opened like a pomegranate and swimming with sticky-sweet juice, was male. I could not help but see him, perfect in an infant's first bundling, as my sword—

Nay, by God, my hand had nothing to do with that deed and the sword had to carry it out alone— My sword hacked my little braided one into the obliterating pieces.

Even Islam did not remove this remedy for wantonness from our daughters. This remedy to erase a man's shame. He must admit—only to a eunuch in a Syrian garden—that it hurts.

Disposing of her lover, her partner in the crime, took me longer. He sat under the protection of his clan who refused to admit to blood guilt in the case of a silly young girl. My hands alone smoked.

But I sought him out when he had no such shadows at the Battle of Uhud. Taking his life then was a pleasure compared to—

"Do not lament so loudly against heaven, my friend, that you will never be a father. Children are rarely an unmixed blessing," I say.

After I know not how long, my scribe rouses me with this snatch at solid ground: "And—about how many years before the Hijra would you say these events took place?"

I'm not certain when the events of that girl's brief life meshed with the long and winding thread of mine own. Indeed, this is the first I've mentioned her since the day of my wrath. Such events are set to one side of history. A daughter who betrays her family must be as if she had never been at all. She should never be spoken of again. But the struggle with one's thoughts—

Ah, little exotic bird—

Well, I shall not speak her name, left unspoken these many years. That name I once shouted joyfully into the harem to bring her running, bright eyes and flushed cheeks, into my arms. That name, like running water, was buried with her just outside Mecca. There, by God, let it remain.

This memory—may it rest at last, beyond peace, even, in oblivion. It has nothing to do with my story, neither in time nor space upon the face of God's earth. Only in the jumble of many times and many spaces that is my mind . . .

But the question lingers: What right have I to look for a daughter in the house of turpentine sellers when this is how I dealt with the first one the Almighty gave me?

God be compassionate if I have spoken amiss.

As compassionate as an empty womb.

18

> My mother, Umm Ruman, came to me while I was playing on a swing with some of my girlfriends. . . . I went to her, not knowing what she wanted. . . . She caught me by the hand and made me stand at the door of the house. I was breathless then, and when my breathing became all right, she took some water and rubbed my face and head with it. Then she took me into the house. There . . . I saw some Ansari women who said: "Best wishes and God's blessing and good luck." Then she entrusted me to them, and they prepared me for the marriage. Unexpectedly, God's Apostle came to me in the forenoon, and my mother handed me over to him. . . . At that time I was a girl of nine years of age.
>
> —narrated by the Prophet's wife A'ishah in the Hadith of Sahih Bukhari

Rayah broke her vow not to return to the top floor. She obeyed the summons to Sitt Sameh's room. She obeyed reluctantly, telling herself she could find an excuse and quickly leave again. She would use the same excuse she'd used for the past two full days of avoidance: Bushra stayed quieter with a cousin to entertain her.

It helped that young Jaffar had gone, still on his stretcher but better, well enough that they heard him jesting with Kefa in the passage. Now, Sitt Sameh's new patient sat on the rug in the middle of the room, unspeaking, unmoving. She had even refused to remove her veil upon entering the harem. Only her dark, wide eyes were visible. At their red lower edge, tears welled and spilled one after another, silently, without a shudder. They left a rim of dampness along the edge of the black cloth that lay across nose and cheekbones. The curtain could not mask the woman's identity from Rayah, however. She knew her at once: Ghusoon, the girl wandering with the jinn in the ruins. All Rayah's resolve to make her excuse and leave vanished in a moment.

An older woman hovered, thin, sharp-angled, with a voice like grit between the teeth. Ghusoon's stepmother, as it turned out, a stepmother who flashed her hands before herself against evil when Rayah looked at her with her blue eyes.

"My daughter, Rayah." That was the first time Rayah had ever heard Sitt Sameh admit this to someone else. Would she do so if it weren't true? A certain anger—or daring pride—blazed in her own blue eyes. "As you have already seen."

This made Rayah forget all promises to herself. She sat beside Ghusoon, between the young woman and the stepmother, near enough to support, but not touching.

Clearing her throat abrasively, the stepmother picked up the tale she'd been telling when Rayah entered. "A jinni, no doubt about it. All good-for-nothing Ghusoon does is sit there like this, not working, not moving, not speaking. I could hardly get her to move to come here. And I succeeded then only when I said this was the healer we would come to, not our usual one, Sitt Imtithal by the terebinth grove. And for all that consideration, look now how she is.

"Just like her mother," the remnants of a sandstorm went on. "Her mother before the demon finally did us all a favor and led her out into the desert, never to be seen again."

"I think perhaps I'd like to see Ghusoon alone," Sitt Sameh said.

Rayah could tell the woman who called herself her mother was making an effort to insert patience in her voice.

"What? Alone?" the stepmother said. "Never."

"We are only women here, and this is an honorable harem."

"What about him?" The woman tossed her head, making the coins sewn on her cap jangle in the direction of Abd Allah, standing dark and silent in the corner.

"As I told you, as he told you himself, he is a eunuch and more protection than harm. But I can certainly send him away while I work with your daughter, if that would set your mind at rest."

"It's not *my* mind that might be agitated. It's her father's."

For the first time in her life, Rayah was glad she never had a father to exercise such concern over her. It must be more stifling than the veil.

"More than her father," the woman ground on, "it's Sharif Diya al-Din."

Rayah felt a shudder go through the silent young form next to her.

"I'm sorry, I don't know the gentleman," Sitt Sameh said.

"The man her father has found to marry her. Such a careful parent."

Marry her? Startled, Rayah stared at Ghusoon. They were nearly of an age, which meant the uncles might soon find Rayah herself some stranger to marry. The thought made a wave of weakness wash over her.

The stepmother continued on, reciting the sharif's virtues: "He's rich, he has slaves, he trades with the Rumi…"

"But he's old enough to be her grandfather, with teeth so bad his breath smells." Rayah's words leaped from her mouth before she could stop them. She didn't know where the impression had come from, but she'd had a sudden vision of the man that made her flesh recoil in horror. He could have been in the room with them.

Ghusoon turned and met her eyes, a look of gratitude there, the first time she'd given any impression that she was other than deaf and dumb.

"What matter is it of yours, I'd like to know, you impudent girl with cursed eyes?" The stepmother's words felt like a fistful of sand thrown in Rayah's direction. "And how would you know, anyway?"

Sitt Sameh visibly controlled her own temper to ask her guest for calm, but the woman was not diverted.

"How would you know, cheeky girl, unless you were possessed by jinn as well as this stepdaughter of mine? How would you know unless your evil eyes cast the demon upon her in the first place?"

She grabbed Ghusoon abruptly by the arm. "Come along, daughter, let's go. We'll get no help here." And she tried to lift the young woman to her feet.

Ghusoon reached out and clasped Rayah's hand. Rayah clung to the ice-cold fingers with ferocity of her own.

When her tugging had no effect, the stepmother thrust her nose in the air. "This harem hides an evil as great as—as great as—"

Sitt Sameh had risen to intervene but grew pale and stood rigid where she was at the word "evil."

"Yes, and I will tell my husband about this, just see if I don't." The woman yanked as if to tear her stepdaughter in two between them.

"Let her go, Rayah," Sitt Sameh said.

Rayah would not.

Then Abd Allah moved. He caught up the inert girl. He startled the two fighting over her so they had to let her go. "I'll carry her home for you, honored Sitt." He bore Ghusoon from the room. The stepmother, when she regained herself, went scolding after.

It was time to leave, Rayah knew. She should have done it before she ever sat down beside poor Ghusoon. But now she was filled with questions and so angry she couldn't leave them unasked. Perhaps more of her anger should have gone toward the impossible stepmother. But Sitt Sameh had complied with the woman's will—and Sitt Sameh was the one here now.

"Could you have helped her?" Rayah demanded.

Sitt Sameh turned away, took up a spindle, and became unduly occupied with the twist of goat hair. "No," she said. "Her father has plans for her."

"Plans that lay her open to the jinn. The marriage makes her too unhappy. When she tries to escape into the desert, they catch her and bring her back to force their will on her."

"But what would become of her in the desert?"

"Death would be preferable, don't you see? And yet they deny her even that. She thinks she has no choice, that she is powerless. It makes her unable to move."

"You have untangled the problem very well." Sitt Sameh nodded, although what played at the corners of her mouth held no joy. "The cure—that is what is not so easy."

"Yet you could do it, couldn't you? You simply won't. You don't dare counter that wicked, selfish father of hers."

"He is looking to the girl's future. A wealthy husband could make her very comfortable."

"Comfortable, but not happy. And comfortable, but not in his bed. She hasn't even been to his bed yet, and the very thought of it makes her sick."

Sitt Sameh twisted goat hair and said nothing.

Rayah's anger flared higher. "You could exorcise the jinni from her, couldn't you?"

"To what end? If I cast out one demon and don't do away with the threat of that marriage, I only leave her open for more Fire Spirits to enter."

Rayah wouldn't let Sitt Sameh stop her. "But you could do it."

Again Sitt Sameh didn't answer.

"How? Tell me how."

"Why? So that you can go and do what I will not?"

Rayah hadn't thought that far ahead. Now she stumbled and said, "I . . .I couldn't cast out spirits."

"Of course you could. You are my daughter."

Now it was Rayah's turn to look away, and she had nothing in her hands to look to. She found herself trembling.

"That is what you meant to attempt, isn't it?" Sitt Sameh said. "Go to young Ghusoon's house yourself and—?"

"I didn't. I couldn't." Rayah's subdued admission only fueled the fire burning around her heart.

"And why not? You have the power, even as I have. You know you do. You sensed just by sitting next to her what the poor girl's trouble was."

"A bad marriage? It takes no power to sense that. They are as common as grains of sand."

"Yes, but the stepmother has no sense of it, the father doesn't. And how you described the bridegroom—"

"Old? From my age—from Ghusoon's—what man is not old?"

Sitt Sameh couldn't suppress a smile. "You have some wisdom after all, my child."

Rayah shifted uncomfortably under the compliment. She was loathe to be beholden for anything to this woman who called herself her mother, loathe to take on praise and what must come with it.

"Not every marriage to an old man is bad." Sitt Sameh spoke almost under her breath.

"Of course it is."

"No," Sitt Sameh said. "You have shown some wisdom. Try to extend it now. I married an old man. Your father."

Her father. Sitt Sameh, suddenly become her mother, had just now mentioned her father.

No. Rayah wouldn't let even this distract her. "And that was the best choice you could have made?"

"Yes, I think it was."

"At least it was your choice."

"At the time."

Sitt Sameh seemed disinclined to elaborate further, but Rayah pushed: "And it has led you to this? To hiding out on the top floor of some stranger's harem. To being widowed early, to raising an orphan—" Rayah stopped herself only by biting her tongue.

"Your father's death, Rayah, was not a fault of age. He did not die a natural death."

Rayah leaned forward, hoping to learn more. Who? Who killed him? If he was indeed her father, she had a right to know. Who?

But she should have known better than to expect such a revelation after all these years. Not now, when the subject clearly lay elsewhere.

"I am willing to accept that the conclusion of an old bridegroom being the cause of the girl's grief simply came to you," Sitt Sameh said presently, after a few more twists in her work. "But the bad, smelly teeth? Tell me how you knew that."

"I . . . I don't know. It just—came to me."

"And you carelessly gave out everything you were given, letting the stepmother know what sort of power you have, making her afraid. Because she is afraid, she has removed her stepdaughter beyond our help. Worse, she has called upon the greatest strength she knows to help her in her fear—her husband. And oh, I would it were not so."

Sitt Sameh dropped the goat's hair, unable to work it more, twisting only one hand within the other. "It would be better if no man knew about me," she continued. "Given one thread, they may tease out the whole tale and then, what shall become of me? Not me so much any more. My life is past. But you, my heart. What will they do to you?"

That Sitt Sameh might have sacrificed the grief of Ghusoon for what she saw in Rayah's own blue eyes sent a chill across the girl's shoulders. But she ignored it. Would Sitt Sameh say that ignorance was a part of her youth? Rayah didn't care, but pressed her case.

"I have seen you heal burns and a bad circumcision. Tell me how you go about ridding a soul of a jinni. I am ready."

Sitt Sameh picked up her spindle again. "And I have seen you raise a little girl, dead from a crack on the head, with the merest touch of your hand."

Did that mean Sitt Sameh thought the skill would come to young hands just like that? Rayah knew that was impossible.

Or did this mean Sitt Sameh was shooing Rayah off to go and play with Bushra once more? The way the goat hair began to twist again in her mother's hands made her think it was this second option. Indeed, Rayah had swung on one heel to leave anyway, although perhaps not to go and sit with Bushra. But the huge form of Abd Allah filled the door and blocked her way.

"Come in, sit down." Sitt Sameh greeted him and offered him a drink of fruit juice for his exertions.

Rayah felt herself definitely dismissed with this. Still, she lingered to hear the answer to Sitt Sameh's question: "And how is the poor girl?"

"Fine, thanks be to God."

"Not fine, in truth."

Abd Allah spoke after his first refreshing swallow. "In truth, she's given up sitting."

"Given up sitting?"

"I placed her on a bed when I got to the home. She didn't move after that."

Sitt Sameh shook her head sadly. "Gone from sitting to lying."

Rayah decided then and there she must think of a way to get Cousin Kefa to take her to Ghusoon's house that very afternoon.

Then, to her back, Sitt Sameh said: "I think, Abd Allah, don't you, that the time has come in your narrative to begin a discussion of how the jinn are to be tamed? For there are cases in our past when this happened."

Rayah turned as if jinn-possessed herself. Sitt Sameh didn't say anything; she didn't even look in her direction. After a heavy beat of her heart, Rayah took up her seat on the rug once more.

"You will recall," Sitt Samah said, "how Sharif Zura of the tribe of Taghlib was jinn-possessed by the wife he'd cast off. And that he—they—had a daughter known simply as Bint Zura—Zura's daughter. My mother. Your grandmother. And one morning, early, when she was about your age, my Rayah . . ."

19

> **A white girl: She rises slowly and sweeps the ground with her hair.**
> **It hides her within its coils, a billow of blackest black.**
> **She shines in its midst like dawn that breaks from the farthest east;**
> **it bends like the darkest night and veils her above, around.**
> **—Bakr ibn an-Nattah, a native of Yamamah**

With a kahinah for a mother, gone into the protection of an enemy tribe, and a father driven jinn-mad, Bint Zura might well have been fated to die. She might have joined any number of other infant girls buried in the sand in those days because no one had the means to raise them. Instead, she was given to the wife of her father's brother to nurse.

Ubayy Abi Ragheb, her uncle, had taken two wives, and they'd borne him twenty children between them. In such a family Bint Zura grew, more servant than daughter. She pushed herself to usefulness from the time she could force milk from a nanny goat's teat or sling a baby on her back, even if his feet bumped her in her thighs.

So the madman's motherless daughter awoke early one morning, grown to her twelfth or thirteenth year, as tired as when she'd dropped to sleep the night before. The dull ache of hunger, a constant companion, lay in her belly.

It was still dark. Guy ropes creaked, and the black worsted snapped overhead, showering down sand. The wind blowing around the tent was the sort of northern blast that blinded the eyes with tears and stole the breath away.

Bint Zura turned onto her side, hoping to sleep some more. Then, above the howl of the wind, she heard the camels as Abu Ragheb prodded them to their feet for the morning drive to the well. It was rutting season and the males, with the swollen, bubbling bladders in their cheeks, were particularly noisy. They could be dangerous, too, snapping at anything that came near with their long, tusky teeth.

Because a she-camel gestates for a year, more or less, there were many bawling infants from last year's mating in the herd as well. And all the beasts protested like old people moving their joints on a cold morning.

Such a fate will be mine all too quickly, she thought. My joints will be old and frozen, and then I will want to be left behind on the migrations to die before, even, I've lived. What more could an orphan cursed with the evil of blue eyes expect?

She gave an extra shove and sent the little goat that had curled up on her belly for warmth bleating away. In such winter cold, every living creature was welcome in the crowded tent. Only camels stayed outside, although they did get jealous and tried to stick their noses under the curtains. When they did, everyone inside had to jump, yelling and beating the whiskered, split-lipped muzzle, or pull at the haunches from behind. Once he got a nose in, a camel would keep creeping forward until his hump was in, snapping tent poles and bringing the whole construction down on their heads.

Stepping carefully over this score of bodies—children, goats, saluqi hounds all in a jumble—Bint Zura made her way to the tent flap. Holding it open to peer out into the graying dawn brought a blast that chilled her to the bone. It also raised a cry of protest from sleepers nearest the door. Quickly, she shook her veil of sand, raising more protests, and adjusted it, glad for its warmth. She scooped up a goatskin basin stretched on a frame of acacia wood at the door and stepped outside, dropping the flap behind her.

Musky fumes of camel draped the chilled air. Abu Ragheb saw her and, rather than thanking her for coming out to help, only grumbled, "It's about time." In the half-light, her uncle's sharp underbite in the middle of his beard made his teeth look like those of a camel.

By the time she'd seen to her own needs away from the tent, the wind biting her bare bottom and sapping every last vein of warmth, the camels were almost all on their feet. Bint Zura's hopes fell. Before beginning the milking, she had hoped to get behind a she-camel just as she stood up. If Bint Zura could catch a stream of thick, steaming urine, she could give her hair a wash. Winter living made the lice bad. Camel urine would kill the vermin, make things more pleasant under her patched veil, give her some of the musky, vital smell, and warm her head in this chill morning besides.

Bint Zura saw the old, mangy gray matron, the last to struggle onto her forelegs at Abu Ragheb's prodding. Pushing between camel backs, crowded close for warmth, the girl made her way to the old dame's tail. The movement made the beast shuffle around on her great padded feet in annoyance, so all Bint Zura managed to get was the very last trickle.

Disappointed, the girl turned and called her favorite's name. "Ya Lataan! Ya Lataan!" Her eyes scanned for the mild-mannered, cream-colored najah. That she-camel might even have saved her urine, knowing Bint Zura would want it.

"Ya Lataan, my beauty, mother of camels," she sang.

Abu Ragheb had given the beast she called for to his youngest son when he'd been born. They'd tied the shriveled infant cord in a sack around the camel's neck as soon as it dropped off. This was the first of what, the Gods willing, would be many, many more possessions. He was a boy, of course, and people could hope such things for him. But he still slept in the leather sling of a cradle from the tent poles.

Her love for the camel made Bint Zura show more adoration for the little boy than she felt, when she was so frequently told to hold and hush him. As long as he still swung from the tent roof, why shouldn't she pretend?

And why shouldn't she pretend she was a great sharif's daughter and owned Lataan all herself? A hundred such. She was, in fact, a sharif's daughter, after all.

Only this sharif was mad, jinn-touched, the leadership gone to Uncle Abu Ragheb, and that was worse than having a herdsman for a father.

"Ya Lataan." It was no use pretending anything when the camel herself was nowhere to be seen.

"Yes, that jinni of a camel has run off." Abu Ragheb came up then, his goad across his shoulders, a hand perched on either end. "May she break her neck in the desert."

"Oh, Uncle, don't say so." Bint Zura touched the amulet of herbs and bits of iron around her neck against evil. "She's just wandered a little, I'm sure that's all."

"Yes? And what's this, I'd like to know?"

There was no denying it. Between his fingers, even in the half-light, Bint Zura recognized the broken hobble she had set around Lataan's legs with her own hands the night before. She always tied it looser than was strictly safe, knowing Lataan would never wander far. It was a secret, just between the two of them. Surely Lataan wouldn't betray her like this—

"She was about to deliver her calf," Bint Zura reminded her uncle, remembering the barreled belly she'd patted the night before. She'd even noticed the slight bulging of the cleft and the ligaments relaxing around the tail.

"Yes, and so she broke her bonds when the pains came on her and ran off to birth in some gully where the hyenas will eat her young the moment she drops it. A pox on Lataan, I say. Half of her young have been born dead. I cannot afford to draw water for such a beast and had better tie my son's cord around one of the strong young foals. Let me but find her, and we'll have camel stew tonight, by Manat and al-Uzza."

"Oh, no, Uncle. You do not mean it."

Bint Zura was clinging to her amulet now. He wasn't blaming her for a loose hobble, since he hadn't seemed to put those details together yet. This, however, was much worse. And he'd invoked the Goddesses with it.

"I will find her," the girl went on. "I will find her and her calf, both safe, if al-Uzza helps me."

Abu Ragheb snorted his disbelief, a camel sound, his breath smoldering in his ash-gray speckled beard. "If you do, I will give you her calf, girl."

"For my own?" She couldn't help it. Hope raced in Bint Zura's heart. But if two Goddesses were to be countered, she must add a third. "Promise me by the three Goddesses."

Abu Ragheb laughed, almost cruelly, she thought.

"Promise, Uncle?"

"By Allat, Manat, and al-Uzza, you blue-eyed curse of a niece. But I might as well promise you a puff of air, a heap of hyena-gnawed bones. I will find that dun-colored najah first and cut her throat."

"Just tell me—where did you find her hobble?"

Abu Ragheb waved vaguely. Bint Zura wasted no time to hurry in that direction, knowing exactly where she'd left Lataan that night with a whisper and a wink: "Ya Lataan, remember. You are bound fast."

In the growing light, she found the place, the large oval mark of the couched camel in the sand, just where it ought to be. Bint Zura knew Lataan's shape so well that she could recognize it anywhere. But the patch of dark dampness she found at the windward side distressed her. Blood.

Bint Zura saw where the padded hooves left a few prints. Their hollows caught the day's first shadow, distinct from all the other shuffling that had gone over them since. They were heading south, toward Jebel Ethtib and Meda'in Salih beyond.

Behind her, the girl heard Abu Ragheb calling his tallest sons to come and do the milking, his daughters to come and help lead the beasts to pasture. He had a benighted camel to kill that would fill all their bellies that night.

Cold dawn banded the salt pans on Bint Zura's left, the same color of bone woven into the tent curtain that divided men from women. Sweet winter grasses had lured the Banu Taghlib much further west and south than their usual herding rounds, deep into the high desert.

Her uncle's tent lay near Meda'in Salih, the Cities of the Prophet Salih, although there were, in fact, no cities nearby. There had been once. Bint Zura knew the story well: God had sent the Prophet Salih to the Arabs settled in this land, the Themoudi.

She dropped her veil and dragged it over Lataan's prints until they disappeared in a patch of gravel. Then she hurried towards Meda'in Salih, the place that had once heard a warning from God.

"Ya Rayah, you must come below." Outside Sitt Sameh's room, Auntie Adilah stood to one side, afraid to look in.

"Let me just hear the end of this story," Rayah found herself begging. The history of the Prophet Salih was retold in the Holy Quran. Blessings on him, they had just studied him in Sitt Umm Ali's class. And here was a different take on his miracle of camels—

"You must come now. Sitt Umm Ali has come to call."

Rayah looked to the eunuch and to Sitt Sameh, hoping they might support her. At least, Sitt Sameh should promise not to continue the tale until she returned. They said nothing. They only exchanged glances with one another and did not even look at her.

"Ya Rayah," Auntie Adilah insisted. "Sitt Umm Ali is asking for *you*. She wants you to accompany her to the baths—alone."

20

> He said to her, "Enter the palace." And when she saw it,
> she thought it a lake of water, and bared her legs. He said,
> "It is a palace paved with glass."
> —The Holy Quran, Surah 27

All Rayah's kinswomen clustered at the bottom of the stairs staring dumbly across to the cool northern wall where Sitt Umm Ali had been given the place of honor. It was as if they'd never seen such a wonder before. They had a pretty good idea what such a visit meant—and they couldn't believe it.

Then Sitt Umm Ali made it plain.

"Speak up, girl," the older woman demanded. "What did you say?"

"I asked after your health and peace, Sitt."

Rayah offered the guest licorice water and a bowl of olives. Sitt Umm Ali took a brief sip, but she seemed to have already quenched her thirst.

"It's been several days since you've joined us in our studies," Sitt Umm Ali said. "Not since Friday prayers."

Rayah couldn't decide whether the bulk of the wealthy man's wife—her neck thick with amber and gold, her hair bright red with henna—was imposing or comforting. Certainly, compared to Sitt Sameh's sharp, fearful angles, there was comfort here; Rayah thought the visitor's voice hinted as much.

"You may have heard," Rayah said, eyes cast down. "It has been God's will that my little cousin suffer a serious accident, and I—I have been helping to care for her."

Sitt Umm Ali sniffed as if at a doubtful smell. "My family, too, has suffered an accident."

"Mashallah. Indeed, Sitt, I am sorry to hear it."

"My brother's son. His life was feared for. His very manhood."

"Jaffar?" Rayah remembered the young man suffering in Sitt Sameh's room. And the tale Abd Allah had read from his parchments about the circumcision in the desert.

"Yes, his name is Jaffar ibn Yusuf."

"I hope, Sitt, that God may grant him a full recovery."

"Yes, the Merciful One. Or—others. It is good to have a healer in the family."

Rayah didn't know what to say then. She looked to Auntie Adilah, leaning beneath the arched doorway. No one gave her any help.

"It is actually about Jaffar that I have come," Sitt Umm Ali went on. "Yes, praise the Merciful One, he seems to be recovering well. Well enough, at least, that we begin to think of a bride for him."

Among the many watching faces, there were actual gasps at this. Still, no one said anything. Were they gasps of delight, of mere surprise—or of horror? With no time to digest how she herself felt, Rayah was obliged to speak. "May God give him joy in his match," she managed.

"You know how men are helpless at such business." Sitt Umm Ali waved dismissively with her arm, deep silk sleeves fanning, bracelets jangling. "Well, they never enter strange harems, so they do not know what young ladies are available. The task falls to us."

Rayah looked to her family for help. Auntie Adilah, she saw, still had both hands to her mouth to stifle her gasp. She did not remove them, even though Rayah begged her with her look. The eyes above those hands held tears. Were they tears of pride? Or tears of sorrow to lose a daughter Adilah had raised as her own?

With a grunt, Sitt Umm Ali began to get to her feet. "I think it is time I was going."

"Finish your drink, please, Sitt," Rayah protested even as she took her guest by the silken elbow to help her up.

"I mean to go to the baths, and the day advances." Now they stood side by side, eye to eye. "I invite you, Rayah, to come bathe with me."

Rayah tried to look away. Again, she sought her kinswomen's aid. Every face reflected back to her the knowledge: Women on the hunt for a bride for their male relatives would insist on inspecting the girl for flaws—in the bath.

Ghusoon's fate had come upon Rayah faster than she'd thought possible. Was she now to answer with Ghusoon's response? To whirl out in the desert with despair? To fall inert? Or, equally passive, just to nod and say, "You know best, my elders. I will do as you say"?

But in all this drama, "What shall become of me?" seemed no more urgent than "What will happen next in Sitt Sameh's story?" Marriage would mean moving from access to such tales. What would become of Bint Zura? The camel? Would it survive the threats of the night desert? And its calf? Would Bint Zura find it in time in the strange pastures near Meda'in Salih—?

Sitt Sameh said this was a tale about her own mother. She said Rayah was her daughter, so Bint Zura was Rayah's grandmother. Perhaps none of it was true, not that this girl in the desert was her grandmother, not that she'd ever hobbled a camel so loosely, nor sought urine to wash her hair on a bitter morning.

The more she heard of Sitt Sameh's tale, though, the more Rayah thought she had in common with Bint Zura in the desert than she had with the girls of her own time and place. In fact—was it just Sitt Sameh's telling for her benefit?—there seemed to be but one blue-eyed twelve-year-old in this harem. The same girl set down in different surroundings, one in Islam, one in the Time of Ignorance.

As she put on her veil in preparation for accompanying Sitt Umm Ali to the bath, Rayah couldn't help but think about the story in the gracious Quran about that same Prophet Salih Sitt Sameh mentioned, which her teacher had read to them.

"Repent and fear God," had said Nebi Salih, the long-suffering prophet in ages past. "Or surely destruction is upon you."

"Give us a sign, and we will believe you," the men of Meda'in Salih said.

"What sign?" The man of God sighed.

"Cause these barren rocks to bring forth a she-camel already great with child." Impossible

"Come along, girl. Are you always such a dawdler?" Sitt Umm Ali scowled back. "That's not good."

Rayah was glad to escape the scrutiny of her family, but the scrutiny of this one woman alone was worse. Rather than the small, new bath in town where Rayah always went with her family, Sitt Umm Ali took the path toward the mosque among the ruins. She turned right at the long columned avenue instead of left. Rayah scrambled to keep up, balancing the lady's basket on her head, full of everything they'd need—luffa, soda ash to cleanse, unguents, towels, wooden shoes, a bundle of sweets—

Four columns different from all the rest—pink instead of the local golden limestone—marked the baths the Roman emperor Diocletian had built for his occupying army. Old as they were, this amenity was still a going concern. With deep bows and profuse well wishes, the bath wife welcomed them to the establishment and accepted Sitt Umm Ali's coin. Because it was women's day, the bath owner himself would keep out of sight, stoking the stove, one wornout slave at his side.

This bath, out among the ruins, was almost a ruin itself. Its aqueduct leaked in a dozen places, making miniature swamps full of insects and miasmas. Inside, the tile flooring was crumbling. Birds nesting in the dome left their droppings on benches and towels. Patrons must have helped themselves to the walls' marble facings, for the plain limestone core was exposed in many places. Or perhaps the owner himself stripped it to sell whenever falling attendance made it necessary.

There was no need to wait their turns at the single working spigot—which Rayah usually did not mind at the other bath, chatting with friends and playing games. In no time at all, Sitt Umm Ali was reciting a prayer to shield herself from the jinn. Then she slipped, crease by white crease, into the water. Rayah slipped in beside her. The water felt good on such a hot day, with a wind starting up that could draw the moisture even from eyes. The pool was far from the near scalding she was used to, however.

People said baths were jinn-haunted. In the loud society of the other building, Rayah had never understood why. Here, strange sounds echoed through deserted archways. Beside her, green algae floated, wraith-like, through the ripples.

Why such a grand woman as Sitt Umm Ali should come to this crumbling bath, Rayah couldn't decide. Just to examine a prospective bride? But the older woman hardly glanced at her budding breasts or her hips to see if they were wide enough to pass healthy heirs. Perhaps, inshallah, there were no marriage plans drifting in the tepid air over the bath, echoing from the darkened corners where rubble could cut the feet.

Or perhaps—Sitt Umm Ali's test would be something else.

Sitt Umm Ali began with the comment, "The Rumi emperor built these baths over the ruins of Zaynab's palace."

Did she mean this to suggest that Queen Zaynab's blue eyes had been covered over and that other blue eyes might expect a similar fate? Did she even know the connection of which Sitt Sameh had only just made Rayah aware? Sitt Umm Ali gave no sign and so, as Rayah watched the ends of their unbound hair float among the algae, black and gray together, she decided she must divert the topic.

Diversion meant to the other tale Rayah could not shake from her head, the one she'd been forced to leave so suddenly on the third floor of the turpentine sellers' house.

"Can you, Sitt, please tell me something of the Prophet Salih?"

Meda'in Salih, other ruins, yet another woman with blue eyes. But Sitt Umm Ali would know nothing of that.

Sitt Umm Ali set her lips skeptically. "The gracious Quran tells us all that is necessary to know about the messenger Salih, blessings on him. Do you know it?"

"I think so, Sitt."

"Only think? You must know. Recite."

And Rayah recited to the rhythm of lapping water:

> "The Themoudi also treated their Apostles as liars.
> When their brother Salih said to them, 'Will you not fear God?
> Shall you be left secure
> Amid gardens and fountains
> And palm trees with flower-sheathing branches?
> And, insolent that you are, will you hew out dwellings in the mountains?
> Fear God
> And obey not those who act disorderly on the earth.'
> They said, 'Ya Salih! Our hopes were fixed on you until now. Do you forbid us to
>   worship what our fathers worshipped?
> Certainly you are bewitched.
> Produce now a sign if you are a man of truth.'"

"And so it was." Sitt Umm Ali closed her eyes in the bath's contentment. "By the power of God. The camel came forth, and her young one. But even with such a sign, no one heeded Nebi Salih. They killed the camel. They killed the calf. They even killed the prophet, blessings on him."

Telling the tale made her flabby white flesh tremble even as she described it: "Then came a trembling of the earth, a storm of dust and fire from heaven to punish the unbelievers. Nothing stood in the path of this judgment of heaven but death and ruin."

"Jews have their prophets. Christians do too," Rayah mused.

"Did," Sitt Umm Ali corrected. "In the past: Adam, who was born circumcised, Ibrahim, Sulayman who controlled the jinn with a ring, Isa ibn Maryam and Yahya his cousin, the Baptizer."

"And Salih was a messenger especially to the Arabs?"

"But he was not the only one." Sitt Umm Ali recited all the names. They blew, twisting, drying, like gusts of the khamsin through the desert: "Hud was the first prophet who came speaking Arabic to the Arabs. Pilgrims in their hundreds still visit his burial ground in the hottest place in Hadramawt. There were Hudun ibn Hud and Dhaniyalah ibn Hudun ibn Hud, for the gift often ran in families. There was Shua'ib, on whom be peace, and Hanzala ibn Safwan, killer of a great bird who once preyed on maidens, and God's prophet Tubba whose tomb is fifteen paces long."

"And who was Khalid—?"

The name made Sitt Umm Ali sit up straight with a splash. "What of Khalid ibn al-Walīd?"

"I did not mean him, Sitt, not the Conqueror." Rayah flinched. "I spoke of prophets."

Sitt Umm Ali sank back in the water up to her chin. "Ah, Khalid ibn Sinan, the most recent of messengers. His daughter was still alive when I was a girl. She went among the Arabs to remind them of his prophecies and to keep his name on their tongues."

"And will another come?"

This question got another bobbing rise from Sitt Umm Ali. "Bite your tongue, girl. Don't I teach you anything? Muhammad, precious blessings on him, was the Seal of the Prophets. There will be no more, for all we need is in his revelation, the generous Quran."

Rayah nodded. She knew that. "Never a woman."

Sitt Umm Ali's bristling turned into an actual sign against evil. She'd taken off her jewels to bathe, among them her lapis lazuli protective amulets, so she merely groped at the air below her sagging chin.

"A woman!" Sitt Umm Ali exclaimed.

Rayah had only commented. She never meant—

"Women who must purify themselves once a month, who in the forthcoming holy days of Ramadhan may not even fast with the rest of the community of believers if they are unclean…"

The lecture went on. Rayah submitted to it with a bowed head, although she'd heard it all before. She knew what precautions she must take the moment that she saw her first blood.

The moment she was ready to marry.

"The ignorance of one girl, however, is of little matter," Sitt Umm Ali concluded. "For God's final Messenger, blessings on him, said: 'When the first night of Ramadhan comes, the devils and rebellious jinn are chained, and the gates of hell are locked.' Because of the purity of the mission of Muhammad the Seal of the Prophets, I need fear nothing still drifting about from the Time of Ignorance."

Rayah dared say no more until Sitt Umm Ali declared their soak at an end. Rayah had asked too much. Would it suffice to reject her as a bride for Jaffar?

On the other hand, she took courage. That wasn't part of her story, to live her life as a fool. Foolish girls, in Sitt Sameh's version of the world, might be the ones most in need of the education of a quick and solid marriage.

They rose from the pool, green algae clinging to breasts and thighs. Sitt Umm Ali complained as she wiped it off but still did not explain why they were at this bath instead of the other.

They dried, partially dressed, prayed. Then they nibbled on the sweets. Rayah, in her worry, had no appetite. Although the cakes were butter-light, sweet with honey, rich with nuts, they stuck in her throat. Sitt Umm Ali, she decided, had brought her to this bath not because she preferred it, but because she wanted none of her friends to see her speaking to this brightest but most troublesome of her pupils. If this were the case, Rayah could allow herself to feel little relief that the marriage was off.

When Sitt Umm Ali pushed the sweets away from her across the worn marble bench, Rayah's suspicions seemed confirmed. "They tell me you have a strange man staying with you, Rayah. In your harem."

"No, Sitt."

"Don't lie to me. I saw him. He helped to carry my brother's sick son home."

A harem crawling with strange men would certainly disqualify her for marriage. But a girl had her honor. "Abd Allah is a eunuch."

Sitt Umm Ali sniffed, as if that made no difference—either his state or the name that declared him a servant of God. Then she said: "You spoke of Khalid ibn al-Walīd."

"No, Sitt." Rayah's heart raced until she feared Sitt Umm Ali must see it through her thin underdress. This came close, too close to what she wanted reserved for the third-floor room. "I spoke of the prophet of the similar name."

"They say this eunuch of yours comes from the Conqueror."

Found out. "He . . . he says he does, Sitt."

"Why would such a great man send his eunuch to a family of turpentine sellers, I wonder. Why should he not send to our house, of all the houses in Tadmor?"

"I . . . I cannot say."

Sitt Umm Ali sniffed again, as if convinced now Rayah was stupid. "They say he visits that woman calling herself Sitt Sameh who lives on your third floor and never goes out."

"He has spoken to her, yes." Even now, he is probably speaking to her, reading her tales I shall miss.

"What sort of woman is she?"

Of course, prospective in-laws would want to know about all the family. Even the members they tried to hide. "She . . . she heals."

"So she seems to have done for my nephew."

Rayah winced. Now came the marriage—

"She must be jinn-possessed," Sitt Umm Ali said instead.

"I don't—I don't really know."

"But she is not of the family."

"I always thought she was." And now I think she is my mother. What would the in-laws say to that?

"She's not of the family, or I would know. I would remember her birth, her wedding, something."

If Sitt Sameh were not of the family, how did she come to have that room on the third floor? How did the turpentine sellers' women come to embrace Rayah so, the men look out for her honor? These seemed perfectly good arguments, but the girl was beginning to feel she couldn't trust them herself. "Yes, Sitt," was all she said.

The older woman's sniffing turned to a snorting of dissatisfaction. Sitt Umm Ali nonetheless decided it was time to go. She sent Rayah scurrying around to find all the things they'd brought with them. The wooden shoes had slid under a bench. Rayah had to crawl on her hands and knees on the wet floor to reclaim them. The rough underside of the bench scraped her back. She twisted around to see what could be so jagged and saw that a plaque from an old temple, carved with figures in low relief, had been reused. Or perhaps it came from Zaynab's palace that lay somewhere beneath her now.

The light was poor there, under the bench, but she could just make the figures out. What she saw made her linger, looking, discovering more. A camel strode across the scene, a woman's enclosed litter on its back. Women completely veiled, their faces mere swirls of fabric, followed after it in solemn, holy procession. Tentatively, Rayah reached out a hand and ran her fingers along the chisel marks that formed the litter's curtains. It was difficult to reconstruct the broken pieces Sitt Sameh had in her room into something like this—

"Come along, girl," Sitt Umm Ali snapped.

Rayah scrambled to her feet, the knees of her skirt damp, the wooden shoes in her hand.

The sun had set at the end of the colonnade when they left the baths. The wind had picked up so that the moment they stepped away from the bath wife's profuse gratitude, grit began to sting and cling to their just-washed skin. After twenty steps, they might never have visited the baths at all.

"They tell me something about that Sitt Sameh of yours," Sitt Umm Ali said, her words like bits of flying sand themselves. "They tell me your uncle—whom you call your uncle—was delivering turpentine to the Encampment of al-Hira when Khalid the Conqueror rode in on the wave of Believers."

"I think you mean my uncle who is dead now, God rest him. Adilah's brother."

"Yes. He who never submitted to Islam until his dying day and so now suffers in hell. He said Khalid asked not, 'Who is your God, O men of al-Hira?' but 'Where is she?' Where is she?" Sitt Umm Ali repeated. "Where is who? Odd, don't you think?"

"Yes," Rayah agreed, the wind blowing her words back down her throat. "But I never heard this story."

"The Conqueror insisted, in al-Hira of all his conquests, that not just the men pass before him and swear submission to his sword at least, if not to his faith. He made the women do so, too. Because they could not touch hand to hand, because of possible impurity, the Conqueror called for a bowl of water, like a small well. Each woman had to plunge her hand into it, veiled to the eyes as she was, as a sign of her fealty."

"What was he looking for?" Rayah asked. Blue eyes, she thought, then pressed the thought from her.

Sitt Umm Ali looked hard into Rayah's own eyes as if she, too, suspected the answer. But "Mashallah, who can fathom the ways of great men?" was what she said instead.

"Did the Conqueror find the woman he was looking for?"

"I think not, since he went on to conquer more, Iraq and then Syria. All I know is, upon your uncle's return we began hearing rumors of this Sitt Sameh up on your third floor. She was with child, they say, a child who would be about your age."

"Then this was before I was born. I know nothing of it."

"Don't you?"

Rayah thought of her grandmother, of the pregnant camel—both of them—in the clefts of Meda'in Salih. Of a pregnant woman fleeing al-Hira where the Conqueror had first seen his woman by a well.

"And now the turpentine sellers' house gets a call from Khalid ibn al-Walīd himself last year, his servant this year. What does it all mean?"

"In truth, Sitt, I don't know."

They came to a place where a gap in the colonnade allowed more sand than usual to blow across the road. Drifts against the far side reached almost to the column's knees. The two women left their footprints as they struggled over the fine substance. Keeping the basket balanced with one hand, Rayah dropped a corner of her veil to drag across her prints. So had Bint Zura done as she went to find her pregnant camel. The wind whipped the end of the veil away like a banner on a battlefield.

But the wind will also cover any sign of our passing soon enough, Rayah thought. Just as Zaynab's palace was covered by baths. And the baths, too, are passing, crumbling. Like the world of banished jinn the Conqueror ushered in as well? If so, can anything at all be counted on to remain?

From the rooftop of the mosque-once-a-church-once-a-temple behind them now came the call to prayer. Only with a difference:

"In the Name of God, the Beneficent, the Merciful.
My Lord and your Lord is God,
Lord of the worlds.
O God, let the new moon bring us
peace and faith,
safety and submission,
and a hastening toward what You like
and are pleased with.
O God, bless us in this month of ours …"

Both turned to look, to listen. Awed.

"Ah, they've seen the new crescent," Sitt Umm Ali said, hastening her steps once the awe passed. "Ramadhan begins."

The women tried to discover the crescent themselves, but the dust was too thick where they walked on the ground. They had to depend on the men's eyes up on the roof to tell them they would begin the fast with the next sunrise.

And the jinn are chained, Rayah thought.

She found herself drawing back her veil to look up at the narrow slash of darkening sky between the clay walls of the houses. She still couldn't see the moon, but a single white star winked down, az-Zuharah, the old Goddess, the evening star.

And as she wearily climbed the stairs to bed, at the same bend she felt it: Perhaps the jinn were not chained at all.

21

> The Themoudi . . .said: "We have consulted the flight of birds and augur ill concerning you and those who are with you."
> Said Salih, "The ills which your bird reports depend on God. You are a people on trial. This is the she-camel of God, and a sign unto you. Let her go at large and feed in God's earth, and do her no harm, lest a speedy punishment overtake you."
> —The Holy Quran, Surah 27

Rayah stood in the doorway to the room on the third floor, panting from her predawn climb. A single oil lamp illuminated the two faces that looked up at her from the meal that must sustain them through the scorching day of fast to come. The one born male, beardless, seemed more female in this light than Sitt Sameh with her angular desert cheeks and chin sprinkled with blue-black tattoos. Her eyes thrummed blue, too, even in this light. A great, dark distance yawned between Rayah and her mother that hadn't been there before.

"So, Rayah?" Sitt Sameh spoke first. "You are betrothed?"

"I do not think she will have me." That went completely against Sitt Umm Ali's last statement the evening before, against every buzzed conversation over the hasty meals below.

How did you come to be in this house? Rayah wanted to be the one asking the questions. Where did you come from? Were you the woman rescued from the Conqueror's bowl of water? What did you leave behind in al-Hira? And before that? Who? Who is my father?

"Sit down, ya Rayah. Break your fast with us. Tell us all about it."

Rayah sat. "The gracious Quran speaks of Meda'in Salih."

"So it does," the eunuch said.

"Sitt Umm Ali and I spoke of that, of the she-camel that came forth by the will of God."

The lamp-lit faces both nodded. They took more bread, broke it, chewed. But they said nothing.

"You said Bint Zura went to Meda'in Salih. She lost her camel there." Rayah felt she sounded childishly demanding. "Did she not believe in God's prophet Salih and in the destruction God caused there at his martyrdom?"

"It's Sitt Umm Ali who asks these questions, not my daughter."

Rayah said nothing but plucked at a loose thread in the carpet.

Sitt Sameh brushed crumbs from her lap. "Drink at least, against the heat of the day, and I will tell you. That is, if you think Sitt Umm Ali would approve."

Rayah made no comment as to what Sitt Umm Ali might think, but took the cup of licorice water the tattooed hands offered her before they picked up their spindle again.

Of course Bint Zura believed in Salih and his miraculous she-camel. She herself had seen the cleft in the rosy rocks where the creature had come forth. And with her, a white calf, for Bint Zura had seen the formations of white salt nearby that were, people said, the shed wool of the young one.

So, though the tents and herds of her people came to forage and to water at the wells that still bore the grooves of the cities' ropes on their coping, no one lingered in the neighborhood.

The family of Abu Ragheb had discussed the place as the dung glowed in the fire the night before.

"And when will another prophet come to us?" Bint Zura had asked her uncle.

"Never," the herdsman answered with a snap of his camel teeth.

Her aunt was not so certain. "When the Gods will it. They say, in fact, that the desert is due to bring forth another soon. The last. The Seal."

"The time for prophets is past."

"Very soon." The mother had had the final word in the family circle, but many of the children had already been asleep when she took it.

Now, as the sun rose and, in a breath, took the worst of the chill out of the wind, Bint Zura remembered. Nonetheless, she walked with purpose toward the cities Salih had destroyed with the God-touched poetry of his mouth.

"And what of the cities of Salih where we camp tonight?" she had asked.

"Hush," her aunt had said.

"Haunted," said her uncle.

"Only Fire Spirits dwell there," said the mother of the tent, touching the charms hanging from the center pole to keep them all, even at this careful distance, safe during the night.

The memory itself seemed to evoke unhuman beings as Bint Zura approached the cliffs of the Meda'in. A whisper of chill remaining in the sand swirled like fetters around her ankles. She knew Lataan was in trouble, needed her. The camel wouldn't have run off otherwise. It was almost as if the girl heard words in the silence, Lataan calling for her. Or what she often heard, in the hum of noonday heat, in the wind at night: the voice of the mother she had never known, speaking from the heart of the desert into which she'd been driven at her daughter's birth.

Dawn altered the bluffs, made them unrecognizable as the same forms that appeared at other times of the day when contours fused. Now shadows split from sun like deep fissures. Dwellings unlike any her life in tents had taught her revealed themselves. Reddish cliff faces formed fluted pillars, steps to doors like mouths open in cries of terror, windows like hollow eyes. Surely such things were beyond human hands and now, by divine hands, they were silent as tombs.

The whir of wings overhead, louder than natural in the silence, made Bint Zura tilt her head skyward. A late-returning bat, perhaps? The place confused the sound so she never saw the creature—until she did, or thought she did, turned to stone on the pinnacle of the closest house. Her heart seemed to change to stone with it and sink in her chest. The spirits of the dead sometimes came to their living kin in the shapes of birds. They were owls mostly—like this one—"Whoo-whooing" for water to ease their dust-parched throats, for the sacrifice of a camel to ease their journey through the afterlife.

Bint Zura looked away, unable to face the stony gaze and beak hooked like a flint dagger. She looked, instead, down at her slowly stepping bare feet. They carried her, she saw, over a rubble of manmade things: broken bits of the containers her people didn't use because they were too heavy to carry from place to place and tended to break on camelback. But settled people used them and called them pottery. Among the shards, too, here and there, were round bits of metal, grown green with age. Settled people used them, too, and called them coins. If one of them fell into the hands of a man of the desert, he held it in such high esteem that he gave it into the safest keeping he knew, that of his wife. She might drill a hole in it and sew it on her veil. Bint Zura did not bend to pick the treasure up, knowing better than to steal from the dead.

Besides, at that moment, she heard a familiar sound. Raised in pain, in fear, still it was a sound of life. She would have known Lataan's voice anywhere. The walls of the cliffs confused her with echoes for a moment. Soon enough she found the proper direction and, within a tight cleft, the dear, familiar shape, just like a pile of sand, appeared.

"Ya Lataan!" Bint Zura cried with joy and then stopped. She blinked. Lataan, it seemed, had grown an extra leg.

Shifting around the animal, Bint Zura soon saw it was no leg but the baby trying to come out, forelegs first and almost as long as its mother's. But there was, as yet, no head. Merciful Allat knew how long this had been so. Lataan groaned and bellowed, to no effect.

"Ya Lataan, easy, my beauty, mother of camels, easy."

Bint Zura tried to calm the clear panic as she stepped closer to help. The animal, however, seemed too pained to recognize her. Lataan kicked out, her toes sharp enough to disembowel a man. Bint Zura knew, and jumped back and to one side. The long neck lashed around in that direction. The teeth snapped and foul-smelling cud spat out. Bint Zura took two steps back and felt the cliff face rise up behind her.

Should she run for Uncle Abu Ragheb? No, he would want to kill the animal. Besides,

Lataan needed her here, now. The camel didn't try any more kicking or biting, but the fevered hisses and moans warned Bint Zura that if she moved, out would come teeth and hooves again. She crouched where she was, not knowing what else to do.

Shafts of light angled off the high eastern crest of the cliff. Presently, from where the light hit on the west, words came. They were words, Bint Zura thought, such as the God of Salih—or mother of camels and all life—might give.

> "You whom madmen and jinn
> worship in their riverbeds
> Bring forth this life."

Bint Zura crouched, her back against the cliffside, and chanted while the sun rose higher, and the shadows sank deeper. There was power in those words, yes, enough to bring forth life. And what more, after all, is ever needed?

When the sun had dropped perhaps a hand's breadth on the wall behind the camel's trembling legs, a change seemed to come over the animal. She still panted heavily, but she seemed aware of Bint Zura now, calmer, and the pained bawlings had stopped.

The girl slowly worked her way to a standing position, shoving her palms, one over the other, against the stone. Lataan's big brown eyes wept between their long, curling lashes. She looked at Bint Zura but didn't move.

Bint Zura took a step. The padded hooves shuffled sideways. Bint Zura sang, "O mother of camels, I will lead you to the sweet well."

The feet shuffled again. It looked as if Lataan were preparing to kick. No. Instead, she presented the part of her in need of help.

Two quick steps brought Bint Zura to the camel's rear. Still half expecting a kick, she closed her eyes, but reached out and laid a hand on the warm hide. She felt a shudder, quick trembling—but no kick.

It was like delving into a well, damp and slick on the sides. Bint Zura guessed roughly where to go by the bend of the knees with their infant patches that would roughen to calluses before a month was out. Then she plunged one skinny arm into the opening up to her elbow. She felt the legs end, pressed against a long, slippery muzzle. She caught it under the jaw and pulled. Too much like tallow, impossible to hold onto. She had to work her other arm in and hook the other side. She pulled, throwing all her weight to the task.

In a rush of fluid, the baby slithered out all at once, the long way to the ground.

Bint Zura fell backward, landing hard. Her front got soaked. The wind nipped through the wool to her bare skin and bunched her belly with cold. Infant hooves kicked her in the face as they went down, drawing blood. But Bint Zura didn't care, weeping with relief.

The calf was born. It was alive.

And, by the oath of Uncle Abu Ragheb, which three Goddesses would make him keep, it—no, she, the calf was a she—was hers.

Lataan gave a great sigh and, with the intake, bent her neck to sniff at her child. She seemed pleased. Although she did not lick her newborn, she stood by, watching the wool dry into tight infant knots on the fledgling hump.

After the sun on the cliff had dropped another hand's breadth, the little thing bleated once or twice. With that announcement, she began to try to get her long legs under her, negotiating the intricacies of folding and kneeling peculiar to camels. The back legs splayed out in two directions, then the forelegs, then one of each. Bint Zura, her tears mopped away, laughed aloud. All the while, Lataan made deep-throated noises of encouragement.

At last the wobbly limbs brought the little face up to the bulging udder. Bint Zura did not rejoice long. She heard another growl. This she knew could not be Lataan. It came from behind her.

The girl turned and gave a little gasp of horror. A lion, drawn by the smell of blood, was fixed there in strong relief, tail switching. He stood poised at the mouth of the cleft, leaving no place to run.

21

> **Then the earthquake surprised them; and in the morning they were found dead on their faces in their dwellings. Verily, your Lord is the Strong, the Mighty.**
> —The Holy Quran, Surahs 7 and 11

Of course, even if Bint Zura could outrun a lion, the baby camel could not, and the girl wasn't about to leave mother and child.

At the first try, nothing came from her searing throat. With the next attempt, she shouted: "Ya! Away, you coward. May your den be always womanless." Hurling the worst curse she could think of, she caught up the ends of her veil and waved them in her arms, trying to make herself look as large as possible. Ears back, the lion snarled. Bint Zura picked up two handfuls of the rubble and threw them at the predator. Nothing more than coins and pottery shards to throw at him—even a stick would have been better.

With that movement, however, she saw that the lion was alone and gray in the mane, not a young female hunting for her young. His ruff was also mangy, ripped out in spots. Saliva dripped from jaws across at least two broken teeth. He bore a torn ear and a long, fly-infested gash along his ribs, the signs of a recent battle in which he had come out the loser. Those ribs stood out stark, his pelvis pinched and lean. He probably hadn't eaten since the fight, unable any longer to catch his usual game. But a newborn calf he could catch. And a young girl.

A pair of vultures had begun to circle through the slash of winter-pale blue above the cleft, waiting for their share. In the magical way those birds learn of such things, another pair took their places in the ring as well.

If Bint Zura were to die—ma laish, what did it matter?— An orphan in a tent of twenty children hadn't much to look forward to, after all. But the little camel, the wonderful little camel, had to die after only a brief morning's blinking at the world with her huge eyes? Well, Bint Zura would just be certain that she herself died first. Life held nothing to live for save this beautiful, new little creature.

Only the baby was not such a little creature. Fearing other things worse than her own death, Bint Zura turned her back on the lion and caught up the calf's weight. That was when she realized she'd never lifted anything heavier. Even the great rolls of tenting she helped unload from the camels every time the family moved were lighter. Those she merely spun off the patient backs, then unfurled, lifting an edge to this pole and that, leaving most of it to lie on the ground at any one time. The calf kicked and bawled in terror.

Fortunately Bint Zura hadn't far to go, just up a pair of stone steps and into the nearest deserted building. She made it through the narrow door, her elbows and the camel's head and rump brushing either side, without the pounce of claws on her back. As soon as they were in, she gratefully let the baby down, where the little body collapsed in a bleating heap.

A heavy, long object on the floor caught her eye. She hastily picked it up and turned back to the door, hefting the good weight. She would stand her ground at the door until death came. The lion would not get around her, through the opening, to the little one.

Outside, Lataan's wise, wide eyes understood where the true danger lay. With a bellow of fury, she wheeled to face the predator. Two long stretches of paws brought the lion to the new mother. Another spring would find him on her shoulder, claws sinking deep, teeth searching for the throat.

Lataan, however, bucked. In a move unlike the usual camel sway of left side, then the right, she brought both hooves down hard. She caught the lion on the head as he sprang, and the thinning mane was not much padding. The blow dazed him for a moment. He sank back on his haunches, but Lataan gave a scream of pain. As the big cat fell back, the unsheathed claws, pulled only by his weight, had nonetheless slashed bloody leather strips from one shoulder almost to her knee.

In a fury, Bint Zura leapt off the steps, yelling. She swung the weapon she'd caught up off the floor of the tomb with all her might, catching the lion's emaciated ribs in the wound festering there. Eyes closed with the effort, she heard the crack of bone. The shock of the impact went all the way to her shoulder, making her wonder if that was the break she heard. There was no time to be hurt.

She'd hit the lion just as he'd bunched for another spring. Alert to the new threat, he twisted his spring midair in her direction. Forepaws as big as her face drove at her. One claw caught through the wool of her skirt to the flesh beneath.

Bint Zura screamed, agony smeared by fear and fury. She tried to swing her club again and found it only half its former weight. It, not her arm, had cracked with the impact. So, though her arm ached fiercely, she thrust the jagged end of the remnant into the swollen, glaring feline eye. Hot breath scalded her arm. One yellow tooth grazed her, then broke off in the tangled thickness of her veil. A snarl turned to a scream.

The meager weapon wrenched from Bint Zura's hand. Lataan's hooves had tripped up the lion's rear legs in midleap. Her horny toes came down on the tawny body. Again. Another buck of her hooves, spraying foaming saliva and blood from her shoulder over all. Then the long, strong camel neck caught the lion under the chest. He tried to curl around the nose to attack with all four sets of claws, but Lataan flipped him. She took a bite of soft underbelly as she did.

One step, Bint Zura picked up new fistfuls of coin and shards. With a yell, she threw them. The next step, she snatched up the broken end of her weapon again. The lion shuddered, like a reed mat shaken to rid it of sand. He seemed suddenly as flat as a mat as well. Bint Zura moved in on him anyway, the heavy knob of her club raised high.

A sharp whistle cut the air. A stone sank deep behind the ragged mane, and the lion lay still. Lataan's hooves raised, determined to flatten the enemy once more. Bint Zura meant to join her, but first she looked where the flying stone had come from and saw Uncle Abu Ragheb striding through the cleft between the cliffs. Shoving his slingshot back in his belt, he exchanged it for his rhinoceros-horn hilted dagger.

And suddenly pain revealed itself behind a mirage of fury, in Bint Zura's leg and her arm. Her limbs wavered, weak, like distant summer heat on the salt flats. And then she sank sobbing to the ground.

"Is he . . . is he dead?" she managed to ask when her uncle drew close enough to hear her whisper.

He let the tawny head drop after study and resheathed his unbloodied dagger. His eyes met hers and he seemed to remember, as if a claw had suddenly come to life and raked him, that her eyes were blue. He looked away.

"Too bad the beast got your calf first," he said.

"But he didn't. She's safe."

Bint Zura rose, pivoted around to the deserted house carved into the cliff. The little one, she saw, stood on unsteady legs in the doorway and began to bleat for her mother.

The weapon dropped from Bint Zura's convulsed hand as, with horror, she saw with her uncle's eyes. Her weapon had been a bone, a human bone, the extended knobby bone of a leg. The floor inside the deserted houses where she'd sought refuge for the calf was littered with such things: the crosshatches of arms and thighs, the basket frames of ribs, the hard, round knots of skull. The cursed dead of Salih Nabi Allah. And among them, drifting, the smoke of jinn. Bint Zura stepped back and retched.

Then, as the creature with its legs three times too tall for head and tiny hump stumbled down the stairs to her mother's calming call, the white winter light fell on her. Bint Zura had watched birth dry from the baby and thought at the time that her coloring was very fair. It wasn't just youth—though camels tend to darken as they grow. She had seen from the start that the daughter was much lighter than her dam. A glance taken in haste with the lion snarling outside had shown her the calf hide gleaming in the house-tomb like the Unbelievers' bleached bones. She had thought them very much of a color and had still not comprehended.

Only now did the realization strike her in the same instant it struck her uncle: The tight little infant curls all over the budding hump, down to the little nose and around the huge, dark brown eyes, were the color of salt.

A white camel.

The baby camel, her camel, was white.

Abu Ragheb found his voice. "A good omen," he said. Then he looked away as the meaning of a blue-eyed girl owning such a creature came home to him.

"I followed the vultures, that's how I knew to find you three, only a finger's breadth from death," he told them.

"Yes, Uncle," she replied.

As he bent between the cliffs to skin the predator, Bint Zura knew she must agree with him on the story.

"The Gods' blessings on you, Uncle, we should have been lost had you not come to our rescue when you did." The accompanying tears might well be for gratitude; she kept the pride in her throat and swallowed it down.

Let him make his lion-skin banner to carry before their migrations with honor, saying he had slain the monster. Let the beast grow much fiercer in his retelling, with bad eye and rotten teeth left behind for the vultures. Let it stick in her uncle's throat like stale bread three days from a well.

Later, back in camp, as she stitched the gash of claws in Lataan's shoulder with thread made of her own hair, Bint Zura whispered in the nursing mother's ear: "You and I would have killed the lion between ourselves, given another forty heartbeats, without Abu Ragheb's slingshot. But for now, your little white baby is safe in my saddle bag on my slow pack camel, and you can follow her every step of the way."

Lataan threw her head, agreeing—and calling attention to the fact that the shriveled cord of the youngest son of Ubayy abu Ragheb had been torn from her neck in the battle. It was lost.

A white calf, white as Nabi Salih's divine calf, born in the cleft of rock in the very center of the cursed cities.

Bint Zura was too old to put her navel cord in a sack. The next time she washed her hair in Lataan's warm urine, she cut out a hank, braided it together, and tied that around the calf's white neck instead. Az-Zuharah, she named the baby, for the Goddess, the evening star, of such perfect whiteness.

"Yes, let them say, too, you are the she-camel of Uncle Ibn Ubayy, my beauty, mother of camels. Ma laish?" More whispers as they marched side by side on to the next pastures, away from the curse. "You and I were there when the cord was lost."

And then she spoke what many another must think when they found their gaze riveted to the white amid so much dusty dun: "Perhaps the days of prophets did not pass with the curse of Salih, as they say. Perhaps heaven may yet speak salvation to the Arabs through a human mouth."

In the warm, close room on the third floor of the turpentine sellers' in Tadmor, Rayah felt a phantom dampness on her knees. She remembered the camel chiseled to the underside of the bathhouse bench. Had that camel, the shrouded women following after, had that camel been white? And did it connect to the woman who had escaped before the Conqueror of al-Hira, of Iraq and of Syria?

"I am glad you are not promised to this Jaffar." Sitt Sameh rose and, cupping her hand in the milk-white of dawn, blew out the lamp. "Time to take the tray back down to the kitchen, Rayah."

And the eunuch Abd Allah straightened his parchments and said: "Then it is time to begin the fast with prayer."

23

> O Mayyah, the wild beasts of the earth must perish,
>   gazelle, oryx, white gazelle—and people, too.
> O Mayyah, the ibex, white-patched of leg, on mountain
>   heights fragrant with wild jasmine and myrtle, will
>   not outstrip time.
> On the summit of a lofty peak, its track chilly below the
>   sky, jutting sharp into the upper air,
> Over it hover black eagles, ravens; below it dun female and
>   male ibex roam.
>
> —Malik ibn Khalid consoling the woman
>   Mayyah for the loss of her brothers in battle

I remember the late spring when I had been caravanning for five years or so. Our train had reached the Way of the Sea. Dunes encroached on the low shrubs—not desert plants, so I didn't know their names—that rattled with dried snail shells on land that could be farmed. Already salt set its tang in the air. Salt—and burning. Something burnt.

Over the rise lay the rural monastery of St. Hilarion. Its four hundred or so monks offered relief to any traveler who couldn't make it the next four Roman miles to the city of Gaza—which offered so many other sorts of relief, and nothing so austere.

We would stop only because my father knew the abbot, and it was a relationship worth keeping in good repair.

My father, leading the train, stopped at the rise of the hill. Camels, numbed with walking and packs that hadn't been moved from their backs all the weeks since Mecca, kept trudging, until noses ran into each others' tails. That roused them from their dullness to snarl and snap at one another. It was a few minutes before I could goad them into behaving so I could go up and stand beside my father.

Then I, too, grew paralyzed.

The monastery was little more than a cross-shaped foundation tumbled with blackened rubble. The mosaic of the floors had returned to colored gravel. We were used to seeing the hillside of vineyards with new, delicate leaf just right for stuffing with flavored grain. These grapevines had been chopped to nubs, along with the olive grove. The honeycomb of monks' cells looked like a raided hive.

"Persians," a monk in a tattered habit, fire-scorched himself, told us. His abbot, my father's friend, was dead.

"Thanks be to St. Hilarion our protector," the monk went on, "things are much worse in Gaza, punished for her sins."

So they were. The colonnaded street leading straight from the desert to where whores had once stood winking under their red awnings; the five towers that had seemed, from atop a camel, unbreachable; the spice market where we were wont to set up shop, near where Omar has had a mosque built, where once stood the famous temple to Dagon and Marnas; even the tomb of the great-grandfather of the Prophet himself, God rain blessings on them both, who had died there on a trading trip—all were plundered ruins. The masts from a few sunken ships poked out between the ruins of the once-busy harbor's piers.

Townsmen were winching a rotting dog carcass up out of the well that had once gurgled under a neat little domed roof, welcoming every comer. The dog came away in soggy bits, a leg here, the head there. The women of the town—we didn't see them, not even the whores—no doubt had been used like this well. Until the effects of the dog could be flushed away, thirst haunted Gaza's streets. Other effects would take longer to heal.

So we skipped Gaza altogether that year.

Jerusalem, Hebron, as far away as Ephesus, Sardis, and Antioch, we were warned, have also felt the Persians' wrath.

The Persians had left their mark everywhere and were now masters of Syria and Palestine, what they'd left themselves of it. What use such ruins could be to them was impossible to fathom.

As for us from Mecca, we had to hurry east, as fast as desert travel could spur us on. There'd be no trading in the west for a while, that was clear.

I had seen Persians before this, of course. Even big, armed men among them under their own bazaar's awnings, however, never seemed threatening, certainly not capable of such violence. I recall attempting the foreign Persian words to cajole them into taking a look at some fine red leather.

After I saw Gaza in smoke, when we met the Persians in their cities, I had no qualms about relieving them of the riches plundered from the direction where there were no profits to be had. After all, the Arabic word for "to conquer" is the same as the one for "to open"—as one opens a pomegranate to blood red. Or a new, ripe market. So we Meccans hardly noticed the change in balance between the greater powers; we got the riches of the west all the same, just in a more roundabout way, with others doing the hard work.

But I do remember that lone monk, clinging to his cell that looked like a lion's paw had ripped it open. "No, God has favored us. Truly, He has granted us freedom. This time it was the Persians. God knows it might just as well have been the armies sent from Constantinople. Heretics. Those Romans, God blind them and harden their hearts, they call their faith Christian, but it is full of errors and they deny us our truth. Persians don't care. In fact, most of their Christians share our true belief. Many of them are refugees from us, fled toward the sunrise across the desert and given sanctuary. The Persians are our liberators, delivering us from sin, from material chains, from oppression in our belief."

"Madman. Grief has turned his mind," my father said, hurrying us east.

But the people in that ebbing of the great western empire were not free. And they were looking for one to unfetter them. Not that they would always think of the Persians in that light.

I remembered that.

"Would you care for a tale of hunting, then?" My scribe and I haggle like the merchant I once was. Before Islam taught me to set my own price—and get it.

He'll settle for hunting. So long as it isn't that woman at the well again.

Very well. So will I. Hunting. And my milk mother, instead.

"A sacrifice," said Umm Mutammim when she had finished trilling with joy and repeatedly reaching up to catch my bearded face in her rough, tattooed, dust-creased hands.

I swear by the Merciful One: The last time she'd done that to my face, she'd been reaching down instead of up. A beard is a better protection against the whisks of bangles, perhaps.

"A sacrifice in thanks for the return of my milk son." Tears ran down the tattoos—to my eyes, like rose petals—on her face. "Would that Mutammim's father were here to see you."

The tent of my childhood, under which I now had to bend my head to enter, was missing something.

My milk brother Malik had grown handsome, with thick black curls curls resting on his broad shoulders. He whispered at my elbow, "Men from the Banu Taghlib killed our father during the Scorcher."

That was it. Nuwaira, my milk father. I'd been in Mecca at the time, during those hot summer months called Ramadhan before the new calendar. Tribes often go hungry then and are most likely to skirmish over camels or wells. I was sorry. I ranted and wept. He'd been like a father to me. More than all Persian-slaughtered Syrians.

"Because you took in the old kahinah they cast off?" I demanded through my tears. "Is that why they killed him?" A man could not suffer powerless grief too long before wanting to find the cause—and the cure.

Mutammim, the older brother, settled against his camel saddle and shrugged. He had had time to feel his pain—and to bind it over. "Or because of something that came from her hand?" he suggested. He, blinded by interaction with Umm Taghlib, might well know the power of her hand.

There, under my milk mother's tent, awash in the fond, familiar smells of dung smoke and dusty wool, a new horror came over me. I'd killed a Taghlibi. They'd attacked our caravan the previous year. My milk family didn't know. I hoped they, Umm Mutammim in particular, never would.

"The sons of dogs," I cried nonetheless, pounding the cushions until dust rose.. Unable to attack Mecca, had the Taghlibi taken it out on my milk family instead? "You must let me ride with you against them while I am in your pastures this season."

"So when you speak of hunting, your quarry is men?" my scribe asks, sharpening another reed in readiness.

"Not so. Not yet."

"*Revenge is already taken,*" Mutammim said, turning his unseeing face with its white eyes to where Malik his brother had taken up his cushions on his left. "*Will you tell it, brother, or will I?*"

It is not proper when a man does his own bragging, but noble when he has a blind brother to turn his deeds to poetry for him. Mutammim told it, in verse.

> "*When he defended my people against the enemy,*
> *He did not refrain from the spears through cowardice.*"

"*They speak of my—our brother now as Amr,*" the older brother said, "*The poet of old, who became chief of his people at fifteen.*"

I was sorry to have missed the bold raid Malik had organized, for he had avenged the old man with speed and ferocity, blood for blood. I was sorry to have missed Malik's liberal, self-effacing distribution of the booty and hospitality afterward. These deeds had made him sharif in his father's place at no more than my age, eighteen. These deeds, and his elder brother, not so much older but wiser, at his side.

"*A sacrifice for Khalid's return.*"

Oh, yes, and his mother. I knew Umm Mutammim, drawing us now from talk of war. I could imagine her urging her son to avenge his father over the old man's still-moist grave. Malik would have had no choice. And she would have driven him to be sharif.

My milk mother prattled, "*That kahinah of the Taghlib said I would regret giving suck to this one, all those years ago in Mecca.*"

Only now do I wonder, did Umm Mutammim blame me for the death of her husband where her sons did not? Did the jinn, through that old kahinah, tell her? Or did she simply guess that—in pursuit of trade, with my jinn-strengthened arm bought at the cost of Mutammim's eyes—at some point or other I had fended off a son of the Taghlib? She didn't say so then, as she welcomed me back to her tent. But had she said so to Mutammim and Malik as they butchered camels to hasten their father's remains on their last journey? (On their way to hell, we'd say now.)

And men tell themselves they are in charge of war, of sacrifice. Perhaps when strangers are by, only then. And Muhammad, blessings on him, did bring some shift—

Umm Mutammim gave no hint of blame as she interrupted men's talk to say, "*As Allat is my witness. Thanks be to Her, I never have regretted it. And here is Khalid, a man grown. A sacrifice, my sons, I say.*"

To what was she urging me, also her son, with such words?

Malik had had no choice but to avenge his father, her husband. Just as he had no choice now but to remember the laws of hospitality. He grinned and rose at the thought of meat, although this time of year, before the first rains, the beasts were tough and practically without fat. "*A sacrifice? To whom, mother mine?*"

"*The Mother of Rain, may She favor us in the winter to come.*"

"The young he-camel, too wild and boisterous by far?" Malik unsheathed his sword, his father's sword, to begin sharpening it on a nearby stone.

"Well, and if that, then a goat besides. The camel, yes, kill him where you catch him—if, Gods willing, you do catch him. But take the goat out by the water hole. Sprinkle its blood around and set its hide on stakes when you've skinned it." Ever practical Umm Mutammim.

"Ibex, ya Ummi?"

"Yes, I've seen their prints at the hole."

"Many?" Malik didn't need to ask if his mother could tell the difference between goat tracks and ibex. There really is no difference—except that if one print is very large, it's an ibex ram.

But Umm Mutammim knew. And what made Malik's eyes brighten with prospects of the hunt meant something different to his mother. "They will knead the water all into the mud if you don't scare them away. A sacrifice and a skin will do the trick."

"And once we've strengthened ourselves on this sacrifice for you, brother," Malik said to me, "we'll go see if there aren't ibex hiding in the rocks off there to the west."

Rut had turned the neck, chest, and shoulders of the ibex bucks dark brown, almost black. Even so, they were very difficult to pick out against the tawny rise of sandstone on which they stood. Malik squinted through his bow, shot, and missed, wasting an arrow. Perhaps he could retrieve the arrowhead, if it hadn't slipped down into a rocky crevice. Fortunately, he was using flints he'd chipped himself. Iron tips, precious as minted silver, had to be bought, by the sackful, from the settled lands.

Startled now, our quarry bounded off, like boulders tumbling uphill instead of down.

"We need to track closer," I whispered in hunter's tone. "Perhaps over that low rise."

Malik agreed, and we set off, taking care where we set our feet, avoiding loud, slippery gravel, and trying to keep downwind. Nor did we leave Mutammim behind. Although he couldn't see, his keen ears had taught him to mimic perfectly the whistles and bleats of the animals in rut. And though every Arab clapping of hands tries for the hollow echoing in the palms, Mutammim could hold his thumbs just so, to make a sound exactly like hoofbeats on rock.

I didn't even breathe a word but pointed. Two bucks, belligerent with each other, and the doe they were fighting over were just where I'd said, springing across a lower rise of rock, one that humans could manage.

A touch from Malik on Mutammim's arm told the older brother to stay while we went ahead and to cover our stalking with claps and whistles.

I was first over the rise. One buck had vanished, but the other and the doe were close enough for a shot. I lost my own arrow because, just as I aimed, the boulder beside me leaped to life. It was the second buck, playing dead as they do, his horns leant away from me looking like part of a low acacia. I truly had not seen him, although my next step might have brought me right on top of him.

"The Gods put a pox on it!" I cursed.

He was off like an arrow, heading for the bluffs and safety.

My arrow was gone. I groped for my sword. Too far, now, for that. Lance. Again too far. Finally returning to my bow, I lost another arrow. The creature had disappeared among rocks again.

If the jinn sometimes strengthened the right arm I had snatched from them, they also knew how to make it fumble when the quarry was a favored animal.

Hot and furious, I turned to defend myself against what I expected to be Malik's taunts and laughter. Instead, I found my milk brother flat in the dust. He wasn't hurt, as I first feared. Instead, he peered intently around the trunk of the acacia tree.

"Get down," he whispered.

I did as I was told. "What is it?" This must be great game indeed.

The eastward landscape over which our flattened shadows hardly extended presented first a flock of ostriches. These were fine enough game, and women liked the feathers to decorate their litters. But what were ostriches to ibex? Then something else startled the flock and they set off to the west, impotently beating their wings against the air.

Just where the horizon turned hazy toward the realm of the jinn, there marched a line of figures that might well have been Fire Spirits rising up to the world of mortals.

"Ah," I said to Malik, figuring there was no need to keep still, not at this distance, not for human ears. "I see you hunt men."

My heart raced in my chest against the dust where I'd dropped. Perhaps these were Taghlib? Perhaps I had not missed the chance to avenge my milk father after all. Or—no. No women's howdahs set their sails among them. A trade caravan, then? People who did not live in the desert and were only passing through.

This thought didn't settle my heart much, however. A trade caravan would certainly be richer material gain than blood feud. My milk brother's stance told me that, unlike my father's train made safe by my presence in these pastures, these traders had no treaty with the sons of Tamim. That made them fair game. If they had no respect for those whose lands they passed through, they could be taught respect. I felt not the slightest flush of guilt to consider robbing the competition so blatantly. They'd do the same if our positions were reversed.

The caravan kept marching, longer than one caravan master could control. And dense, too, not traveling single-file as traders do. Had two or three caravans joined forces for protection? If so, at this time of year just before the rains, the wells—if they got to them—would not quench them, beasts and all. Fools. All the more deserving of being plundered. I half got to my feet.

Then through the haze, I saw the fire glint of metal. Metal on metal. Even swathed in cloth against the punishment of the sun's rays, there was no complete concealment, not of so many coats of mail, of so many spearheads, sword hilts, helmets. And now we heard the distant plod of marching drums, setting the martial pace.

"Persians," I gasped, breathing low dust once more. The dust might have been the smell that had hung above Gaza that day.

Malik watched silently this invasion of his land.

"Bound for Rome?" I asked. "I wonder there is anything left there to attract them."

Malik shook his head. "Bound for the Encampment, al-Hira, I'll wager. To exercise their power upon Arabs who've grown settled and fat."

"So will you hunt Persians?" My heart raced faster still. "For crossing Tamimi land without permission, for drinking at your wells?"

"My few men? Against so many, and so well armed? No, my brother. In this I must disappoint you. The Arabs of al-Hira have made themselves like ducks sitting in the Iraqi marshes. And I cannot feel sorry that so many of them are sons of Taghlib. We will use the defenses of our lands here. We will watch. If need be, we will pack up our herds, our women and children, and move out of their way, into the inner desert at this season, if necessary. The Persians will not know that the pastures of Tamim were ever more than wasteland."

I agreed. The Persians had leapt over this place on their way to Rome. But did they now understand that they had to control the land in between in order to assure access? Did they understand this would be like walking on quicksand between solid islands?

With only a shade of disappointment, I said, "So much for hunting today, I suppose."

We got to our feet and went back to Mutammim. The older brother hadn't stirred, but he had stopped clapping. He stood unmoving, the staff he used to feel his way balanced across his shoulders with a hand slung over either end.

"Hush," he warned as we approached.

"What?" we demanded, more concerned with Persians than anything.

"Don't you hear it? Them?"

We heard nothing.

"That way." He pointed left. "Two of them."

"Two Persians?" My first thought. And that we could take them, if there were only two.

Off Malik and I went to find, just over another rise, a second pair, not of soldiers but of bucks. They had locked their horns in combat, which now was to the death. They'd been thus, each the prisoner of the other, for so long that thirst had overcome them both. One, in fact, had fallen, pinning the head of his opponent to the spot. The strong one set up a new lurching struggle as we came, but the other didn't have the strength to rise to more than his front knees. It seemed a good omen. Taking them was as easy as taking locusts when the camp is swarmed: Children and old women can gather baskets full, simply by sweeping their veils here and there, a graceful dance through the air.

"Great Hubal keep me from the throes of love like this," I joked to Malik as we each cut a throat, let the blood into the dirt as an offering to the old Yemeni god Athtar, and prepared to return to Umm Mutammim with our prizes.

At some point on the way home, amid talk of bucks dying over does and Persians, Mutammim said, "Perhaps Rome and Persia are locked in a fight that weakens them both. Perhaps it leaves them prey for the first small power that comes upon them."

Malik and I laughed aloud. Who could have believed such a future at that time?

"It hangs on Adi's Hind," my milk mother said upon our return, loaded with our prizes, including news of the Persians, to her tent.

"Adi's Hind? Who is Adi's Hind, ya Ummi?" I asked to the ghru-grug of her churn. There would be melted curds to enrich the toughness of our game.

"Mark my words," she replied. "This matter of Adi's Hind will bring changes to the tents of the Arabs."

"She speaks of jinn princesses," Malik, swollen with a hunter's successful pride as he gutted his kill, dismissed her.

"Only rumors of a princess from the settled lands." Mutammim was more tolerant of women's talk.

"On the individual rather than on great armies," Umm Mutammim pressed.

"Spoken like a true mother of Arabs," I laughed.

And al-Harith ibn Suwaid, the boy who'd been lost, then found, in this desert, squatted at the outer edge of the tent, listening, awaiting his portion of the kill for his old mother. He had grown but slightly, with hardly a wisp of beard and thin as a reed. He labored now as my milk brother sharif's herdsman, just like his father before him.

"Just don't forget Adi's Hind," Umm Mutammim said with the repetition of curd making.

I remember it now.

24

**There is among trees one that is pre-eminently blessed, as
is the Muslim among men; it is the date palm.
—Muhammad, God's Messenger**

And I remembered the woman's talk of princesses several months later, at the end of that winter instead of at its beginning.

"Don't forget Adi's Hind," my milk mother said as she handed breakfast over the harem curtain. She must already have heard the women's gossip among the gathering tents.

Ah, the Days of the Arabs. Yes, ah, the Time of Ignorance. Ah, that spring day when I swaggered with my milk brothers into the pilgrimage town of al-Hira.

Straightening his parchments, my scribe stops me.

"Tell me more about your cousin Omar—may God preserve him as leader of the Faithful."

He thinks I cannot tell, but I know he's not writing. He thinks because he's written this before, he need not write it again.

So I pretend not to hear him. "Ah, when I was eighteen and the wells of the Encampment winked beneath the sun of the eastern desert like gems on the neck of a well-dowered woman," I recite, watching the play of sunlight in the fountain.

"Omar ibn al-Khattab is now the khalifah, the Leader of the Faithful," my scribe prods like an annoying gnat. "All the world is interested in him."

"The world will remember Omar without my help. It is the time by the wells of al-Hira I want to remember this afternoon."

"The Christian girl again?"

"Christian? She may have carried palm fronds, but I wouldn't call her Christian. Not in the end."

"You know whom I mean, master, anyway."

"As you know my meaning. How many can I mean by 'she'?" Many. Too many.

"I thought we put her behind us with the naked Christian hermit."

"Who does not recite the Quran's first Surah at least five times a day?" And I begin to do so: "In the name of God, the Compassionate, the Merciful . . ."

My scribe submits, joins me. "You only do we worship . . ." The words sparkle like the water, but he doesn't know what I mean.

That morning, camping near al-Hira for the pilgrimage, we ignored my milk mother. That was the morning when, after we'd eaten the curds scooped up with dates she'd handed us, my milk brother swaggered into al-Hira, the Encampment, the new power of a chieftain with him. Mutammim and al-Harith swaggered, too, because everything of their sharif's was something to be either shared or emulated. And I swaggered, not to be outdone.

Ah, but there was something in the air of al-Hira that made the lowest smith's son swagger. The townspeople say that one night slept in al-Hira is worth a year of nights in any other air. Of course, those of us who ride the fat-humped ones, we admit no purer air than the desert affords. But we had to confess there was much in al-Hira to lure us out of the desert, else al-Hira would never have come into being at all.

"To make Arabs fat and lazy," Malik liked to say, though he was no less attracted to the settled place.

A great high wall surrounded each settler's home, distant from its neighbors, as if each were a Damascus or a Homs in miniature. In each compound a lord lived with his family and small clustering of retainers and clients. Well they might cluster, for they remembered the tales from their father's father's time, how attractive al-Hira looks from the desert in a bad year. They stood on their high roofs and watched us swagger in. And they remembered the birthright of the desert they had sold for a mess of pottage, as a Jew or Christian might say: the bondage of four walls.

The desert blew through the spaces between enclaves. Some of the space was cultivated, of course, groved with palms and sown with grain and vegetables watered by a canal dredged, in those days, all the way from the Euphrates.

And wells pockmarked al-Hira like my face. To this day, I cannot tell their number, though I am called lord of that place. And at one of those wells, before the sand drifted in, I met—

But I wasn't thinking of that when first we swaggered in. It hadn't happened yet.

My milk brothers and I went first to pay our respects to the pair of great and ancient pillars that marked the Encampment in the name of the God as-Sabad.

The Gods of that Time of Ignorance—false Gods, demons, jinn, as the Prophet, blessed be he, has since taught us to call them—were Gods of the desert. Like the men of the desert who worshiped them, they were attracted to this fertile strip of land between the river and the wastelands.

Those who would discredit the antiquity of the site by the Euphrates, who forbid it to vie with Mecca's days of Ibrahim and Isma'il, tell a more recent tale of the pillars' origins. They say a son of Lakhm, king of al-Hira, used to drink himself into blind and reckless states with two favorite companions. During one of these binges, as a sort of madman's lark and not knowing what he did, the king ordered his friends to be buried alive. He did not come to his senses until it was too late to do aught but mourn the dead and place two great stones as monuments upon the spot. The Two of Blood, they were called, and the well-sobered king offered the blood of one of his subjects every year to appease the wronged and thirsty spirits of his friends.

I do not speak this aloud to my scribe, but I think it: If you had seen those pillars in the Days of Ignorance—before I had the Muslims tear them down and bury them like the king's servants, before they became but a monument of senile fancy—you would know that they were older than any son of Lakhm. I find their image at the very edge of memory, those twin erections of alabaster. Perhaps that is why I feel they must have been older, even, than any son of Ibrahim. Toppling them has somehow upset the balance of the earth—

No. I will not entertain any demon that tells me I did wrong to order idolatry torn down and hidden from the face of the One True God.

One year King al-Mundhir, another son of Lakhm whose reign some I knew as a youth could remember, made his sacrifice in a way none could forget. In a raid he led against Roman Haleb, he captured four hundred nuns from their convent. They refused to be fertile; he would fertilize with their blood instead. They served as his sacrifice upon the stones that year.

The leading family of the Encampment, the sons of Lakhm, had been Christian for a generation now. Christian or no, the Lakhmids had not torn down the pillars as we Muslims would do later. And that spring day as we arrived, the crowds circumambulating were greater than ever. Many of them believed it best to face the God as he'd brought them forth, naked under the sun. The dancing raised dust to bare knees, to buttocks.

"But even religion cannot have drawn a crowd such as this," Malik said.

The sons of Tamim and I couched our camels as close as we could and then pressed closer on foot, as much from curiosity as from faith. We could see nothing for all the people.

"There," *I told my milk brothers.*

A cluster of three small boys clung to the top of a nearby date palm. I threw stones at them until they scurried down. I tucked the skirt of my robe into my sash. Then I climbed up myself into their place, curling my bare but calloused feet around the prickly stumps of spent fronds like the steps of a ladder.

The tree was perhaps thirty years old, for it lifted me about so many steps into the sky. There, in the crown, the female blossoms, like pearls threaded on strings, had hardly begun to bend with the weight of their fruit into the graceful arcs they would hold at harvest time. Diligent husbandmen had corded spines of waxy, cream-colored, star-shaped male bloom into the midst of the pearly sprays. The fragrance of their love reminded me of the fruits to come in the fall: sticky sweet.

The tree was newly pruned to provide thatch. Or to provide the Christians with the branches they needed to welcome their Isa ibn Maryam to his death. Some folk circling the stones bore them even now. I wonder, did I grip between my knees the very tree the woman I would see by the well used for her palm frond?

What caught my eye from my new height, however, was near the center of the stones. Here, surrounded by an empty ring of respect himself, stood a man in the silken trousers and turban of a Persian noble. In his entourage, besides a number of milling men similarly dressed, were women completely veiled, and wails of grief rose like a cloud from them.

The tree shuddered beneath me. "It's an-Numan, king of the Lakhmids," *said Malik, who clambered up behind.*

Other Persians stood by the king, well armed, flaunting the pilgrimage; they had him under arrest. I heard one of them say: "The Shah-in-shah of the Persians then asked me, 'Can you control the Arabs for me? They are a difficult race for one so lacking in numbers.'"

The Persian soldier—of some high rank, it seemed—went on: "And I replied, 'Yes, sire. If you but get rid of one of them for me, an-Numan who calls himself their king, they'll be as tractable as lambs.' So we are rid of an-Numan now, and the Shah-in-shah shall reward me well."

Up in the tree, though in its shade, I felt myself go red with shame. It wasn't as if an-Numan were my king, a Quraysh from far-away Mecca as I was. Nonetheless, I was still an Arab and, fight among ourselves as we might, an outside threat to one threatened us all.

"Fool," Malik muttered, telling me he felt the same way. "To think one man can control the Arabs as one man controls the empires, both east and west. We are herders, we are not herded."

The king had already abandoned leather boots, as any man must, even those who did not think the God commanded complete nakedness in his precinct. As we watched, retainers helped the king to remove turban and royal diadem, outer robe stiff with gold thread, softer inner tunic and trousers, until he stood not quite naked, but like a hermit, a cloth only about his loins.

The Persian soldiers moved in to take him. Would he go thus, without a fight? I felt more shame still. Then, although stripped, an-Numan raised a hand for leave to speak. His voice rang regally, and the circling throng strained to hear him.

"Arabs, free people of the desert, my brothers. Parvez Shah, Shah-in-shah, emperor of all Persia, has ordered me to stand before his throne on the matter of the poet Adi ibn Zayd."

Murmurs rose in the crowd. Not every Arab had agreed with an-Numan's imprisonment of his clerk Adi as a curb to ambition, for daring to look on an-Numan's own daughter. "The matter hangs on Adi's Hind," I remembered my milk mother had remarked just as we left. But no one would mention the princess's name in such a public place.

The spectacle of the king stripped, going to meet his judge the emperor without a struggle, having no choice, made a strong impression. His flesh underneath the silks, untouched by sun, seemed white and weak.

"The Shah has taken my sons hostage. My wives and daughters, however, my armor, symbol of the Arab's freedom, I leave to the safety of the desert." An-Numan was not lost to all honor, then. "A small, disjointed people without state or standing army, we cannot hold, neither against Persia on this sunrise side of the desert, neither against Rome where the sun sets. We are ground between them like grain between stones."

I remembered my father's words: how we Arabs played the big powers off against each other, the way a smaller wrestler may use his opponent's own weight to throw him. I remembered too the ibex bucks, killed when they locked horns. But an-Numan, who had dressed like a Persian and played by Parvez's rules, had to obey those rules even when they turned against him.

He had begun to pluck out his beard in clumps now, saying, "I leave my treasures in your care, in the care of the desert, knowing no place contains more honor, even unto death."

A retainer handed the old king a length of white linen, then helped to wrap it around him. His shroud. He went to Ctesiphon knowing full well it was to his death, knowing the Shah would probably even deny him burial. He went as prepared as a man could be for such an event, prepared to do the office for himself. He took up his shroud much like the izar a number of the pilgrims around him were wearing, it being the common garb of men of the desert. It is the garment worn by pilgrims in Mecca today.

"And so, my brothers," said an-Numan, last king of the Lakhmids, "I bid you farewell."

"We should stand up to Persia." I turned to tell Malik this, clinging to the palm trunk at my foot.

"And how should a few scattered tribes do that?" he retorted.

Back near the center of the circumambulation, another figure stepped forward. Rather than Persian silk, this man wore the woolen robe of the desert over his simple izar.

"My lord an-Numan," this man said. "I accept the charge of your armor, of your harem, of those you leave behind you."

"That man I don't know," Malik said.

"But I do," I replied, my heart thumping with pride to be able to say so. "That's Hanzala ibn Thalaba, sharif of the Idjl clan of the Banu Bakr ibn Wa'il. My father has horses with him."

The Persian soldiers recognized the man, too, or at least the threat he posed. They moved to take him into custody as well, spears meshing like iron basketry around him.

Hanzala merely chuckled at the attempt. "I do not give myself into your hands as my lord king here does. Instead, I claim the immunity of the moon."

Persians cared nothing for an Arab's holy month, even though their Nowruz was at the same time. They drew tighter, and their captain slung an iron-studded gauntlet against Hanzala's face.

Hanzala hardly flinched, though the blood flowed thick into his beard.

The crowd could abandon an an-Numan, but not one from the desert who showed such courage. "For shame, for shame, not during the holy month," they shouted, and they began to tighten their own circle around the soldiers. "Not here in the sanctuary. For shame."

The Persians, whether they understood the chanted Arabic or not, understood the meaning. Overcome by unarmed men, half of them completely naked, the soldiers stepped back, then broke, taking only an-Numan, the one-time and compromised king of Lakhm with them.

Hanzala laughed out loud as they went and the worshipers cheered. "Every true supporter of the Lakhmids—no, every true Arab—will stand with me, even to the death, taking up our own shrouds."

"The Gods have gifted Hanzala with a great hand with the wind-drinkers," I told Malik as soon as unconsidered cheering strangled in my own throat. "But if he has taken on the charge of an-Numan's armor, my horses are no longer safe with him. Come. Let me down."

We scrambled from the palm in time to watch as King an-Numan made his final farewell, in spite of being a Christian in name, to the baytels of his family: He made his last circumambulation. Then, followed by retainers pouring dust in their hair and women tearing their veils, he made his way. In a funeral procession of the living, they moved toward the Euphrates and the sun rising to bring death to the desert.

"I've got to save those horses. And yet—" I spoke to myself, since Malik had waved a hand of *dismissal and trudged back to regain his camel."—With the right leader, we Arabs could do it. We could throw the weight of the bigger power, light on our feet as we are."*

I had just seen it done.

25

**In the name of God, the Beneficent, the Merciful:
When the sky is rent asunder, obeying her Lord in true
  submission;
When the earth is stretched out and casts forth all that is
within her and becomes empty, obeying her Lord in true
  submission!
O man! You labor hard unto your Lord and you shall meet
  Him.
  —The Holy Quran, Surah 84**

The eunuch set aside his parchments and wearily rubbed his eyes. They stung, he announced. "This jinn-filled wind sucks all moisture, even from the eyeballs." Fasting, too, gave him a headache and parched his tongue. There would be no more reading for the day.

Reluctantly Rayah left the third-floor room and dragged her hunger- and wind-weighted feet downstairs. Little mounds of sand had already blown into the corners of the steps, though she had swept them well first thing that morning. Over the wind, she could hear sounds from the kitchen, saw the smoke mingling with the flying sand in the court. The rest of the women had already begun work on the meal that would close the day's fast as soon as the sun set in a haze of orange.

Just as she made the turn where the jinn hid, grinding sand between their teeth, Rayah saw a figure materialize from the smoke and cross the court to sit on the fountain's coping. It was Auntie Adilah, carrying a slab of cheese, chopped cucumber, and a few olives balanced on two rounds of new bread.

Rayah continued down the stairs and stopped to wash the grit from her face at the spigot. She was careful not to let a drop pass her lips, though her swollen tongue longed for it.

Adilah began to eat, tearing bits of bread and wrapping them in bite-sized morsels around salty cheese and olives, succulent cucumber, and washing them down with hand scoops of water. She took her other piece of bread, however, and, between mouthfuls, offered it to Rayah.

"I'm fasting," Rayah said.

"You're not a woman yet," her aunt reminded her. "A full fast is not required of children. 'God,' they say, 'does not want to put you to difficulties.'"

"But we are encouraged to fast as much as we can, to practice discipline and patience."

Adilah nodded—somewhat sadly, it seemed.

"Besides, I can't eat in this killing wind. You aren't fasting?"

Rayah had let a note of disapproval into her voice but was immediately sorry. "Guard against the sharpness of your tongues during the fast," the Prophet, blessings on him, had taught. Her impatience was more than the fasting, however, and she knew it. If Sitt Sameh were in truth her mother, why had Auntie Adilah, whom she loved and trusted, never told her? Why, in fact, had she lied to her all these years?

Adilah's thoughts were elsewhere. "My same affliction. It's returned." She sighed.

Auntie Adilah had a flux of blood, more than other women. Women during their moon time, or just having given birth and nursing, were not required to join the rest of the community of Believers in abstinence. They did have to make up the missed days, but because most of the turpentine sellers' harem cycled together, those times later in the year meant no great hardship. Rayah knew all this—but not her parentage.

"The greatest hardship is how alone I feel." Adilah sighed again. "Now—and later, when others eat and I do not."

Rayah settled herself on the coping next to her aunt, sitting carefully with her back to the southeast, to the desert. Although she'd tried to dry her face and hands on her skirt, she could feel new sand sticking to them with each gust, like air bellowed from a furnace.

Adilah was ready to change the subject away from her own sad lot. She forced a grin. "But you are certainly doing well for yourself, my heart. Did you hear? Sitt Umm Ali sent to our house this morning while you were upstairs. All our women are invited one evening next week to her reading of the gracious Quran for the holy month."

The sudden burn of dread in Rayah's stomach had little to do with the khamsin.

Oblivious, Adilah went on. "You should hear them chatting about it in the kitchen. I expect she will call on you to recite, to show off. And I shouldn't be surprised if her brother's son listens at the door when you do."

At this news, Rayah wanted a mother more than ever, and to whom did she first turn in this need? Not to the woman on the harem's third floor. "Will you come, too, Auntie?"

"God willing. But I don't know that I'll be well enough. You don't look happy about the prospect."

"I wish . . . I wish I didn't have to . . . have to do. . ."

"Do what?"

"Oh—anything."

"It's called Islam—submission."

"I wish it were not!"

Rayah covered her mouth with her hand and closed her eyes. She expected lightning to strike out of the swirling dust. It didn't. God bless Adilah, no scolding passed her lips. In a moment, Rayah dared to open her eyes again.

At the same time, the demand that she submit had not gone away, any more than had Adilah's affliction.

Rayah studied Auntie Adilah, more closely than she'd ever done before, this woman who'd made up for the slack of Sitt Sameh—for the lack of any mother, truly. She wasn't very old, this woman she called auntie. Young enough still to chase around a fountain, not old enough to be her real mother, probably beginning those duties at an age younger than Rayah herself was now. Then there had come that year or so—to the child Rayah, it had seemed much longer—when the older woman had been married off. But she'd come back, the husband having no use for a wife who bled three weeks out of every moon and bled away his seed as well. He hadn't divorced her, only taken a second wife, so Adilah had returned to her father's house again. Only by that time, her father's mind was no longer in it, gone to his fathers, although his body lingered. But Rayah still was, and that had been enough.

Rayah watched the pretty, thin cheeks chew their food that, in this time of isolation, was only necessary toil, no pleasure. The girl remembered what Sitt Umm Ali had said about Auntie Adilah's brother and Sitt Sameh, about the child who had been born after the fall of al-Hira.

Considering this, Rayah suddenly blurted: "Who's my father?"

Auntie Adilah choked.

Rayah jumped up and thumped her aunt on the back—if the dear woman were in truth her aunt.

When she could speak again, Adilah said, "Mashallah, child. What makes you ask that?"

"I just wondered. If Sitt Sameh is in truth my mother—"

"Who told you that? Did she tell you that?"

Rayah found herself unable to answer the anger in Adilah's voice. Of all the people in the world, she loved Adilah best, had never been afraid of her. This love had made Rayah always choose actions to please her aunt. Now the anger—or was it fear? Fear in the older woman sent throbbing fear into her own heart.

Adilah sighed, repenting her tone and seeking to control it. "Well, of course, all you had to do was take one look in Demiella's mirror. All you had to do is see you two together. The gestures, the very way you hold your head. Those eyes— And if Sitt Sameh herself has decided finally to tell—"

"They told me my mother was dead. You told me."

"I don't think I did. I tried never to actually lie to you about—about this whole business. Others, maybe, but I tried— It was safer that way. You can understand that, can't you, Rayah? As you come to know Sitt Sameh better?"

Rayah shook her head, but because she had turned her thumping into massage, Adilah could not see it. The fear she'd seen in her auntie's eyes still niggled her.

"I thought it was safer this way," Adilah repeated. "We all did."

Safer? Safer from what? "Who is my father?" Rayah insisted.

"Your father is dead."

"If he's dead, how can it matter?"

"Oh, it matters. If you understood who your mother truly is—"

How can I, when no one wants to tell me? Rayah massaged harder than ever in her constrained anger. "Is it Khalid ibn al-Walīd the Conqueror?"

Adilah smiled indulgently. "You are ambitious, my heart."

"Is it he?"

"Is this what the eunuch has told you?"

"No. Not in so many words. But he hasn't reached the end of the story yet."

The smile vanished and Adilah sighed again. "It's true that everything has changed since that sexless one came. Came prying into the peace of our harem on behalf of that conquering master of his. I wish he'd never come, this Abd Allah."

"So I would still think my mother was dead."

"That I was the closest thing to a mother you had. And you, the closest to a child of my own." Auntie Adilah touched Rayah's cheek with a wistful hand.

"Auntie, your brother is dead, may rain moisten his grave. He brought my mother here. From al-Hira."

"That's true. I remember—"

Rayah added up the details. "Is he my father? And so we are blood kin? Are we truly aunt and niece?"

Yes, Rayah found she could live with that. But Adilah evaded that question, too. "Yes, some—some have given you his name."

"Islam forbids an adoptive child to take his new parents' names. The lineage must remain clear and pure."

"Then you should not take my brother's name, honored though he would be. All I know is that your father was already dead when my brother met Sitt Sameh." Of this Adilah was definite. "And that I was never supposed to ask more. Maybe it doesn't matter who your father was, only your mother. And now that you know . . . Accept that, and be at peace."

"But he—your brother, blessings on his resting place—he brought Sitt Sameh from al-Hira. Where Ibn al-Walīd was the Conqueror." Where he fell in love, first, with my grandmother, Rayah thought but didn't say. "Yet your father never converted? Is that true?"

"He died fighting the Arabs." Adilah folded another little packet of olive, cucumber, and cheese and popped it in her mouth. She chewed quietly a moment before she said, "There is submission, I suppose, and submission. Islam and Islam. My brother first made it possible for our family to become clients of the Quraysh, so we could continue our trade. Yet then he turned around and— Well, and saved your mother. Only how it is called saved when she no longer recites poetry—?"

"My mother recites poetry?"

"She did. Created it, too. I heard her. At first. Then no more. It was too dangerous, coming from—well, a different inspiration. A jinni, I guess you'd say, instead of God. Perhaps she could no longer hear her jinni, here behind walls. But of course, by then, she had you to think of."

"I silenced her? When she paid me so little mind that I didn't even know she was my mother?"

"That, too, was fear, perhaps. Ask her."

Rayah thought she might—and then decided she didn't dare.

"You understand, I was very young that day I stood beneath the silver protective hand with its blue eye and looked down the hall as my brother went out the gate that last time. He had to fight. He knew Khalid ibn al-Walīd and his Arabs would win, Syria would fall, and he would die. But he placed you—very young—in my arms and said, 'I submit to heaven's will. I leave you this banner waving. Waving even in a harem, and no Conqueror shall topple it here.' That is your name, you know."

"Rayah." She had never thought of it before. "A banner."

A banner floating in the khamsin in a harem. It was ridiculous. But was it any more ridiculous than that Bint Zura's Uncle Abu Ragheb should have taken her lion skin and set it before his tent as his own ensign?

Adilah looked down at her bread and made a face. "The sand's got into it," she said, and she threw it to the chickens and to the young sheep the family was raising for the Eid celebration.

"I'll go get you another," Rayah offered.

"No, thanks, my heart. It will be sunset soon enough, inshallah."

And they would submit, even to sunset.

"There is submission to the Conqueror," Rayah mused, "who has found us out even in the harem. His conquests have made an army that moves with the speed of God's own lightning, and moves with one will—God's—like one man. But what place for the sickness of one woman in all of this? What of her own personal grief?"

Rayah scrambled off the coping and came to stand before her aunt. She stopped the older woman as she caught up her jug to get more water for the kitchen and to get back to work. Fasting and the wind made Rayah lightheaded. Holding her auntie by the shoulders, and hardly thinking what she did, she blew against the khamsin and into Adilah's face. Instead of Quranic verse, she recited:

> "By You whom madmen and jinn
> worship in their riverbeds..."

Adilah rubbed her neck and smiled. "I do feel better, my heart. Mashallah, what healing hands."

Yes, but who, besides God, was responsible for those hands? Sitt Sameh, surely and—a man, perhaps, who had fought against the Conqueror and the Islam he brought? But many had done so, then submitted and were forgiven, either as Muslims or as taxpaying, protected Christians or Jews. And if her father was dead, what did it matter? Why did Sitt Sameh still need to hide? With Adilah, Rayah couldn't be angry. Adilah was young. Adilah was afflicted and knew only what others had told her.

Rayah regained a steadiness. "If I must go to Sitt Umm Ali's recital," she said, "I want you to come, too."

"It will be as God wills," Adilah said, getting up with a sigh and a last wan smile.

26

**You whom madmen and jinn
worship in their riverbeds...
—al-Hasan ibn Hani**

Sitt Sameh shifted her room's single lamp so it would not gutter so much in the hot wind snapping the room's tenting walls. The lamp caught her tattooed face for an instant as she sat on her rug, picked up her spinning, and began the story once more.

And the tale she told made Rayah wonder if a search for fathers must be the curse of all girls of her lineage, born with blue eyes.

Word came to the inner desert that King an-Numan had gone to meet his fate before the Padishah in Ctesiphon. Even more discussed was the rise of a new holy man at the Encampment of al-Hira. A follower of Isa ibn Maryam, his name was Ahudammah, and he had great skill, so the report ran, at casting out demons by the finger of his God. He had, in fact, cast the jinn out of the one-time sharif of the Banu Taghlib named Zura.

The young orphan Bint Zura had always assumed that her father, whom she'd never known, must have died in the last wadi to which his jinn had led him. Now here he was, alive, no longer possessed. And he had sent a message to Uncle Abu Ragheb for her through a passing pilgrim.

"Has he—has he found a husband for me?" she asked doubtfully.

Always she had dismissed as impossible the fantasies she let invade her long hours on the march or watching the herd in their pastures. Every girl must dream of marriage to a prince, but Bint Zura had never known it to happen to anyone. How much less so to a girl with her history? That she would mother greatness, that was something else again. This came to her on what she knew to be a truth-speaking wind, whispering with her mother's voice. Now, for one wild moment, both seemed possible.

"The Gods willing, yes, if you call Isa ibn Maryam a husband," her uncle replied. "To repay this Ahudammah, he means you to become a nun among the Christians of al-Hira. Something about helping to replace the two hundred—or was it three hundred?—nuns from Haleb that the former Lakhmid king of that Encampment is said to have sacrificed to his God of stone."

And so, at the next pilgrimage, Abu Ragheb brought a herd of twenty-five camels to find buyers among the caravan drivers. He also brought his niece and dropped her off at the great iron-studded door of the church, not caring to enter the building himself.

"Father?" she said to the first of the pair of black-robed strangers who welcomed her in.

The word choked her. She did not know what that word should make her feel. Worse, she felt the stifle of buildings all around, death-dealing to one who'd only known the breathing walls of a tent. Stale and too-sweet incense oppressed her lungs. No wonder her uncle had refused to join her inside.

Not knowing what else to do—she certainly didn't want to embrace the man before her—she dropped to her knees, veil and skirts puddling around her and shedding their sand.

"I am not your father, child," the man said. "I am Bishop Ahudammah. This is your father."

The man and the other with him looked alike, in identical robes. In the church's dimness, she tried to make out the difference between them. Bishop Ahudammah's black figure was that of a man who asked no questions, solid in his mastery.

How such a man could cast out Fire Spirits, Bint Zura decided, was a wonder. She doubted a gust of desert air would even make his hem stir. What could he know of jinn?

"Are you also a bishop?" she asked her father.

Ahudammah smiled indulgently. "Your father has just been called by the grace of God to serve as wazir to the new king, Iyas ibn Qabissa, whom the Persians have placed on the Lakhmid throne."

Bint Zura thought it odd that a wazir could not speak for himself. Ahudammah was certainly more interesting, not to say threatening, than the man who was supposed to be her father, a shadow in a monk's black robe. They had announced that her father was alive. Truly, he seemed dead, standing in the choking smoke of incense, against a background of painted images propped against the walls, golden, wide-eyed, flattened people. Her father allowed Ahudammah to do all the talking. Apparently, the jinn had lately abandoned him, leaving an empty hull behind.

"This is the icon your father created in thanksgiving to Maryam's son for his healing," the bishop was saying. "It is of the Magdalene, the saint from whom our Lord drove seven devils."

Nothing made this painting stand out among all the others to Bint Zura's eyes. In fact, they seemed all the same, like the two Christian men here.

The bishop gestured. "Here, a tablet on which he had memory of the miracle engraved: 'Zura ibn Taghlib did this with praises to Ahudammah, bishop of al-Hira, in whose hand the finger of God moved.'"

The more Bint Zura looked at the icons, the more these bits of pigment on board unnerved her. They seemed like real people, trapped. True, they were trapped in boxes of gold that leapt and gleamed in the lamplight, but they were trapped nonetheless, in a world that allowed them no depth. And they all looked at her, straight on, impassively, with huge, round eyes. Perhaps such eyes were meant to show them as people of soul. Not one had blue eyes, however.

Her father seemed one of them, rolled onto a golden box in his black robe. His eyes avoided her.

"Shortly we will take you to the convent that is to be your new home," the bishop told her. "You will like it there. There are many good, faithful sisters and a lovely garden."

The word "garden" to a woman of the desert meant something akin to "paradise." She would probably have to die to go there.

Ahudammah explained that part of it to her. "But first, I think you must be baptized. You haven't been baptized, have you, child? Sprinkled with water in the name of Isa al-Masih? Your father said he omitted the rite when you were born because it was in the desert and you were, after all, too young to know your own mind."

"I try not to waste water the herds might drink," she said.

"Waste?" She saw anger flash through his dark eyes—but only a flash. It vanished. "Come, child, with me."

Bint Zura held back. "Excuse me, sir."

"Yes, child?"

"First I must know where I should keep my camel."

"Camel?" Bishop Ahudammah stopped in his tracks, another flash of anger.

Bravely Bint Zura pushed. "Yes, sir, I have a camel. Az-Zuharah is her name, for the Goddess-star. She is white, a good omen. Abu Ragheb would like to have her in his herd, I know only too well. But she is mine."

"Oh, a sort of bride price. An offering to the church upon your admission. I see. Well, we do have a herdsman into whose charge we can put it."

"No. She stays with me wherever I am to lodge."

Tears had begun to smart in the corners of Bint Zura's eyes. But she wouldn't back down, less now than from the lion who had tried to take az-Zuharah from her at the camel's birth. Over the years, she and az-Zuharah had grown together. Although no one should ride a white camel or put loads on it, Bint Zura had trained the animal herself in secret.

She'd begun with the commands to kneel and rise, using words of her own devising so only she and az-Zuharah should know. Bint Zura had pierced the camel's left nostril with her own carpet knife. Az-Zuharah wore the lead with as much pride as a woman wore her nose ring. Bint Zura taught her camel to take a burden, then herself as a rider on bareback. The last step was a litter, which she was certain the camel could manage, if she ever had the opportunity.

No doubt about it, of all things, az-Zuharah had learned pride. If anyone else tried to control her, they would find the task impossible. On foot, Bint Zura led the camel at the head of any migration, beneath the lion-skin banner. Abu Ragheb could flaunt the animal as his own, but if someone asked him directly, he would have to confess the truth of the matter.

"You cannot keep her at the convent," Ahudammah stated. His tone demanded obedience without question.

"Then I'm afraid I can't stay in this garden, this paradise, of yours."

Ahudammah and her father exchanged uneasy glances.

"Those eyes," Zura said, the first words she'd heard from her father's lips. A hollowness echoed there, like a well run dry. "Just like your mother's, those evil eyes."

Even though the heavy doors had been closed against it, a desert breeze blew through the church then, swaying the lamps on their chains. Leaving the men's black robes untouched.

"You—you who were born in the very holy qubbah when your mother kicked out the Gospel books."

Bint Zura saw her father twitch, a shudder run the full length of his black robe. A little groan escaped his lips.

Another gust, and two of the lamps blew out.

Zura snatched up the skirt of his robe and in anguish rent the fabric in two. In a voice yet more distant, not his own, he cried out: "What have I to do with you, Handmaid of al-Uzza?"

Ahudammah stepped quickly to his disciple's side. "Zura, fight it. Call on the Lord Isa, say his name, Zura."

"Is—" Zura screamed, but the second syllable strangled in his throat.

"In the name of Isa ibn Maryam, I abjure you, ya shaytan—"

"Our Father who art in heaven— Our Father— My Father—" Zura tried to recite, but he got no further before he pitched forward onto the floor, tearing the dark robe from him.

No word of "Mother," Bint Zura noticed. A struggle, rather, to avoid it. She watched in horror as the body beneath the heavy black wool was revealed. He was like some desert-drifted stump of wood, wind-whittled. Some Great Hand, it seemed, had drawn a blade across his jugular and bled him dry. Against the sun-blackened color of his skin, the simple goatskin about his loins stood stark.

Ahudammah was on his knees, trying to make some ritual signs to cast the spirit out, but he lost dignity with every thrash of the afflicted limbs. Her father had begun to bite his own hands now, so deeply that lamplight glistened on the blood he drew.

Bint Zura wanted to say something to ease such suffering. Ahudammah, she thought, was going about this all the wrong way. The bishop was trying to rid her father of what possessed him completely, which would leave him as hollow as before, and defenseless. She spoke only what long days in the desert had taught her: "A shaytan, adversity, is not all bad. Embrace him as you wrestle him, like a lover. Don't do it from a distance."

"Why, you very spawn of the jinn," Ahudammah cried. "This is all your fault."

Bint Zura turned and ran. Throwing all her weight against the heavy wooden door, she managed to open it. In the brilliant sunlight of al-Hira, she could breathe again.

With the khamsin still burning her nostrils, Rayah longed for such fresh air. "Auntie Adilah says she heard you recite poetry. And little Bushra said so, too."

Sitt Sameh didn't answer. Rayah hadn't meant it to be an accusation. The look the older blue eyes exchanged with the eunuch made her press further: "Is it just the purity of desert air that brings poetry to our people?" Rayah knew that the Arab people of old—who could carry nothing with them except in their heads—had appreciated this art that was painting and sculpture, books and pottery to them. "Or is it actually the jinn who touch the tongue?"

As if coming to Sitt Sameh's rescue, Abd Allah suddenly found great interest in his parchments. Pulling the single lamp to him, he said: "Ah, Khalid Abu Sulayman, my master, had something to say of poetry. Yes, here."

And he began to read, more rapidly than usual.

27

Did the poets leave no tune to sing of?
—the Qasidah of Antar ibn Shaddad

I had seen Hanzala ibn Thalaba, sharif of the Banu Bakr, swear before the sacred stones to keep the Lakhmid's armor against the might of Persia. I made the calculations. I'd leave my milk brothers to go in search of the mares and high-tailed stallions that bore my father's brand. The spring had come, the holy month. The horses would be sleek and strong and handsome. If Persia were going to go after a set of armor and some royal women, they would pay well for my animals.

And, besides every other faith, the Encampment, al-Hira, was also sacred to those who knew no God but the one the Greeks called Mammon.

But first, youth had to escape distractions . . .

Our camels tripped around the town's promiscuous assortment of Persian, Indian, Arabic, Roman, Egyptian, and Sabaean goods. Stalls were ripe with cosmetics, spices and oils, textiles, saddles, grain, fruit, livestock, jewelry, slaves, weapons, tools.

I was used to such rites of worship from Damascus, Homs, even Mecca. But my companions' tongues—with perhaps the exception of Mutammim's poetical one—could not name half of what glimmered and danced before our eyes like sunlight through cut glass.

The herdsman's son al-Harith grew wide-eyed as we rode. "In al-Hira a man sells Roman raisins one day, Indian spices the next from the self-same bags."

"In truth," Malik agreed, "his cousin under the next patch of shade is selling Persian gold work the first day and his own daughters out of poverty the next."

Even as he said it, his camel brayed in protest and pulled up short. Mine had almost run into its tail, and Malik's mount was a particularly foul-tempered beast. With a billow of dust, an accident had happened in the crowded market. A camel in the slow-moving caravan in front of us had suddenly dropped its load.

"A seller of camel saddles," Malik shouted to us behind him, "who could find no place better to set up shop than directly across the main thoroughfare."

"No doubt he'll attract attention there," Mutammim replied, shifting his ears rather than his eyes around the close-pressed crowd for the chuckles he hoped his joking would rouse. There were none.

I caught a sidelong view of Malik at the head of our group of four. Beneath the shade of his headcloth, his young, narrow face gazed unblinkingly at what lay before him. He wasn't smiling at all. Then I saw that this was not just some leather-stitcher who had set up shop to one side of the road. Nor was it an accident, a broken girth sending goods tumbling across the way. This spill been done with deliberate aggression. And just for us.

A stranger's voice rose loud and clear:

> "Lo, a lean camel, journey-worn to a remnant,
> with sunken loins and a sunken hump,
> worn lean by kicks and bites of rival males."

Is the stitcher reciting poetry to lighten the business of his own fallen camel, so we won't be too unhappy about him blocking the way? That's what I thought, what I hoped.

Then Malik said, "We come to the pilgrimage, O sons of Taghlib."

Taghlibi. The blood feud. They had killed my milk father Nuwaira. His son Malik had killed some of their number. Now they were after revenge in their own turn. My heart began to race. Maybe I hadn't missed the fighting after all.

"They come to mock us, these dogs of Tamim," someone shouted.

"We come unarmed," Malik insisted, "in the peace of the moon."

"Yet you still wear your warriors' locks," another man said.

It was true. We hadn't had time to shave our heads yet, as pilgrims do.

Malik's hand, under cover of a blown-back cloak, reached for his dagger. I reached for my own. We'd left our swords with the baggage and the tents, as the pilgrimage required. But even on pilgrimage, one needs a dagger to perform the sacrifice. Perhaps the stones of al-Hira would see other bloodshed today. I felt my own blood pulsing.

The Gods who had set life coursing in my veins wouldn't be pleased to have their sacred month sullied. Or again—they might shed my blood just for pleasure. But if Malik would fight, I would back him.

Al-Harith shuffled his camel to recede. He was in no mood for a fight—ever.

I urged my camel forward into his place, to cover Malik's left, to make a phalanx of my milk brothers and me. Now I saw better. The kneeling pack camel and its spilled goods made a barricade across the dusty road. Behind that safety stood seven strong young men wearing the green cords of Taghlib to keep their headcloths in place. Their hands were empty, but they all stood with their outer cloaks open, making sure we saw the curved silver sheaths and rhinoceros-horn hilts of their daggers.

At the center of their number stood yet an eighth man, older than the rest. His white beard was goatish, his keen eyes set in a nest of wrinkles. Teeth broken rather than filed cragged what was either a grin or a sneer.

Old man, go drink your broth by your fire, I wanted to tell him. Leave young men to this bloody work.

I even opened my mouth to say it, but found I was too dry. I strove to bring up more spit. I had to admit, even if we could trust Mutammim in his blindness to take on the old man, I still didn't like the odds, seven Taghlibi to only four of us. And one of us was al-Harith.

Before I could say anything, the old man spoke, whistling around his teeth:

> "Lo, a she-camel who bears you twins every year—
> evil issue, every one of them rebellious."

Malik's dagger glinted openly in his hand now. But I had seen how loosely this old man's mantle hung down, how he wore only one sandal, even to cross hot sands, and how, under his headcloth, only one side of his hair glistened with oil. This man lived in two worlds—he was a poet.

"Destroy the peace of our pilgrimage, will you?" shouted one of the younger men. "The Gods curse you for it." He and two of his fellows spat.

Mutammim caught his brother's dagger hand just as it began some threatening gesture in return. Then he turned his blinded face to the Taghlibi and said:

> "I ride my camel at high noon when
> the mirage shimmers as if aflame,
> or I curb her to a pacing gait
> like a dancing girl
> trailing her white gown before her lord."

A common enough image, that of the camel as dancing girl. Instantly the old son of Taghlib replied:

> "When we engage a people in battle, we are
> as two wild camels, racing bonded, till
> one, our enemy, totters, and we triumph.
> We are the firmest men in duty
> and the truest of men to the oath once taken."

I saw that, in deference to the holy month, the Taghlibi had set a trap for us. We were ambushed into a contest, and it would have to be of words, not blows.

In those bygone days of the Arabs, we recognized great power in the driving force of poetry. A tribe would celebrate over the birth of a poet come to his words as much or more than over the birth of a strong-limbed boy who might grow into a warrior. Then, a poet's words were powerful enough to raise the jinn; they had often turned the tide of battle. Now, only one poet—God and His Quran—counts. These are different times.

My heart sank. Everything I prided myself on was useless in such a trap. Malik, who had led the brilliant raid, was also no good at this. Mutammim was the only one among us with any claim to the name of poet. I hadn't heard much of his work since my recent return among the Tamim, but I knew well that, unlike war, poetry was a skill that got better with age. Mutammim was very young. He—we—had given his eyes to the jinn. That sign of dwelling in the two worlds marked his very flesh. But was it enough?

My milk brother had matched the rhythm scheme set by the older poet in his first improvised responses. That was expected. So far, however, he had not come close to matching that fierce opening cut. The Taghlibi poet had suggested that not only our she-camels but also our women suffered the kicks and bites of other males. We felt that keenly.

Silence seemed to stretch a very long time in the spring air between us. By Hubal, I thought, Mutammim has already come to the end of his words with that silly image of the dancing girl. Sweat from my hands could be wrung from the braided wool of my reins. I might have to cut the old man's throat anyway. But what honor would be in that with the ban of pilgrimage on us?

Then I saw that Mutammim was just waiting for the violence to leave his brother's dagger arm. When Malik put the weapon back in its sheath, the older son of Nuwaira let the arm go. Then he turned his full attention to his adversary.

The next thing out of Mutammim's mouth was a guttural order to his camel. An echo of the sound came from the beast's throat and, forelegs first, it rocked to its knees. This was never a graceful process, and I could only think that at least mounted we had the advantage of height. We could, if worse came to worst, drive our animals over the barrier of saddlebags and panniers and through the standing sons of Taghlib. Or, if we wanted the name of Tamim to ever be a byword for cowardice among the Arabs, we could turn our camels' noses and soon have the men on foot outpaced.

But Mutammim, with a dignity that belied his twenty years, dismounted and stepped around his camel's knees to stand directly in front of the Taghlibi poet. He greeted him with a dignified bow, hand on his heart, then gestured for the old man to sit first. He did, and then Mutammim squatted opposite him. One of the younger Taghlibi drove the camel that had acted as a roadblock out of the way, although most of the litter from its back remained. The two poets faced each other over it, there in the pounding sun. The crowd that had backed off when they feared we might come to blows began to regather. No one made a sound, however. They didn't want to miss a word.

To my right, Malik let his mount kneel. Behind us, al-Harith followed the example of his sharif. Finally, so did I. I did not leave my saddle, however.

When at last the dust from all of this had settled, Mutammim said:

> "We split the heads of warriors and slit
> through their necks like scythed grass.
> There you see the skulls of heroes like
> camel-loads flung down on the pebbles."

I'm not sure how much of the kneeling and bowing was a cover while my milk brother composed this verse in his head. Even so, and even to my dull ears, it was impressive: the Taghlibi's same martial rhythm. And a grand, sweeping gesture over the scene as Mutammim said the last line caught up the very images of the barrier of goods before us. He picked the figures of speech up and threw them like pebbles. The crowd murmured "Oohs"—so did one or two of the Taghlibi—as if the words actually stung like pelting stones.

The old poet left references of camels altogether now to get to the heart of the matter. He addressed the God of al-Hira's pillars:

> "O as-Sabad,
> if you had suffered loss like me
> and your father had been buried,
> you would not have restrained me
> from killing my enemies."

Openly, then, he referred to the blood that stood between his lineage and that of Nuwaira. That blood cried for blood and, if as-Sabad were any sort of God, He would not have established the pilgrimage month to get in the way.

My poet of a milk brother retorted:

> "Why, O Taghlibi, do you give ear to
> our traducers, and scorn us? Why, O sons
> of Taghlib, should we be your underlings
> and abject slaves in your own house?
> You threaten and menace us—yet when,
> pray, were we your mother's menials?"

I exclaimed with the rest. The questioning Mutammim used in this pass might have seemed a weak retort, but now he had brought the other tribe's mothers into it.

> "I have to this day pledged to bear
> my Indian sword strapped to my hip.
> When I stand forth to take
> my revenge, I need not repeat the stroke;
> So when the folks rush to arms, you'll find me
> impregnable, my hand gripping its handle."

Mutammim replied to the Taghlibi:

> "When he saw me up against him,
> he bared his grinders
> and not in a grin; I ran him through with
> the spear and pierced him with my Indian
> blade of shining steel . . ."

He spoke as if he were Malik in these verses. Now I could see just how Malik, in spite of youth, had managed to hold on to his dead father's place. He had Mutammim to speak for him.

But Mutammim wasn't finished. The same stanzas driving on, he dared evoke the image of the Taghlibi's fallen kinsman:

> *"And as the day*
> *spread out, he lay before me, head*
> *and arms red as if dyed with madder,*
> *a hero like a clothed sarha tree,*
> *shod in boots of tanned leather,*
> *and no runted twin."*

Two of our young foemen gave a cry of loss, of rage, then scrambled over their own barricade toward us. Although I rocked on my saddle as if the beast beneath me were moving at a solid lope, I kept my seat and didn't answer their threat. Beside me, Malik did so with greater ease. He had faith in the words his brother brewed behind the white steam of that eye.

Their fellows called the Taghlibi back, telling them not to shame themselves by actions too rash. The old poet warned:

> *"When we haul our war-mill against a people,*
> *they turn to grist at the encounter.*
> *Its sack reaches to east of Nejd,*
> *and the grain it grinds on is all Kuda'a."*

Our turn.

> *"Give ear to our word of truth: how*
> *we take the banners white into battle and*
> *bring them back crimson, well-slaked;*
> *how in days of old, long and glorious, we*
> *opposed the king, and would not obey him.*
> *And many a tribal champion, crowned*
> *with the crown of rule, guarding those*
> *who flee to him, we routed, leaving*
> *four horses standing over, their reins*
> *upon their necks, one foot on tiptoe;*
> *the tribe's dogs howled behind us as*
> *we stripped our border enemies of their*
> *arms, like a tree of its thorn-bristles."*

Mutammim managed such a long burst, I realized, because he borrowed portions of it from the well-known qasidah of Amr ibn Kulthum. But he did well to call the enemy to task for their dependence on the Persian Great King with the mention of a "crown," a Persian word. True men of the desert were their own masters. What could the Taghlibi say to that, when so much of their power was that of the settled places?

> *"There will come a turning to your pride:*
> *but that is the way of mankind;*
> *the sorceresses cannot ward off death."*

With the old man's hiss of words, a wind of the desert came up my back. He referred, of course, to Umm Taghlib, the old kahinah who had sought refuge with my foster father from these, her own kinsmen, and whose protection Malik had inherited. She was a bone of contention between the two tribes greater than that of spilled blood, perhaps. Her existence had led to the blood in the first place. I hadn't seen the old woman since our bartering over my right arm in my childhood so long ago, when she asked for my sacrifice to the jinn for the return of the missing al-Harith. Indeed, I was surprised to learn she still shadowed the Tamim encampments and had not already been swept away by the night wind.

I shivered in spite of the hot al-Hira sun on my back. The Taghlibi had branded the kahinah evil and put her from them. And the sons of Tamim had taken her in. If the Taghlib depended on the Great King, the Tamim trusted in an even darker power, one that belonged to the desert. Mutammim must have surely realized this, every time he tried to look through his jinn-bartered sightless eyes. Even after all these years, I wondered if my milk brothers would have done better if they'd copied their enemies and removed their protection from such a kahinah.

Mutammim's discomfort was clear. His bad eyes blinked rapidly and beyond his control. Much of the pause given him to compose did not go into verse.

Finally, my milk brother, playing on the verses of Antar ibn Shaddad, which sounded around every campfire, said quietly:

> "Yet the poor of the earth know
> my generous hand and the rich,
> my glorious deed. O blamer! pleasure
> and war divide my life—could you
> grant me immortality? If you cannot
> shield me from death, let me then dare
> it head on with all I have."

> "He takes shelter with unadorned women
> and disheveled and nursing women like the jinn."

The Taghlibi poet threw the lines back in my milk brother's face. Mutammim responded:

> "When a boy of ours reaches his weaning,
> tyrants fall down before him prostrating."

But I could tell my milk brother had fallen back to the curses of common poets, and he let the older man have the last word in a different and finalizing meter:

> "He who disobeys the proffered spear-end of peace
> bows to the sharp tip of the spearhead of war."

That was the end, although neither side had won a decisive victory. The crowd repeated the best of the verses among themselves as they pulled the spilled camel saddles out of our way. The closing argument was only promise of more blood to come—when the moon of pilgrimage should pass.

And it was just after leaving this scene that I came to the well where the mad Christian preached. And where the young woman with blue eyes swung a palm frond so enticingly over her shoulder.

28

> May the morning clouds refresh his grave with heavy rains;
> My dromedary was frightened by the grave built over a
> liberal and bountiful man.
> O she-camel, do not fear him, for he was a drinker of wine
> and a wager of wars.
> If I did not have a long journey to face and a barren desert
> to cover,
> I would have slaughtered her at his grave.
> —Hafs ibn al-Akhnaf al-Kinani

Jinn haunt tombs. Everyone knew that, and to Rayah it seemed as if Tadmor itself rose a mere mirage behind them. Whole pilgrimages of Fire Ones engulfed the tombs.

"It's the old charcoal burner at his work," the womenfolk assured her. Then she could pick out the gray smoke of the old man who turned fall-wood from the mountainside's figs and other scrub trees into charcoal. Yes, she could distinguish him from the breaths of sand carried on the last gasps of the khamsin wind—and from jinn.

"We'll have to visit him afterward." The kinsmen expressed their own interest. "We could use another load of charcoal in our workshop. And we must see what the juniper berries that grow among the figs are like this year. They make a fine oil to sell."

The turpentine sellers and their families always came to visit the dead at the midpoint of the holy month. But the Ramadhan fasting had crept forward through the year to hotter and hotter days, and this year the khamsin penetrated midmonth. At first the adults thought they'd have to put the long trek off. The wind had died somewhat during the night, however, so they'd decided to undertake it after all.

The Christians of Tadmor buried their dead beside their churches, and many Muslims were beginning to do so in their own graveyards. Families who had been at the oasis since time immemorial, on the other hand, each had their own tomb tower in a valley that was a morning's donkey ride to the west. The Valley of the Dead lay under and between the folds of the scrub-covered ridge of hills. Each tower stood at least two stories high, large enough to contain all the souls of large clans; upper floors were reached by inner spirals of stairs. They were lifeless, dark stone erections that might well stand sentinel between the land of the living and the one beyond, where the jinn dwelled.

Although the Muslims had battered in the faces of many another statue among the ruins of Tadmor when they'd come here, they feared the dead more than God's tenet against idolatry. They'd left the towers intact. Some of the towers had carvings inside and out: the deceased lying in stone shrouds at peace, some reclining on couches, some depicted in busts with individual features so finely drawn that Rayah would have recognized them had their lifetime coincided with hers. The only difference was their stony pallor and the haunted pits of their unblinking eyes.

The family of turpentine sellers entered the tower with their name carved in letters that no one alive knew how to read over the pillared door: tongue forgotten but not the blood. As she entered the ancient stone tower Rayah recalled how Bint Zura had sheltered her newborn camel in the ruins of the Prophet Salih's cities.

Inside was cool and shade, escape from the rigors of the khamsin's sand biting into the skin with every step. Here was a musty sweet smell, gum arabic and myrrh only just covering the stench of corruption, the smell of the tombs so akin to turpentine, the smell of the living. Body-length vaults were set into the walls, four by four on each face. When they were filled, masons sealed the space to let the dead sleep behind silent stone.

The family began by sweeping the tomb of all the sand that had drifted in over the year. With the sand went the red worms, blind, with scales that whispered over the stone in the dark, none shorter than Rayah's foot. When brought from the land of the dead to the land of the blinding light, the creatures writhed and quickly died in heaps beside the door.

Then the family made trips back and forth to the spring trickling like magic out of the hillside: an emblem of the eternal springing of life from that which seemed dead. Denying themselves the refreshment all the while, they carried it from bust to bust, from vault to vault, pouring out a measure for each.

As they did, the elders said what they could of the deceased: "Ah! Do you remember her pastries? No one could make them as light as she could, even when her hands grew so crippled."

"Do you remember his laugh? Even in the harem we knew when Uncle heard a good joke."

"The bowel complaint carried her off when she had only just begun to prattle, the little one. But her mother always said, 'Mashallah, she is the brightest of my children.' I'm sure it was a mother's pride in the girl that brought down the evil eye."

And every account ended with "Alas."

More of the dead were beyond anyone's remembrance than within it, and yet none of these were the people who had been given names and life in Sitt Sameh's room. Rayah sighed to herself. Were the stories told by that blue-eyed desert woman mere fables?

Then her cousin Demiella said, "This was Uncle Yaqob, may his time in hell be eased. You know, Adilah's brother. He died away from here and is buried where he fell. This is only a plaque, for remembrance. A pity Adilah is not well enough to join us today. A pity he had no son. He has no one else to remember him."

Rayah stood and stared at the stone sealing an empty vault. He has me, she thought. If only I knew something to remember.

"But wait." Rayah stopped the family as they turned from the empty tomb. "Adilah's brother? Isn't he my father?"

"No, dear. You are mistaken." That's all they said as they bustled away, things more than mourning on their minds.

Why had they stopped telling her that? When? Just now. Rayah trembled with the realization. The whole conspiracy of her origins must have crumbled, so as one voice, they'd all stopped saying it. And what had eroded the conspiracy so suddenly? The arrival of Abd Allah the eunuch with his parchments, of course. The things in that record, the things Sitt Sameh told her, they must be true. Disturbing as they were, disruptive to her whole world, they must be true, and everything else lies. For a moment, those lies made Rayah burn with hatred of the people who had loved her so.

Still, no one denied that this Yaqob had brought Sitt Sameh from the wide world and secreted her in their harem. Away from Khalid, opposing the Conqueror. Yaqob, the man who had died elsewhere and had no one to remember him.

"I will remember you," Rayah whispered. She touched the cool, smooth stone.

The rest of the turpentine sellers' party went out to sit in the shade and doze through the hottest hours, stupid with hunger and thirst, until it grew cool enough to begin the trek home. Leaving them, Rayah found herself returning alone to the spring. After the long procession in the rising sun, the work to clean the tomb, the clear, cool splash tempted her so. But she resisted breaking the fast and caught only enough to bring another measure back to the tomb. This she let run down the stone drapery in front of the empty tomb, living water echoing dead stone.

"A brave man." The sudden voice behind her made her jump. She turned and saw it was no demon. Her heart settled. It was an old man, soot-grimed and reeking of smoke. The charcoal burner who lived among the tombs.

"You knew him?" Rayah asked.

"Of course. He was younger than I, but still a young man who commanded notice. Full of honor, even though he fought for the wrong side. Or not the wrong side—the side that lost. Forgive me. I watched you fetching the extra measure of water, and I just wondered. The blue eyes and all."

Tufts of white hair smeared gray stood on cheeks, chin, under the rag round his head. His words whistled through stubs of teeth along with threads of saliva. If anyone had a jinni… she thought. And what had she always been warned about being alone with strange men, particularly in deserted places? She found she'd taken a step backward until the folds of the stone veil of the tomb pressed into her back. She pulled one side of her own veil across her nose to the other ear. Nonetheless, calming herself and, she hoped, the man with a prayer, she asked, "He died fighting Islam?"

"Yes, at the battle of Yarmuk." He eyed her keenly, uncomfortably so. "That would have been the year you were born, little girl, or thereabouts."

Rayah edged along the tomb wall toward the entrance. The forms of the dead, slipping along her spine, were of more comfort than the living.

"Yarmuk, where Khalid the Conqueror came whirling out of a desert everyone said could not be crossed," the old man went on. "Yaqob died there with so many, as the great Roman army went down in defeat. He was a fool to go, young Yaqob. But an honorable fool."

An honorable fool? That indeed sounded like the product of a deranged mind. "Why do you say he was a fool?"

"Because he knew the Arabs would win, once Khalid brought them through that desert as if by miracle. He had seen Khalid's work before in Iraq, in al-Hira. He had told us all about it as we men sat debating events in the marketplace."

There. She was around the tomb's last corner. The old man didn't stand between her and the land of the living any more. "Did he win anyone to his side as you talked? Did anyone fight next to him, who survived? Whom I could find to talk to?"

"Ah, not a one, my girl. We were all for letting the Arabs have our city peacefully. We'd seen a lot of bloodshed over the years as the Romans marched eastward and then got driven back again. We wanted peace. The Arabs were, after all, closer to us in blood than either Persians or these strange, arrogant Rumis from across the sea. Besides, we were—we are still—Christians."

"Then I would think you'd want to fight on the side of Christians, I mean on the side of Rome." Rayah found that the breath to ask these questions came a little easier now, even though she had been taught that the morality of followers of the Nazarene left a little to be desired.

"Not at all. Romans are the Christianity of power, whereas Isa ibn Maryam, while he lived, was a man of submission. Of *Islam*, as the Arabic word is."

The charcoal burner had stopped fixing her with his keen, smoke-stung gaze and looked at the tomb instead. "The Romans degrade our Lord by dividing his nature in two, the human and the divine. Sometimes even three—Father, Son, and Holy Ghost—while we know we must worship the unity and majesty of God."

He reached out one sooty hand and touched the empty tomb, leaving his prints on the newly washed surface. "Because the Romans had the imperial army behind their mistaken belief, those of our faith, unarmed as our Lord was unarmed, were persecuted, even to death. The Roman Church likes to speak only of how the heathen emperors sent them to the lions and used their burning bodies to light their banquets until Constantine saw his sign. Selective memories. They do not think of what they did to us, or to the Jews, in our eastern provinces. Such deaths and worse."

Consumed by his tale, Rayah had forgotten the unsavory cast of his mouth. She remembered it only now as he took the dirty end of the rag on his head and used it to wipe away extra spittle and some of the grime.

Then he went on. "So when the Muslims came promising us, as fellow monotheists, to leave us our faith in peace, we and the Jews knew we must embrace them as liberators, not conquerors."

"So how was Uncle Yaqob an honorable man, if he fought on the side of a greedy, godless power?"

The charcoal burner kissed the empty tomb as if in farewell. He said nothing for a moment while his echoing footsteps crossed the newly swept tomb and came to stand between her and the light of the door again. This time, the positioning didn't frighten her as it had before.

"On the side of one greedy power against another? And if those are the only choices given a man—"

The charcoal burner let his voice drop, considering, for a moment. "Few of my co-religionists would agree with me, I suppose. But I have time to think all these things over as I sit out here tending my kilns. If I had the gift of poetry like some of those who speak to jinn in the desert, I would have made a poem to remember Yaqob, full of the mystery of good and bad living side by side in one man. I've tried—but it is not my gift. Only the stacking of a good chimney."

Recalling this work, lonely but demanding, he stepped out into the sunshine as if to leave. Rayah found herself scrambling after him. "Please, Sayyid, don't go. Tell me more."

He blinked down at her as if he couldn't, for a moment, remember what they'd been talking of. "You see, my girl," he said presently, "no one could hide himself in those days, hardly even women. And as for men—a man had to stand with one side or the other. And Yaqob made the braver, more honorable choice. To stand with something older than either holy man, on the side of a woman with a child who had claimed his protection, even though he knew it would cost him his life. As long as Yaqob lived, the Conqueror would be able to trace the woman he sought to hide through him. No, it was better to die."

Rayah's vision blurred then, and she pulled close her veil, knowing tears flowed down her face.

"Mashallah, child, there you are!" Demiella scurried around from the shady side of the tomb tower to the south-facing door where Rayah stood. "I was beginning to worry."

Demiella didn't see the old man making his way back to the inferno of his kilns. Nor could Rayah give the answer to Uncle Aharon's question as they trekked back to town. "What do you make of this, my brothers? The burner has added an extra five bushels of charcoal to our load—at no cost. Mashallah, who ever has done this has certainly earned his keep today."

The evening star rose before them as they returned from the Valley of the Dead to the living. That night, over the remains of breaking the fast, Rayah listened to Sitt Sameh tell her grandmother's tale until the long day caught up with her. Rayah fell asleep curled up on the carpet, still listening for explanation of the empty tomb she'd seen that day, receiving none.

29

How beautiful the gait of the gray camel!
It is Sita sewing small shells in a pattern on its litter.
—a song of the Rwala tribe

Once out of the stifling church of the Nazarenes, away from her father's madness, Bint Zura meant to get out of the Encampment too, as quickly as possible. If once she got on az-Zuharah's shaggy white back again, they would ride out into the desert together and never look back. That she had no tent, no tribe to go back to? At the moment, these things hardly mattered.

But the shadows cast by clay walls confused her sense of direction to where her uncle had pitched his camp. Where her white camel awaited her return.

Perhaps she could find where her friend Layla bint al-Minhal of the Iyadi tribe was camped. The girls knew each other only from pilgrimages, for their people dwelt in different parts of the desert during most of the year. Nonetheless, Layla would take her in. Layla's people always pitched their tents closer to al-Hira than Bint Zura's own—and Bint Zura could find az-Zuharah from there. She realized, however, that she was not even going to be able to find the Iyadi without help.

She must ask someone. But whom? She pulled her veil more tightly around her. Most of the people she saw were men selling a dazzling array of products in the market. She tried not to let them see her and clung close to walls of clay and those of hair pitched between them. A woman alone in a town was truly in trouble, as everyone had always warned her.

Her steps led her around the rear of the tent belonging to a saddle maker. She could tell because rejected frames cluttered the narrow alley here between guy ropes and tent stakes. A shift of sand blowing between the booths made her notice one frame in particular—a woman's litter. Great loops of sacred tamarisk had been bent and then bound with brightly colored wool. It almost seemed to call her name. Not Bint Zura, as everyone called her, but another name she knew as her own although no one ever said it: Amat al-Uzza, handmaid of al-Uzza.

The litter had lost its curtains. The wool bindings were unraveling and one of the wooden loops was broken. And what was the use of a litter, she told herself, if she could never find her camel again?

Bint Zura tucked her head under a rope and around a side curtain of the saddle maker's tent to see if she could make a dash across the open space to the next protecting wall. What she saw in the open space before the tent made her stop, but not retreat. The men of two tribes confronted each other over camel saddles.

Her first reaction was relief, almost to the point of tears. On one of the sides were sons of Taghlib. She recognized their great poet, gray-bearded Abu'l Ghul. They would lead her home.

If they didn't lead her back to the church, to answer her father's vow. That possibility always existed, didn't it?

Hesitation at this thought gave her time to stop and see exactly what was afoot. Rather than with lances and swords, in honor of the holy month the tribes battled with a sharper weapon: poetry. Bint Zura forgot her quest, even her safety, to listen. She saw other women listening too, peering around curtains and over clay walls, out of the men's sight and thought, but seeing all.

Shayatan blessed these tongues with excellent poems. Abu'l Ghul she had heard before. But the young blind man on the other side also knew sacred adversity as the closest of boon companions.

> "There you see the skulls of heroes like
> camel-loads flung down on the pebbles."

Bint Zura found one of her hands gripping with the onslaught of such power. It was the rim of the broken litter around which her knuckles grew white.

> "There will come a turning to your pride:
> but that is the way of mankind;
> the sorceresses cannot ward off death."

Abu'l Ghul's use of the word "sorceress" brought further realization. The men standing opposite her tribe were the young sharifs of the sons of Tamim. The tribe with which there was such bad blood.

The tribe—she'd heard whispers—that had taken in her mother when her father had become prey to the jinn.

> "When a boy of ours reaches his weaning,
> tyrants fall down before him prostrating."

Some gesture of the blind Tamimi on that word "weaning" drew her attention from his white-eyed face to that of another who was standing support to his kinsman—or rather, not. Pacing with impatience at words when he'd rather swing a sword, he was the most remarkable man Bint Zura had ever seen. He wasn't handsome. She couldn't say that of a man so short in stature, whom the pox had ravaged in his face. But something about him she couldn't name—

"Do you see your destiny, child?"

Bint Zura cried out. The voice had whispered just through her veil. Reflexively gripping the qubbah's frame with both hands, she fought to keep her feet while her heart raced and her sight grew white with the start.

An old, ragged woman had parted the saddler's tent just behind her and sidled up to speak to her of destiny. How all the charms about the old woman's neck had not clinked a warning with the movement, Bint Zura could not tell.

"I— No, Aunt. Not at all. I merely like the poetry."

"And does not prophecy come to us in poetry, in words beyond common knowing?"

"I wouldn't know. I am not a poet myself."

"Are you not?" The strange woman seemed clearly surprised. "I thought perhaps that might be your destiny."

Bint Zura tried to soothe the woman's obvious disappointment, although she wondered why a stranger should be disappointed. "It is not the Gods' will."

"Then the litter, perhaps?"

Bint Zura looked down to where her hands gripped the tamarisk wood still so fiercely. "I beg your pardon, Aunt. I do not have the means to buy and so should not have touched your wares." She let the litter go and hid her hands for shame beneath the ends of her veil.

"And yet it called your name, didn't it?"

"I—"

"Do you have the camel to go under it?"

"Yes." The certainty of her own answer surprised the girl.

"Not a white one?"

"I— Yes. I do."

The old hands grasped an amulet as if it might set her sailing into the sky. "Al-Uzza be praised."

Bint Zura found she had to look away from the old woman's gaze. She watched the battle of poets breaking up, but her mind was so full of other things now that the sight made hardly a shadow on her mind. Except for the one pockmarked young man as he made his camel rise.

"But think of what this litter might be," the strange woman persisted. "If I get the saddler to replace this broken arc of tamarisk here. If you take it and wind it with new wool spun of your own hands and dyed in the black and green of the sons of Taghlib. Drape it with white gauzy fabric, sew it with bells and cowrie shells, here, here. Tuft the crest with ostrich plumes. Why, the Goddesses themselves might ride in such a conveyance, at the head of an army of jinn."

Bint Zura gave another little cry of shock. She could see it, yes. Only too well. Swaying on az-Zuharah's regal back across the Taghlibi pastures in the green of spring. The vision was beautiful. Yet the old woman's delivery was too desperate, too much like that of a merchant to be trusted.

"I cannot buy a litter, even a broken one. I beg your pardon, Aunt."

"Call me but mother instead of aunt and you shall have it."

"I must go to be with my kinsmen."

"Very well, Amat al-Uzza."

The name ran through her like the stab of a thorn. More distressing still was the old woman's reaction to having spoken the phrase. Great tears welled up in the eyes one would have thought all dry within their sand-blasted rims.

"They call me Bint Zura, Zura's daughter," the girl said.

"And no mention at all of your mother, all she suffered."

"I beg your pardon, Aunt."

Bint Zura stepped out between the guy ropes to the safety of her kinsmen, finding herself nearly trod on by the striking young man whose camel strode away, unseeing. She watched him go.

Her kinsmen were throwing the saddles to one side so the path was clear once more. "Odd of that strange old woman to get us to build this barricade," commented one.

"But didn't it work out well, thanks to the Messiah?" replied his companion.

Bint Zura whirled back to look at the rear of the saddler's tent. It was only then that she realized what had made that strange gaze so piercing, so different from any other. The deep eyes in their nests of wrinkles were iron blue.

"Mother—" Bint Zura cried.

But the old woman had vanished into thin air like a dust devil when the wind dies. Along with her had gone the broken camel's litter.

30

My soul has become the caravanserai of cares . . .
—an anonymous pre-Islamic poet

"My soul has become the caravanserai of cares," the poet says, "Because I have not taken action and thus sent them speedily on their way."
This same source provides the best remedy:

"For the enfeebling impulses which befall me at night
I am preparing a strong, lean she-camel and an empty saddle."

Swift, demanding activity was what I needed. I needed it at once, or I should have been satisfied to stand with my lips pressed against the bronze-studded church door forever, debilitated and pacified into a soulless nothing. I came out of my daze when I heard Malik say, "So have you wasted the water and become a Christian, O Khalid?"

At first I stared at him blankly, uncomprehending as he leaned over the horn of his saddle to study me. But then, there was my former life of swagger, there where I had left it, just waiting for me to pick it up out of the dust.

While my scribe stops to sharpen a pen, I remember those days when poetry lay as thick as oasis air around me in al-Hira. I remember I found three of the men holding my horses that very first evening after the poetry contest. That should have been enough. Now, in my garden, I cannot understand why it was not enough. Certainly it was enough for my belly. I took the herders' generous hospitality (until I was sick to my stomach) and their promises to have the horses brought in from pasture before two sunsets had passed. My shrewdness would have satisfied my father. But I was eighteen . . .

Of every man I wanted to ask, "Do you know such-and-such a girl with honey cheek, blue eyes, and silver anklets?" Good manners forbade it. And what purpose served all my swagger if I should never see her again?

"The Nazarenes keep their religion in a skin of wine," Mutammim had remarked wryly before I left him earlier.

Where did the sip of wine taken in worship end and the drunkenness begin? Sprawling senseless *from the wining booths that adjoined every church and wine-making monastery, we sons of the desert couldn't tell. In those days, before Muhammad, blessed be he, had spoken and made it law, the saying "We of the desert do not become intoxicated" was just that—a saying. If we did not become intoxicated during the course of a normal day, it was because strong drink was not available in the desert.*

My business done, I rode to the section of the Encampment where I found my milk brothers. Beneath palm trees, the undersides of their fronds lit by torches, wine mongers had set up their booths. I heard the driving rhythms, the click-click-click of gaming pieces. I heard the exotic and alluring gurgle of date wine, thicker than water, as it flowed like blood from the jugs and skins.

Then came the wives and daughters from the tents. They plucked at my reins and called to read my fortune. They could have given this much correctly from their piles of salt and magic pebbles: my milk brothers and I would all be as drunk as Christians before we left the Encampment. Or, as the Christians say, "Drunk as a son of the desert." Constant contact with the powerful blood of their God taught them a temperance we had yet to learn in one hard lesson.

The wine seller who greeted me as I made my camel kneel was fat and pale from his indoor work. He sat before his jugs like some great pastry, undercooked and attracting flies.

Beneath his blue banner, a sign that he was well-stocked, I pressed by him and made my way to my milk brothers and their herdsman, playing the game of chance—and drinking. They said they were learning "A way to unburden one of the day's heavy gain," "A cure for headache," and "Hot gazelle's blood to fire one up to the deeds of a man."

I didn't feel myself in need of any of those effects that night. I was still lightheaded, and I had the inkling that a drink of anything could only make it worse. What I needed was a magic to free myself of the spell of a pair of well-blue eyes.

But Malik ibn Nuwaira insisted. "You must at least try. No, don't even shrink your own pouch for it. I myself will pay for a goblet of the best our host can pour out."

The pasty wine seller left his post by the door and came to answer Malik's wave.

"There," Malik said. "Sip at that and keep us company while we empty his skins and force the fellow to withdraw his boastful banner."

Only the sagest of men knows how to refuse a luxury when it is offered. And no man is sage at eighteen.

Well do I remember that first sip. It was a Syrian wine—grape, not common date—thick and sweet and mulled with cinnamon and myrrh. That is quite enough, I thought, and set the goblet down. But, alas, I found as I tasted the wine's remnant on the roof of my mouth that the standing-stone impression of the Christian girl began to erode from my mind.

"I hope you don't come across sons of Taghlib again in this condition," I told my milk brothers.

I sipped at the goblet again—I was now on my second at least—and chanced to spill a drop or two across my knee and onto the carpet. A swirl of sand bore new holes into the sacrificial stone of my heart.

"Never mind," Malik said. "The carpet is blooming with a pattern of such flowers already."
We laughed.

I went from goblet to bowl, from wine to wine, until I found stinking date wine delightful, and I lost all my horse traders' hospitality on the wine seller's rugs.

My scribe protests that he doesn't care to portray the Conqueror of Islam in such a light.

"Does it comfort you to know, my friend, that for all our efforts, we did not drink down the wine seller's blue flag that night?" I ask of him. "You may be sure he was businessman enough to reserve supplies to put off his day of folding up booths and packing empty jars until later on in the month of pilgrimage."

"No, not much comfort," he says, the emerald in his ear winking with religious jealousy.

Is it better to suppress from this writing what happened when I heard our host say, "Cursed whelp of desert bitches," as he saw us out and ordered his boy to clean up our mess?

I wanted to make him take that saying back at sword point, but Malik and Mutammim were too full of their next plan for the night's entertainment and stopped me. Do not think by this suppression that I am or ever was a man who takes insults lightly. I've taken a belated revenge on every fat Syrian wine seller I've met since then: cut them neatly in half and exposed the fermented insides to grow sticky and attract flies upon the paving. I consider my hearers—and move on.

"O al-Harith." Malik had, by this time, noted the red kerchiefs blowing tantalizingly from the center poles of other nearby tents and made a new plan. "This stay in al-Hira might make a man of you."

Al-Harith flushed red to the rim of his ragged headcloth. Suwaid, his herdsman father, had not been able to scrape together the price of a bride for his son. Al-Harith was the only one of us four who at eighteen had neither a beard nor yet the bud of a harem. Marriage alliances are more important for the noble than for the common herdsman, and yet a man without a woman in the desert is tempting death and destitution. Sharif Nuwaira, as a charity just before he died, had made arrangements with another poor herdsman that instead of paying him a debt he would give his widowed daughter to al-Harith.

The woman, however, had died just before the wedding. Her malady was not known. But she had been al-Harith's senior by several years and precocious. It was rumored that she had betrayed her father by taking a lover, someone more dashing and attractive than simple al-Harith, and had conceived by him. Such a dishonor was best to get rid of sooner than to let the whole tribe learn about it in a few months' time. Even a poor herdsman has some family pride. The woman's father had paid the debt in camels instead, which satisfied Nuwaira, but in no wise could it satisfy al-Harith.

The women who called al-Harith their "strong, virile man" from beneath the flapping red kerchiefs now made him blush his beardless blush at Malik's teasing.

Mutammim had begun to sing a song of worldly love. Unlike his poetry, his singing was prone to triteness and at first, remembering the miracle of the woman by the well, I was as offended as al-Harith. Then, under the wine, Malik's triteness became, if not subliming, at least arousing.

> "A lady of wealth, chaste like an egg,
> I often ravished in her private tent—"

Malik's plan, after having introduced me to the mysteries of wine, was now to introduce al-Harith to the mysteries of women. And so it was from a blue banner to a red one that we weaved, staggered, sang our merry way.

Beneath the red kerchiefs meandered the string of low tents, each big enough, only, for a family of two. On their guy ropes and curtain edges roosted rows of doves, the Goddess's birds. The birds' low murmurs were indistinguishable from the murmurs that came from inside the closely drawn curtains. For no matter how late the hour, there were men for whom the pilgrimage of al-Hira would not be complete without this rite. Indeed, the power of the pilgrimage struck me here suddenly as it hadn't done before. I was young, and the mystery of life ending in smoking blood on the Encampment's pillars meant not nearly so much as the mystery of life's start here.

In the center, a single tent stood open. Beneath its kerchief, dropping like a dagger's shadow into the light, a single wick in an oil lamp attracted insects. Such lights the poets usually ascribe to night-watching desert monks, but practitioners of other forms of petition used them, too. On the low table with the lamp sat a number of small clay idols in very suggestive poses, around which curled the heavy, choking smoke of frankincense from a brazier.

And, like the idols grown large, the better to receive mortals' worship, two women danced to the driving beat of a drum played by a third. The women wore very little over the sweat sheen raised by the hot, humid night. Strips of white translucent linen hung from their shoulders down front and back almost to jangling bracelets about each ankle. The garments were slashed open at the sides. Heavy, low-slung belts of bells caught the linen briefly in the middle and emphasized the deep, grinding, almost too-slow rolls of hips in the dance.

The women did veil their faces, however, as priestesses, as the Goddess—the demon Goddess—was said to have done when she descended into the underworld to save mankind. This is the origin of all our women's veils, some say, revealing to the profane only the breathtaking mystery of dark eyes and brows. My mouth went dry as my heart lurched to meet the drum's rhythm. That sound thrust its way through every nearby tent: men's grunts and women's high peals of passion took up the same beat.

Being in the lead of our small band—Malik helping Mutammim along and al-Harith most reticent of all—I had stepped into the opening first. For a moment, I stood there alone. Hips first, one of the dancers glided up to me, closer than was comfortable, and grasped my hand.

"Come to worship the Goddess, O son of the desert?" she crooned. The breath from her unseen lips stirred the veil. "Come to make your pilgrimage complete?"

The scent of cloves came from her breath. Heavy black kohl ringed the glinting beauty of her eyes.

It made them, in the yellow light, seem sunken like the sockets of a skull, the conception of life in the midst of an image of death. The henna on her hands made them appear heavy, hot, engorged.

She dragged my hand within the slit of her linen just above the bells, holding it there on her moist skin, all the while continuing the movements of her dance—

"I will write no further," my scribe declares, throwing down his reed.

31

And it is lawful for you, besides, to seek as wives by means of your wealth those women whom you enjoy . . . Verily, God is All-Knowing, All-Wise.
—The Holy Quran, Surah 4:24

My memories shattered by my scribe's tantrum, I find myself back in this tired old body in this garden of retirement. "What is your difficulty," I ask him, "eunuch that you are?"

I am met by a barrage of such piety that I might as well have stayed at home in Mecca and listened to Cousin Omar.

"My own body betrayed me," I tell him. "What can I say? It was a lesson to me, if not to you, that if God is One, He is not a very moral divinity."

"But surely there were not such women? At a pilgrimage?"

"Of course there were. For all I know, they ply their trade there yet."

"Not in Mecca."

"Perhaps not. Not now, not under Omar. But they did."

"'The whore and the whoremonger—' the Quran says. 'Scourge each of them with an hundred stripes.'"

"So much for the compassion of God," I smirk.

"'And let not compassion keep you from carrying out the sentence of God, if you believe in God and the last day.'"

"Yes, Omar did charge out of his house one day, whip in hand, reciting that. He declared if he discovered any man had contracted a temporary marriage with such women, he would personally see him stoned to death."

My scribe sighs with relief.

"But these aren't—or weren't—whores," I insist. "We married them properly—for a time. An hour, maybe. A day. More, on merchant journeys."

"But men don't call such a contract a—a marriage."

"Well, that's what we called it. One of the four permitted forms of marriage during the Time of Ignorance, as A'ishah, the Prophet's wife, declared herself. There were rules. The duration of the contract had to be stipulated. You had to pay a bride price."

"A pander's fee."

"Call it what you like, but it doesn't show the ladies the respect we felt for them."

"Respect!" He sputters with indignation.

"Of course respect. Even a little fear. They represented the Goddess, after all. And could, we believed, grant or withhold fertility, just as she did."

"Why, society would fall apart without proper marriage, without a system to raise the children."

"But there was a system." I look up through the trees, the fronds' shadows making shapes of things that are past. "My good friend Amr ibn al-Asi was the product of such a union, and he got raised. Well enough to conquer Egypt. You had to leave your name with the women, of course, and they made a note of it, as part of the legal contract. They would come looking for you through all the desert if a child did result. You agreed then, in the heat of passion, to be the infant's support. I do suspect, having control of fertility as these women did, they had the means to let no child come where the man didn't seem worth their while."

My scribe persists. "They knew no husbands, these demon-servers."

"Of course they did. They gathered twenty bride prices in a day. As the Prophet—blessed be he—used to say, 'Don't put your private parts where you don't feel safe putting your dirhams.'"

"God's precious blessings on him, he never—"

"Of course he did. I heard him with my own ears." That keeps him quiet. "Yes, these women gathered fatherless children about their tents, children with similar abundance and diversity—black, brown, and fair, all calling one another siblings. The mother's own tribe, her own varied brothers, claimed and protected these children. They were proud, in fact, to take on the burden. Sheer numbers of offspring gotten by these means indicated what good effect such worship might have upon one's flocks or fields. And some of the brothers, too, would dress the part of the Goddess. For those of the devout who prefer such things."

"God must curse such a world."

"And yet He didn't." A bird preens in the fronds and then flies down to feed. A hoopoe, his crest at rest, unalarmed. "Muhammad himself—"

"The Prophet, blessed be he, never—"

"No, he himself did not indulge. Not that I know of. He had plenty of wives, after all. He was allowed more than the four he let the rest of us have."

If my scribe had a feathered crest, it would rise in anger. I let him squirm at the wistfulness in my voice before I continue. "But I do remember the time he came with a number of followers to make the lesser pilgrimage, and the priestesses of Mecca got themselves all dressed up for the occasion. His followers complained that they were lonely. They had left their wives home in al-Medinah—so Muhammad allowed it. And what of the merchant, traveling with his caravan to strange places for months on end? Would you have him live in sin, just to earn his bread?"

"I won't believe it."

"You are a eunuch, my friend. The God you—and Omar—imagine must be like that, too, not the real God of this real, vital world."

"I still don't believe it."

"But the Quran says—"

"'An hundred stripes,' as I've quoted."

I fold my hands over my old man's paunch and say mildly, "The Surah on Women. Twenty-fifth verse or so."

He scrambles among his parchments to consult his sacred text. But I begin to recite before he's found the spot.

"'And it is lawful for you, besides, to seek as wives by means of your wealth those women whom you enjoy. Give those women their appointed wages; it is no fault in you in mutually agreeing after fulfillment of the wage. Verily, God is All-Knowing, All-Wise.'"

He has found the place now, and he begins to read, just to show me how my mind fails—"'And it is lawful for you, besides—'"

He stops and looks up at me with a face full of such horror that I cannot stifle a laugh. "The written word, my friend, will betray you sooner than the mind. Haven't I told you I don't trust it?"

"There must be some explanation. Some wise man, wiser than I, can offer some explanation."

"Oh, I have no doubt there will come interpreters to put a thousand faces on such a thing, to preach their thousand interpretations from a thousand pulpits. Yes, even to send young men off to die for their interpretations. God knows, I was one of those young men—once. And God knows I didn't die. Yes, go and find your wise mullah this very moment—"

He goes.

Alone in the garden, I say, with only birds to hear, "But I was there when that verse was revealed. I know what it refers to."

When my scribe returns, he gives me a long, pious speech to which I listen—doze off—and listen some more.

"Fine," I tell him when he seems ready to run out of camel-dung fuel. "You may run your castrated life according to that fashion. You may even write this all down in a nice treatise if you want. But this is my life I'm paying you for at the moment, and you interrupted me in one of the more exciting parts. I don't know if that can be forgiven."

"I won't write lasciviousness," he says with a pout, like some spoiled brat. In truth, I suspect, in his condition he's only jealous.

"What is lascivious?" I am nearing the end of my patience, and I never had much of that. "I didn't marry a woman. Not that night, at any rate. Although I did at other times, other pilgrimages. You may have forgotten the vision of my woman by the well, but I had not. Besides—"

"But think for whom you write this. Writing is not like simple spoken words. Anyone can read or have it read to them. You must burn these pages to stop the spread, not just look over your shoulder and hope for the wind to blow them away. Think who might read this."

And I think. She comes to me, the image of a girl with tousled hair asleep on a rug. She is too young to be my daughter. And no doubt just a dream. But I press the story on.

Rayah dreamed about the Conqueror in the cool of his garden. Then she realized where she really was, on the carpet in Sitt Sameh's room, and that the eunuch was gently lifting her up into his arms. Auntie Adilah had come to get her, and she and Sitt Sameh were speaking quietly together. Rayah pretended still to sleep, the better to hear what they would say.

"Thank you, Sitt, but I think I will pass on your potion this time."

"Thank the Gods, your flux has ceased then?"

"Yes, and I have that sleeping child to thank, if not the Merciful One. She blew in my face, countering the ill khamsin, and brought me again to health."

Sitt Sameh had nothing to say to that, so the great male chest beneath Rayah shifted to carry her from the room with Adilah following after.

Perhaps it was another dream, but after a while she did hear Sitt Sameh in her desert accents murmur, "So she does have such gifts, my daughter, and cannot deny them. She will help the world, but Goddess help her."

The words echoed in Rayah's mind still as she awoke to another prod from Adilah, which seemed only moments later. They echoed as she scurried to help the aunties set out the breakfast before another scorching Ramadhan day should break and as she listened in the pre-dawn to more of the eunuch's reading.

"Khalid!" Malik chided as he entered the tent, Mutammim on his arm, to find my hand on the priestess's slick hip. "We haven't money left to pay bride price for you as well."

"And there are only three of us unoccupied," said the woman, gesturing toward her comrades, but all the while keeping a keen count of how many heads entered her tent. "Someone would have to wait." The way she kept my hand fast to her skin told me she did hope that someone wasn't me. "Or two of you may marry one, if you like, but that does cost you double."

"Only al-Harith," Malik insisted, shoving him forward. "To make a man of him."

The woman nodded, beginning to see how things were. Thank Hubal, she'd stopped grinding her hips into mine. "Five dirhams," she announced.

"What?" Malik exclaimed.

Even I choked a little. Who would have thought that such a simple service could demand such an exaggerated price? I'd heard a handful of dates or a worn cloak was often all the price a man needed—particularly if he was a young, well-favored man.

"I thought the traditional price was a tent and a spear."

"So it is, although I don't appreciate being told what the traditions of my cult are," the woman said with a narrowing of the splendid eyes above her veil.

I couldn't help myself. I had to plant a kiss to the edge of one of those fine eyes. She didn't even blink.

"I could buy a tent and spear for one dirham," Malik said, the wine slowing his bargaining powers.

"Not now, not with the shops closed. And I see you don't carry such things with you. The size of tent I want, after a long day, would make you bend double."

She didn't have to hold my hand on her hip to make it stick now. The "bend double" gave opportunity for a very suggestive movement in Malik's direction. Mutammim, lacking eyes to be enticed this way, found the drum and shimmering bells more than enough. Only al-Harith continued to hang back, and he was the most silent of all.

"In silver, it's more," the woman said, just to remind him we were bargaining a marriage here. "The Goddess likes imagery—the spear and the tent, the sword and the well. The imagery isn't there in coin. That's why it's more."

"Oh," Malik said, as if he believed her. "We'll give you ten, then."

I knew he didn't have more than ten and some odd coppers left in his pouch. And the price was supposed to go down, not up.

"Ten," the woman said. "And the time—an hour, by that hourglass there."

"No, all night," Malik demanded. "Give the poor fellow a proper wedding night."

"Perhaps we should give this up," Mutammim suggested at his brother's side. This bargaining ploy might make the woman think she could lose us altogether. Or perhaps the wine was about to put our poet to sleep.

Although the rest of us had come to doubt the wisdom, if not the good business, of the plan, it had become a point of pride with Malik to see this initiation accomplished. No one had more doubts than al-Harith. Poor herdsman. He had now met the ladies face to face, seen their strength of character.

The woman had pity—or pretended to. "Very well, until a black thread can be distinguished from a white one."

I had no idea how far the night had progressed myself. There might be only an hour of darkness remaining—or less.

Who would have thought that a tent full of simple women, unguarded by men, should refuse to be bargained down? Instead of their succumbing to our manly prowess, we at length succumbed to their womanly wiles. Now, I ask you, who is the God there?

"So which one of you is it to be?" she asked.

I think she could tell. She'd initiated young men before, and the fact that al-Harith still hadn't stepped beyond the shadows must have given her plenty of hint. But before Malik could give up his hand on Mutammim's shoulder for the other companion he had to lead in, the woman turned back on me with a wrath as startling as it was divine.

"And as for you," she said, "as for you who touch virtuous women, kiss them without the proper *rites of marriage. You don't want me. You want—a spell. You are under a spell already. A counterspell. A spell to conjure—someone. Another. Who? Ah—give me her name and the rest of your coins, and I'll work one for you."*

It was too keen an insight, too jinn-touched, too close. She could give me a spell that would help me find this girl from the well—even nameless, perhaps. At that moment, I would have died for that spell. I certainly sobered.

But sober, I couldn't think how to explain, not in the presence of my milk brothers. And I didn't know her name. I would come in the morning, alone, with coin of my own, less limited. It was, after all, the pilgrimage. And pilgrimage has its rites.

Malik shoved me one direction, al-Harith in another. The young herdsman disappeared around the curtain as if he were going to his death, and an ignominious death at that.

The women left behind had a pleasant little song they began as they added more incense to the brazier: "This deed, well-performed, will swell herds with fertility." Pleasant little laughs.

So the three of us—Malik, Mutammim, and I—left, trusting the priestesses to a full knowledge of their creed. Trusting I would return soon with coin of my own.

32

**What's left to lean together with, longing against,
When life's outlines get swept away?**
—the Qasidah of Imru'l-Qays

"Come dawn, the butter skin began its song in my milk mother's tent again. *Ghru-grug, ghru-grug*. Like the first Surah, like a poet's refrain."

Having recited the first Surah in her dawn prayer, Rayah thought of it now as she listened to the scribe Abd Allah read his master's words. Birds, God's faithful creatures, had greeted the dawn with similar praise, a brown-and-black pied hoopoe among them with his far-carrying "Poe-poe-poe." And she'd thought, instead of divinity, of the hoopoe in the Conqueror's garden in Homs and of the fronds making shapes over his head.

The eunuch read on. "'The matter,' my milk mother said to us as she swung the skin, 'hangs on Adi's Hind.'

"'Our dealings in the market were something of a disappointment yesterday,' Mutammim said.

"'Must you remind us?' Malik sighed.

"'Ten dirhams for the good golden she-camel,' Mutammim persisted, shaking his head. 'We got three times that last year for her mother who, by al-Uzza, was an older and weaker animal.'

"'The matter,' my milk mother said again, 'hangs on Adi's Hind.'"

"And so, indeed, it did." Sitt Sameh paused her spinning for a moment to interrupt the scribe. "The Conqueror's milk mother was right. But before you read more, ustadh, let me return to my own mother, to Bint Zura, for she, too, learned much on this subject of Adi and his Hind."

"Although my master never said, I always suspected that is at least one reason why he had me write his tale. So you would tell yours."

Sitt Sameh nodded and picked up the spindle again, speaking to its rhythm. "I'd left Bint Zura beside the saddler's tent, having just had a vision of her mother—driven from her at birth—appear, then just as suddenly disappear. Even as she stood staring at nothing, the sons of Taghlib, her tribesmen, came from their poetry contest. They collected her, scolding. Rather than taking her to their tents and to her camel az-Zuharah, they insisted that she go back to her father and the future he had planned for her.

"'But he is possessed of a jinni,' she protested.

"'Nonsense,' they said. 'It is the Holy Spirit that has possessed him since the coming of Bishop Ahudammah.'

"Interesting." Sitt Sameh interjected the comment in the middle of her story. "The old poet, Abu'l Ghul, alone stood up for her."

"How should that be?" Abd Allah asked.

"He knew whence inspiration comes," Sitt Sameh said. "'It may be that the Gods have a different fate in store for her,' he said."

"In those days," Abd Allah nodded, "a man's tribe had more to do with the Gods' acceptance, even when most of his kinsmen were baptized."

Sitt Sameh went on.

In spite of the fact that he was a tribesman and had just held his own in the battle of words against their dreaded enemies, the Tamimi, the old poet's opinion was overruled. His victory had not been as decisive as one would expect from a seer of his gray hairs. Perhaps he was losing his gift. Perhaps the jinn meant to grant it to another.

As Bint Zura followed her kinsmen back to the church, reluctantly dragging her feet, she did happen on two people who showed that her fate, indeed, might be different. The first was her friend Layla bint al-Minhal of the Iyad whom she had hoped to find at the pilgrimage. Layla was such a plump, pretty, merry girl. Walking together but still toward the church, they had been handed palm fronds by Bint Zura's kinsmen in honor of the day.

"I would like to come to your tent tonight," Bint Zura told her friend.

"But of course."

"They—" Bint Zura tossed her head with a clink of the cowrie shells on her veil toward their escort. "They want to put me in a garden where I cannot keep az-Zuharah."

"You would be welcome to the tents of the sons of Iyad," Layla assured her.

Then, before Bint Zura could turn their path, they came upon her father. Nearly naked, he was dancing around the rim of a well chanting in a deep, hollow voice. Bishop Ahudammah was trying, in vain, to get him down and back into his black robes. A crowd of pilgrims had already been drawn to the sight. Some knelt, asking for the spirit-possessed blessing. But even those wearing the blood of sacrifice from the stones of as-Sabad did not laugh.

"Let's go another way," Bint Zura said, grabbing her friend's arm.

But that was when her father saw her. His body grew rigid on unsteady legs. "What have I to do with you, O daughter of a kahinah?" he said. Then, pointing one bony finger at the end of a bony arm, in a voice that wasn't his, he shouted, "Behold, the coming salvation of the Arabs."

A bolt of lightning seemed to run through her from that finger, having first transfixed the unknown man in front of her. The stranger felt it too and turned—their eyes met. She saw it was the pockmarked son of Tamim again, from the poet's battle. Hastily, she looked away, almost forgetting her father for a moment. Or feeling herself torn between the two men. She could sense the stranger following even when she didn't look back, even with the company of her kinsmen.

In the end the church seemed the best, closest haven. There, four strong men in black brought her father and held him down on the stone floor so he couldn't run off again. There, Ahudammah, calling loudly on the name of Isa, tried to tame the demon with the Christians' blessed bread and wine while the congregation knelt, prayed, and sang. Mostly, Zura's thrashings spilled a lot of wine that matted his hair and beard like blood.

"Poor man," Layla murmured, touching her own desert amulets against evil as the people around them made the sign of the cross. "Can you do nothing to help him, Bint Zura?"

"Nothing. My mother put the curse on him. He must make his peace with her to get it removed."

"But you said the curse arose this time when he saw you, not her."

Layla was right, but Bint Zura didn't like to admit guilt for something she never meant. She had spent all her life trying to hide the fact that she had any power.

"Besides, a knowledge of such things may descend from mother to daughter," Layla insisted. "It is well known."

"Even when I have never met my mother?" Bint Zura said nothing to her friend about the old woman behind the saddler's tent who claimed to be—no, who must be—her mother.

"Maybe." Layla shrugged.

"It is when he is well that they want to sprinkle me with water and lock me away from az-Zuharah," Bint Zura complained.

Layla nodded sympathetically. "But you are not telling me you don't have some idea of what must be done to help him."

Zura's screams echoed now within the church's hollow ribs. Lamp lights writhed on their wicks and every brown eye glared at Bint Zura from every golden icon box. Tears of anguish had begun to flow down her cheeks, and she wiped at them with her veil. Her mother had done so little to raise her. What did she owe her, after all?

"I know a plant that grows in the desert," she said. "Perhaps it—"

"There." Layla whispered, for some of the chanters were turning to scowl at them. "I knew something would inspire you."

"I know where this plant grows in our dirah, where I usually herd our camels. I don't know where it grows around al-Hira."

"What is its name?"

"Baaras, for its flaming color. A kind of rue."

"But I know a vale where it grows."

"Near here?"

Layla nodded. "The sons of Iyad almost camped there when we first arrived at the pilgrimage, until someone pointed out the shrub, grown nearly as large as a fig tree, and said we ought to move. To step on the plant unwittingly in the dark is to invite the very possession its root can be used to cure."

"Come. Show me." Bint Zura grabbed her friend's arm and steered her through the kneeling crowd, away from the sounds of a tortured jinni toward the door once more.

They entered the cool of the evening air. Bint Zura held her friend back without a word for a moment on the steps as she saw the retreating back of the son of Tamim, his lovelocks lifting from his shoulders in the breeze. The man whose fate a jinni speaking with her father's tongue had bound up with her own.

"It may be that the spirit tormenting my father does him good as well as evil," she said, following where Layla led through al-Hira's lengthening shadows. "Or the world good, perhaps. It does keep me from the garden."

"If you know how to get the herb without ill effect, you must use it. He is your father," Layla insisted.

And so they got the herb and drove the demon from Zura that very evening.

33

How oft, by God's will, has a small force vanquished a large one?
—The Holy Quran, Surah 2:250

Sitt Sameh picked up her spinning once more and encouraged the eunuch scribe to pick up his parchments.

That's all she's going to say about the cure? Rayah wanted to scream, but she held her tongue.

"Where was I? Oh, yes." Abd Allah read the Conqueror's words: "'The matter,' my milk mother said again, 'hangs on Adi's Hind.'"

Again Sitt Sameh stopped him. "Oh, but I forgot to mention Adi's Hind at all, didn't I? Yes, that comes next."

Rayah could hold her tongue no longer. "But how did Bint Zura—my grandmother, God rest her—how did she take up the herb and cure her father? What is the plant and where does one find it?"

Sitt Sameh's eyes met hers sharply. Rayah had to look away. It was no use pretending why she wanted to know. The silent jinni of Ghusoon's suffering still lingered in the darker corners of this room, the evil spirit that made Rayah's young friend immobile with dread at her upcoming marriage. What mattered whether Rayah tried to wipe the direction her thoughts wandered or not? Nothing could be hidden from her mother's keen blue eyes.

Then, just as if she hadn't guessed the purpose of the question, Sitt Sameh told the tale in every detail. Rayah scrambled in her mind to pick up the pieces as they were tossed to her—shoving, she feared, some memorized Surahs to one side in her scramble to store it all. But the Holy Quran, after all and thank God, was written down. This knowledge was not.

Sitt Sameh concluded: "So she brought the root fixed in the iron ring back to the church just before midnight when, they say, 'Christ is risen.' When, they say, the Ones of Fire have most power."

They also say it was the risen Messiah who healed Zura ibn Taghlib just at the time of Isa's rising. But his daughter knew she was the one who undid what her mother had done. She was the one who pushed past the four burly monks still holding him on the floor to press ring and root to his nose.

"Ah, good," Ahudammah said. "Here is the girl we must bring to the waters of baptism."

And he turned to a basin he had nearby.

Even as he did, a shudder ran the nearly naked length of Zura ibn Taghlib, a shudder so violent it threw all four monks off. The freed Zura broke through a screen of icons and ran to the altar, clinging to it as if he didn't dare or couldn't let go.

"Alas, why do you wish to be rid of me?" cried a voice. It came from Zura's grimacing lips, but its tones were those of a woman in travail. "I who have been your lover all these years, ever since the blowing sands of ad-Dahna, closer than your heart."

"Mother?" Bint Zura stammered, staggering back. A mist thicker, darker than the already thick incense collected around her father's mouth, winding in his beard and mustache. Gold-boxed icons rocked to the floor and lamps trailed out golden oil as he continued to cling.

One long, last wail—"Alas!"—and the mist shot toward the dark night.

It tumbled the baptismal basin to the stone floor, spilling the water all over the skirts of Ahudammah's robe as it passed. Water wasted in the desert when the oil spilled on the altar cloth suddenly leapt to life—

With a sigh and a great groan, Zura fell back from the flames, his arms like Isa ibn Maryam's on the cross. Bishop and monks hurried to smother the flames, then to help him rise. He was as weak as a kitten and wanted only to sleep. But he was himself. Himself, womanless, without an adversary. Sterile.

Water wasted to the desert stones spared Bint Zura baptism that night. It did not spare her the Nazarene nuns' garden, however. There they took her, very late, when their rites in the church were over, having parted her from Layla.

"I am Hind, the mother of this house." The woman who greeted them at the gate introduced herself.

The word "Mother" had always sent a prickle of longing across Bint Zura's shoulders and up to her eyes, having felt the lack of such a person all her life. She bristled, however, at the thought of anyone claiming that relationship who did not deserve it. "Aunt," perhaps, "Mother's sister," but not this.

The white veils the woman wore let not a finger's width of flesh show. Whether she was old or young, it was impossible for Bint Zura to tell, except that her voice, by its muffled tones, sounded unused, ancient.

"I am sorry we woke you so late at night," Bint Zura said when the two of them were left alone. She half hoped that disturbed sleep might make the woman say: "Go away. Come back at a more suitable hour," giving Bint Zura time to think of a way to get back to her tent and az-Zuharah.

"Not at all," the dusty voice said from amid the folds of fabric. "I sleep very little, lending my voice to prayer at night, when the world most needs it." She seemed kind, though this lack of sleep was bizarre enough. Would Bint Zura also have to pray all night in this garden?

She could smell it all around her now, the growing things in soil that wasn't sand. It was too dark to see, however, as Hind led with the eyes of a bat over familiar ground.

Then Bint Zura had to ask her hostess: "Hind? You said your name was Hind? Adi's Hind?"

The rumor had run through every harem in the Encampment. While the men had seen and spoken of an-Numan going off to see the Padishah in Ctesiphon wrapped in his shroud and of his armor left behind, the women spoke rather of this.

The flow of fabric in front of her suddenly dammed itself up and Bint Zura knew it was true, although Mother Hind presently said: "I have forgotten the name of Adi and remember only Isa ibn Maryam as my Lord."

Now Sitt Sameh, spinning in her upper room, seemed to have run suddenly into a dam herself, as if her mind had wandered, or as if she were ready to hand the story back to Abd Allah and his parchments. She set aside her wool and took an earthenware jar from the assortment against her wall, beneath which the Goddess idols hid. She lifted off the lid and sniffed the opening. The ring she wore in her nose chinked against the baked clay. A dry, lemony fragrance reached as far as Rayah where she sat watching, legs folded under her, on the rug.

"Is that the herb my grandmother gathered in the desert to drive the demon from her father?" Rayah asked.

Sitt Sameh looked up and smiled, the expression reaching even to the blue eyes. "No. It's a sort of artemisia, southernwood. The herb her mother had set, tied in the knots of a cord, under the saddle cloth of young Khalid ibn al-Walīd as he paced at the poets' battle. An herb that would draw that Tamimi's foster son from his home in Mecca to his fate with her abandoned daughter."

And that was the end of the stories until the blessed cool should come again.

Although the khamsin had settled, the wind had left not a petal to any of the lilies and roses in the court that were usually Cousin Demiella's pride and joy. Instead, Rayah begged a scrap of red silk gone to pink through its incarnations as a woman's gown, then underdress, then something smaller for Bushra. Through that long afternoon when it seemed impossible to move, Rayah twisted the fabric into three budding roses, knotting them together with a bit of green thread.

With this posy, Rayah made her way, through alleys and over rooftops, to Ghusoon's house.

It was considered a good deed to visit not only the dead in their silent towers across the valley but also the afflicted during the holy month. Rayah knew no one more afflicted than the girl a jinni had possessed the moment her father promised her to an old man with bad teeth. All the same, she hoped time and the holiness of the month—the doors locked against the jinn—might have worked a cure. Then she could go back home and not worry about this any more.

"You'd as well have gone to visit the dead again, God rest them," Ghusoon's stepmother greeted her. "She doesn't eat—even after dark. She doesn't speak. Just lies there with the evil spirit pressing the life out of her."

Rayah saw it was true. She knelt on the floor beside the low bed in the darkened room and offered her silk flowers to the shallowly breathing form. When this got no reaction, she set the flowers aside upon a low table and picked up one inert hand.

"It's hard, I know," Rayah whispered, hearing the tears in her own voice.

Sitt Sameh would not cure this girl, which was as much as to let her die. Rayah could not let that happen, a girl so much like herself. She didn't have the root, but she knew how. Knowledge wasn't enough, however. There had to be the gift. Did she, Rayah, the daughter of the desert woman, have this gift?

The little light coming from the doorway was suddenly blocked, and a fierce tirade began: "What, have you come to comfort my daughter? The bitch. She won't marry my good friend? We'll see about that."

Rayah recoiled against the wall as the big man with a beard like camel thorn took two more steps into the room. Ghusoon's father, Rayah assumed. She wanted to take back her hand to protect herself from possible blows but, feeling a sudden, begging pressure from the girl, she took a breath and did not.

"I suppose you're just like her—like all girls—full of lust that must be curbed with a good whipping. Like balking donkeys."

"I beg pardon, sir," Rayah stammered. "I only thought—"

"But that's just the thing. Girls don't think. They just feel. Beat them until they go numb and can think for a change. Think about feeding their children. About making a decent, comfortable life for their future instead of love. Can you eat love, I ask you?"

"That may be as it may be." Reacting to the pressure on her hand brought a stiffness to Rayah's own form. She edged away from the wall to kneel more upright—and did not let go of the hand.

"Oh, right. Look at you. Evil eyes, the eyes of a demon. I wouldn't be surprised if you encouraged my daughter's behavior. That you caused her possession, with eyes like that."

"My eyes are God's will." Rayah felt a sudden surge of power as she said these words, words that took the responsibility out of her hands and submitted them into Another's, greater than hers.

"She will marry Sharif Diya al-Din, I say. It is *my* will."

"No, sir. All things are God's will."

"Do you contradict me?" The big hand raised.

Rayah did not back down. "You will not get her married until after the fast is past, in any case. And after that—it's God's will."

"I will be master in my own house."

"Inshallah. Still, there is one Master over us all."

"She will, I say, the bitch."

"Inshallah. If God wills."

Such power in that word that seemed to give all power to Another. The man's fist did not fall, either on Rayah or on the girl whose hand she held. Finally, with a snort, he left the room.

When he had gone, Rayah persuaded Ghusoon to drink a little water. Because she was sick, she did not need to keep the fast. That was the first drink, the stepmother said, that the girl had had in days, despite all the heat and wind.

"I'll be back, Ghusoon," Rayah whispered to the girl when finally she rose to go. "And it will be as God wills."

Inshallah. Not only her blue eyes. The power that had come through her hand to heal Bushra, from her lips to heal Auntie Adilah, both were God's will as well. And who was she to go against the All-Merciful?

34

> At eventide she lightens the black shadows
> as if she were the lamp kindled in the night
> by a monk at his devotions.
> —The Qasidah of Imru'l-Qays

"And now I will relate to you the story of my red turban," I tell my scribe. I take the thing off and run my hands, trembling, over its worn folds.

"Now?" he demands. "Now, in the midst of wine sellers and whores?" He is angry, betrayed. He seems ready to throw the reed from him in disgust again, this time for telling what last time I would not tell.

"Wait and see," I say to him. "Wait and see."

A breeze rattles in the fronds overhead and a single rose petal just the color this turban once was drifts down to float in a quiet corner of the fountain. Like a clot of blood.

In al-Hira that night, Malik continued in his rare, roiling mood. He consulted his slack coin pouch as if it might have gained more weight by magic. With the wine still in his blood, he declared to the night sky over al-Hira, "I've been cheated."

Mutammim with his blindness fared better in the dark, allowing his brother to lean on him. The wine hadn't helped him, either, however. And I, my blood and sense likewise wine-thinned, let Malik convince me he was right.

"Help me think, fellows. How shall we even the score? Extract revenge of this old Encampment?"

Then Malik stopped in his stumbling tracks and caught both of us to him by the elbows. He was suddenly silent and, if not quite sober, at least very serious.

"What is it, O Malik my brother?" I giggled.

"Did you not hear the gossip in the market today, O my brothers?" he asked us.

"What gossip?" I was unable to open my mouth without giggling, even though I could tell full well that the time for silliness was past.

"About the most beautiful princess in all al-Hira."

"Who's that?" I asked.

But Mutammim knew the answer at once. His voice was the echo of his mother's. "Adi's Hind."

The moon was high, just past the full, indicating the holy month. It caught ridges and corners of the darkened town with a soft white light. It might have conjured the souls of the houses and palms to rise from their dull, everyday slumbering in mud to soar with it in dreams of ethereal wonder. The girl by the well came to me. With that memory, my spirit was suddenly filled with light, too, caught up by the edges where only dulling wine had been. I wanted to be left alone to this dream of higher things . . .

But Malik persisted. "We must find Adi's Hind."

"Adi's Hind," I said, "has forsworn the company of men."

There was anger in my voice, first at Malik's repeated interruption of my dream and, second, to cover the panic I felt. As we were speaking of al-Hira's beauties, my tongue might stumble and betray she whom I knew to be the most beautiful of all. And I could not, must not sully her with such company.

"Do you know what a 'convent' is?" Malik asked.

"Yes, of course," I snapped. "It is a house for such as Hind bint an-Numan who would forswear all men."

"No men are allowed within," Malik instructed me. "It is a monstrosity of a household, all women, unprotected, unchaperoned. Many are committed to the convent while they are but girls and remain forever virgins. You can see them passing in town on their way to their churches—veiled from head to toe. Their hands know no heavy work, their skin no touch of the burning sun. They sit in the shade of their gardens by cool fountains all day at their prayers. If that is not a flaunted temptation to rip away mystery, I don't know what is."

By God, Muhammad, blessed be he, never described Paradise half so invitingly, so worth death to attain, as Malik described a convent that night.

"Shall we not climb these walls and find a lovely, lonely Hind or two for each of us with never a copper coin spent?" Malik concluded his preachment.

Yet "Have you no fear of their God?" I protested. The moon's divining influence was upon me.

"None," insisted Malik. His tone was enough as to say, "I shall relieve myself on the sacred stone of this God when I shall find Him."

"The women might be guarded," I tried again. "The Taghlibi are Christians. They might resent it and come with more than poetry this time."

"These are women who have forsworn men. Who wastes his energy to guard such women?"

My brother's heavy, wine-bearing breath was right in my face and served as another draught of cheap drink, a cry of "Coward" to dull my moon-enlivened soul. Before I thought clearly again, I was boosting my milk brothers over a convent wall and being hoisted up after them.

We landed in the soft, newly cultivated and dew-moistened earth. Melon vines strung over it; overhead palms would shelter them from sun come the day. Tomorrow's blossoms folded into buds: the white hands of a girl beneath her cheek, smoothed by an innocent and peaceful sleep.

Mutammim's feet tangled in the tendrils. He fell headlong across the plants. He came up unhurt, in fits of silly giggles.

The plants did not fare so well. They had shrunk, the breath of life forced from them in one gasp. They had grown yellow, too, beneath the moonlight, and brittle like an old woman's hands. All in an instant, they had become as herbs in the inner desert after a fierce and lasting drought.

I stood and stared at the wantonness of this destruction. For a man of the desert, any garden has something of the miraculous. The very word "garden" contains in its roots every connotation of Paradise, and this garden was above the ordinary use of words. A nightingale exchanged verses of wordless poetry with an invisible fountain. The air sighed under the heavy, sweet burden of herbs: lovage, rosemary, thyme. Fragile jasmine. Sharp citrus.

Everywhere, in every nook and cranny, between rocks as well as from the dark and mounded earth of carefully spaded beds, multitudes of plants grew. They grew without compulsion, responding to the women's hands—just as a lover cannot do enough for the beloved. He feels himself slighted if she thinks of no impossible tasks for him to accomplish in a day. The plants of this garden loved to grow, loved the life that let them send roots down into the soil and luxurious foliage into the well-sheltered air.

It is a mystery and a wonder among Christians that three are equal to one. I will never come to see that reason. This place, however, demanded similar faith.

The house was just an ordinary house Hind had inherited from her mother's side of the family. But within this house, these women were creating a sanctuary, a harem in the aspect of that word that means a sacred place the outside cannot profane.

"The coming salvation of the Arabs" entered my mind again by the light of the moon that made all life in the garden appear in ghostly spirit alone. I, gross of body, drunken of mind, how dared I to set foot in there?

I could not climb the wall again without a boost from my brothers. I had to follow the way Malik led to get out of the mangled melon patch and onto a path laid down in moon-white pebbles. Mutammim caught my arm for help to find his way and I, blind fool unable to help myself, stumbled on after him.

Men would have set a guard against the evils of the night and kept a watch fire burning. These women alone had not bothered, for they preferred to trust a single God of both day and night. Blessed be that single Merciful One Who did not betray them that trust. He Who sees everything touched a sleeping tongue with thirst that night.

She had been watching us for some time, perhaps ever since we had tumbled over the wall and into the bed of melons. I knew this because I felt her presence long before I actually saw her. How weak and clumsy were my eyes compared to the surety of my heart!

Then, at last, I did see her. I knew it was she, the young woman from the well, though the moon was at her back and her face in deep shadow. She had crouched down and was observing us through the railing of an upstairs balcony.

I said nothing of her presence to either of my milk brothers. My intrusion was blasphemous enough.

Her will was to do nothing for some time. Perhaps our appearance had so frightened her that she took a while to gather her wits in order to take action. More likely, she was proving me again, testing my faithfulness and my ability to respond to her messages of the spirit.

"The coming salvation of the Arabs" rang in my head, she its core. "I remember you, young Arab. Don't you remember me? Then why do you disappoint me so?"

"No, no," I tried to assure her.

And I must have muttered it aloud, for Mutammim, gripping my elbow, urged, "Come on, O Khalid. Show me the way."

Malik saw her only when she at last stood up. Or perhaps he heard the jangle of her bracelets when she began to move as any other woman would have done long before. "Aha," my milk brother said to us in the hush of a hunter who has spotted his ibex. "There is one now."

Malik found a staircase to the balcony. He began to take the stairs with careful movements; he had only climbed irregular mountainsides before.

Then the young woman began to run, anklets jangling. She pounded on the doors she passed and shouted alarm.

I hesitated, and Mutammim did because I did. Malik called back, "Don't worry, you two. They're only women. She's only waking up a pair for you."

I could have killed my milk brother then and there for his blasphemy. But the young woman had reached the end of the balcony, a dead end and a trap—except that it contained the convent's sematron with which they called to prayers. She picked up the mallet, gave it a great, arcing swing, and let it drop upon the suspended, hollowed palm trunk.

When Malik heard that wooden gong, echoing alarm over all the sleeping Encampment, he stopped his pursuit across the balcony and instantly sobered. I saw his face over the railing, white as spirit, white as stone, white as the moonlight had been making most other things for hours.

"By al-Uzza, let's get out of here," Mutammim urged, blindly grasping my elbow.

"By the three hundred and sixty gods of the Ka'ba, I think we may be too late," I replied.

Malik was down the stairs in a moment, shoving us on, but already we could hear the pound of horses' hooves, the shouts of men aroused outside the walls. A nun crossed the garden at a run to unlock the gate. Dressed in white, she stood out against the dark plainer than my woman in her desert black. Other nuns' cries unfurled through the night.

We made it back to the ravished melon bed. I boosted first Mutammim and then Malik up on the wall. Malik reached down a hand to me. I made a leap to catch it, but it moved. In a panic, my milk brother pointed over my head.

I turned and saw the shadow of a man no more than twenty paces from me. I had assumed the nuns' protectors would be men from al-Hira, settlers whose idea of self-defense was a high wall. If once that was breached, they were helpless. This fellow, young and powerful, balancing his spear for the throw in our direction, was a man of the desert. He was my equal if not my better in any combat. The feathers dangling from the shaft of his spear, the weave of his outer cloak: These told me in the first flash of recognition that he was a son of Taghlib even though it was too dark to see his green headband. I had no doubt he was one of those who had stood on the opposite side of the camel baggage in the street the day before. But a Taghlibi didn't need an excuse to kill a son of Tamim. Now that his God had graciously allowed one to fall into his hands, it would take him half as long.

The spear flew. It was meant for Malik's heart. I do not blame my brother for dropping off to safety and letting the spear sail by into the night. At least that weapon of long distance was spent without harm. But there I was left, my only escape cut off.

The Taghlibi was a larger man than I. Before reaching for my dagger, I tried my luck with my legs first. I scampered off through the gardens, leading him as the plow behind the bullock to harrow up the rows of radishes, spinach, and tender young lettuces.

My legs proved faster than his, but he had friends to call for aid. Whistled-up shadows appeared here, there. I jerked to avoid them. In no time at all, I found the wall of the house curbing my free run across the garden. I could not pass too many more pillars, turn too many more corners, before I'd find myself encircled and outnumbered.

A stone-carved water trough glinted in the moonlight. I determined to take its height for my advantage. I'd gain it and turn and fight as best as desperation could make me. Just as I took that decision, a hand reached out from a darkened doorway. It plucked at my sleeve.

35

> **The likeness for those who take to themselves guardians instead of God is the likeness of the spider who buildeth her a house: But verily, frailest of all houses surely is the house of the spider. Did they but know this!**
> **—The Holy Quran, Surah 29:41**

For one moment, every part of my being froze. Death himself was reaching for me in the house of my enemies, inviting me into his eternal abyss.

Then I knew it was not. I knew the hand was female. More than that, I knew it was hers.

"The very hand that called the alarm on you?" My scribe cannot write for panic. "What horror did she call you to now?"

"I really did not care."

"But she had called the alarm on you."

"On Malik and Mutammim, not on me. I trusted her implicitly."

"You trusted her, master? The Quran teaches us that he who puts his trust in any but the One God 'is the likeness of a spider who builds herself a house.' To be destroyed by the first passing wind."

A spider has built her web in the arms of a succulent plant arcing near my cushion in the garden. I consider the fragile tissue, pulsing in and out with a passing breath, as I say: "And surely the frailest of all houses is that of a spider, even to the dwellers in the wind-whipped hair tents. Yet there was the day when Muhammad, blessed be he, owed his life to just such an insignificant creature."

"You speak of the time he and Abu Bakr were escaping from their enemies and hid in a cave?"

"Of course. The Compassionate One sent the little creature to cover the break in the rock. Praise be to God, it did it so quickly that the enemies were certain nothing could have entered any time recently and passed on. There is a whole Surah devoted to telling the story." My scribe raises his pen, thinking of the best words to set down his version.

I stop him. "So you do not need to write it here. Were he not the Prophet of God, had Abu

Bakr not been there by his side to add his witness to the miracle, I would swear Muhammad stole the tale from me."

To avoid going in that direction, the scribe asks: "But what of the red turban, master?"

"Patience, boy. It's coming."

The woman from the well did indeed seem to be no more substantial a barrier than a spider swinging on a web of filigree moonlight. She shoved me down and into a black hole that I know not how to name but that it smelled of damp plaster and probably crawled with scorpions. Within this cave I did my best to silence my panting and my heart, which pounded like the sematron to my ears.

She stepped between me and the drawn dagger that appeared at the opening. I moved a foot to play the hero and drag her from harm's way. Only the spell of dumb security she had set upon me kept me from betraying the both of us. Then, while I looked out in awe, the blade stopped a mere span from her breast.

"Praise be to Isa al-Masih," I heard the Taghlibi say. "You were not harmed in this damnable intrusion, niece."

She must have smiled and made a gesture to assure him of the fact, for his next words presumed some communication although she did not speak. "Well," he said, "It simply convinces me of what I have felt all along: A man should never let his woman sleep anywhere but under his own roof until it be under her husband's. No matter what your father and his preachers may say in favor of the holy life for women as well as men. Your father is mad. The old ways are more secure.

"Accursed sons of Tamim." He spat into the night. "Damned litter of a mongrel bitch. Who'd guess even they'd be so base as to try such an attack upon our honor? Brother's daughter, let me but find the one left loose in this place. Let me spit this vermin upon my dagger, and I'll bring you safely to our own tent where you belong."

Here she must have communicated some wordless protest to him, for he said, "No, this time I will not let Zura your father talk me into changing my mind. You will come home with me tonight."

She spoke, not without some note of relief: "As you wish, O my uncle."

The man smiled, revealing a camel jut to his lower jaw. He sighed with contentment. "Was ever a man blessed so?" he asked himself aloud. I could have knocked the weapon from his hand as it came around her back in a fond embrace. I was covetous enough of that embrace to risk all our lives to do it. Thank the Merciful One, I refrained.

Thus satisfied, the Taghlibi and his dagger ran off to hunt for me elsewhere. If she were indeed, Manat forbid, that man's niece, I now knew enough about that woman to call her by at least one name: Bint Zura, daughter of Zura and of the Taghlib tribe.

Daughter of my milk brothers' hereditary enemies and of my own.

Bint Zura sighed and swallowed with relief. Then she stepped back into the cave. She stepped back onto my toe, which caused her twice the pain and surprise it caused me. So close, her scent enveloped me as if a spice merchant had just opened his sack beneath my nose: sweet and sharp and musky.

"Why are you here?" She nearly wept when she had caught her breath again.

Oh, how I loved the sound of her voice, like the flowing of rich waters over the stones of my mind!

I wanted her to speak and her alone, but I finally forced myself to reply, "You brought me here." I said it as gently as I could, trying not to disturb the sweetness her words had lent to the air. I loved to make my words feminine for her. "You stood as a spider on her web between me and your bloodthirsty uncle. You caused him to think that no one had disturbed this place in ages."

"But you should be gone," she insisted, close to tears. "Would you wait around for him to return and find you? I meant for you to be gone at once, up those stairs."

"Stairs?"

I had not realized there were any stairs behind me. I ignored them even after she pointed them out. I strained instead to see her face. All this time, since I'd first caught sight of her at the well, I had never glimpsed more than a curve of cheek, the point of her chin—those blue eyes. It hardly seemed fair. Either she kept her back to me, or she stayed in shadows, or the fall of her veil hid her. Did she do so on purpose, to provoke me?

Now she hurried past without reprieve to show me the stairs, to climb them before me, and to fling open the shutters of a small second-storey window at the top.

Bint Taghlib sighed as I slowly climbed the last two or three stairs to her side. My step and the way my gaze searched the darkness where she stood told her I had other interests besides the saving of my life. She sighed as a mother may, with exasperated patience at the child who will stop and look at pretty pebbles when a rapid migration is of the essence.

She refused me her face again by the ruse of looking out the window to the ground below. What she saw there challenged her determination. She turned back from the window and began to fumble with the clasps of her clothing in the dark.

By Hubal of my fathers, my thoughts reeled within me. Shall I have a virgin in a convent after all? Given to me of her own open generosity and free will . . . ?

But again I was a foolish child looking at pretty pebbles. She shoved the product of her fumbling into my hand. It was a length of fabric, generous in proportion, the red silk of an underdress.

"The window's too high," she said. "You would kill yourself. I will let you down."

I took my turn to peer out the window. It was not so high as all that, I wanted to proclaim with great manly courage and virile pride. Quite soberly, I was certain I could drop from the ledge with no more harm done than a broken ankle. Contrary to the cautions of womanish physicians of the settled lands, a man in desperation can run as far as he has to on a broken ankle. Bonesetters in the desert even encourage the exercise.

I wanted to do brave and wonderful things for her. The exchange was already weighted too heavily in my favor. Nevertheless, I swallowed my pride and took the further kindness of the underskirt she offered me. I showed her soft white hands—like folded melon blossoms—how to wrap the fabric about the central post in the window so they would not have to bear any more strain than necessary. Then I jumped to the sill, swung my legs out over the void and began my descent. Warmth from her body permeated the silk between my hands.

I had just passed the sturdy safety of the sill when I felt the first ripping jerk. Her hands did not betray me; they were as strong as they were small, used to hauling ropes at wells. It was the faithless *material of the underdress. I had meant my descent, this lingering contact with her, to be drawn out as long as possible. But now I hand-over-handed it as fast as ever I could. Still, when the final, total rip came, I fell no short way. The greater part of the underdress floated down like a rose petal in water after me. Like a clot of blood suspended in water.*

I ignored the shock to my legs. I sorted myself out of the folds of red silk and waved them to her, trying to think of a way to return them. But our stifled gasps as the fabric tore must have been heard, or our hurried conversation, or perhaps the fall itself. Or perhaps the man of Taghlib had only reached an empty cul-de-sac and returned to beat upon every doorway of the convent until he found me. For there was now a great row within, shrieking women and cursing men. The Taghlibi was being blamed with intrusion. Or had he discovered his sister without an underdress?

Outside the convent wall, just around the corner from my view, I heard the coughs and low murmurs of men, the stomp and nicker of their horses. The men keeping the Taghlibi mounts, missing the action, were restless and alert, ready to do anything to save their master's honor. I tucked Bint Zura's red silk dress up under my arm and ran for all I was worth in the other direction.

36

> In the Name of God, the Compassionate, the Merciful
> Have you not seen how your Lord dealt with the army of
> the elephant?
> Did He not cause their stratagem to miscarry?
> He sent against them birds in flocks . . .
> And He made them like stubble eaten down!
> —The Holy Quran, Surah 105

"You're certain, Sitt, you will not come with us?"

Rayah found it strange to hear Abd Allah speaking words of his own emotion. He actually wanted Sitt Sameh to leave her room and come out for the evening. Was this for Sitt Sameh's benefit? Or was he urging her to more efforts of maternal support as her daughter went to a difficult meeting with potential in-laws?

Abd Allah was childless, a eunuch so he would always be. More, he was a scribe: He took down what others said and then called it up again. He might have been parchment himself, with no more feeling. Of course, no one could imagine the Conqueror of Syria and Iraq to have such a reedy voice as his messenger did, for all his confessional protestations of short stature and pox-ravaged features. No more could a glance at pale parchment evoke what Khalid ibn al-Walīd must look like. Still—

"Certain." Sitt Sameh pressed her thin lips together.

Strange, too, to see Sitt Sameh down the stairs in the courtyard.

The rest of the turpentine sellers' women, having broken their day's fast with no more than a sip of tea and a handful of dates, scurried through the evening's first gloom. They were readying themselves for Sitt Umm Ali's Quranic recitation. As each one passed, she had something to say to Rayah, some adjustment to make in the costume that had been a group project since henna the night before.

But it was Sitt Sameh's low murmur Rayah strained to hear instead. "I cannot listen to one voice when another booms in my head."

Stranger still to see the desert-tattooed hand reaching out to someone else. Yet, here was Sitt Sameh reaching out to smooth the dull, grimy pink fabric bound over the eunuch's rounded paunch. Not the main sash, a bright, contrasting flowered brocade. It was too worn for that. She'd made him wear the Conqueror's red silk. No one would know, of course, unless Abd Allah—or Rayah herself—told them. And how could Rayah tattle, when she suspected Sitt Sameh had set a spell upon its knots? On all the Conqueror's things: turban, sword, and crumbling litter.

Fortunately, none of Rayah's dress had come from her mother. Though she needn't fear a spell, didn't real mothers take care what their daughters wore? Well, Sitt Sameh had offered to pierce Rayah's nose for a ring to match the dangling gold Cousin Demiella had offered for the holes in her ears.

"Thank you, no, Sitt," Rayah had replied. Too much of the desert for meeting Sitt Umm Ali's—Jaffar's—kin.

"Take care of my girl, won't you?" the kahinah told the eunuch, averting her eyes from the object of her concern.

Pretended concern it was, for Sitt Sameh must realize that those who stay inside, locked on the third floor, could never truly affect anything. No, not even with a dozen spells knotted into an old silk sash, invoking the jinn. For weren't the jinn, too, locked away since the Prophet's coming, blessed be he?

"Ya Rayah," Auntie Adilah called from the doorway. "Come, come. You're the one they want to see, not us."

At just that last moment, when every other woman had already disappeared giggling and chatting with excitement down the tiled corridor, Sitt Sameh turned to Rayah. With the same caressing hands she'd applied to the eunuch, she carefully wrapped the black outer veil over the new dress, up to the blue eyes Demiella had carefully outlined in kohl. As if thin black cloth could in any way defend a girl once she stepped from beneath the lapis-lazuli hand of protection over her harem door and out into the world. The outside world that had begun to work with new weapons since Sitt Sameh's girlhood in the desert where the greatest danger was the demon desert itself.

"Let Rayah know, ya Abd Allah. She doesn't have to marry this boy if she doesn't want to."

When, with the speed and force of lighting, the other blue eyes flashed up at Rayah from their clouds of desert wrinkles; she saw there were raindrops there. Then, like a night owl, the figure had flown up the stairs once more, disappearing just at the jinn's bend.

Bint Zura was a hawk, soaring as if she were one of the smoky Spirits of Fire. On wide wings, she flew, following the river north and toward the rising sun.

Below her, the desert vanished and canals cross-hatched a world of aching green fertility. Here the Euphrates grew close to its twin, the Tigris. Bint Zura flew over them, and then she saw a great city, the center of an empire. It dusted the horizon like a mirage, a trick of the jinn. Its core was an ancient white palace behind walls fourteen times the height of the tallest man.

She circled outward again, to the edge of the sprawl, saw the silent towers where vultures picked at the innumerable dead such a mass of humanity produced. Her raptor's eye attracted her there, but the part of her that remained a girl found it too ghastly and would not linger. Between the towers and the white walls in the middle lay all that could cram in. The warrens of the living twisted and knotted onto blind alleys. And there, on the south, spread a new palace complex: baths, treasury, the mint, a stable, a well-stocked game preserve for the king of kings' hunting.

Between stable and preserve lay a dusty field. Men-at-arms bounded the space on three sides. In unflinching ranks, they stood according to their divisions from all the armies of the empire. Armored cavalry mounted on Persian horses, so much heavier than the delicate horse of the desert. Scale plates sheathed man and steed completely. The metal caught the sun like fire. Near them, the Immortals stood with lances stiff at their right sides and red-dyed horsetails pluming from their conical helmets. Standard bearers in white tunics twisted their headgear with white turbans against the glare and spiked them with feathers. Other warriors wore rounded casques from which chain links draped like women's veils. Like women, their features were obliterated. Cunning metalwork outlined only slits, every pair a uniform, evil-eyed glare.

On the northern border of the dusty field stood the imperial bodyguard, three thousand to a flank. At their apex presided a score of magi priests, veiled to keep their breath from contaminating the sacred fires they tended, sacred cords girding their waists. They stood their ground in the cosmic fight of good against evil as bravely as the men-at-arms, the might of Persia, stood against the physical manifestations of that battle.

And, at the very core, shielded from the sun by a richly embroidered canopy, Choroes Parvez, the Padishah, king of kings, sat upon the peacock throne. He perched stiff in his brocades, weighed down by his heavy-banded crown.

Above all the company on the dais, Bint Zura saw an enormous lance-shaped arc of baked-clay brick. The entry into the great audience hall of the imperial palace reminded the girl-bird of a gorge in the desert near Meda'in Salih, the place where her white camel had been born. She soared between walls where pigeons cooed and preened, tempting as prey to her bird nature. She soared out again and saw that the magi took her presence, contrarily, as a good omen for what was to transpire.

The martial splendor of these spectators did not overwhelm but rather accentuated the lean, lone figure at the center of the field. Wrapped in nothing but a white shroud, the Arab stood solitary, chained to a stake in the midst of dun dust. Bint Zura could not help but feel her wings lifted on the updraft of his pride, his honor. His single might swelled by sucking the strength of those who had amassed to bring him down.

Then great battle drums began a steady, solemn throb. Balanced on either side of shaggy camels with two humps instead of one, the instruments were encircled by jangling bells. The solid wall of armored men parted to open the way for the bull elephant, one great gray beast. Rings of iron spikes banded its ankles, honed iron tipped the long scythes of its tusks. A grim-faced mahout sat cross-legged on its massive neck, urging the steady forward pace with his sharp-hooked prod.

The man on the field in the shroud pulled away from the approaching monster, as far as the chains would allow. He must have felt the beat of the drums match the tread of the great feet to the very trembling of his knees. He neither screamed nor flinched, however, until a kick of one spiked ankle opened a gash in his side and laid him flat within his shroud upon the dust.

One monumental foot stepped on one of the man's knees, one on the other. Both joints turned to powder, mortared with the neighboring bone. At this, the condemned man could not suppress a groan that echoed off the unmoving walls of steel and sent the pigeons flying from the arch.

The mahout's hook backed the elephant, then lumbered it around to the other end of the man whose blood had begun to darken and lay down the dust of the field.

On command, one weighty foot came up and settled, gently, gently, on the victim's bare head, as gently as a mother hen upon her egg. A gesture from the peacock throne made the leg balance there. Only the drums did not let up, pounding a heartbeat of terror now.

The Padishah rose in all his gold brocade stiffness and stepped down from the carpeted dais. Ranks of the bodyguard in tow, he stepped to the center of the field until he stood and looked down into his enemy's face. The pain-filled eyes, set in sun-wrinkles, opened and met the kohl-lined royal ones in their puffed pouches. Hands clasped the shroud but King an-Numan didn't flinch.

"You may still live," the king of kings crooned. "You would never walk again, of course, but I can yet have the mahout back his beast off, and you may live. Only tell me with which faithless tribe you have left your armor and your women, your emblems of power. Order them to be given up, and you shall live."

An-Numan said nothing, only managed to rock his head a negative in the dust. The Padishah could hear the man's skin rasp against the animal's with the gesture.

Choroes Parvez flung one satin-draped arm dismissively. Before he quite had time to step away, or the guard to close behind him, the great foot came down with all the elephant's weight, crushing the head like an egg beneath a mallet. Bits of brain clung to the golden braid at the hem of the Padishah's robe.

And in the sky, Bint Zura felt the support of air beneath her wings vanish. Flap as hard as she might, she plummeted out of the sky. She fell toward the dust where the elephant was now given its head to step and step, over and over, all the length of the body until the shroud could no longer contain the damp morsels. They spilled and then became one with the dust the last king of the Lakhmids had so loved.

As the blood and dust came slamming up at her, Bint Zura screamed—

Then she awoke to find Hind, an-Numan's daughter, the mother of the convent, sitting on the floor beside the mat where she'd been sleeping. Full daylight streamed through an open door behind her.

"You've dreamed, my daughter," Hind said.

"It was nothing," Bint Zura said, trying to calm her heart that throbbed still to the thunder of the battle drums. "I . . . I just remembered those evil men who broke into your sanctuary last night."

"And how, now, you sleep without the red silk of your underdress."

Bint Zura flushed but could find no answer to that veiled accusation.

"Nonetheless, it is true," Mother Hind said after a moment, "that dreams can be prophetic, telling what is, or is to be. This is particularly true of those with far-seeing eyes."

So, Bint Zura told the older woman what she had seen.

"My father, he is dead in Ctesiphon," Mother Hind said, and she recited a prayer of the Christians for his soul. Tears glittered in her eyes. "My Adi, whom my father imprisoned and killed for loving me—he is avenged." And she recited an even longer prayer for that man.

"Will you now leave your seclusion, lady?"

"No. Never." Mother Hind turned hard as flint. "It is fated that whoever shall enter these walls shall die within them."

"And yet, I cannot do so, for my fate." Bint Zura had to take a breath to find the courage to say it to the abbess's face, but she did. "What escape is this? To behave like the ostrich hen, sitting on her nest, who lays her long neck along the sand when she is startled? She thinks her enemies may not see her, but she leaves the great bulge of her belly exposed. Is that truly the way to escape all that is evil and unfair in the world?"

37

> "If you stand near a blacksmith, you will get covered in soot, but if you stand near a perfume seller, you will carry a sweet aroma . . . with you."
> —a hadith of the Prophet, blessed be he

"The ostrich laying her neck along the sand..." Sitt Sameh repeated the words of her mother thoughtfully. Rayah even read guilt there, as if this woman realized her years spent in this little room deep in a harem had perhaps been a mistake. Or—perhaps not. Without further pause, Sitt Sameh went on with her story.

That question of evil was something to which Bint Zura was destined never to receive an answer. For at that moment, one of the nuns of Mother Hind shadowed the open doorway.

"Mother, a visitor. A man at the gate."

"Who is it? Can't he wait?"

"It's the same son of Taghlib who helped chase the intruders from our walls last night."

"My uncle?" Bint Zura asked.

Working her way to her feet, Mother Hind said, "I did not give him all the thanks he deserved, because of the late hour."

Bint Zura was before her, out the door and to the convent gate.

"They tell me," her uncle greeted her from high on his saddle, not bothering to couch his camel beyond the studded wooden slats, "you lost your underdress last night. The red silk I bought last pilgrimage in the Encampment."

Abu Ragheb's eyes studied her as if trying to make the decision to lower his lance toward her heart then and there and so retrieve his honor.

"It could not be helped," she began, knowing the reply was weak but having no other excuse to hand.

Her uncle snorted skeptically, chewed on his jutting lower lip, then said: "I've come to tell you of another loss."

And instantly, with another thorn of fear in her heart, she knew. "Az-Zuharah. My white camel is gone."

"They tell me she's not here."

"You thought she might be here?'"

"I thought perhaps she had wandered here looking for you, niece."

"Camels may wander to a place, where they were born, or where they remember particularly lush pasture. They do not feel such attachment to people."

Abu Ragheb shrugged. "I thought this one might be different."

"I did not take her or call for her, if that's what you think." Bint Zura remembered the courage of an-Numan in the Padishah's dust. It seemed to lift her wings again and she said: "I must tell you I will not stay here in this garden my father has planned for me unless I may see az-Zuharah—every day. You see how she wanders off without me to keep an eye on her. You and your herdsmen are too careless. This isn't just any camel, uncle. This is the white one, born spirit of the Taghlib."

"And you, born in the holy qubbah yourself."

"What does that have to do with a lost camel?"

Abu Ragheb gave no answer. What reply could he give? Bint Zura was right on every count. More, he had tried to cow her and failed.

Finally, he said, "Well," by means of departing phrase. "I must move on to try to find her. Too many people about here at the pilgrimage. Who knows who may have taken her?"

Bint Zura leapt out and caught his mount's bridle before he could turn. "O father's brother, take me with you."

Behind her, Mother Hind said something about no woman leaving the garden once she had entered, about a baptism planned for that day.

"By the lion skin you hang in front of your tent," Bint Zura insisted to her uncle, "you must let me help you find az-Zuharah."

Abu Ragheb looked at Mother Hind. Then he shrugged. He reached down a hand to his niece and, as she set one bare foot against the camel's side, pulled her to perch precariously on the rear of the hump.

Their first stop was back at the tents of the sons of Taghlib so Bint Zura could mount a camel of her own to help in the search. There, she was able to study the imprint of az-Zuharah's couching of the night before.

"Nothing strange," her uncle assured her.

But there was something strange. Footprints—a woman's, by their small size and high arch—there at az-Zuharah's head.

The turpentine sellers' women, the eunuch holding the torch high before them as if he were their purchased slave, made their way to Sitt Umm Ali's door. Just inside, they were separated from the men coming to a similar gathering downstairs and ushered left, up a steep stair, until they found themselves in the spacious women's rooms. Rayah had come here before, for Quranic lessons, but she'd never seen it decorated to greet guests, draped with rich fabrics, stuck with bright blooms in vases, twinkling with jewels in ears and around necks like the starry heavens come to earth.

In spite of the heat of the night, a brazier burned at the door. Bangled hands threw golden lumps of frankincense onto the coals. Clouds of the deep, sweet fragrance clogged the alcove. One by one, as helpful hands removed outer veils, each woman was invited to throw her skirts over the brazier and stand so the twisting wraiths of smoke could fumigate her.

When it was Rayah's turn, Abd Allah preceded her and took charge of her veil. She saw the ripple of comment run through the women of the house: "Heaven help us, a man?"

"No man, a sexless one."

"In the service of Khalid the Conqueror."

"Ah, we are honored."

And as he stepped aside for her to approach the brazier: "Is this the one?"

"This is she?"

"Will she do for a son of our house?"

"Not bad."

"Remember which son we're talking about."

"Yes, Jaffar."

"Mashallah, not bad."

"Not bad at all."

"Wait till you hear her recite. Wisdom is more than looks."

"But you know—those eyes."

Trying not to hear, but hearing all the same, Rayah straddled the copper basin on its three thin legs. She saw the precious lumps of perfume upon which many a Tadmori fortune was built, including that in this house. Packed in saddlebags worth more, rotl for rotl, than the weight of a slave, the scent went to fuel Rumi churches and Persian fire temples. Without them these religions could not function, and now those religions were conquered by the very Islam that provided them this necessity.

Rayah saw the lumps turned to powdery ash—blown away on a breath of wind—in order to be of use but once in their lives. She saw the eery, jinn-like twist of smoke—then dropped her skirts to capture it to herself.

She felt the heat, felt the fragrance cling first to the sweat on her skin brought on by the walk through the hot town's night. The warmth worked its way into every fold of cloth, purging the smell of turpentine that had been about them before, so much a part of her since her birth that she hardly noticed it. The incense forced its way into every fiber, then began work on her body. It filled the hollows in her nose, under her eyes. It curled into every pore, every crease, the hollow behind her knees, her navel, the shadow beneath each budding breast. Even her most private parts, smoke tickled, then filled until, flushing, she had to step away.

"Please, stand longer," they invited her. But she would not.

Rayah knew this rite was meant as an honor, but she couldn't help but think it was meant to rid everyone of even her original smell, to make even her air the same as the household's. She listened to the smoke, for it filled her ears as well. Almost, it seemed, the smoke could dull the effect of her eyes, turned them gray at least instead of the disquieting blue. Incense, she understood, drove jinn away, for Fire Spirits preferred the stench of latrines and tombs and the burning excrement used to heat bath houses. If she had any jinn in her, the fumigation took care to send them flying. And if she married into this house, the smell, the condition, would become permanent. So different from turpentine.

Beyond the reception alcove and the small chamber where Sitt Umm Ali had always held their lessons, the women were taken to a great plastered space. Grape arbors fringed it on every side, filtering the night and biting into the lingering incense with their smell of ripening fruit.

In the center space open to the sky, Rayah tried to get her bearings by looking up but found there was still too much sand in the air. Or perhaps, the clouds of too much incense. Or too many lamps burning, evenly spaced around the low wall. The women of the household knew the direction of the qiblah without recourse to the stars and invited their guests to pray with them. Then, according to the rank of their honor, they found seats on cushions around the walls of the rooftop.

"Sit here." Sitt Umm Ali brought Rayah to a place nearer her own than age should allow.

A supper to break the fast soon came forth, wonderful things: roasted fat-tailed sheep ladled their grease over cracked wheat as well as a basin of rice. Ewe's milk made another basin of rice rich and creamy. Platter-sized bread, still warm, rose in heaps it took two women to carry. Garlic, cardamom, and pepper flavored a tureen of chickpeas sharp enough to bite back. Salty cheese, olives, cucumbers, and figs decorated platters like great flowers in bloom. And as for the sweets, they could have created a fine mosaic on the floors of a palace. Sitt Umm Ali might not have the time to be much of a cook herself. With such a numerous family, however, there were plenty of other women who enjoyed nothing so much as the chance to show off their skills with holy day ingredients. Generous Ramadhan indeed.

Calling for the removal of several platters from the center of the rooftop, Sitt Umm Ali at last called for two of her kinswomen to replace them with a long, low table. Upon the table lay an odd assortment of writings: parchments of different sizes, vellum, papyrus, the broken half of a pot, a stack of dried palm leaves, even the shoulder blade of a camel. This was the collection of Quranic verses which Sitt Umm Ali's pious relatives had gathered from their travels—to Bosra, Damascus, Jerusalem, Egypt. They bartered in this small oasis for the word of God, in this great market for an assured recitation in the exact cadence of the Prophet, and with an extra lump of the finest frankincense, a fair Kufic copy thrown in. The family owned nearly all of the sacred book now, each Surah written separately on what the reciter had to hand. By passing the copies upstairs and down in the hands of children, the men could read it—and then the women.

Sitt Umm Ali settled her silks before the holy writ, cleared her throat, and prepared to begin.

Rayah's belly ached with being stuffed almost as much as it had ached with hunger all day. She groaned and tried to find a more comfortable position. In so doing, she looked up through grape leaves rustling with roosting pigeons. Was that the first cooling wind they'd had since the khamsin began? Hard to tell, it was too weak and faint at first. Rayah thought she could pick out something now: One streak of the River in the Sky—for heaven could not be a desert—was blurrily visible, as if writing the first "B" on the first page of life. After, of course, the alif for Allah, God.

"B," the recitation began, "Bismillah . . . In the name of God, Most Gracious, Most Merciful." Every woman present, without exception, knew the Fatiha, the Opening. They chanted along.

38

> Just such wrath We will send down on those who divided
> the Quran into random parts,
> as have made the Quran into shreds as they please.
> —The Holy Quran, Surah 15:90–91

Sitt Umm Ali recited the first eight chapters in a feat that could not help but impress. She had the whole by heart, the palm fronds and papyrus she made a show of shuffling between merely aids to memory. Those first chapters were the longest, most difficult ones.

After Sitt Umm Ali had finished "Surely God is well-acquainted with all things," At al-Anfal, or The Spoils of War, she paused to take a sip of water. The ninth chapter, Surat at-Tawba, Repentance, was the first of the long ones Rayah had managed to get under control, all one hundred and twenty-nine verses of it. She prepared to hear the familiar words.

"Now," Sitt Umm Ali said. The everyday word sounded out of place, and Rayah thought for a moment she didn't understand it. "I will have Rayah bint Tadmori, my prize pupil, recite this one."

Under the layer of incense that seemed to be drying into a skin tighter than her own, Rayah felt herself grow hot. Her eyes, her blue eyes, filled with tears and, looking down, away from scrutiny and comment, let the moisture drop, darkening her bodice. She knew the verse. God willing, she would have no trouble with it. The only trouble was with the honor—and the thought of what it might lead to.

Hardly knowing what she did, she rose and took her teacher's place behind the Quran table. The camel blade bone—that was what it was written on. She pulled the item to her over spent rags and shards. She saw, however, that, even with the household's women rising here and there to trim the lamps so they'd burn brighter, she couldn't see much of the writing. It was as if the bone had been drawn out, cracked and blackened, from a fire. The recitation would all be from memory. Her mouth went dry.

Then Rayah caught a glimpse of the eunuch, standing with his arms folded across the red silk at his waist. So she began, hearing her voice thin and reedy, but not missing a beat: "A declaration of complete absolution on the part of God and His Apostle, from all agreements made with idolaters." The exchange of the honor of a man's own word as the highest value for that of his obedience to a will made divine by unity in numbers.

Rayah knew that few of the women in the audience knew what the Arabic words meant, speaking only Syriac for the most part. But they, like her, could feel the power. It rose from the hum in the throat, lifting the skull, tingling to heaven. It sank to the chest and stirred the very heart, just the bodily act of it, without comprehension. Her breath, moving over the words, worked like winter wind, stinging her eyes until she wept. Other eyes did as well, kohl running, smeared on cheeks.

All the while she couldn't get the red silk out of her mind. Am I just like Abd Allah? she wondered. More parchment for the words of another? Certainly the other in this case was Almighty God. But what should it mean to create words of one's own with power? Rayah knew power. She had healed Bushra and Auntie Adilah—who sat also weeping with pride at her charge's recital. The actual healing had come from God, at least God had allowed it. But the hands He used in this case, the breath were hers. As the words on Abd Allah's parchments were the Conqueror's, so were the deeds, for a eunuch never could have done such. And yet—Abd Allah was the one who gained entrance to the turpentine sellers' harem where naked power did not. Abd Allah opened doors that could not be forced, not even by the Sword of God. He did it by being who he was—or by who he wasn't.

Then it was over. Gratefully, Rayah returned to her seat. Some discussion followed. Mostly it had to do with the girl and the performance, not what was read. The immediate concern: Was such a reciter worthy to marry Jaffar? The answer tended to yes. As for the reading, what was revealed was revealed. One of Sitt Umm Ali's kinswomen, however, a thin, sharp woman with a birthmark on half of her face which she veiled closely to disguise, wanted to know about one passage.

"Those who believe . . . and jihad with might and main in God's cause, with their goods and their persons have the highest rank in the sight of God; they are the people who will achieve salvation."

Rayah had to repeat it to be sure of the phrasing.

"The Almighty holds out salvation, then, only to those who practice jihad, holy war?" the voice from within the veil asked. "Is there then no hope for us women?"

The notion sent murmurs through the hearers. Some said they'd always thought it was true, that women led lesser lives. Sitt Umm Ali had nothing to say and let the subject drop as women found everyday matters of marriage more interesting.

Sitt Umm Ali won't admit she doesn't understand it all, Rayah thought. I know the interpretation she has taught me, but I don't dare question it. Neither, she saw, did any other woman on the roof. The skin of incense tightened around her as Sitt Umm Ali called another to take her place and the recitation went on.

"Mashallah, you read very well." Two girls about Rayah's age, twins, nieces of Sitt Umm Ali's who came occasionally to the classes but seemed to prefer other, livelier activities, squeezed in beside her. The one on the left whispered in her ear.

"Praises are due to God," she replied. "Thank you."

"Our aunt tells us you're going to marry our brother," said the one on the right, pressing a tray of sesame sweets drenched in rose water and warm honey on her.

Rayah didn't know what to say. To hide her confusion, she took a square of the candy and bit into it, so sweet it hurt her teeth. Finally she found that very useful word, "Inshallah. It will be as God wills."

"Look, she's blushing," announced the left.

"See how it contrasts with her eyes," said the right.

"Hush," said the women to either side of them.

"Don't you like our brother?" asked the left, trying to be quieter.

"I . . . I have never met him," Rayah replied.

"I thought he was at your house."

"They carried him there when he was so sick."

"Into your harem."

"When your kahinah cured him."

"Yes." Rayah finally got a word in between them, although her body was having a harder time in the squeeze. "But certainly I was kept out of the way then."

Both girls nodded, as if one were looking into the mirror. "But come. You will see him now."

"And you'll find he is very worth your interest."

Each took an elbow and brought Rayah to her feet. Stifling giggles, they left the open roof and led her down a short corridor until a balcony opened onto the floor below. There, the household's men were enacting their own version of what the women were doing above. They were running a little behind the recitation: Surat at-Tawba had just been brought to them on the shoulder blade. And the reader—Rayah blushed harder to learn from her two hostesses—was none other than Jaffar.

The pallor of his illness seemed to cling still to this thin boy. He needed some help to get over the more difficult passages. What interested her was that, when he finally retired, the discussion of the men—and it was more lively than that of the women—centered on the same passage as Sitt Umm Ali's kinswoman had found so troubling above.

"Does salvation, then," one asked, "belong only to the men who carry jihad beyond Iraq, beyond Syria, beyond even Egypt now? Is there no jihad in a trader's camel pack? In the boiler of turpentine? How are we who stay at home to attain salvation, if it is as the scripture says?"

"Jihad means struggle," Rayah murmured. "Any sort of struggle. Perhaps just the struggle to be best what God created you for."

Her companions had no interest in such musings. "We want to know what you think of our Jaffar."

"Is he not handsome?"

"He did not answer the question very well," Rayah replied.

"But does that matter at all?" She heard growing disappointment in their voices.

"I suppose not," she said. "He seems very nice." After all, she hadn't been brave enough to give any answer herself among the women.

"So does this mean you agree to meet him?" asked the twin on the left.

"Meet him?" The very thought seemed a brink from which there was no turning back.

"Yes, he will not take our word for it."

"He says he will marry no girl he hasn't first met for himself, stubborn boy."

Such a demand was something in his favor, Rayah supposed. "Yes, I will meet him."

The girls squealed their pleasure, hugging her until coughs from below said they were disturbing the men. They had to run back to the women, stuffing their veils over their mouths to muffle the sounds.

Rayah slept through part of the remaining recitation, curled back against the wall. Finally, the birds began to sing in the grape vines overhead. Prayers, a final bit of food and water, and a white-hot dawn broke upon the rooftops of Tadmor. The women of the turpentine sellers gave their humble thanks and began their trip home.

"Let me carry you then," Abd Allah said, making Rayah realize she had stumbled along through two or three alleys, asleep.

She agreed and he lifted her in his arms. His sharp, male scent scoured the last of the frankincense from her nose in the dusty morning air.

"God bless you, you read very well."

Rayah felt herself smile but couldn't find the strength to give any more of an answer.

"I understand you agreed to meet young Jaffar," the eunuch said.

She was too tired to puzzle out whether that was disappointment in his voice or something else.

The eunuch voice squeaked, "Whatever you will, little Blue Eyes."

Was it just her imagination, or did he say it with the same tone people used when they said "Inshallah"?

As if the words came to her in a dream, Rayah heard herself reply, "How can I look to the future when I don't know the past? Without the future, how can I know my jihad?"

"Very wise. Your mother, you know, looked to the future when she carried you to safety in hiding. Khalid the Conqueror, God rest him, was so busy making what he thought was the future that he didn't think about it seriously until it was all in the past."

Rayah struggled in vain to get her tired mind around such ideas. "It seems nothing is solid out in the desert, where my mother came from," was all she finally managed to say. "Not even the Gods. Not like here in town." Maybe it wasn't the desert. Maybe it was only her mind.

"Not like after Khalid made his choices." And then the eunuch began to tell something that must have come from one of his master's parchments—only he said it without reading, as if it came from his own mind after all.

39

> O sweetheart! O you with a white spot on your forehead!
> And today, where are you, treasure of mine?
> I followed your footprints, every little while halting,
> And yet I found neither the mistress true nor my dear mare.
>
> —a song of the Rwala tribe

My milk brothers greeted my return from the trap of the convent garden to the tents of the sons of Tamim with nothing short of jubilation. They had only just finished telling everyone that they despaired of ever seeing me alive again. Mother, sisters, brothers, slaves all crowded to hear and wonder at my escape, but I was loathe to cheapen the tale by putting it into every ear. So I told them nothing at all about the young woman. Instead I satisfied them with a rousing account of blows exchanged with the fearsome Taghlibi. The dress I explained as something I had taken in a moment of brilliant foresight from the convent's clothesline to let myself down from the second storey.

Malik laughed aloud and slapped his knee with pleasure. "Ah, Khalid my brother, you are the only one of the four of us who returned with any trophy of this night save headaches and shame."

This comment turned my thoughts from myself to others. I saw al-Harith among the faces staring at me with the sort of admiration that is usually reserved for the heroes of ancient poetry. Of all the people there, I hated to feed him with a braggart's lies. He, if anyone, let the deeds of others suppress his own possibilities with a helpless shrug: "Oh. I could never be so brave and strong." More than that, I could see through his looks of glowing admiration that al-Harith had been crying.

I asked, "How can this be on the very night we paid a small fortune to see you made a man?" I should have kept my joking to myself. The herdsman's son blushed fiercely and left the circle without a word.

"The women laughed him from the tent," Malik explained when I asked what I might have said to offend him.

"They what?"

"Just what I said," Malik replied.

"The harlots? Why? He couldn't do it? Or what?"

Malik shrugged. "It's not something he's going to go telling all the camp and bragging about."

"Perhaps when he fell . . ." my milk mother mused quietly.

"What do you mean, Mother?" I turned to her and asked.

"Nothing." She waved her hand and pretended total ignorance, which is often a woman's best defense. "It is something that happened when you all were very small. You wouldn't remember."

But I did remember, very well, the time little al-Harith had run away from camp and fallen down the chasm. Who could not? Mutammim was blind because of that event. I worked my right arm nervously, remembering what I, too, had promised. I remembered the jinn of the desert—and Umm Taghlib, the old kahinah who could speak with them. The name had deeper resonance for me that early morning, for there was a daughter of the Taghlib I knew now. Nevertheless, I took defense from such thoughts along with my milk mother in her feigned ignorance.

"But we paid them good money," I insisted to my milk brothers. "What else is a whore for if not to make a man give the performance of his life? By Hubal of my fathers, we should go and make them give the money back if they have the nerve to laugh at someone for their own failures."

But continuing to speak of it was like trying to goad a dead camel, and the warmth in my cheeks told me I had said more than enough already.

"Al-Harith begged us not to," Mutammim said quietly. "It would only embarrass him further."

Malik rescued us from a very uncomfortable silence then by the rediscovery of the red silk, twisting and untwisting in my hands. "Aha," he said. "So convents have red flags, too, just like harlot's tents."

He held the cloth up for examination. I swallowed nervously, then gratefully, for it was torn beyond all recognition. Still, it was a very good piece of silk, too good to throw away. So Malik proceeded to rip here and there until the silk took the form of a headdress. When I fell asleep at last, it was with the tail of this new turban, wrapped Persian style, scented with her body, held like a rose before my mouth and nose.

"So now you know about my famous red turban," I tell my scribe. He is silent, doesn't know what to say. I say it for him. "Almost too ignominious to be believed, is it not? That the conqueror of Iraq and Syria should have gone about the world for fifty years with a woman's underdress on his head."

"It might have been defiled."

"Indeed, it might."

"With women's impurity, with clots of blood."

"Indeed."

"It was a joke?"

"Of course it was only a joke. At first. A joke stretched to its limits. Made to fit the height of my great bragging lie. We laughed long and hard about it that night in the tent. But before this joke had quite run out, wearing my turban had become a matter of pride and something of a good-luck talisman."

"What do you mean?"

I reach up, and the worn silk runs like water through my fingers. "She wore it first next to her body. It partakes of her spirit. To this day, I have never had the courage to take it off. Or to switch it for another."

"Courage? Why would taking it off require courage?"

"Here among your reeds and inks, you know but one sort of courage."

"The deeds of the battlefield, those are deeds requiring the greatest bravery. At such things, master, none in the world is braver than you."

"But what sort of courage did it take for Muhammad, blessings on him, to walk into the marketplace and obey the demands of the angel?" I quote from the holy book itself: "Declare in the name of your Lord who created, Created man from clots of blood. . ." And expound to my scribe in my own words, "To know that he was nothing, slow of speech, that they, pagans all, would laugh at him, stone him, perhaps. And still he would declare himself God's Messenger. 'Declare! For your Lord is most Beneficent.'

"I haven't such courage," I continue, there in the safety of a garden. Shortly the muezzins will call evening prayers from all four corners of a Muslim city, tuck us safely into yet another Muslim night. "I never have had. Such courage is what it would require to walk into the open without this scrap of cloth, after all these years. Such was Muhammad's courage. Such, too, was the courage of the daughter of Taghlib, and it fills every fiber of this silk. If I were to try and stand without it, I would be admitting that all my deeds of glory are like the first mock bravery of rape on a drunken night. Would have been better left undone."

"You are suggesting this bit of women's silk drove you to your deeds, not the truth of submission to the divine?"

Best not to shock the boy too much just as he packs up his pens for the night. "Because I wore this," I say, "men pointed me out on the battlefield. I could not hide anonymous among the fleeing crowd."

"Of course. Yes, I see."

And while he truly doesn't see, while he is consumed with the fitting of this reed into this slot in his case and the inkpot into that indentation, I brush the turban off my head. The movement makes him turn and stare. What use would he be in the woman's bath house, I wonder? But I have eyes only for the silk in my lap.

Age has dulled the color, I see, as I finger it once again. I ache for the vanished brightness that was suitable for a young man to swagger beneath out into the markets of al-Hira, to cover up the splitting headache of last night's wine. But that color would hardly do for the retired Sword of God, a sober old man in Homs, fifty years later.

I could not have been sleeping long when the saluqis, a jumble among my milk mother's cushions, suddenly lifted their sleek heads. The bitch arched her feathery ears, and the male dog growled deep in his throat. Umm Mutammim reached for her veil and threw it first over her hair, then her face. Mutammim opened his milky eyes so wide, they shone like lamps.

"Who's there?" Malik challenged.

He rose in a single movement, snatching up the lance stuck in the sand at the tent door. I was not a step behind him. The son of Taghlib, I realized, must have followed me here, looking for revenge. I could never forgive myself for having brought such danger to my foster family.

Behind us, the dog had begun to snarl. I threw back the curtain for Malik to step through, spear at the level. Both dogs pushed past us into the night. A dark figure stood stark against the spangle of stars, an inhuman point to his head.

The dog leapt for the throat. The figure raised an arm, which the canine teeth caught instead. The dog fell back with a whine of pain. Malik let his lance sail. It stuck the figure full in the chest, but the weapon dropped harmlessly to one side.

"The Gods save us, it's one of the Fire Folk," murmured al-Harith behind us, touching Umm Mutammim's centerpole and its amulets.

The dagger in my hand began to feel a soft and useless thing.

"Such things do not walk during the holy month," I heard Mutammim say, but he couldn't see what we saw.

At a steady pace, the figure kept coming.

40

> I gathered to meet the chances of Time
> a hauberk flowing, a swift strong steed,
> Stout and hardy, a grooved blade that cleaves
> helmets and coats of mail in twain,
> And a straight spear shaft that quivers when
> I poise it, aiming it straight and true.
> —Amr ibn Madikarib, a great champion in
> the early days of Islam

The saluqi bitch, smaller than her mate but no less fierce, and having a bundle of pups to guard, had gone for a leg instead. She didn't reach flesh any more than the dog had, but she caught the long skirts of the figure's robes and held on, snarling. The figure dragged a little to that side and waved an arm as if to rid itself of that annoyance, but that's all it could be, an annoyance. The bitch didn't halt the threat in the least.

I reclasped my dagger and found it solid. I thought, Bint Taghlib, this I do to free you of your kin. And to free myself, even if it be of this life I'm obliged to live without you. To you—

And I jumped for the throat.

Pain burst like camel thorn to my elbow. I dropped to the dust with a gasp. But I'd heard the clang of metal on metal, knew the jinn could not abide iron, knew this was a man. It was a man encased in that rarity in the desert, a full suit of armor. But it was a man.

Moving through pain, I made another lunge, for a leg. He threw me off as easily as a cloak, kicked off the bitch, and made a lunge for Umm Mutammim's center pole.

"O lady, I claim sanctuary of your hospitality."

The voice, coming through the nasal of a helmet, had the jinn-like quality of echoes in a well. Mutammim had his father's sword down from where it customarily hung at the highest peak of the tent. He had it free of its sheath, waving it blindly. But he, too, recognized the figure as human.

I picked myself out of the dust. The saluqi dog had recovered from the damage done to his jaw and made ready, with a snarl, to leap again.

Umm Mutammim, however, moved faster than us all. She whipped off her veil and threw it over the stranger's head.

"Sons, cease," she cried. "This man has the protection of my veil."

And we all knew there was something stronger than either blade or chain mail, and that was a woman's veil.

"So you are that Hanzala ibn Thalaba of the Bakr ibn Wa'il about whom all the desert is abuzz, like bees over the spring meadows." This was Mutammim's poetry.

"I am," said the stranger.

"My father, al-Walid Abu Khalid of Mecca, has horses with you," I said.

"Yes, Khalid ibn al-Walid. I heard you were gathering up your herd early."

But could that be why he had come? To seek me out? It hardly seemed likely. Such a man would expect me to go to him—and he brought no horses with him.

Then a wry little smile appeared at the corners of Hanzala's mouth, as if he were teasing a child. "Afraid of the Persians, are you?"

"Me? I'm afraid of nothing." I reacted as I might have to a knock upon the knee. "Are our animals well?"

"If it is the Gods' will. I haven't been out to our pastures to see them in a while. This is not why I have come to your tents, O Arabs of Tamim."

He was a jovial man, this sharif of the Idjal clan of the Banu Bakr. Even when he was in deadly earnest, humor twinkled in his eyes as they caught the light of the fire restoked with dried camel thorn and dung. Or did he think he'd played such a grand joke on the sons of Tamim by coming at them in armor at night?

"We have bloodfeud with your Arabs," Malik growled.

With whom did the Tamim not have bloodfeud, except the Quraysh?

"In my father's father's time, we fought and our blood lies thirsty on the ground," Malik went on. "Have you come to pay the camels you owe us, or do we take it from your veins?"

"I will give you camels, I swear," Hanzala chuckled, "and women, too, if that is your desire—"

"My veil is over him."

This was my milk mother speaking. She had reclaimed her covering from off the helmeted head and now used it to make herself part of the shadows. But she did not retreat to beyond the harem curtain. Because of her veil, for all intents and purposes, the son of Bakr was now a milk son of hers as well as I. And the armor took all light to itself anyway.

"Let him say what he has come to say without talk of blood and camels," Umm Mutammim added.

Hanzala nodded her his thanks. A grand nose and square, strong shoulders made up for what he lacked in height, once he took off the helmet. He wore a glossy black beard with a distinctive curl at the end of it, and bits of gold decorated the brown wool cloak he threw back to reveal the armor entirely.

"This I wear is the armor of King an-Numan, that which he entrusted to me when he went to his death under the elephant's feet before Choroes in Ctesiphon," he said.

In the dance of firelight, we could all see what a beautiful piece of work it was. The long-sleeved coat of Persian mail moved like water over Sharif Hanzala's stocky form. Although it seemed light enough, even on his figure—and without question, it had been made for a larger man—we all had ample proof of its strength. We'd seen he had enough flexibility to walk. Clearly, however, it was more comfortable for him to lean against Malik's camel saddle with those legs stiffly outstretched than to try to cross them under the thigh-length skirt of the hauberk.

The helmet he had removed and set to one side so that Malik and I could take turns examining it. Four triangles of the hardest iron made the crown, fused and reinforced into a cone. A ridge at brow level gave place for the turban to wind. From the level of the ears fell a veil of mail, as if he were trying to emulate women. The scowl of brow, however, was very masculine and fixed permanently in purest gold.

Then there was the turban itself: bright purple and gold silk studded with gems. To all but a warrior, this would seem the costliest part of the attire. Warrior's eyes, however, coveted the greaves formed of long slats of metal threaded onto soft leather for the shins. Armored knee coverings served that part of a horseman always most vulnerable because they met his enemies' stabs head on.

And there were the weapons: A fine sword the sharif drew from its sheath so we could appreciate its keenness, the blade with which to scythe a chill through a foeman's heart. The spear whose cunning I'd already met almost too closely. A quiver of tang-headed arrows with superb fletching. A great bow the stranger strung for us there, but of such a tight, backward bend I thought few men could perform the deed as he did. I wasn't certain I could do it myself.

"A beautiful armor," Malik admitted.

"And a great honor to have been given the care of it," Mutammim added.

"I wear it at all times," Hanzala ibn Thalaba confessed. "Ever since I returned from standing up to the Persians when they led an-Numan away from the sacred stones."

A man could feel invincible in such a tortoise shell, I thought as I passed the helmet on for Mutammim's hands to appreciate. But let us remember such things are not of the desert, and for good reason. The afternoon sun on such works of art caused the Romans to nickname their armor clibanus, after their army's portable ovens.

"No man may take it from me while I live," Hanzala declared.

"It's good you do wear it all the time, by the Gods," I commented. "Even sleeping. For the sons of Tamim are not the only ones who will try to kill you in the days to come."

"The Gods willing, I will die with my honor intact."

No wonder we find him wandering the desert by night, I thought. For sleeping in such a thing could not be easy.

"And how you will escape dying, I cannot say," Malik remarked. "If you get enough lances thrown at you, even in such metal, sooner or later, like fate-arrows, one will find flesh."

I was thinking of all the fine horses I'd sold to the eastern side of the desert over the years. I meant to add those of this very Hanzala to their number and sell some more. I knew the vast army that would ride those beasts. "You have all the Padishah's empire against you now." Another reason not to sleep easily in such armor.

"It will be as the Gods dispose," Hanzala said, shrugging the shoulders of the mail shirt. "I have my honor and the poets will sing of me."

I was beginning to think the man something of a fool—and the same of an-Numan, for entrusting him with such a prize owning so little defense.

"They say you keep those who are behind an-Numan as well." Umm Mutammim spoke from the shadows.

"The king's women I have sent with my people to the inner desert, where your horses are, young Meccan," Hanzala replied. "There they will be hard enough for the Persians to find, the Gods willing, and safe."

"Didn't I tell you? I knew this had much to do with Adi's Hind," said my milk mother. "But you, O son of Thalaba, you are not so safe."

"I am going among all the tents of the Arabs here on pilgrimage to see who will stand with me."

"Against the Persians?" I blurted out. "Such men would be mad. Or you are. Or both."

"It is a matter of honor," Hanzala replied. The armor shimmered as a chuckle rose from his belly with his usual good humor. "All true Arabs understand honor."

"There is honor and then there is madness," I said.

Malik did not jump so hastily to his conclusion as I had. "What success have you had?"

"Not much," Hanzala admitted.

"I could have predicted that," I said. "Perhaps there are no true Arabs, as you say."

Graciously, Hanzala chose to ignore my comment. "The Persians have given the throne of the Encampment to the sons of Tayy and of Taghlib, of course. Their tents to the south and west I must completely avoid. We Bakr have long had bad blood with the Banu Taghlib."

I almost said something about the wisdom of such men, but the name of Taghlib stayed my tongue.

"We, too, have a feud with the Taghlib," Malik said.

"News of your poets' battle fills the desert tonight." Hanzala nodded toward Mutammim, then realizing he couldn't see added: "Honor fills this tent."

"Next time, the Gods willing, more than just words will fly," Malik vowed. "It has been so, ever since the Day at the wells of ar-Rumah."

"That is why I dared to come to you under night's veil."

What did this division among eastern tribes matter to me? Let them beat themselves against each other or against the wall of Persia, as they chose. We Quraysh would make ourselves rich selling them all horses.

And yet—the Taghlib. The fact that this tribe chose to side with the Persians gave me pause. It was the most sensible side, surely, for who could even dream of going against such an empire? My heart felt a great need to win, trained in the horse markets of the desert's edge as I was—but never at the cost of profit. There would be no winning on the side of honor this time. Fine and impenetrable though this armor of King an-Numan may be, it covered one man, in one instance, and had its gaps where a blade could slip.

And yet, the sons of Taghlib were my enemies. They were my enemies because they were the enemies of my milk brothers, yes. More, now, they held Bint Taghlib from me. Could I join the fight against the whole Persian Empire for the sake of such a girl? I couldn't hope to win. I would have to be mad. The ache in my head told me I probably was.

"Ibn Thalaba, you've yet to tell us who does side with you in all the desert," Malik said.

Hanzala spoke around this bush and that for a while in broad and optimistic terms, but the conclusion I reached was that, aside from his own Banu Bakr, he had no firm allies. In fact, it sounded as if he couldn't even count on the Banu Hanifa, a lateral but powerful clan of his tribe.

"I told you it had to do with Adi's Hind." Umm Mutammim yawned with satisfaction in her shadows.

"Or with Hind's Adi," replied her second son.

Mutammim said: "O son of Thalaba, our mother's bread and salt is in your belly and her veil is on your head. We may not be able to commit to your cause, just though it may be. We grant you, however, the customary three days' hospitality in our tents."

"For that, I am grateful," said Hanzala ibn Thalaba. "But I expect I haven't the liberty to accept even that full measure. Should I stay long enough for any on the Persian side to find me, I lose life, armor, and honor. You would, too, for harboring me."

"Should the Persians come now, we would be honor-bound to do our best to protect you, with the help of the Gods." Mutammim might well have been speaking the jinn-images of poetry.

"Other than that, I can't promise," Malik said, more frankly. "Give us leave to think on what you have said. This night, with the Encampment's wine in our heads, is not the time for clear thinking."

"Although I think a promise of neutrality, pulling back to the safety of the desert, is all we can promise," his brother suggested.

"Even if I promise you camels to slake the thirst of your dead at my father's father's hand?" Hanzala veered just short of outright begging.

"Honor may be appeased for the moment. But a promise of camels that may all be lost in a battle with the Persians is certain to bring no honor to the name of Tamim at all."

And so they left it at that. We slept in the cool of the early dawn, even the saluqi bitch among her pups. And my head I cradled in the red silk of one who was, as yet, neither friend nor foe.

Among the well-worn folds of red silk, my scribe finds the sanctity of the lock of the Prophet's hair. Half black, half an iron gray, each strand separate and true to its color, with a slight curl. That keeps the boy with me until the call to prayer comes, and I am forced to have his company with me for the rite. He would even set the little bit of hair tied with camel yarn at the head of our rugs, to the south, so we face it along with the holy cities.

And I set the faded silk in the same place, casually, without comment. I had had evidence of its powers for good from the first time it took my weight out into the dark of a night in al-Hira's ignorance. And more was yet to come that very next day.

But first, as one last line to scribble on the parchment before all light fades—

Al-Harith, his tears and shame forgotten, came running back into the tent that early morning to the ghru-grug, ghru-grug of my milk mother's churn.

"What is it, O al-Harith?" Malik asked. "You look as if you'd see a ghost, a fire spirit, a jinni. Have the Persians found Hanzala's already?"

Instead, he gasped: "A camel."

"Yes, we have lots of camels, praise the Gods," *said Malik placidly, for all that his head, like mine, must have been aching from the wine.*

"A strange camel among the herd. Mashallah, this camel is all white."

41

God has not sent down an illness without sending down a cure for it.
   —a hadith of the Prophet, blessed be he,
      related by Ata ibn Abi Rabah from Abu Hurayra

Late that afternoon after the Quranic reading, Rayah paid another visit to Ghusoon, who lay inert and possessed on her bed. There was no change, only the father was away, passing the long hours of fasting with his friends in the mosque. Rayah got some more water and a little juice down her patient's throat. The girl looked so much worse than on her previous visit, however, that Rayah wondered if there'd be anyone left to tend when next she called. It must be as God willed.

What made her think she could heal a soul who clearly had no interest in her own survival?

Rayah's hurrying back to the third-floor room to hear more from Abd Allah's parchments felt like a retreat.

It was the time of the fast day when the sun seemed to hang pinned to curtain of khamsin haze against the western sky. Would it never set? Empty bellies led to lightheadedness. Or irritability. Or both.

Sitt Sameh was waiting for her. The older woman had even laid her spindle aside and merely sat, Cousin Demiella's mirror in her lap. One thread-calloused finger traced the rim, around and around. The eunuch scribe was not there.

"Excuse me." Rayah stopped in the doorway, the beaded curtain clinking softly behind her. "He must be visiting with the men in the majlis. I will go and help my aunties prepare the fast-breaking meal until he returns to pick up his parchments again."

"No, child. Wait," her mother said. "Come. Sit."

Rayah did as she was told, although she wasn't comfortable. This woman, her mother, by the grace of God—or so they said—was no easier to sit with than a strange man. Rayah wanted the soft, patient eunuch as chaperone to ease matters between them.

Sitt Sameh tried to pass the mirror from her lap to Rayah's.

"Thank you, no." Rayah averted her eyes. "I know my eyes are blue. Finally. Now."

Without pushing her voice, rusty still with years of disuse and the foreignness of the Syriac tongue, Sitt Sameh insisted.

Again Rayah tried to refuse. "You are my mother. I accept that, with the help of God. But I don't need any more of the smoke trickery of mirrors."

"Trickery? You don't say reality. Which makes me think you don't believe the witness of your own eyes at all."

Rayah looked at the ground, not between the two of them but between her own folded knees, and said nothing.

"Mirrors are not known in the desert," Sitt Sameh went on, a sense of loss twisting wistfully around her words. "We have the land of mirage, of course, always with us. And wells, sometimes. Waterholes, when the water is still and black. These can provide ways to see into the Other World. I understand people here in the settled places use mirrors, however. I thought we might try. You might try. Children, they say, are the best mediums. Their innocence easy to impress. I was, when I was young."

"Those Beings of the Place are too dangerous. I don't want to stir them." The image of a hornets' nest settled in Rayah's mind.

"And yet you try to heal your friend whom they have possessed. How can that be possible without entering the realm where they dwell?"

Rayah found the mirror in her lap. She had hoped for retreat; there was none. Only a new and more dangerous path of entry to the strange world she now inhabited. Wasn't there a tale of Zarqa of Yamamah who had had her blue eyes gouged out because of what they had seen and she had prophesied?

"Sit where its surface can catch the last of this sun," Sitt Sameh said. "Catch the colors of red and orange on the black."

Rayah did as she was told, the colors glinting in the back of her skull making her more lightheaded than ever.

Her mother then dipped a thumb into a pot of blue paste and wiped a smear of it on each of her daughter's eyelids. There was definitely olive oil in the mixture, and there might have been some indigo as tint, but the color was closer to ground turquoise. In spite of all the cost of such a concoction, that is what it must have been, for Rayah could feel the tiny grains as a heavy weight. They and the smell blurred her vision with tears as if a swirl of wind had blown sand into her eyes.

Satisfied—she who was never satisfied with anything—Sitt Sameh then brought out her three female idols. "In the desert, we might drop one or more of these in the water, but here—"

"No. Please put them away." Rayah knew the Most Merciful could never bless idolatry. "I...I will have to do it my own way."

What did she have then but her own flesh and blood, sweating in the khamsin afternoon? Her own tearing eyes? Rayah circled the rim as her mother had done earlier. The finger spread soon to a full hand. She circled her palm as if to wipe the surface clean, only without touching, as that would smear the surface.

Then, taking a breath, she took her hand away.

Rayah saw only her own eyes, the blue emphasized by the turquoise. She'd been right. She would see nothing by demonic means. God was gracious and all-powerful.

Her hands closed on the rim to return the object to Sitt Sameh or, preferably, to Cousin Demiella, whose vanity seemed a harmless pastime in this light.

Then Rayah gasped. The eyes turned dark, to those of a curly-haired boy with a glint of mischief. Something in those eyes reminded Rayah of her patient Ghusoon, as if this boy had stolen the light that had once enlivened the girl's gaze for his own play.

"What is it?" Sitt Sameh urged.

"Nothing. Just a boy. I don't know him."

Her mother seemed content, too, that there was nothing in this, especially when the face quickly vanished and Rayah blurted with recognition, "The lion skin. Bint Zura's lion skin that her uncle took for his own to lead his people on their migrations."

If asked, Rayah would have had to admit that the shift of sun on the mirror only looked a little something like a battered lion skin, head down on a pole: two dangling streaks of paws, a blur of head, that was all. But she was beginning to see that seeming was a very great part of what the jinn showed to mortals.

42

And today they wander, a trembling herd, their herdsman Death.

—an anonymous man of the tribe of Khatham

"The miraculous white camel isn't yours, Hanzala ibn Thalaba?" my milk brother Malik asked his guest. "Left you as the prize of all his treasures by King an-Numan?"

"It's not mine. That's my plain riding camel over there. Never have I seen such a wonder as this." The stiffness that must have set into Hanzala's limbs from having slept in his armor left him as he stared with the rest of us. "But I take it as a good omen upon my desperate cause."

My father will soon be returning to al-Hira, well-laden from Bahrain, had been my first thought upon groaning awake again—after remembering the daughter of Taghlib in the convent shadows. *Father comes to collect his horses and his son. I have work to do.*

But when I awoke in my milk mother's tent that morning to al-Harith's announcement of the wondrous white camel among the Tamimi herds, it was with a throbbing head. My mouth felt like the inner desert after five years' drought. Worst of all, my own sweat soaked the rugs and matting under me. Horses should be put through their paces or moved early, before the heat. I was already too late. The day would be wasted altogether if I didn't get going.

But then there was the white camel. Holding my head, my hand sticking with sweat to the red silk there, I staggered out to see the spectacle with all the rest.

"A good omen," Malik repeated Hanzala's words.

"Where can she have come from?" Mutammim asked, running his blind hands along the wonder he could touch but not see.

"Well, she balks from me," Malik complained.

"She may not let any but her owner control her," I said.

"Her owner may be the Gods," said Hanzala.

"She is well-cared for," Malik said, studying the lead threaded through one nostril, the colorful tassels hanging from her jowls.

"Who would not care for such a good omen?"

"And yet they've allowed her to wander."

"Wasn't the news of the desert that the Taghlib had a white camel born to them some years back?"

"Taghlib?" Hanzala spat and Malik joined him.

"At Meda'in Salih, so I heard from some sons of Tayy who made the trip just to see."

"Taghlib," Malik repeated. "May their wells give them all the cramp, those Persian eunuchs."

Hanzala said to Mutammim: "Thanks to your shaytan, who caused you to crush them with your words yesterday."

"If this is their beast, then I don't see that it's brought them the best of luck," said Malik, reminded of the battle of the poets—had it been just the day before? "Probably we should kill it."

"And have it for dinner tonight?" Shock sounded in Mutammim's tone.

"Why not?"

"But such creatures are sacred."

Malik studied the little buds of ears on the animal. "This one hasn't had its ears clipped to show it belongs to any God."

"The Gods themselves have marked her if, as you say, she is white."

"Yes, she's white, as white as a cloud."

Mutammim might not remember even the sight of clouds from before the curse, but he didn't contradict his brother.

"At least if we were to sacrifice her to the stones of as-Sabad, either by slitting her throat or by simply turning her loose there, the Taghlib wouldn't be able to accuse us of theft."

"That is a worry, isn't it?" Hanzala agreed, shifting under the weight of his entrusted armor. "But it is a good omen. A very good omen, that she has left their tents and come to yours. Such a camel, they say, can serve as the very spirit of a tribe, leading them to victory against the starkest odds."

I could tell, even through my headache, that this sharif of the Banu Bakr was trying to find a way to get my milk brothers to lend this omen to his own hopeless cause. He couldn't ask for it outright; that would be the end of all honor. If he praised the animal over highly, they would be obliged to give it to him, and that would lose honor, too. But to walk this fine line between honors for the great honor of such a beast—that was worth the risk.

Mutammim did not see his guest's subtlety—or if he did, he chose to ignore it. "If she is theirs, the Taghlibi's," he said, "the feud of ar-Rumah's wells and the death of our father may flare up again with more than just poetry. If she is discovered here among our tents."

Malik lashed his camel goad at empty air. "So we have the blame and danger of a raid—during the moon of pilgrimage besides—and none of the pleasure. And all because somebody can't keep their own beast of good omen fettered."

"But she was fettered, Master." Al-Harith spoke for the first time, having silently scouted the ground around the new camel all the while the two brothers had conversed. I had been sick into a clump of camel thorn.

Mutammim's headache must have bothered him, too, at the moment. "How can you tell?" he asked.

"See the broken line about her foot?"

"Yes," Malik agreed. "But just see what a flimsy thing it is. A newborn might have broken it."

"So the owner must have trusted the beast and—"

"And?"

"Something happened."

"Something?"

"Perhaps the owner died, the Gods forbid, or— Well, we'll probably never know what."

"Yes, we must make a decision with the Gods' help, not knowing what happened." Malik lashed his goad at nothing again.

"But just look at these footprints." Al-Harith had not fuddled his mind with so much date wine the night before. Shame before women, bad as it might be, left a clearer head.

"Don't tell me this camel has the prints of a jinn beast?" Malik said, touching the amulet around his neck against evil.

"No. A stranger's prints. Those of a woman."

Holding his head, Malik squatted to study the slight indentation his herdsman pointed out. Then he straightened stiffly. "A sharif should know the prints of every one of his clansmen. And while not kin, I believe she may be one of us. Aren't those the prints of Umm Taghlib?"

"The kahinah?" his brother asked as if coming to sudden understanding.

The name struck me as well. I had taken to calling the young woman I'd seen by the well Bint Taghlib, for I knew nothing else. Was there a connection between this old mother of that tribe and this young daughter? It made my head hurt to consider.

"Who is this woman?" Hanzala asked.

Mutammim explained.

Malik said: "I always knew I should not have extended our father's protection to her."

"No, brother," Mutammim chided. "It is better to grant her protection than to have such power against us. Don't you remember our father speaking of how she put the curse on the wells of ar-Rumah?"

"And of how she saved me?" came al-Harith's quiet voice.

Saved you for ignominy before women. Besides losing Mutammim the use of his eyes. The thought hung in the air for a moment, but no one, not even the blind poet himself, urged that as reason for a witch hunt.

"Nonetheless, I must go and learn what she means by playing this dangerous prank on us." Malik began to move.

Mutammim followed the moving voice more slowly, working his stick before him over the rough gravel. "You will go cautiously, brother. Perhaps she means this as a beneficence for us."

"Or perhaps, after all these years, she means to bring her tribe down on us, that accursed race from whom we've protected her out of our high sense of honor."

"I, too, would go meet this woman," Hanzala ibn Thalaba said, following after his hosts with the chink of his mail at every step.

"It is better for you to stay in my mother's tent," Malik told him. "The Gods forbid what might happen were you to be discovered abroad in that armor."

Then my milk brother resumed his long stride toward his camel to ride it after the old kahinah's footprints, which led away from the rising sun. "Well, let us just see how my honor repays such a woman's treachery."

I'd just been sick again. Groaning, I realized how high the sun was, and how I must leave the sons of Tamim to their own fate with the kahinah. I couldn't even be off about the girl I had seen, not in this condition. I must be about the business of gathering my father's horses before the pilgrimage drew to a close.

My milk mother stood just before her tent, the wind catching at her veil and skirts as she, too, looked at the wondrous white creature. She held the tent flap for her guest to return, but he excused himself to struggle, the call of nature against his armor.

Umm Mutammim's curds set out on the roof of the tent had begun to dry. She tried to talk as she pressed some of them wrapped in a cold slab of bread on me.

I ought to talk to her, I told myself. I ought to speak to my milk mother. About the girl I was calling Bint Taghlib. Were the two appearances, hers and the camel's, just coincidence? Both had something magical, from the other world of the jinn, about them.

If Bint Taghlib had nothing to do with the kahinah and the appearance of the camel, still I had narrowed down the girl's parentage. I had narrowed down the number of tents Umm Mutammim had to search, as only a woman can, going from harem to harem, drinking water sweetened with herbs—and by a well-chosen word, turning the gossip.

One question to the right ears ought to give me a father—yes, even a bloodthirsty uncle—to put with those blue eyes. My milk mother might find someone, anyone I needed to ask, to load with coin, horses, camels, whatever it took to buy her. Or yet which tent flap I'd have to creep under to raid it of its prized possession—if she ever came out of the convent. Yes, I'd even do that, at risk of my life, to gain the girl. Women in their veils often continue to visit in harems where their men would be murdered at sight on the other side of the curtain. Would my milk mother, for me, dare go to the encampments of her enemy? She would if I asked her. If I said, "Yes, Mother mine, you are so right. Adi's Hind is the core of it all, here in al-Hira. And for this reason, I must ask you to go into the tent of our enemies—" She might not thus guess my true purpose and distraction.

Something in Umm Mutammim's face, too, invited confidence, now that my milk brothers were gone about the white camel. Unfortunately, even after a bowl of salty, lukewarm camel's milk, my head still throbbed, my tongue felt like sand. Horse dealing, I decided, would take all the effort I could muster that day.

43

In the Name of God, the Compassionate, the Merciful.
Happy now the Believers,
Who humble themselves in their prayer,
And who keep aloof from vain words,
And who are doers of alms deeds
And who restrain their appetites
Save with their wives, or the slaves whom their right hands
possess: for in that case they shall be free from blame:
But they whose desires reach further than this are
transgressors.
—The Holy Quran, Surah 24:1–7

My father bought horses from the Tamim and other tribes of the eastern desert in the autumn, just before the rains, when prices were lowest and the people most desperate. These tribes, as is only too well known, breed the best horses in the world, without question. Their stock, it is said, is all descendant from the heavenly mare God first gave to Isma'il. But at that season, the animals are emaciated. Even if they could cross the Syrian desert to the markets of Damascus where the Roman Empire bought them for its generals, they would never win the commander-lavish prices from the Romans who can see only skin deep. The animals had to be over-wintered on the sweet pastures of the inner desert, to grow sleek and strong by spring when my father would collect them.

The desert pastures are the sweetest in the world. They are never thick enough, however, for a horse to eat himself fat and lazy. And they could not support more than a horse or two at a campsite, rarely three, never the herd of twenty or more my father liked to buy. So he left them with their old masters, branded to him, but scattered. The Tamim were allowed to take the colts, if the winter rains should bring them, and use the mounts for their raids. Yet they were responsible to see that neither wolves nor drought nor enemy arrows took an undue toll. As security for his scattered interests in this region Father liked to leave some trusted man—a cousin, a nephew. The year that I was ten, I was that man. I took the honor with pride. My milk brotherhood was already proving most useful.

By the time I was eighteen, that all-important pilgrimage at al-Hira, I was not simply left to over-winter with the Tamim. I was given chief responsibility for the regathering of our animals in the spring. My milk mother had weaned a man indeed.

When I threw my saddle on my camel that late morning after the night in the convent and then tried to ride, the movement made me sick to my stomach. I had to walk about my business instead, all the way to the tent of al-Minhal of the tribe of Iyad ibn Nizar. He was pitched at some distance from the Encampment, at the head of a wadi surrounded by high yellow rock walls. Here the wind had blown hillocks of sand up against the roots of widely spaced salt brush.

And here I found the one the Arabs called The-Beneficent-Iyadi-Like-Unto-An-Ever-Flowing-Spring appropriately squatting on the rim of a well. He had drawn water and was letting a mare dip her nose in the leathern bucket. A swarthy man with sunken hollows beneath prominent cheekbones, perhaps his most remarkable feature was his feet: the last two toes of either foot were webbed together. I noticed the distinctive prints in the mud beside the well when he moved to greet me. They had sunk heavily toward the heels where the squatting had set all his weight, but I would have known them anywhere.

I wondered briefly how my milk brothers were getting on with their search for the owner of the other prints, with the source of the white camel. Then I pushed that thought aside and wished al-Minhal a good day full of light.

The man's high-pitched voice was hard on my head, but the dryness of the wadi air enlivened by water on dust helped. I took another deep, fresh breath to rid me of the last of the wine's poison and swore again that some day I'd have my revenge on all Syrian winesellers. I also spared a thought for Bint Taghlib—that other sweet breath of air to my mind—while my host's rush of greeting washed over me.

I drew a bucket full of water myself—it was a long drop to the echoing splash. I drank deeply. The water was brackish, tasting something like mold, but I thought, all the better to make a sturdy horse.

Then I threw the rest of the full skin of water over my flushed and sweating head, leaving it to run down, for the wind to dry through all robes. Al-Minhal made no comment, but after that, he had me draw again to do the same favor to the horse, which others would have watered first. I sponged her down with a corner of my robe to cool in the heat of the day. With the dust slurried from her, I saw that this was indeed the mare I'd come for, our brand like a row of shark's teeth riding on her flank. She was white, dappled all over with markings that made her look like fine marble. Her face was a dish of alabaster, the black and indigo tassels of her harness hung with protective rings of silver onto her forehead and from beside her ears, like earrings.

"She looks well," I said.

"Ya'uk bless her," al-Minhal said carefully so my praise wouldn't make the jinn jealous. "The honor is not mine. Rather praise Ya'uk of my fathers and the sharif your father, who gave me this horse in trust."

We all called on pagan gods in those Days of Ignorance. Al-Minhal would have submitted with the best of Muslims to the One God if that God had only willed that he live long enough to hear His Name preached. Much of the world blew markless through al-Minhal's forgiving mind like wind through a sieve. In one thing alone did he have superior understanding, and that one thing was horses.

"But don't leave her in the shade," he said. "That weakens them."

I hobbled her near a sunny patch of thistle that might still have some tender shoots on it. I always did as al-Minhal bade, for animals never failed to bloom beneath his care like wildflowers under spring rain. As I turned from the hobbling, I saw a tear had settled within the hollow under each of the old man's cheeks. He felt, I saw, gratitude to be allowed to witness such wonders as the glistening marbled skin before us.

"She's not over big." I said this in part because I did think I'd been rash in my jealousy-causing praise earlier. I hefted each dainty foot one by one as I did so, testing their light weight and seeing at the same time how very strong clambering over desert rocks had made her.

Al-Minhal grinned with awe, his form of pride, through his tears. "Horses bred in Persia grow bigger," he said.

"The better to carry their heavy armor."

"But they are coarse." And I agreed with him.

No one could call these pretty, dancing feet coarse.

Father would be pleased with this success. We would make a fine profit in Damascus. My deepest frustration with al-Minhal was that he kept trying to give the animal to me as a gift. "I am your servant, O son of al-Walīd, and the servant of your father and the servant of Ya'uk my God. Please, accept this Little One as my humble due to you." It was all I could do to refuse to let him make me a thief without hurting his host's sensibilities.

Al-Minhal had no other name for the filly than to call her his "Little One," a name that had no doubt served for others before and would again in the future. The dam and the sire meant nothing to him, unlike the great sharīfs who follow pedigrees back to Isma'īl's first single-hooved mount.

"Let us, however, seek the shade," he said, leading me toward the dark swell of his tent that stood, its back to the wadi winds.

Once my eyes adjusted to the welcome dimness, I saw fresh tears glinting just above the line of my host's gray-streaked beard. I followed his gaze and met nothing but the black-and-red-striped curtain separating the men's section of the tent from his women.

That was when I finally allowed myself to remember that al-Minhal had a daughter as well as a mare. And that, in the fall, when we'd struck the deal for purchase of the horse, my father had spoken for the girl as well—for me.

Al-Minhal's only objection to the match, and he apologized profusely for it, was that his daughter was but a girl, just seeing her twelfth year. Granted, wives are often made of girls younger. The Prophet himself, blessings on him, married his beloved A'ishah when she was only nine. Al-Minhal, however, worked with horses. He knew the dangers of bringing a mare too young to the stud and pleaded for more time.

So now this little girl had had the better part of a year in which to grow into a woman. What should I do? My unspoken, unspeakable, impossible devotion to the daughter of Taghlib stood newly erected like a rock wall—not just a camel-wool curtain—between me and any other women in the world. I would have a difficult time even feeling faithful to my first wife in Mecca. I simply could not match al-Minhal's unreserved and guileless welcome. Still, it would betray the most sacred trust of a host to crush his hopes of a good match for his daughter, and I could not do that. I saw no escape.

Faster than it takes for water to boil, a bowl of warm camel's milk appeared over the top of the dividing curtain. The bowl was of the best blue Persian fritware, a rarity in the desert where such things must crack in saddlebags. Perhaps it had been bought in the market of al-Hira—just for this occasion. The thought brought back the morning's wine sickness; this was not my milk mother's offering.

In the salty liquid, al-Minhal steeped the herbs that had come over the curtain with the bowl to raise this above usual fare. Thyme and basil tanged the air all the while I struggled to settle my stomach enough to drink and my host asked after the peace of myself and all connected to me. I told him peace was everywhere, thank the Gods, but in fact I'd never felt further from it. We didn't even begin to touch on the disruption of King an-Numan's armor loose among the dunes and wastes of the Arabs' lands, too disturbing to be polite in first talk. And as for the other things that bothered me—

Once the milk was duly and successfully sipped, the old man had nothing more with which to occupy his transparently anxious hands than a small tuft of wool. He kept carding it between fingers, spinning, knotting, and then undoing it all again. Had al-Minhal persisted in playing thus with his bright Yemeni dagger, I would have been less unnerved. I was convinced that this little fluff of wool was to be the token of the bridal bargain. It would be pressed, felted with the sweat of his palms, into my own the moment I but spoke the word.

A second wife—and one with such good connections, a constant source of the very best horses in Arabia—what should I have against that? I did not have to love her. I did not have to be with her any more than with the first. I would give the easiness of this match up for something that was no more than a nighttime dream? Something locked within the impenetrability of a Nazarene convent, no less? Even if my last night's dream did prove obtainable in life, what should be wrong in taking a third wife? A man's third wife is often the love of his life, they say: the first for family, the second for business, and finally, the third for love.

Nevertheless I drew out all other conversation as far as it would go. I managed to reach late afternoon before having nothing left to say but: "How is the peace of those behind you?" I meant, in a polite fashion, those al-Minhal had behind him, behind the harem curtain.

All somber tension broke from the old man's face like a crust of dried mud beneath the cloudburst of his smile. He leaned back and slapped his knees with his hands, the absurd tuft of wool forgotten for the moment in his relief. He'd been afraid I might never get around to it.

"My daughter Layla, thanks be to Ya'uk, has been blessed with such good health and growth during the past year—the Gods shield her. Her hips have broadened and her women's courses have come. Praises are due to Ya'uk—and to all the Gods of the Ka'ba, too. You don't believe me? Will you believe your own eyes? Let me call her forth."

I tried to indicate that, no, it was not necessary to disturb the sanctity of his harem. I believed him full well. But the girl was already called, and she came at once. After all, she had been waiting on that side of the curtain as long as her father on this side.

Like a demon Goddess's sacred dove, Layla bint al-Minhal fluttered into the men's section. I was being shown, no doubt, that she was a girl of devotion. It was obvious by her loose and flowing costume and hair and by the daubs of gore on her forehead that she had attended the rites at the sacred stones, the Two of Blood. There was even something familiar about her, as if I'd seen her out of the corner of my eye while my attention was centered just to one side.

The flush of the afternoon, the exercise of youth, the heat of the harem, all were a heavy veil upon her. Praise God for that veil, for there was very little else she wore. Her pilgrimage dress did drag properly on the ground in back the way the poet likened unto the tails of well-fed cattle, and she looked wild-eyed and bovine as a young heifer. But that same dress was scanty and shawl-like enough above where her thirteen-year-old breasts started from her rib cage as if in surprise.

Layla bint al-Minhal was of that age—the first perfect bloom of womanhood—when no girl can be ugly, and most are beautiful. And some, like this Layla, like a piece of popular poetry cannot help but have an emotional effect on any hearer. It may be cheap and contrived, but it is emotion all the same. My eighteen-year-old heart softened within me.

Al-Minhal's face glowed like sunrise to see his child. One might easily have interpreted his blush as lust, but those of us who knew him could not imagine that he had ever even lusted after the child's mother. Lust requires a greater sense of selfishness than my host was capable of.

A few smiles from me, a few kind words in her direction, and Layla bint al-Minhal knew nothing of shyness or reserve. Whatever attention I gave her, she returned threefold. I continued to give it not because I especially wanted to flatter her, but because I myself enjoyed being flattered. And what started as a game grew and grew, throbbing throughout the rest of the afternoon, until none could call it playing any more, giggle over it as we might.

Layla bint al-Minhal circumambulated me with her flirtation. Our courting was a rite, fixed by tradition and precisely followed. The rite needed only a young man and a young woman to flutter and dance around him as they do (or used to do, before the Prophet) around the sacred stones. The women's gestures and words are prayers asking that we—stones or men, it little matters—grant them good marriages and babies.

Layla was body but not soul. My heart was softened and lifted but not pierced.

Presently, and almost apologetically, her father suggested, "Our guest would be more honored to take bread and meat from your hand than mine, or from the slaves'."

And the girl went at once back into the harem. Al-Minhal watch his lively daughter just as he watched his horses, finding Ya'uk, the God of his fathers, ever-present in them. Horses and daughter he would have worshiped, but he was too simple to construct a worship ritual of his own.

Layla might have been what I had swaggered into al-Hira thinking I longed for. But in the lively exchange with eyes and blushes that accompanied her departure, I reached up to touch my turban to see if it was on straight. That was when my hand met the red silk, new and crisp on my head. Then I knew better.

And just then, as if the touch to my turban were a magic taught to me by Umm Taghlib to evoke the jinn, a second party rode up to al-Minhal's tent. The host stood to recognize them as honored guests.

I rose, too, to survey a man on a war camel. Behind him on another, tamer beast floated the woolen curtains of a woman's howdah. Something about that howdah . . .

I couldn't give the howdah the attention it needed. By God, I knew the man at the head of this party. I knew his swagger, the weave of his cloak, blue on black, the green band to his headdress, the camel-jut to his lower jaw. The black and white feathers dangling from the head of his lance. He was the very son of Taghlib whose dagger I had only narrowly escaped in the convent garden the night before.

44

The fig is a fruit descended from Paradise because it has no pit.
   —a hadith of the Prophet Muhammad

When Rayah next prepared to visit Ghusoon—and she did so yet again the next day—she looked down the hallway from under Fatima's protecting hand. She heard her boy cousins rowdy there, heard the dull talk of the men as they endured the fast and the wind. She thought of Bint Zura, the girl of the Time of Ignorance, her camel and her freedom in the desert snatched away. Rayah turned back, knowing that the men would not permit her to walk to her friend's unescorted.

Instead, Rayah pulled the ladder from its place at one end of the courtyard and set it against the low roof of the house next door. This was the way grown women moved about the town, using the back ways and the roofs. Rayah thought not so much about being grown-up as about avoiding the male-dominated street level, avoiding the scrutiny of Zabbai the gatekeeper. Was it so for all women, then?

At her feet, as she scurried across the pressed plaster from roof to roof, leaves of trees growing in courtyards lashed in the wind; no one was out in this. Gusts made ropes of her skirts and tried to tug her from the edges, unprotected by railings or walls. Hardest of all were voices she couldn't quite make out, calling to her in poetical rhythm as they swept past. By the time she slid down a wall to reach the stairs at her friend's harem, there were actual words in her head.

"If she doesn't improve by the end of Ramadhan—" Ghusoon's stepmother, bringing the smell of cooking onions and cumin from that evening's awaited feast with her, threatened her still-inert stepdaughter while Rayah sat there. "We will do to her what her mother did to herself. We will take her out to the desert, tie her to a tree, and let the jinn take her completely."

The thought of food and the growl in her stomach made Rayah's head reel, more than the threat to her friend. Rayah tried chanting to the song she'd heard—still heard—in the malevolent wind outside, trying to cover the stepmother's threats with words just for her friend. Most people grew listless during Ramadhan, during the khamsin. But not even a squeeze of protest came from the hand Rayah held. When she rose to leave, Rayah felt that the struggle to move the ladder and cross the rooftops had been a waste of time. Ghusoon's listlessness had almost sapped her into the same state, so she began to feel that joining the jinn in the desert might be the best that could happen.

On Rayah's return journey, her heart heavy with such news, one of the old women who lived in the house next door was watching for her. The crackling old voice called from the depths of their court as the girl passed on the roof overhead: "Ya Rayah, look what the devil wind has done to our figs."

Rayah looked down, refusing to become dizzy at the height of two narrow floors. What she saw sickened her more. Wind still whipped the old fig tree's branches, but most of the hand-shaped leaves were gone. In the newly appeared gaps she saw green and purple fruit littering the pounded earth of the old woman's floor. An over-sweet smell, which seemed mixed with the dust of tombs, rose on the heat to reach her nostrils; the humming of sated wasps came, too.

"Tell your aunties to come and claim their fill, or everything will rot. Mashallah, and my sister and I hoped for such a good crop this year."

"Thank you, auntie. Inshallah, I shall."

That small house next door that made such a good bridge to the world beyond had been tucked in beside the turpentine sellers' as an afterthought. The buildings shared a common wall, requiring only enough rough and crumbling bricks to be made for three walls instead of four. The builder and owner of this product of harder recent times lived elsewhere. He left the domicile to his two aunts, the widows of two brothers who never gave either of them children. Both were so old, they rarely made the trip up to the roof any more. The turpentine sellers' women, all of whom were much younger, usually ignored the widows. "They are Christians. Leave them to their old ways of three Gods instead of One."

But Rayah used their roof to cross to town. "We can't expect them to change at their age," she worked to convince her family. Besides, she thought, the grand old tree itself had stood since before anybody'd heard of the Messenger of God, blessings on him. "And when they are neglected by their nephew—who of us could live like that? Women of any creed must stick together. We cannot travel like men to be only with those who believe as we do."

So the women of the turpentine sellers came in a body to salvage figs. They were just the year's first crop; many would dry bitter instead of sweet, especially those blown from the tree untimely.

"My sister and I just gather up enough for our breakfast every day," the old woman said. "We haven't had strength to dry them this year."

"I offered some to our nephew's household to whom we owe favors, but they won't come, so take them all." The second old woman made this comment as she leaned on her cane and watched her neighbors stooping and gathering the bruised fruit into baskets. Her face was rough and leathery like the fallen leaves with their wind-borne coating of dust. "They will not wait for those who are too grand to bend for them."

"But of course we will give you the owners' share." It wasn't Rayah's place to make such a promise for her large and Ramadhan-hungry family, but she made it anyway.

She was glad when Auntie Adilah repeated her, as if she had been head woman. "Of course we will, Mothers."

"But that neglectful nephew of theirs—" Cousin Demiella insisted, "I wouldn't cook a meal for him unless it would curdle in his stomach."

The baskets went from hand to hand up the ladder and over to the turpentine sellers' roof. The women accomplished the task with only one mishap—Cousin Demiella stung by a wasp on the cheek whose smoothness she admired so much.

"Sitt Sameh will help it, so there is no scar," Auntie Adilah said above Demiella's overblown wailing.

Rayah looked to the curtain before the little room on the roof. Even in this wind, it didn't stir. If Sitt Sameh and the eunuch were speaking, she couldn't hear them.

Rayah felt the anger welling in her like another khamsin preparing to blow. Sitt Sameh would enjoy the figs as well as the next person in this household. Why didn't she think she had to help with the work, even to heal those wounded in the effort? But it was no use Rayah taking her anger out on Demiella, whose tears were right here and now.

"I'll take care of you, ya Demiella," she offered.

Quickly, Rayah tore several branches from the pots of basil growing by the fountain in their court. She chewed the leaves—careful not to swallow and break the fast—then pounded them to a salve with a hard, unripe fig that made her dry mouth pucker with its gummy skin. She added more of her own spit, difficult as it was to come by.

Demiella's moans increased as Rayah daubed on the gray-green paste. Rayah withdrew her fingers as if she had been stung. It wasn't her cousin's wail; she could have worked that. It was the feeling in the tips, like the crackle in the air before a thunderstorm. When she touched the red and swollen flesh again, she understood: It was the venom, drawing out through her own fingers, healing.

"O God, Lord of people, remover of hardship, heal!" She took refuge in the words of the Prophet, blessings on him, that Sitt Umm Ali had taught her. "You are the Healer. There is no healer but You, with a healing which does not leave behind any illness."

But she didn't stop until all the salve had been applied and her fingers stopped tingling.

"Don't look in your mirror," she advised her cousin. She forgot that Demiella was her elder; she only remembered the first sight of her own blue eyes in that shiny surface. She also remembered how avoiding being seen by the men that morning—which was something like looking into a mirror—had not helped her confront Ghusoon and her parents. "Not until it's better."

Leaving Demiella to keep Bushra company in the cool, dark arbor—young children didn't have to work, no more than they had to fast—Rayah went back upstairs to help with the figs. The fruit filled every basket and bowl from the two houses now, and her aunties shifted them around and on top of each other to make room for her to join them on the rooftop.

The best fruits the women set aside and Adilah carried them down to the kitchen. She would make sweetmeats of them, stuffing them with ground pistachios and dipping them in honey. Then she would carry at least half of the sticky treats back over the roof to the widows next door in thanks.

Fruit of lesser grades the aunties dipped first in a lightly salted brine boiling over a fig-wood fire. "Cousin Kefa blusters like a fig-wood fire." Auntie Adilah pulled her veil up to her mouth, half to giggle, half to cough in the smoke as she spoke. It was good to have this fire on the roof rather than down in the courtyard where the fumes and heat would linger, trapped. "All smoke and no heat." Everyone else forgot their hunger for a moment to feast on that rich image and to laugh out loud.

Deft, stained hands then twisted each fruit of the middle grades, tucking the eye and stem in toward each other and flattening the soft flesh. These the women threaded, thirteen to a length of fiber, and looped to dry. "Thirteen for our Lord and His apostles," said one of the widows watching from her courtyard, and no one stopped to correct her. Muslims honored Isa the son of Maryam as a prophet as well as Christians, and the shrines of his apostles were still known as places of blessing.

Fruit of the lowest grade went over the edge of the roof to the poultry and goats foraging below. Figs to be dried whole the women used their knives to open up. One on top of another, they pressed the fruits into wooden frames then dumped the blocks like brickmakers onto straw mats to dry in the sun. This bitter, chewy leather went well with the richness of lamb.

All the while, the women struggled to keep from licking the juice that dribbled all the way to their elbows so as not to break the fast. And they fought against the growing sting of fig smoke in their eyes, even with the khamsin carrying it away, against the white fig milk irritating their skin. Rayah thought she should make a salve from the grease of sheeps' wool to help those hands afterward, and cucumber juice for the eyes.

As she squatted to join these tasks, Rayah suddenly noticed one hand with blue-black tattoos among the rest. Lingering clouds of anger drifted through her mind. She looked up and met the eyes so like her own. So the blue-eyed kahinah had left her room and come to join the work after all. Rayah couldn't remember a time when that had happened before, and she could tell there were some among the women who were uneasy about Sitt Sameh's presence now. Not the widows, however, who knew what it was to be outcast.

No wonder the people had a saying, "A fig tree which turned out to be a ruin of mosquitoes." Someone actually quoted the saying now: Sitt Sameh.

She said that proverb because no one else seemed inclined to chatter much with her there.

Out of the corner of her eye, Rayah saw one desert hand cradling a fig. "Look," said Sitt Sameh into the silence again. "A wonder, God bless us. In spite of all the wind, this one still has the wings of the female fig wasp caught in the fruit's opening. How like the curtains of the sacred qubbah marching across the desert."

The women on the rooftop shifted to a nervous jangling of anklets.

"And the fig is like a harem," the unnerving accent went on. "The wasp enters, looking for a safe place to lay her child."

Rayah felt blue eyes on her and her cheeks burned hot.

"The wasp child cannot grow without the fig, yet neither does the fig grow without the wasp. But the wasp must shed her protective veil of wings at the harem's door."

Sitt Sameh attempted a nervous laugh as she held the fruit up and the wind finally caught the gauzy wings away. "So the wind comes out of the desert. 'Ask no favors during the khamsin,' as another proverb says, because it makes people too irritable, unable to think of anything beyond their own comfort. But even in the khamsin, the harem joins together to save what can be saved."

Sitt Sameh had her string of fruit full and ready to dry. Having knotted one end to the other, she reached over and laid the circle like a necklace around Rayah's neck.

"There was another khamsin, wasn't there?" The lone voice persisted. "Thirteen or fourteen years ago, it came out of the desert riding not on sand but on horses and camels. Men. Men brandishing swords and a new belief. And within the harem, you have rescued what can be rescued of a world—"

Sitt Sameh stopped herself. Too many people around them were shifting uncomfortably, clenching hands around fruit already too soft to handle. No one said anything for five or six figs apiece. All eyes stayed diligently down on the work.

After another flick to fig flesh with her knife, and another, Sitt Sameh got to her feet without a word and went back to her room. Rayah's clouds gathered again. How could anyone claim to be her mother who didn't join when the women did work like this?

The withered old woman in the courtyard pointed up toward the lumpy necklace Rayah had forgotten she wore. "We wore such necklaces in the old days," the neighbor widow mused. "When a girl became a woman, her mother presented her with one of these."

Isa ibn Maryam and his apostles again? No, for the other widow said, "Like the thirteen stars in the Bull that rises in the spring of the year."

Quickly Rayah took the pagan ornament off and hung it among the rest to dry.

But after the family had broken their fast, Rayah took a few stuffed figs into the little third-floor room and stayed to hear more of the tale of Bint Zura in the desert.

45

> Look forth, O friend, do you see ladies, camel-borne,
> that journey along the upland there above Jurthum well?
> Their litters are hung with precious stuffs, and thin veils thereon
> cast loosely, their borders rose-red, as though they were dyed in blood.
> Sideways they sat as their beasts climbed the ridge of as-Suban...
> They went their way at dawn... straight did they make for the vale of ar-Rass as hand for mouth.
> Dainty and playful their mood... and faces fair...
> And the tassels of scarlet wool in the spots where they dismounted
> glowed red like ishrik seeds, fresh-fallen, unbroken, bright.
> —the Qasidah of Zuhayr ibn Abi Sulma

Uncle Abu Ragheb recognized the man in the horse breeder's tent the moment after Bint Zura herself did. He stopped in the midst of his opening pleasantry to al-Minhal and jumped to an attack with a lightly balanced dagger. "Stand, O vile son of Tamim!" he cried, his lower camel-jaw jutting. "And look upon your death at the hand of Ubayy abu Ragheb."

Al-Minhal, who had come out to greet the new arrivals, laughed. He knew not what else to do in the face of such inexplicable violence. "Peace, O Abu Ragheb," he said. "That is no son of Tamim. Would I insult the honor of your visit by the presence of one whose tribe I know you hate? This is Khalid ibn al-Walid, a son of the Quraysh of Mecca. Why, he is as close to a son of al-Minhal as I ever hope to see. So put up your dagger." Still, the poor host could not keep a tremor and a squeak of fear from his voice.

"Good," Abu Ragheb said. "I shall not kill him under a false identity then. But I shall kill him nonetheless, be he the Great King of Persia, for his devilish prank in the convent last night. By the heat of summer and the Scorcher I do not forget that face, however he may change his headdress in his guilt. It is he. And, if I mistake not, he was there with the sons of Tamim when our poetry lashed their souls as well."

Through a gap in the woolen curtains of her howdah, Bint Zura saw now just what the Qurayshi stranger was wearing: her own red silk underdress. Worse, she felt his gaze on her. Well, not on her exactly, as she sat still within blowing gauze, but where she would have been if drawn curtains had not been in the way. It was the same sensation as the night before: He could feel her presence as she could feel his. She blushed and grew confused just when she knew she must do something, quickly, to snuff out her uncle's violence.

Now al-Minhal saw his guest was in earnest and would not be laughed from his murderous stance. "The holy month," he pleaded. "Would you break its peace and solemnity and start an endless war of wickedness?"

"The sanctity of this month has already been broken." Abu Ragheb spat. "Last night, this dog's son broke into Hind's convent with God-knows-what fiendish designs upon our holy women. I declare the wars of wickedness already begun, and I shall play the part of righteousness in this."

Al-Minhal grew paler and paler with every unretractable word. He looked up at the Qurayshi stranger for a sign of denial but really did not hope to receive one. His look changed to a helpless one that told Khalid, with a shake of the head, "Alas, son of my dear friend. If only we had married you to my Layla sooner, you would have had no need to go rummaging about Taghlibi convents for your satisfaction, so far from home."

Bint Zura felt herself blush from a new cause. Her friend Layla had mentioned that her father planned a marriage for her with a stranger, a Qurayshi, and Bint Zura had wished her joy. But not this man, not *this* Qurayshi. That was all wrong. The hand of the Gods meant something else for this man. Ridiculous thought. If her uncle cut the man's throat in the next moment, the Gods planned his death.

The Qurayshi was al-Minhal's guest and, scold the young man as a father all he would, the host was honor-bound to die in the stranger's defense. The graybeard stepped forward to stand directly in front of his visitor. He drew no sword, took no defensive stance, simply stood there as a lamb about to be sacrificed.

"Let me fight my own battles," Bint Zura heard the Qurayshi say. "And I'm sorry I brought this to your tent."

But it's no use saying such things to a man so piously constrained by duty.

Abu Ragheb shrugged, then rebalanced his stance to take on two instead of one. The Qurayshi reached for his own dagger.

Bint Zura scrambled from the howdah. The Qurayshi's face registered shock. It couldn't be that he hadn't sensed she was there. Very well, he must realize now she wasn't the beauty moonlight had fooled him into thinking. He was going to marry Layla, after all, and Layla was a beauty. Yes, maybe now he could see for the very first time that Bint Zura's eyes were blue.

Nevertheless, she walked without fear up to her uncle's revenge-maddened side and laid a hand upon the wrist that held his dagger.

"What is the matter, O my uncle?" she asked gently.

"Get back in your litter, daughter of my brother," he said. "I am going to kill this bitch's son."

"Why?" she asked, trying to sound surprised but not afraid. "What has he done?"

"This is the very vermin who invaded the convent last night."

"You saw him so well, then?" She put a hint of reproach in her voice, scolding the Qurayshi for having been so careless as to let his face be seen.

"I saw him."

"There must be some mistake. I have sworn this man's protection."

"You're trying to tell me you know this devil?"

"Whether he be devil or saint I cannot say. But if you kill him, you kill him under the shadow of my pledge of safety and thereby defile the sanctity of your own harem."

She left her uncle's side and stepped between his dagger and the Qurayshi's heart a second time. With one hand, she reached up and touched the red silk of the Qurayshi's headdress—her underdress. "O uncle," she asked, "don't you remember this length of fabric you brought me as a gift from al-Mada'in?"

Her uncle snorted. "Any man who has the coin and the vanity could buy himself such a bit of red silk."

"But I know this piece. You simply bought it and stuffed it in your camel bag. I spent three days with the needle over it to make myself a garment. I can see the pattern of the weave in my sleep. I know this fabric as you do not. It is mine, I swear before Isa."

With a quick and spontaneous gesture she whipped the fabric from the Qurayshi's head, leaving him bareheaded and, she knew, ashamed.

"This is mine," she said further, and she produced from the folds a small stamped bronze amulet sewn to a section of the silk. The Qurayshi had not known it was there; all his rough tearing and tying to this new shape had failed to discover it the night before.

Bint Zura not only knew just where the talisman would be but also produced its exact twin, still clinging to a last scrap of red, which was now appliqued to the bodice of her blue-black outer gown. When she said a final, emphatic time, "This is mine," the evidence convinced everyone.

"Very well, it is yours," Abu Ragheb said. "I can see that. What I want to know is how he got it before I cut off his hand for being a thief."

"I gave it to him," she replied.

"You gave it to him? Along with your honor, perhaps? What has any son of any foreign tribe to do with anything belonging to Taghlibi women? I shall kill him first and you afterward for being a shameless harlot."

At this, rather than cowering in fear, Bint Zura laughed out loud.

"Now, by Manat and al-Uzza." Her uncle shifted his stance in her direction. "I shall kill you first for mocking me."

"Uncle, uncle." She laughed again, raising her hands before her as one does to defend oneself from a toddler's fists and not a grown man's dagger. "You know only too well that I have no interest in the love of men. Haven't I refused every offer of marriage you ever found for me? Hasn't my father decided I should marry Christ alone? I do not even know this young man's tribe—Quraysh, you say?—much less his name. He simply seemed to me to be the sort of fool who would get himself into trouble wherever he found it, and so I thought I would give him what sort of protection I could."

This version of events wasn't quite the truth. Bint Zura had never wanted to leave the desert, for example, to come here to enter the convent. Yet, she knew, her uncle would like how this version gave him more control over her. His honor so enhanced, it would sound true to him.

"Remove your protection, brother's daughter," Abu Ragheb said. "If this fellow is not made an example, any other dog's son may take it into his head to disturb your sacred life."

But the irrepressible fire was gone from his voice. Hearing Bint Zura call the Qurayshi a fool was all the satisfaction he craved. With a gesture she tried to make lacking in any care, Bint Zura tossed the red silk back to the stranger.

He caught it with one hand that remained held out to her as if to say, Can't I offer this back to you? I am already so much your debtor that I can't live with myself. Won't you even cut off the little bronze cross and reclaim it?

But she replied, "You keep it, stranger. My uncle bought that fabric for me, trying to tempt me from a life in Christ by showing me the vanities I would be giving up. For his sake I wore it, but red is hardly the color for one who intends to take the vows in but a few month's time. God knows, this is not the last time in this life you'll need its protection. Put it on your foolhardy head. There's a burning sun out there."

Abu Ragheb nodded stiffly to al-Minhal as he stuffed his dagger back into its sheath. "Peace be unto you, al-Minhal, my friend," he said. "I hope you will allow me to postpone acceptance of your gracious hospitality until a more convenient time."

Al-Minhal nodded his all-too-willingness, letting out the breath he'd thought might be his last, and the men made to part.

"My uncle," Bint Zura cried. "Must I go, too?"

"Of course. I will not kill him, but I will not have you dwelling on the same stretch of desert as he if I can help it."

"But I must ask my friend Layla bint al-Minhal if she has seen az-Zuharah."

"Into the harem with you at once, then, while I wait," Abu Ragheb said fiercely to prove he was still master. "Not a hair outside the curtain for any reason. Al-Minhal, I'm entrusting you with my dearest treasure."

"You honor me," al-Minhal stuttered. "By Ya'uk my God, I shall die before I let so much as an untoward wind enter my tent to disturb her."

"And let that son of a dog stay where I can see him."

Without looking at him, Bint Zura sensed how quickly the Qurayshi stranger moved to obey. Or was that to keep her in sight for as long as possible before Layla's harem curtain dropped behind them?

Bint Zura stumbled into the harem, past the water skins and set-up loom, the tangle of dried thorn to feed the fire. Here was the smell of a woman caught within wool, so different from the woman-smell of the convent, which the priests tried to cover up with incense. Into Layla's exuberant embrace she stumbled, into the other girl's whispered questions as to her health and how it was that she was no longer in the convent. Bint Zura answered, but briefly, allowing one part of her heart to follow what was happening with the men—a skill she knew men did not possess in reverse.

"My niece has a white camel that has gone missing," she heard Abu Ragheb apologize.

Through the crack between the dropped harem curtains, Bint Zura watched as he walked with al-Minhal to reclaim his own mount, to wait for her from there.

Layla said something, to which Bint Zura merely nodded, more intent upon listening to her uncle say: "I need only ask if you've seen such a beast. You, sir, need only shake your head no, and I'll ride on my way, out of this enemy's sight. But women, you know, take longer to ask even such a simple question. So I will wait while she does so."

"You know I would have seen such an animal if it came by us here," al-Minhal said.

"I know, old friend. But I must look—and women must talk."

Abu Ragheb shot an evil, arrow-like glance in the direction of the Qurayshi. Bint Zura could not see the stranger, but she could tell he'd become agitated, tried to make signs to al-Minhal, perhaps. Part of her knowledge came from her uncle's glare in that direction. But part of it—she just knew.

That was when she knew something else. She knew he knew. He knew where az-Zuharah was. Now the harem curtain had tumbled down to seal her in a place beyond any man's prying thoughts. And though he knew, the Qurayshi wasn't about to tell her uncle a thing.

46

Know that God loves forbearance, even over a few dates, and He loves courage, even if only to kill a snake or a scorpion.
   —a hadith of Ibn Asakir in Tarikh Dimashq

So I found myself but a curtain away from my beloved—and yet, with her uncle glowering outside, a vast desert might have separated us. The Powers that put us in that circumstance must have been Lords from the Time of Ignorance, for this stroke of wry humor. Muhammad's God, all praise to Him, never jests.

Those old Powers, however, never left a man completely helpless. Hadn't they contrived to let me know where the white camel was? But how to let my beloved know?

My dreams had told me that, given the chance, without veil or darkness, I would be content to gaze at Bint Zura endlessly. But from daylight's truth, cowering from her uncle in al-Minhal's tent, I had in fact turned away and cast down my eyes. I had not felt such confusion since I was fifteen, knocking over my womb mother's Persian vase when I thought I had cleared it. My face, my God! Smallpocked like a cheese, like a sponge! She had seen it, my beloved had cast her blue eyes upon it.

Any fellow who reminded me of my disfiguration in my youth—I'd beat him senseless until my face had become a thing of general respect instead of derision. She made me crave a veil to hide behind, the protection of her harem. The glance of her blue eyes had not healed me.

And yet, in a way, they had. Bint Zura's spirit worked a curious sort of drumming on me, taking over my life and marching it to her rhythm like a well-disciplined Roman mercenary.

That's when it occurred to me. What man of the desert does not recite the old poems—or Surahs of the generous Quran—when they suit his tale? Or his situation, to console him in bad times, to exult with him in good.

> Her hips are two sand drifts sprinkled with light rain
> And rest on two calves like the rollers over which the well ropes pass.

Those were the first verses that occurred to me, the pet phrases of anybody's youthful love. But I knew that was not right. The drumming in my heart was the meter to another poem, more heart-touching than the first. The second poem was one the poet composed not for others, for profit or for flattery, but for his own private consolation upon the death of his wife of many years. Her hands had prepared some cheeses for him just before she died, and now that the stones of her last hearth marked a barren spot in the desert for a grave, he partook of the ripened curds. They caught on the sorrow in his throat and he coughed, sobbed them out into his poem. These are the first lines of that poem:

> She revealed in my heart a stream of love with underground source.
> She was nearer than my jugular, and kinder.

These words took over my heart that afternoon and consumed me. And yet, such a recitation, in this time and place, would get me nowhere.

I stepped back into the shadows of al-Minhal's tent where a worn patch in the worsted roof let in gray rather than deep black. And I spoke:

> "Contrive to stay 'til the White Maiden rises.
> Then shall your al-Uzza rise again, too."

It came out just like that, just like the love poetry throbbing through my head, in a couplet, a shaytan whispering in my ear, no words of my own. Never before or since have I come so close to the gift of prophecy. Just that, and no more. Cryptic play on the name of her camel and the morning star and the time by which, just before sunrise, I was certain I could get the animal here to al-Minal's tent.

I spoke loud enough for anyone on the other side of the harem curtain to hear. I hoped, however, that no one outside the tent would be any wiser. Al-Minhal had chosen to stay out there, to keep company with the girl's uncle, the insulted guest who wouldn't descend from his camel. Al-Minhal did hear something, however, and stepped in to ask: "You said something to me, O Khalid ibn al Walid?"

"No, sir, not at all," I replied. I heard a stifled giggle from the other side of the curtain, so I pushed past my host and out of the tent altogether.

At first sight of me, the Taghlibi raised his spear to his shoulder. Al-Minhal scurried between us yet again, pleading for his honor. I ignored the threat. Instead, I reached our host's Little One at her hobble. I had her bridle loose and was mounted bareback before the spear sailed just beyond my ear. And once I felt the Little One's desert-hardened muscles beneath me, I knew the Taghlibi, on his camel, would never catch me before I reached my foster family's encampment.

The sun—large, flat, and blurred—had set by the time I reached that safety. Bats had begun to circle through the dust raised by gusts of the evening wind. The veil of that airborne earth was so thick, the day's heat had not yet broken through it to freedom. Nor could I yet see any stars. The Goddess wanderer az-Zuharah—or, as others called her, al-Uzza—would not appear until, near the thin moon, she rose in the east as morning approached. I had plenty of time to return to al-Minhal's tent with the white camel named for the Goddess-star.

For surely Bint Zura would understand my hurried, cryptic message to her and contrive to stay in her friend's harem until dawn. Would a white camel serve as a brideprice for such a young woman?

I couldn't say, but it would declare me a man of good will. At the very least I hoped to open the doors to further negotiation.

If my milk brothers hadn't decided to eat the damned creature in my absence.

The first man I came upon as I approached Umm Mutammim's tent was al-Harith. The herdsman's son was just finishing up the evening milking, standing up beside the camels' flanks, holding the skin basin in his left hand and working the teats with his right.

"Is the white camel still here?" I demanded of al-Harith.

He nodded and pointed to the right with his milking hand. "They've decided—" *he began. Maybe he was even trying to warn me of something?*

I didn't stop to listen, but swung off the sweaty back. "Here. Cool down this filly for me. See her watered and fed," *I ordered him carelessly as I tossed him the reins.* "I may also have to have you take her out to the desert with the rest of my herd."

I first remembered the camel I'd rode out on and abandoned at al-Minhal's tent when al-Harith looked up at me in wonder. His headcloth was damp from the camel flanks, his own flesh red with the contact. The camel I'd abandoned—well, let them milk her that night. Bint Zura's soft hennaed hand— I'd be back to claim her—and more—soon enough.

She was easy enough to find, that az-Zuharah, her white coat gleaming in the twilight. She couched, placidly chewing cud. Even in such an attitude, she seemed more glorious than ever, now that I understood whose soul was connected to hers.

"Come, sweetheart," *I said, quietly making girl and beast one.*

I decided right then I probably shouldn't ride the camel where we were going. The sons of Taghlib might not take kindly to my using the spirit of their kindred in such a fashion. I'd do best to borrow a riding mount—and another saddle—from my milk brothers and lead az-Zuharah to al-Minhal's. Such was the sacred aura about her, both girl and camel.

The camel didn't bolt to her feet at my approach. I took hold of the bridle to bring her up, stroking the beautiful neck with my other hand. Girl and camel had grown so close in my mind that the wool of the neck might have been the neck of my beloved—

A jab of pain fired my hand. I gasped aloud as it blazed, throbbing with every beat of my heart, rising higher and higher up the right arm with which I grasped the bridle.

I swore loudly. With my first clear thought, I knew what it must be, although I couldn't see the little monster in the gloom. A scorpion.

I refused to let such a tiny—I gasped again—thing stop my plan. Pain making my right hand stupid, I reached for the bridle with my left. Now I screamed aloud. A second jab took that hand. The camel continued to chew and to blink at me with wide, placid eyes.

Cursing heaven, I turned to stagger to my milk mother's tent—and nearly tripped over the wizened, ragged figure of Umm Taghlib instead. She was small and birdlike, yet malicious, something between a sparrow and a vulture. With those blue eyes like nothing else in the world—except my beloved's, I realized with the poison pounding at my temples.

She gave me no time to sort out what that coincidence meant. "Ah, so it's you," *she said.* "Come trying to steal the spirit-camel. Didn't I tell Umm Mutammim you'd be trouble, all those years ago?"

Was it just the agony in my hands, working its way up to my brain, or did her words really jab in my head like yet another stinger? "All those years ago." Did she mean the time when we had come to her, begging her to find lost al-Harith? My arm itched with poison. And with remembering the cloth I had stolen from her magic, as if it was still tied around my arm.

"I've been stung by a scorpion," I gasped. "A pair of them."

"Of course. You don't think I'd settle down for the night leaving the White One unprotected, do you?"

"You? You set those monsters on the camel?"

"I conjured the Ones of this Land. This is the form they took."

"Jinn?"

"I wouldn't carelessly say their name like that if I were you. Not with their venom pumping through me."

It was true. I could feel my heart racing, coursing the poison like a wadi in spate, fire through my veins. I tried consciously to stop the muscle moving that force but of course had no effect. My head began to reel.

"You might have hurt the camel," I tried to say. "To allow scorpions to crawl all over her."

"Nonsense. The Fire Ones knew what they were there to protect. Well, come along."

She caught my elbow, and I withdrew it with a shriek that made me tremble to my toes. I didn't know if I could keep them under me much longer.

"Don't you want me to see if I can draw the Fire Ones off? Since they've attacked at my bidding, may they not better retreat to the same orders than to any others?"

This made sense to the wild fever in my brain. In fact, I doubted very much whether I could make it through the rest of the camel herd to Umm Mutammim's tent. It seemed a day's journey through a well-less lava bed to me then.

Umm Taghlib's tent, her same little rag propped by one short pole, was much closer. I saw it now by the wink of a few small coals in her hearth: jinn's eyes. Terrors of childhood regripped me at the sight. For one horrible moment, I thought I went there to die—or at the very least to lose the strength of my right arm, which once I had so carelessly bartered. But I had lost its use now, anyway.

In the end, she supported my arm—higher up, under the shoulder. I never would have made it otherwise. I let her lay me down under the scrap of rag that left my feet out under the stars. The stars that were swiftly turning to al-Uzza's rising.

Here followed hours I cannot number, hours of endless numbness, of vomiting, of blinding pain, every breath a gasp of fire. Why would the old kahinah want to save me, that arm I'd promised then reneged?

I'll answer before my scribe can ask it. I doubt she saved me at all.

Strange visions came to me in my delirium. Umm Taghlib's leathery skin seemed to click with her crippled, old movements like scorpion scales. They gave rhythm to her chants, but after a while, clicking caused the hard carapace to crack down the middle of her forehead. The old crone moulted, revealing flesh glistening with youth and vulnerablity beneath. The single pair of eyes, however, multiplied to five glinting in blue rows along the firm angular line of her new-formed face. I recoiled from the eight arms tending me, from the stinger that curled up over her back.

In this guise, she managed to capture the scorpions that had stung me. Her old form restored, she held them between claw-like fingers and dropped them live in the hollow of a stone. Here she ground them to pulp, then forced me to drink the mixture slicked with a little sesame oil. She lanced my wounds and drew the venom from them into her dry, stale-smelling mouth.

These were hours choked with incense rising from a hollow slab of chist, which Umm Taghlib addressed in mumbled chants.

"Not incense," she snapped at me when I tried to say something over my swollen tongue. "It's one of the Dwellers in the Land, naturally."

And after that, the twist of smoke did seem to dance with sinuous curves as if it were alive, responding to her exhortations like a celebrant to the drum.

Then, at one blurred moment that seemed part of a nightmare, Umm Taghlib hoisted her skirts and straddled me, trying to get my vital juice to respond. "A sure way to purge the poison," she assured me.

By that time, froth was foaming at my mouth as if I were a camel in rut. The scorpion woman remoulted to view, young enough to tempt, but hideous. The male scorpion sometimes injects the female with his venom to calm her so he can mate. Then, often as not, she eats him. I felt ready to die. I wanted to die.

I was as incapable of performing as al-Harith had been the previous night with the women in the red-kerchiefed tents. Umm Taghlib looked at me with something between disgust and despair. There was nothing for it now. I couldn't perform, I would have to die. It couldn't be helped. Just the thought, through all my pain, shot stars before my eyes. And that reminded me—

I struggled to get up. She held me down between her thighs.

"I must go," I gasped. "I must get the white camel to al-Minhal's tent before—"

"The white camel is going nowhere," Umm Taghlib assured me, still wriggling her parts over mine. "Doesn't the poison coursing through your veins tell you that?"

"But I know to whom the star—I mean the animal—belongs. I must bring the wanderer back."

"As I know to whom she belongs as well. But she never wandered. I led her."

"Bint Zura wants her spirit-camel back." I moaned.

"And so shall she have her, for such a gift the Gods do not grant to everyone."

"Bint Zura—I promised—" I panted.

"Bint Zura." Umm Taghlib turned from me, offering a glimpse of her curling stinger before it vanished. "Her name is Amat al-Uzza. What has Zura to do with that child? May the Dwellers of this Place twirl his wits to madness. She is mine."

"Yours—?" Had I been trying to give brideprice to the wrong place? Had I so badly misunderstood? Not that it really mattered much now, since I was going to die.

"She is my daughter whom an evil man stole from my arms. When she comes for the camel, that will bring her back to me. It is the magic I have worked for all these years. I hope you let her know—somehow—that you knew where the camel was? A verse of poetry, perhaps?"

I was too overwhelmed by the pain—and by what I was hearing—to do more than nod. I had been used. My desire used for other ends. Did that mean it counted for nothing?

"Good. Then, yes, it will work. She will come. It is prophesied. Such is the destiny of all women of this line, whose eyes are marked blue, like desert wells. My daughter, Amat al-Uzza, was born in the holy qubbah. Try as her father might to destroy it and all old ways, ways of the Dwellers in this Land, it remains her destiny to ride as the spirit of her tribe in the holy of holies. Her destiny is to lead her people to victory."

"Then she should stay with her tribe. The camel should go to her, not she come to it."

"But the Taghlibi are cursed. I have cursed them. To the salvation and victory of the Arabs."

I remembered Hanzala and his armor. "The Taghlibi have the support of the Persians," I said, though it made my head spin to argue thus. "Things cannot help but be safer on the side that does not go against the great empire."

"Ah, that shows how little you know what is written in the sands. How poorly you read what is in the sky."

I was weeping now, with pain and frustration. "All I know of the sky is that the morning star, az-Zuharah, will rise soon. I promised her the camel would return by then."

"And do you not see how the great Sky Warrior—al-Babadur whom the Greeks call Orion—was banished to the heavens for his rape of the Goddess against her will? In our tongue the names of the stars make his shape: Rigel, his foot, Saif, 'Sword of the Giant.' Betelgeuse, his armpit, the red star at his shoulder where the red star of the scorpion sank home."

She slid off me then, making a sound, more of her own kind of disgust. This quickly turned again to something between longing and renewed prophecy. "Bellatrix—the Female Warrior. She is there, in the heavens, too. Do not dream, even in your delirium, that your magic can defeat mine, all these years in the making, and written ere now, centuries, in the skies."

I tried once more to rise, but even with her gone from my hips, I found I could not. I rolled and wailed with pain, impotence, and shame.

47

**Sons of our uncle, peace: scrape not the bark from our terebinth tree.
Walk now gently a while, as once you were wont to go.**
—al-Fadl ibn al-Abbas ibn Utbah ibn Abu
Lahab, a close kinsman of the Prophet

"Shouldn't you stay home?" Cousin Kefa asked Rayah. He was loading adzes, axes, and scrapers into the donkey's panniers in the predawn light. "Turpentine can't be good for your hands. Shouldn't you be getting beautiful for your meeting with your intended?" He sounded as if he thought such a feat would take more hours than there were in a lifetime.

"Jaffar's not my intended," Rayah insisted, handing her cousin the next tool to prove her usefulness.

"Not yet, and he certainly won't be if you don't make an effort to please."

"How can it please any man to see a possible wife who doesn't know how to work?"

Rayah had awakened to a strange stillness thrumming in her head: During the night, the khamsin had died. The morning was cool and fresh and blessedly still. The swelling of the wasp sting in Cousin Demiella's cheek had almost disappeared, so the young woman was allowed her mirror again. And little Bushra was up and dancing to break her fast.

Rayah saw and was gratified, thanking God in her prayers. But that made her think the healings were none of her own doing. God alone was the Merciful; it didn't matter what a person did, beyond submitting. Certainly Ghusoon only got worse under Rayah's human hands. She also remembered what Sitt Sameh had said over the figs the day before: "Within the harem, you have rescued what can be rescued of a world—" How had she meant to finish the sentence? Or were all the words she told of days gone by a conclusion to that same sentence?

No matter. Rayah had risen from her prayers having decided what she must do. She told her cousin: "You need the extra hands among the pine groves. The heat of the khamsin set the juices running more than usual, during the days when you couldn't go out to the stands for the wind. The scrape is no doubt clogged with sand and dried up as well. My meeting with Jaffar isn't until tomorrow. Sitt Sameh will give me a salve for my hands. Today you need my help."

Someone else needed Rayah's help more than the men—Sitt Sameh.

"If you want to learn the healer's art," Sitt Sameh had said yesterday, "You can begin by learning to keep up my stores. Turpentine, for instance. I have run out."

The older woman picked up the vial from which the household's piney fragrance wafted with even more intensity. She turned it upside down to show that, indeed, it was empty of everything but odor. "During the khamsin, more people suffer difficulty breathing. Their wounds fester. They need turpentine."

Rayah took this information to heart, as if building her own wall of healing stores. "Our people here make turpentine," she said. "Nothing easier than to send Cousin Lutfi to the shop for some."

"Perhaps," Sitt Sameh replied. "And so have I done all these years. But its strength would be much improved were your hands to be in it throughout the entire process, from the beginning."

So, "You need my help," Rayah told her cousin. She said it all, everything she could think of, pursuing a speech-dry Kefa from doorway to donkey and back again. Finally he threw up his hands in surrender and went in to eat and drink the last little bit before dawn prayers and the fast began.

The desert wind had indeed made a mess in the terebinth grove. Sand and broken twigs coated the channels and catch-cups, drying the yellow coagulation beyond use. Fasting though they were, the men set to work at once with their sharp tools to reveal the raw wood, to set the tree wounds bleeding again.

The piney scent filled the grove once more, sometimes so sharp as to bring tears to the eyes. It got trapped beneath the dusty gray canopy of leaves hung with ruby berries. Rayah remembered coming to the same place as a very young child, riding on Auntie Adilah's back. When she'd been set down, she'd played in the fragrance, as if within a mother's skirts after she'd been purified with incense at a party. Now the odor even pervaded the wool of goats that tiptoed in the shade with her. A pair of old nannies, their udders swinging, jumped up into the boughs to nibble leaves.

Had the herd not included some of the family's own animals, the menfolk might have driven it off. A number of the animals, in fact, had already been picked to be the sacrifices at the Eid celebration. Trimmed with proud woolen tassels and splotched between the shoulders with red or yellow or green dye, they were like a party of children showing off bright new clothes. So they all were left to browse.

"I wonder that your animals would eat such bitter leaves," Rayah commented to the herdsboy when she passed him between tree trunks. "And won't it make the milk taste like medicine?"

"The best thing for them," replied the moon-faced fellow. "They give little milk in this season, and the terebinth keeps worms out of their guts."

Rayah wondered if the same thing would work for people. She would ask Sitt Sameh. Or she would try it herself on the next case of worms she learned of.

A dog the color of slate came running among the herd. Rayah took him for the herder's dog until the boy pulled out his sling and drove the creature off, whining, with a few well-aimed stones. Then she saw how painfully thin the creature was, its ribs standing out like veins in the its sides where the stones hit. This told her it was wild like most dogs, unclaimed even by a pack of its own kind, perhaps even mad. The herdsman was right to drive off the hound, almost as dangerous as a pack of hyenas.

"Turpentine daubed on the sores they get also helps the healing." The herdsboy forgot the dog the minute it was out of sight, thinking only of his flock again. He passed on, drawing his flute out of his belt then and charming his charges.

Rayah's uncle and some of her cousins broke off bits of turpentine scrape. Though probably breaking the fast if they were to ask the imam, they popped the crystals in their mouths and chewed on them. The act was more a penance than indulgence, proof of manhood; the resin was very bitter. "The Padishah of Persia ate such at his ascension," they told each other, "to keep mindful of the bitterness of life. This was after he'd eaten a frail of figs, for life's sweetness, and before drinking the sour milk which taught that what is sweet may, with time, go bad." Speaking of food, particularly that found on royal tables, was a favorite way to while away the long, hungry hours.

"Since the coming of Islam," added another uncle, "there is no king in Persia any longer, so we common men may take the lessons of his ascension for ourselves."

Rayah didn't know about padishahs, or even about being a man, but she thought she would see how the health of these kinsmen equaled that of the leaf-eating goats.

Like eating turpentine scrape, preparing the trees was not work for a girl. It was heavy and required a certain level of skill so as not to cut too deeply into the dark heart and kill the tree. They set her to cleaning the cups and then to attaching them to catch the new flow. She worked her best, trying to put healing into each movement to infuse the product as Sitt Sameh said she should. She had the unhappy feeling that the more conscious she was of the desired results, the more they eluded her, like trying to pick up quicksilver. How was she supposed to make powerful turpentine if that was men's work and they wouldn't even let her near? And of all the uses she knew or had just learned for the pungent liguid, none of them was a cure for jinn possession such as her friend Ghusoon suffered, the thing uppermost in her mind. Nonetheless, she kept at it.

She also cut the few herbs she found still fresh after the killing wind; wild onions, thyme, and capers among the rocks, some for curing, some merely for cooking, some for both. She stored these in the tied-up corner of her veil. No one could say this wasn't woman's work. What else were veils for?

"Ya, Rayah. There's no need to cup that one," Kefa called to her as she walked to one tree set aside from the others. "We never cut that tree." At his warning, she saw the terebinth, taller than all the others, its lower branches draped with bits of cloth.

The Mother Tree. Such a one as perhaps Khalid ibn al-Walīd might have cut down in his conquest—only this one he had spared. Probably because he never knew of it. As he never knew of Rayah herself.

A breath of wind, the death rattle of the khamsin, stirred in the Mother Tree's branches. The sound turned into a low growl. Fear prickled down Rayah's back. She backed up a step when she saw it was the mangy dog, still hovering about, as if waiting for scraps from fasting humans. The brute had no concept of the holy. And yet, of some things, he did. The dog, she saw, growled not at her, but at the wind in the Mother Tree. As Khalid the Conqueror might if he were here. Just before he cut the idol down. The dog's hackles rose. He growled again. The dog could tell, unlike any of the humans fasting for sharper spirituality, that jinn were present in the tree. Rayah didn't think that made the creature mad. With this hint, she could sense the Fire Beings, too. She almost heard them speak the name of her friend, Ghusoon.

Should she cut the Mother Tree and take the powerful turpentine from its trunk for herself?

No. Some things were too strong to handle. Rayah tore a scrap from the hem of her underdress instead and tied it among the others in the lower branches. She spoke the name of her friend. Then she moved on.

Her heart had hardly returned to a normal rhythm when the charcoal burner came by. He came to discuss deliveries of his stock to the rendering sheds and to see if there was any fall wood among the terebinths he could add to his next burn. Rayah looked away and pulled up her veil, pretending to concentrate on her work. It was none of her business, a strange Christian man as he was. But as he went by, going to get his donkey for the load, he hissed at her under his breath: "Yaqob, he still sleeps with honor in your family's tomb." Yaqob, this man she'd never known, still haunted her.

The heat of the day had come upon them. Because of the fasting, the men's strength gave out early. They spread themselves about in the shade under the trees, wrapping the corners of their headgear over their eyes.

The younger ones, with some energy left, went off with a wildly ambitious plan. "Ya Rayah, inshallah, and if you don't disturb us, we will catch a hawk."

"The sharif, inshallah, will give us gold for such a prize."

That left Rayah to take the donkeys to the spring for water. That was woman's work.

She saw the dog again, this time with her cousins after it, throwing more rocks. Kefa even set off with a bit of donkey halter, trying to catch it.

She shook her head. These boys of the town. At least the hawk was safe.

Rayah was as gummy as the men, her fingers sticking together, her skirts clinging to her legs, and her veil resined to her braids. She took the opportunity, while the animals drank, to step down into the spring and scrub the worst of the terebinth off. Afqa was the name of the spring, the place, so they said, where Queen Zaynab came to bathe. The stonework surrounding the cavern was easily so old, probably older. For without the water bubbling from the earth at blood heat, smelling vaguely of sulfur and iron, renewing and healing in its properties, Tadmor would be as dead as the desert around it. Rayah resisted the temptation to break her fast with a drink but left the dampness in her clothing, to help keep her cool.

As Rayah stepped up the stonework to lead the donkeys back to the terebinth shade, a scrambling sound among the bushes stole her attention instead. Bending down, she saw the slate-colored dog tied to the large leaves and thick stems of a plant growing about waist high. The dog whined as she approached.

"Ya, you poor thing."

"You can let him go now, Rayah," her cousin yelled from the top of the next hillock. "We didn't want him eating the bait, but the hawk has flown off now, so it doesn't matter."

Dogs, she could almost hear Sitt Umm Ali say, were unclean. But as she knelt and parted the leaves to find the end of the cord, Rayah realized just what sort of a plant this was, revealed here beside the life-giving spring. How did she know this? She couldn't say. Except, perhaps, for a whispering from the water itself. "Baaras." From the nearby Mother Tree.

At last. After a day of sap and medicated lungs, here was something that could work against possession. Her cousins hadn't even known what herb they touched. And yet baaras could be very dangerous. Even harvesting it could cause the root such pain that it would scream aloud. And the scream of the baaras could pierce the skull and kill a man. Still, such superhuman sensitivity was what a healer wanted in the plant.

Rayah took a breath to steady herself and moved closer. Instead of releasing the dog at once, she dug in the soft, sandy dirt around the base of the plant until she saw that, indeed, it had a long, thick, fleshy taproot. The dog fawned, sensing liberation. Rayah couldn't meet its eyes.

She freed the root as well as she could, so it wobbled in its matrix. Then she stepped back.

Something to lure the dog forward. Her family had no food with them but the rabbit her cousins had trapped, then skinned for the hawk. She got this and waved it for the dog.

"Here, boy."

She knew she ought to say some words of power, and all she knew were those of the Holy Quran. Closing her eyes against what might be a force so strong it could kill the dog—it could kill her—she recited:

"'I worship not that which you worship.'"

With her eyes tight shut, she heard the scream. Was it the baaras root? Or only herself?

"Ya Rayah, what happened?" Kefa demanded as he ran up to her.

From behind a veil pulled closer than was needed for a young kinsman, she pointed. The dog, its bit of donkey bridle dragging, was gulping down the rabbit carcass. Had there been bad effect on him? She thought maybe he had gone deaf. At least, none of Kefa's curses had any effect on the poor creature. And there were maggots dropping out of the slate-colored ears. But maybe the wounds torn by the teeth of other dogs had always been festering there—she just hadn't been close enough to see before.

Rayah didn't worry about that, more than to hope some healing terebinth sap might stick to those ears and scabs. Hidden against her breast, she clutched the almost infant-sized root, smelling of earth and, she thought, a little jinn smoke that make her own hackles rise.

What else was a veil for?

48

> Ah, how beautiful your arms, O Sita,
> With blue tattoo marks!
> How beautiful the noise of the attack of her kin
> And the sabers blood-dyed as if with henna.
> —a song of the Rwala tribe

That evening, Rayah sat down eagerly to break her fast in Sitt Sameh's room. Her mother laid aside her spinning to accept the vial of new turpentine from her, sniffed at it tentatively, then nodded in approval.

The cold lemon drink on Rayah's throat, parched from the terebinth plantation, made her lightheaded with relief. "Praised be to God who teaches us to fast so we may know His gifts," she recited.

Equally wonderful to Rayah that evening was what she held in her heart: appreciation of her own healing stores. With the help of the dog and the murmur of the spring, she had something Sitt Sameh didn't have: the baaras root, the plant one needed to drive away demons. She said nothing of this to Sitt Sameh as the older woman turned her back to set the turpentine among her herbs and drugs. Rayah wasn't exactly sure what made her hesitate to seek her mother's acceptance. But even as Sitt Sameh began to conjure the world long-gone with her words, Rayah made plans for a world of her own.

The star al-Uzza rose over Bint Zura's friend's tent, and the Qurayshi, the man her uncle said was an enemy, did not return. More important, no az-Zuharah came, tossing the tassels on her head with a teasing pride. For all his annoying attraction, the Qurayshi was a liar.

Or no. Perhaps the sense Bint Zura had taken from his words, cryptic as a poet's, was not what he had meant to say. She rolled the couplet over and over in her mind:

> Contrive to stay 'til the White Maiden rises.
> Then shall your al-Uzza rise again, too.

What he had meant, however, remained a mystery to her.

Once he'd chased off Khalid ibn al-Walīd the Qurayshi, her uncle felt better about leaving her in Layla's harem. Better to have her stay quietly there than gadding all around al-Hira after him, looking for that camel.

So, Bint Zura had spent the night with her friend, half in gossip, half with her mind on the strange Khalid's words.

"You know Khalid ibn al-Walīd?" Layla asked her guest as they lay together on the cushions, looking out the tent curtain at a triangle of stars.

They decided to tattoo one another, although no doubt Hind in the convent garden would not approve. In the stifle of a breathless tent, Layla pricked ash saved from numerous fires beneath Bint Zura's white skin with a sliver of smoothed camel bone.

"The son of al-Walīd," Bint Zura repeated, catching her breath at the pain but admiring nonetheless the pattern beneath the little beads of blood on her own ankles. She admired it by the leaping fire, fed by more camel thorn than was really comfortable, just to provide enough light. Bint Zura would have to trust her friend as to the beauty of the line across her forehead. "So that is his name. You see, you know him much better than I."

Although if this were so, Bint Zura was surprised that Layla had not recognized him at the well when her father had spouted his mad prophecies. Khalid following them as they swung the palm fronds over their shoulders to the church . . . Bint Zura had recognized him. Indeed, it seemed as if she'd always known him.

"We're to be married, Ibn al-Walīd and I," Layla said.

"Is that so?" Bint Zura said, unnerved by how sad the news made her feel. "Isa ibn Maryam set joy on the day."

"He lives in Mecca," said her friend. "I shall have to go there with him."

"Now, that I dislike. Will you have to live in a heap of mud brick instead of in a tent?"

"I . . . I don't know."

"Mecca is very far away."

"But you are going to enter the convent," Layla said defensively, "which is even farther away, if not in space, then in spirit."

"Don't you want to marry this man?" Bint Zura asked as she took the camel bone needle between her own fingers to work on her friend: magic circles about the breasts, a dotted line from navel to the furred mound of pubis. The drawings would frighten away evil jinn, spare the sight only for a kindly husband. Bless the children to come. "Or are they making you marry him for some trade alliance?"

"Oh, no!" Layla did her best to cover her intakes of stung breath with giggles and a whisper. "He is the most wonderful man I have ever seen."

"Then he is worth going any distance for," Bint Zura said. "He is worth giving up family, home, everything for, if he is indeed so wonderful." She heard the serious doubt in her own voice.

Layla took the words as if they'd been a scolding. "I know you," she said defensively. "I know you. You give up all men for the God-man Isa. I heard you say it today."

A falling star shot across the tent opening, God casting a jinni down to earth. "Then you don't know me at all," Bint Zura said, and it saddened her. Did even she know herself?

She saw that she might have hurt her friend. With her words? Or just with an extra-sharp jab? Bint Zura said, "She has great power."

"Who?"

"My mother."

"How do you know this? You've never met her."

Bint Zura said nothing about her meeting behind the saddle booth the day before. "She is a familiar with the jinn. It is a gift to the women in our family, this power over the Fire-Born Ones of the desert. Zura my father married my mother while she was yet a child in his attempt to control the power. So it devolves upon me, this great responsibility."

"You are only a girl! Nothing is so much your responsibility. Come, I would make one more mark, here, at your wrist."

"Yes, so when my sleeve slips away, men will see the hint of blue marks revealed."

"This mark will give you the good graces of the sun Goddess," Layla said, concentrating on her work. "She-We-Should-Not-Name can be fierce and unmerciful if provoked to jealousy."

To Bint Zura's father, that same sign might be the cross of Isa. The two figures differed from each other in no more than a careless slip of the needle.

"So they would like," Bint Zura said.

"What?"

"That as girls we have no responsibility. Christianity was the thing that first and most fiercely opposed my mother and her power. I rejected it at once. But I have given the matter some more thought. My entering a convent will cement my father's alliances. Is the convent the only possibility for one such as myself who feels an inhuman power inside her and a desire to have continual contact with the will of heaven, as I was born to do? For my father, such power must be stifled and so die with me. There is no place for it in the world that is coming. At least this way I shall spare future generations the pain I have known.

"So I have been vowed to Mother Hind." Bint Zura tried to put a definite finish on her tale, however unsatisfied she was with it. "You may marry that Khalid what's-his-name, Layla, and with my blessing. You might as well be in Mecca as in the eastern desert for all I shall be able to see you. You'll be no farther from my prayers at any rate."

Layla didn't like where Bint Zura's mouth took them. She puckered the sore pin pricks in her forehead and then took command of their conversation, filling it with simpler things. After this, therefore, Bint Zura watched the stars and listened to her friend's babble like a stream passing by. No other star fell, not that night.

And the white Goddess rose without sign of the white camel. Without sign of Khalid the son of al-Walīd.

Toward midmorning, her uncle returned, exhaustion carved in the very sag with which he sat his camel.

"You have not found her?" Bint Zura asked, rising and coming to the door of the tent.

"No," was his grumbled reply as he made his own camel sink wearily to its knees. "May maggots infect that creature to her very eyes."

"Uncle, say not so." Bint Zura touched the amulet about her neck against such a thing happening.

"But I have been to every tribe encircling the entire encampment and no one has seen her. How can a white camel not be seen?"

"Unless it is by the power of the Dwellers in this Place." Again Bint Zura touched her amulet, this time against the jinn—or for their aid. "But are you certain? Every tribe?"

"Well, except among the sons of Tamim where, of course, I dare not go, at price of my blood."

"But that's where she is, of course." Suddenly the Qurayshi's words made sense. He'd just been trying to tell her where az-Zuharah was, even if he couldn't actually bring the camel to her.

Abu Ragheb looked at his niece. Her certainty penetrated him. "Yes, of course. I wouldn't put it past those sons of dogs to have resorted to such a theft. And in the holy month of pilgrimage, no less."

"We must go and get her back from them," Bint Zura urged, grabbing his arm.

Uncle Abu Ragheb pulled away, as much from the idea as from a woman's touch. "I couldn't go there. No son of Taghlib could. I'd only return without the camel—and probably without my life."

"But what are we children of Taghlib without the soul of our lineage? The white camel, sent to us by the Gods—?"

Her uncle turned from her with a fury, tapping his camel goad against his leg. "Christians don't approve of the qubbah litter, you know. 'Pagan,' they call it. They don't want you to keep az-Zuharah in the convent garden, either."

"Although they worship human faces painted in golden boxes."

Uncle Abu Ragheb worked the camel-jut of his lower jaw as he gazed out, down the wadi and toward the Encampment. The smoke of many camel-dung fires blurred the view. "The Christians are joining with the Persians in an attempt to regain an-Numan's armor. I think we must unite with them."

"If the sons of Taghlib are going into a set battle, not just a raid, you must have an ensign in the lead."

"You're right, niece. My lion skin will not be enough."

Bint Zura held her tongue with effort. She could feel her heart racing. What did it matter that the lion had really been her kill? Hers and the camel's. Her uncle was going to help her get az-Zuharah back. But she could also tell there would be a cost. The miraculous white camel might cease to be hers altogether and belong to the whole tribe. The quiet of Mother Hind's convent garden suddenly had its attractions—if she couldn't run away to the deepest desert with az-Zuharah. But father, uncle, tribe, or abbess, none of them was ever going to let her find her own destiny.

"As I went from tribe to tribe yesterday," Uncle Abu Ragheb said, "I heard that Hanzala ibn Thalaba has been going among those same tribes just ahead of me. He is showing off that traitor an-Numan's armor, trying to get the tribes to support him in that impossible conflict."

Bint Zura could tell her uncle wasn't really talking to her. He didn't think she could understand such things, such male things. But she did understand that a white camel had been born as she watched in the cleft of Meda'in Salih, and that colored her understanding of all things.

"Yes," her uncle said with sudden decision. "Hanzala ibn Thalaba was seen with the Tamim night before last, so I heard. If I take this news to my brother—your father—I need not lead my clan alone against those sons of dogs, the Tamim. I will have the might of the king of al-Hira backing me in our old feud."

"You will get az-Zuharah back for me then?"

"For you? For all the sons of Taghlib."

So it began, the division of herself among all the people. First they would take her camel, then her every waking thought, her every silent prayer.

"Yes, I'll get her back," Uncle Abu Ragheb went on. "And I will crush the Tamim."

The Tamim. To which Khalid the Qurayshi, Layla's betrothed, was connected.

49

> How prettily her camel to its feet is rising
> Adorned with purchased ornaments.
> —a song of the Rwala tribe

"May the heavens hold their rains from them," Uncle Abu Ragheb cursed on toward evening of the same day. Then he turned to apologize to the regal company he'd brought out to this abandoned stretch of camel thorn with him. "The sons of Tamim must have heard of your coming, sire, and fled to the desert."

The upland strewn with pebbles where the sons of Tamim were known to camp each year for the pilgrimage was empty. Many camels had nibbled the thorn in the recent past. Their droppings were drying everywhere in the sun, attracting flies and dung beetles. No other sign of Tamimi tent or Hanzala ibn Thalaba in the dead traitor king's armor remained. Nor of the sacred white camel.

Bint Zura, slipping out of her litter as her borrowed camel knelt, wasn't surprised. Unlike a mere raiding party moving while the moon was small, this company her uncle had garnered from the new king created enough fanfare to let the whole desert know it was coming. It must have raised a column like a sandstorm to herald them wherever they went. It would not take much to guess that the usurping king had been urged to break the pilgrimage in order to gain his purpose in the easiest way, by picking off one rebel clan detached from all the rest. Seeing such an apparition on the horizon, any sensible tribe would have wasted no time in packing up and heading to the inner desert.

Khalid ibn al-Walīd had, no doubt, packed up with them. Bint Zura scratched at the tattoos on her wrists and ankles, still tender.

Then, at once, Bint Zura knew it didn't matter. The upland was not completely abandoned—not quite. While the armored men all around her held their mounts—camels and horse together—to shout recriminations at one another and debate what they should do, she saw it. At first, it was just a shimmer, a puddle of mirage in the distance, something of the jinn arising out of nothingness.

She began to walk—then run—toward the vision. By the time she was running, her uncle goading his mount after her, she knew exactly what it was: a tiny wisp of a tent with a solitary camel kneeling outside.

A white camel.

"Az-Zuharah, az-Zuharah!" Dust filled her mouth, but Bint Zura kept shouting.

The camel turned her regal head at the sound of her name and struggled to her feet. She gave a greeting bawl. Bint Zura saw the animal try to run to her—then saw that a solid hobble prevented her.

The girl was a stone's toss away from throwing her arms about the beautiful white neck when suddenly she skidded to a stop. A small, wizened figure had stepped between her and az-Zuharah. Hardly more than a heap of rags, yet the figure threatened.

More, Bint Zura had the strangest feeling that she knew the woman.

Tears stood in the old woman's eyes, then began to spill down her tattooed cheeks. Such unexpected emotion, a veil thrown unashamedly back before strangers—these things were unnerving. Bint Zura retreated a step.

Then she heard her name, as she had only heard it whispered behind the saddle maker's tent—and inside her head—before: "Amat al-Uzza." She took another step back, clutching both veil and her amulet against evil.

"Amat al-Uzza, my daughter, my child." With open arms, the woman who knew the black magic of her secret name made up that step; two steps closed the gap.

"What . . . what have you done to my camel?" Bint Zura spoke defensively. Having had, before, eyes only for the animal, she had not noticed the construction of wood and curtains that now sprang from az-Zuharah's hump. It was strange, but beautiful, definitely something floated up from the world of the jinn.

Then Bint Zura remembered the bare litter frame of bent acacia wood behind the saddler's booth, the old woman who'd encouraged her to touch the arcing construction. This was the same woman. They met, blue eyes to blue. Bint Zura's lips moved. They tried to form the word "Mother" but failed.

"Don't touch her, you fire-blackened kahinah."

This was not Abu Ragheb who spoke. Her uncle had pulled his riding camel up some distance away the moment he'd come to an awe-filled understanding of what he saw. The speaker was Bint Zura's own father, Zura himself who, in long Christian robes, had ridden after the war party on a donkey.

"Get behind me, shaytan," Zura said further.

Had he truly meant that scripture he spouted, her father ought to have climbed back on that donkey and headed back to the safety of al-Hira's walls. Instead, he dismounted and came on foot, step by threatening step as the support of a force of twenty armed men at his back him gave him courage. He held the great iron cross he wore around his neck before him like a shield.

Her mother didn't blink but shot back with a derisive snort. "Shaytan? What know you of shaytan, you who have run to a priest's robes and the walls of a town? I know—I am the desert.

I know a shaytan when I see one, and mine has always been you, O Zura of the sons of Taghlib, since you forced me as your bride. With that union, I embraced you, my shaytan, and you gave purpose to my entire life. Every breath I take, every grain of incense with which I invoke the Fire Ones—it has your name on it, Zura—Zura—"

Bint Zura saw her father stagger backward at the sound of his name, although how it was, she couldn't explain. Her mother seemed half his size, and sand-blasted besides.

"Remember Jacob struggling with the angel in the wilderness," Ahudammah the bishop said, stepping up to second her failing father. "Stay strong with the good so in the end you may be chosen as was Israel."

Well, let them struggle with their shayatan, Bint Zura thought. She wriggled between them and ran to embrace her own guiding spirit.

"Ah, az-Zuharah," she crooned when she had the familiar bridle in her hand once more. The kahinah's words had made her understand just how much and in what supernatural fashion the camel had always inspired her. "You have always been my shaytan, haven't you, my spirit camel, my soul? Always encouraging me to brave deeds, to be more than I was before."

Bint Zura loosed the hobble. Anyone who had to keep az-Zuharah restrained like that did not deserve to have the animal. Bint Zura ran her hands over every span of the dear, white wool, crooning all the while, and saw no harm done. She sank her face deep into the fragrance of warm camel wool.

Then her hands found the qubbah perched on the animal's hump, and she began to explore that with even more wonder. She knew she was looking into, touching, the place she'd been born, the very matrix of her being. She found herself weeping with wonder, tears she scrubbed off again and again on az-Zuharah's hide, raising the familiar scent of damp wool. What lay within the gauzy white curtains? A Goddess? A jinni? She didn't dare part the drapes to see.

"This animal. Here." Her father's shout came right behind her and made her jump. "Slaughter it. See, see what an emblem of pagan misbelief it is. To worship a dumb animal. And this—this shrine to demons—"

Zura reached out a profane hand to tear aside the qubbah's curtains. Bint Zura tried to knock his hand away, but he gave her a stinging slap. Fortunately, her shaytan made up for the strength she lacked. Az-Zuharah kicked; she spat through her split upper lip. She tried to take a bite out of Zura's shoulder. The man stumbled backward over the skirts of his black robes.

Bint Zura caught az-Zuharah's bridle to keep her from kicking more. Those hooves could kill a lion, the girl knew. A man, once he'd fallen, had little chance.

"Put that heathen beast to death," Zura shouted from his seat in the dust.

Uncle Abu Ragheb didn't lend his fallen brother a hand up but dropped to the dust himself, on his knees before Iyas ibn Qabissa. The new Persian-appointed king of al-Hira had come with the party. He was a round man, soft, a lump of clay as yet unbaked in the sun. The only thing kingly about him was the plain circlet of a crown from which sweat ran from his forehead into his eyes. He did not descend from his regal horse but gazed at the squabble, trying to be above it. The hands he rested together on one of the four wooden horns of his saddle showed white at the knuckles, indicating the effort with which he kept them there.

Uncle Abu Ragheb spoke, brother against brother: "Your Grace, do not kill this animal. Since the hour of its birth, my tribesmen have seen it as the spirit of our people. They will not fight half so fiercely if this camel and her litter don't ride before them, an ensign to protect. I fear that if your orders should kill it, the sons of Taghlib will not fight for you in the coming conflict at all. They will return to our dirah in the desert, just as these accursed Tamim have done."

Uncle Abu Ragheb gave a gesture across the abandoned upland, then concluded, "Your Grace will not see a warrior among them again."

"Your Grace—" Zura attempted, dusting himself off.

But the king raised a soft hand for her father to desist. "Abu Ragheb has the right of it. Prayers are one thing, warriors another. In the coming conflict against these rebellious tribes, we need warriors more. Abu Ragheb has remained with his people, not escaped to a monastic life, and understands his fighters' mood. Besides, our Persian overlords upon whom we will depend greatly in this same coming conflict—they are not Christian either. They are followers of Zoroaster, worshipers of the sacred flame. An army made of banners of all the different faiths over which they hold sway would please them. An army made over according to strict Christian vision—well, that would disquiet them. Their greatest enemies are the Christian Rum. The Persians might refuse to aid us. I must win an-Numan's armor before I am truly king—and I must have Persian and Taghlibi help to win it. The camel lives."

"My lord, do not fight against the Bakr." This new voice, strange among the usual council voices of men, belonged to Bint Zura's mother. The old kahinah stepped to the king as Uncle Abu Ragheb had done, but she didn't kneel.

"What does this old woman want?" King Iyas ibn Qabissa asked the lackey who held his horse, as if the woman were a dumb beast they were discussing.

Before the lackey could reply, the kahinah proved she had a tongue: "I say, do not attempt to take that armor from Hanzala the Bakri's sharif."

The king chuckled shortly. "By Isa al-Masih, women don't understand anything. This throne of mine means nothing as long as the armor of the Lakhmid stays out of my hands."

"It has been revealed to me—"

Bint Zura found herself listening intently to what her mother was about to say. Prophecy? True prophecy, not dead and in some book? Something that had to do with her, her own flesh and blood?

"False prophecy, Your Grace," Zura spouted. "All she says is false."

Bint Zura wanted to fly at her father for interrupting. Fortunately, her mother was not a woman to be interrupted.

"The Arabs shall win this coming conflict," the kahinah said in a voice echoing with authority.

"The coming salvation of the Arabs," Bint Zura heard the bishop Ahudammah murmur behind her.

"And so they shall," the king replied. "My Arabs—supported by the might of Persia."

"No, no, those are Persians, not true Arabs." Quantities of white had begun to show around the blue of the kahinah's eyes, and her movements grew jerky.

"She is possessed," Zura accused, but he couldn't keep everyone in the company from watching in fascination. From listening to the rolling singsong.

> "True Arabs rise from the desert.
> True to their honor they stay
> and do not stifle it
> under the allure of power.
> Do not try to take an-Numan's armor
> from the man to whom he entrusted it."

The kahinah shuddered, shook herself, then returned to normalcy as if nothing whatsoever had happened. "This is why I stole the white camel from the sons of Taghlib. Such a miraculous creature does not ride for the losing side. My daughter, my only child, must not ride for that side, either."

Bint Zura felt the heart rise in her—all the way to her throat. Might she truly return to the qubbah of her birth? She who could only remember having no place in her uncle's crowded tent. Might she ride—? Take on that greatest honor that could come to a daughter of the tribe? Even though her father's madness had fitted her only for the suppression of the convent? Her mother said she'd seen— Her mother spoke in a voice not her own, the voice of revelation. Yet her mother was a known kahinah. To ride— Bint Zura stole another look at the qubbah. Her mother was asking the Taghlib to join with their traditional enemies the sons of Tamim, to ignore blood feud and ride against the great empire to the East. It seemed a hopeless wish.

Beneath his crown, King Ibn Qabissa flushed with anger. Zura saw his chance.

"You see what an evil woman she is, my lord? She admits to camel theft. She has slept with a jinni, committing adultery with Fire Spirits. This I know as her husband. How else could she presume to prophesy? She is a famous kahinah, besides. Just now her words set a curse upon your hopes for battle. You must put her to death. Or allow me to take a husband's right. Stone her, that she may stop tormenting your life." And mine, he might have added.

"Yes, to suggest we can fail is treason. Such words might well set our efforts to naught, backed by black magic." The king considered.

"Stone her," Zura shrieked. His whole body trembled, as if the demon prodded his flesh, looking to regain entry.

Bint Zura had to pull hard on az-Zuharah's bridle to keep the camel from trying to bite her father again. The animal spat instead and groaned her displeasure.

King Iyas gave a sudden and decisive nod on his doughy neck. "Yes. Bring her along. I heard her give our cause no hope with my own ears."

"No!" Now, for the first time, Bint Zura dared to speak before the king. In fact, she had no choice. She dropped the camel bridle and threw aside her veil. Everyone would understand this traditional gesture that meant her plea was so earnest, she forgot modesty. It made up for other words she could not say.

Her father caught her arm, until she thought he might break it. "You should have stayed in the convent garden," he hissed at her, and he slammed her veil up with such force, it set her nose bleeding.

Bint Zura waited until the stars left her vision, holding her veil to her nose to staunch the blood. A pair of comforting arms sustained her. Presently, she saw they belonged to the bishop, Ahudammah, and although she never thought she'd be beholden to the man for anything, she was grateful. She was even grateful when the arms kept her from moving to her mother again. And her uncle did much the same to az-Zuharah.

It was impossible to go against the squadron of huge armored men that closed around the wizened figure at their sovereign's order. Bint Zura had never known a mother. She'd caught but a fleeting glimpse of such a woman, a brief vision of the world beyond this one. To have that mother snatched away again seemed only fitting, the way the world always worked. The soldiers hustled the old woman to the tail of a camel and lashed her there. They were going to make the old woman walk all the way back to her fate in the city, three men with spears marching to either side.

Bint Zura tenderly touched her own nose. Wracking sobs kept her nose running, mucous and blood mixed. Then, for one moment, blue eye met blue eye again.

"Never mind me, child," she thought she heard her mother's voice. But she'd thought she'd heard it so many times before in the shift of sand, the wind in the desert. Was it just the voice of a tormenting jinni? A shaytan?

The voice continued: "I have seen you once more. They couldn't take you from me forever. What I see makes me very proud. I know you were meant to have those eyes, to see what others cannot, to lead.

"And now you are reunited with your camel, as you were meant to be. The salvation of the Arabs—it's to come through our blue-eyed blood. Don't you know that? No matter what such men as your father say or will say of others in the future. Haven't you sensed that before? For me, nothing else matters."

That blood, blue-eyed or no, was growing stiff on Bint Zura's veil. The caravan of king, soldiers, father, and uncle had moved on, beyond hearing, so Bint Zura knew she couldn't have heard what she thought she heard. She murmured one sngle word—"Mother"—then ran until she caught up and could bury the rest of her blood and tears in despair in az-Zuharah's sleek coat. Her uncle spat through his jutting teeth in disapproval and shifted to lead from the other side. She could only imagine that every step took her away from the desert forever.

And all the while she ignored the pair of men's feet left sticking out of the tiny rag of a tent they left behind.

50

> I was seated once in the house of the Prophet, precious blessings on him. He passed his hand over his head and said, "Make use of henna, the best of all dyes. For henna strengthens the skin and increases sexual energy."
> —a hadith from Abu Rafi

"Ya Rayah." Auntie Adilah came to the doorway and interrupted Sitt Sameh's story with more immediate concerns. "To avoid shame, you cannot wait another moment before getting ready to be seen, inshallah, by Sitt Umm Ali's nephew Jaffar."

Abd Allah let his parchments curl closed on their own and, in silence, he and Sitt Sameh watched Rayah rise and go.

A breath or two of air outside that close little room made the spirits vanish. Rayah scurried to bring in the towels and other items on the line. The women would want them to get her ready for Jaffar's visit.

"Never you mind about that laundry," Auntie Adilah said, filling a basket with her own quick movements. "I'll get these things. You go down to the other aunties. They're ready to set out for the baths."

Adilah had all she could carry now and headed for the stairs. "Come on."

Rayah stopped with one sun-lit length of linen draped over her left arm. That was all she meant to carry down, but under the linen, which should have been warm, she felt her hair rise as if from cold. Two months ago, before the coming of the eunuch to their harem door, she would have dismissed the sensation. Or perhaps she would have recited a quick "I seek refuge . . ." and hurried about her business.

Now, she recognized it as the touch of the jinn—and knew she couldn't just escape to refuge. When the world declared the Fire Spirits chained, those who felt them free and strong were left on their own.

Rayah cast her gaze toward the stairs. Not there, not in the shadowy corner.

She turned to look over the rooftops instead and saw—a black-draped figure on the neighboring roof. Who was this woman, watching her?

"Peace on you and yours," Rayah called out. This could be no jinn, she assured herself. Relieved, she waved.

To her surprise, the figure started and ran. She saw just enough to know, before it dropped down the ladder and disappeared, that the figure moved faster than either of their old widowed neighbors could. Taller than an average woman, remarkably flat-chested.

And it stumbled in the veils in a way no girl brought up to cover herself would do.

After baths, after sunset and prayers and the breaking of the fast, the turpentine sellers' women gathered around the cool of the fountain. With Cousin Demiella's quick movements over her bowl, the earthy scent of moistened henna flowers rose. This ancient ceremony was often reserved for the time when a girl actually became a bride, but mere presentation to Jaffar was occasion enough for the full treatment. Rayah had to offer her feet as if they were creatures separate from herself. Painted with the intricate designs of delicate twining vines and birds, they were then swaddled in rags for the dye to set overnight, away from her control. Teaching her to be a wife.

Then came the hands.

New stars would have time to wheel to the open air overhead before the work was done. As soon as she could no longer use her right hand, bundled in linen as if with a serious burn, Adilah had to be her fingers. Her auntie began plying Rayah with figs and dates. No shadow of hunger must appear in her face for the prospective bridegroom, be it Ramadhan or any other month. And over Rayah's head, the women chatted their hopes for herself and the whole family. She could not fail to please, inshallah.

"Inshallah," Rayah repeated quietly. "May it be as God wills." God, however, often willed something else entirely than everything humans labored for.

Rayah thought of Bint Zura and her friend Layla, giving one another the more permanent marks of the desert, the blue-black tattoos, in al-Minhal's tent when the white camel was missing. She thought of Khalid, gone to get the white camel and defeated in that by the small, stinging things of the desert. How had he fared after that, this great Conqueror? Al-hamdulillah, must she become a bride before she learned? No, she would never hear the tale then, if she had to leave this house.

Even as she thought it, Abd Allah the eunuch appeared on the stairs. She knew him by the glint of the emerald in his ear in the lamp light, by the arms grown unnaturally long, which he wrapped around his parchments. By the self-effacing way he moved through the world that had been made for others. Or rather, that he had been made to elude.

The turpentine sellers' women fell suddenly silent. The paintbrush grew still in Demiella's hand.

"Good evening, ladies," the voice tried to set them at ease but failed with its strange reediness.

Abd Allah tapped the bundle of parchments under his arm. "I have here tales Khalid the Conqueror dictated to me. Of his life and exploits. Would you care to have me read them to while away your time this evening?"

"Tales of the Conqueror?" Cousin Demiella repeated.

"I told you that was what they were doing up there," Adilah insisted. "Nothing demonic."

"Mashallah, yes, that would be very good," was the final conclusion. "We in this house can be as proud as Sitt Umm Ali with her Quranic recitations."

"But Rayah, what is your opinion?" The eunuch's gaze held hers steadily, not pushing, just waiting for her to make her own decision. She who couldn't even move to feed herself. Trying to cram more of the story in before the bridegroom should come and she could hear no more.

"My aunts will not have heard it all," Rayah said.

"Never mind that," the women chorused. "No one has ever heard all of the epic of Antar at one sitting, have they? We will hear what we can hear, and later, when it becomes as great as Antar, we will say we were the first to hear the Conqueror's heroics."

Abd Allah continued to look at no eyes but Rayah's blue ones. Rayah gave a quick nod, then pressed her unfinished hand to Demiella.

Abd Allah pulled a lamp nearer and cracked open his writing. Rayah looked away when, out of the corner of her eye, she saw a shadow move. It was Sitt Sameh, not the figure on the roof the jinn had pointed out to her earlier. Sitt Sameh, descended. Unseen, she bunched her dark skirts under her and sat on the stairs, just at the corner where the jinn dwelt. Listening. Watching her daughter become immobilized with henna. As an antelope may freeze with fear before the hunter.

Not speaking about the women, the past.

Only listening.

51

God made the desert when He wanted to be alone.
—an Arab saying

"The coming salvation of the Arabs." By God, how I craved it! I could almost reach around that curtain and touch it! A haunting spirit had crept out of the wonted abode of such beings and into the soft, smooth flesh of this daughter of the desert. She in turn had set her spirit in the red silk underdress I would wear on my head to my grave.

I awoke from such fevered dreams to find myself alone under the thin shadow of Umm Taghlib's rag of a tent. Both arms still ached dully from scorpions' stings, but I managed to sit up—brushing my red turban against the roof. The kahinah was gone. My milk brothers and all their tribe, whose tents had filled this upland when last I was conscious, they, too were gone.

The white camel was also gone without a trace, vanished into the world of the jinn whence it had come. And with the white camel—my hopes of the girl, Bint Zura.

A last trickle remained in a leaky skin of water. I drank it, then had to relieve myself. I passed a deal of scorpion poison, or so I hoped. I looked back at the rag tent, then around at the empty upland again. I howled in my frustration. The void swallowed the sound so it hardly reached my own ears. I wanted to escape the glare of this morning. But on what animal? The white camel wasn't the only one gone. They all were.

How many hours, days, had I been asleep? I studied the tent again, with its eery collection of bones and amulets hanging from the pole. I couldn't make myself crawl back into its shelter, with its earthy smell of herbs and roots. It might even be the death of me to do so, to fall asleep here, alone in the desert.

And so I began to walk. To lurch. To reel.

At some point after walking—I knew not how long—a troop of seven or eight tribesmen on horses came out of the heat waves to overtake my staggering steps. They were not all of one lineage, but Taghlib, Ibad, and Namir and perhaps another clan I didn't recognize, their various insignia clashing, the brands skirmishing over their animals' flanks. Powerful weapons, however, united them: bright, new swords, bone-crushing maces, and hauberks and helmets to resist the same in the hands of other men. Persia had equipped them—and thus forged such unnatural allies together in spite of their births. As allies they meant to ride with the empire against Hanzala ibn Thalaba, one man in the desert with but a single suit of armor.

Such was the apparent strength of the Persian Empire against nature that the men had even forgotten the first rule of the desert, to offer me a drink from their water skins. And, compared to their empire, I was obviously so insignificant a being, unmounted and armed with just a dagger, that they didn't bother to ask after my origin. Giving them glare for glare, I tried not to spare the energy to admire their well-grown horses as they stood between me and the westering sun.

Taghlib? I had no interest in that tribe, I told myself. Oh, once I'd loved a girl of that blood—but that was long ago, before scorpions and the desert sun had baked that foolishness from me. In any case, I couldn't suggest such a thing to such a warrior.

"Our new and rightful king, Iyas, favored of the great Shah-in-shah, is about to mete out justice." One of the Taghlibi did condescend to offer me this news of the desert, but he did it more as a boast, and I listened to it with but half an ear, as such boasting deserves. "We go to see him stone a kahinah."

"Such purity will definitely bolster our cause against the benighted Hanzala," agreed an Ibadi.

When have sons of Ibad ever agreed so with sons of Taghlib? The marvel so distracted me that I never considered who the kahinah might be. The world is full of old women, is it not? And even for a man just attacked, then healed by such a woman, there cannot be too few of them, be he young enough. In spite of the fact that I stood reeling in the heat of the day, it occurred to me no more than to the Iyadi that night, benighted, could come as a blessing.

I gnashed my teeth vainly on the horsemen's dust as they rode on in the direction of the Encampment.

Half dead, and toward evening, I made it back to al-Minhal's tent in its wadi, to his well and to his daughter to draw and cook for me.

"The Gods shield me and forgive me for speaking what might be considered envy," al-Minhal greeted me, "but you don't look well at all, my friend."

I showed him my still-swollen arms. "Cursed scorpions."

"Ah, hush, do not speak their names lest you draw such spirits here to my tent."

"Of course. Forgive me."

Al-Minhal touched his tent pole for luck.

Presently, hoping against hope to receive more than just form in reply, I asked, "What news of the desert?"

I asked it after a long pause during which silence I had tried to sense something, anything, from the other side of his harem curtain.

I felt nothing. Nothing but a panting anticipation from his own daughter, Layla. The girl who interested me was gone.

"The sons of Taghlib have found their white camel." This was al-Minhal's great news about Bint Zura's tribe.

"The Gods give them joy of it," I grumbled.

"War between the Persians and the tribes is more and more likely by the day."

"The Gods spare me from any of it."

"I do not think I can avoid it," al-Minhal mused.

"Which side do you join?"

"With the king, Iyas ibn Qabissa. And the Persians, of course. It's the side my tribe has chosen, though the Gods may will little honor there."

"What good is honor if you're dead on the other side?" If my milk family, as appeared likely, had gone with Hanzala ibn Thalaba, they deserved their fate. Although rank stupidity was not something I credited my milk brothers with, especially not Mutammim. Malik did have his honor. I would do best to avoid them, too.

Al-Minhal nodded sadly. Then, as if to change the subject: "And there's to be a stoning. In al-Hira, by the two great standing stones."

I seemed to recall having already heard this news, but it didn't impinge on me. I didn't care.

"And how fares my Little One?" Al-Minhal asked for his own news.

His mare. Yes. "I've sent her out to a fine pasture with the rest of my herd," I told him. "In the care of an excellent herdsman, never fear."

It was a hopeful lie. I really had no reason to believe that anyone among my milk family would have bothered to pick up my abandoned responsibilities. Al-Harith perhaps? I couldn't count on it.

As I said these words, I realized where I would have to go next. It was the only place, in truth, I could go: out to that meadow to check on that herd. I must give up my dreams of love and gather up the pieces of my mundane life again.

So I did, as soon after there was enough food in my belly not to be rude. I ignored the horseman's subtle hints that I marry his daughter then and there, to take her to safety along with the horses, away from the brewing fight. I took the camel I'd brought to al-Minhal's the first time, ignored the fact that it was night, and headed out into the rain-blessed but Taghlibi-arid desert.

Glad I was to find, as the sun rose, the basin called al-Lussuf unpopulated and as yet, save for my herd, ungrazed. There, among the pools of rainwater scattered like silver dirhams, was pasture enough for my herd for several weeks. The sweet grass and sweet-smelling wildflowers were fresh and glossy as fine Persian enamel. But such fertility and beauty, in my frame of mind, served only to suggest the well of my desire left behind in the Encampment.

Al-Lussuf lay at the very edge of the desert. On a clear and settled day, from a height in the basin, one could see the line where peasants' barley fields ended, the farthest point to which the Euphrates' water could be dug, canaled, or hoisted. A night's ride, and I could find myself in al-Hira once more—

But the herdsman's son al-Harith, I discovered, had in fact come safely with the Little One and stayed on to help my own slaves and herders when he had discovered my absence. I gave him just a nod of thanks, although he deserved more. A man who could not perform with women made up for it in other ways.

Horses are always skittish to be away from their homes and with so many new animals. We had mostly mares, of course, but I'd also purchased two fine stallions. These had to be kept not only from each other lest they fight, but also from trying to mount too many of the mares in a day lest they wear themselves out with passion.

Like myself, I thought. And I nodded again to al-Harith over the dust the hooves raised.

Others mares were due to foal soon. There again was care to be taken.

So I was obliged, for purely practical reasons, to forgo the desires of my heart. I was, in fact, glad of the distraction.

By the afternoon of my arrival, storm clouds draped the western sky.

"More rain, so blessedly late in the season," al-Harith said, "to fill the hollows of al-Lussuf, the Gods willing."

I should have been glad for the hope of more lush grass to come. "But thunder might stampede the herd in the night," I reminded him.

"Even though these horses are bred not to mind the clamor of battle?"

"Without every hand to contain them, the Gods forbid, a year's work might be lost."

I had our two small tents moved out of the wadi so as not to let a flash flood catch us. I set them in the open plain itself, about a hundred paces apart. I made the men hammer the stakes in deep and reinforce them with stones. I had the horses brought in from their pastures and hobbled in the space between our hair houses for greater security.

Then, with a prayer toward the point where the sun would rise again come morning and another toward the heavy clouds, I retired with one of the slaves to one tent. This slave was faithful Nuri, of the childhood escapade with the camel bag. Al-Harith with another slave and two guard dogs went to the second tent. My third slave would stand the first watch.

I tried to sleep, but did so poorly. Now that things were quiet, the scorpion stings came to life again. The threatening storm kept the desert from cooling off. The air grew more oppressive, rather like the steam baths the Syrians so enjoy. I find they only stupefy the wits.

And, in spite of how hopeless I knew my case to be since the loss of the white camel, I began to rehearse what I would say to Umm Mutammim my milk mother when I asked her to go visiting in Taghlibi tents. I rehearsed, too, what I would say to the son of Taghlib who'd tried twice to skewer me with a spear and no doubt looked forward to the next time, when he would not miss. And finally I rehearsed clumsy words of love to the young woman herself—who wanted to be a nun. Even the first suit, that to my own milk mother, was probably a fantasy. This sliver of reality—that I imagined it all—might have allowed me to sleep. I didn't consider for a moment.

Sometime during the night, there was thunder. Lances of lightning ran along the northern horizon, filling the air with the smell of burning. Then it looked as if the storm would pass north of us. Clouds hid the moon from the moment of its rising.

Closer to dawn, I came out of a shallow sleep. Had the one slave come to waken the other, to take the watch? I got up from Nuri snoring through his ruined nose to check.

The palest line of white formed a margin in the sky toward the Euphrates. All but the morning star had faded. The sight brought a stab of pain. I had to look away, remembering how I had failed to meet the one soul on earth whose good impression I most desired at the rising of that sun a few days earlier. The storm had blown on. It was the dogs barking that had awakened me.

"Somebody's there," I said to Nuri.

I stepped out. I smelled the horses rather than saw them, the dew heavy on their coats and the night's droppings. Cupping my mouth, I called to al-Harith. He'd naturally be awakened, too, being much closer to the dogs than I.

"The watch never returned to waken us," he told me when he'd crossed the distance between our tents, hunching into his thin cloak against the morning chill.

We each set out with our slave and a torch, though whether a little flame on the end of a bunch of brush helped us see better or worse in that odd light, I'm not sure. We set off to make a circuit of the encampment, calling the missing guard's name. I saw no footprints I didn't recognize, nothing to rouse suspicions.

"Nothing," al-Harith called to me from his tent when I had returned to mine.

"Must have been hyenas," I shouted back, although I had seen no canine prints save those from our own dogs. Jinn, maybe, I thought but didn't say. Dogs were known to raise their hackles when Fire Spirits passed.

"But where is your third slave?"

That I couldn't answer. My father had given me the most trustworthy of our slaves. And only the rawest of captives would attempt a break for freedom with the desert all around, crueler than any master. The Gods willing, when the light got better—

Knowing sleep would elude me now for good, I had Nuri milk one of the riding camels for my breakfast. I helped myself to some water from the skins cradled in a nest of scrub. It had the alkaline taste of the local wells, mixed with the fetid taste of goat skin. There was a little more light now, the world outside the tent a pearly gray and my camel a shadow, nuzzling her companion and waiting for me.

The dogs barked again as I finished off the wooden bowl of warm and salty milk that black Nuri had handed me. Before I had a chance to call to the other tent, the hounds fell silent. Al-Harith must have hushed them, so I ignored the alarm.

I reached up to readjust the red silk on my head, just because I loved to touch it. I turned to tell Nuri I was going to ride in search of our missing guard, heaved the saddle I'd slept on to my shoulder, and bent my head under the sag of tent opening.

Something hard and heavy hit me from behind.

52

> Oh, that I had but grasped death with my own hands
> and had not had to suffer the kind of death which is
> assigned to enemies.
> —a poem of Adi ibn Zaid

I came to almost immediately. *My face lay in the camel dung Nuri had gathered for the fire. Horses were milling, stumbling in their hobbles, whinnying from nerves.*

"My young uncle, are you all right?" Nuri set his hand on the back of my head where a lump was already forming. I gave a yell of pain and scrambled to my feet. My pilgrimage shave had given my skull very little protection—only the red silk had kept the blow from breaking the skin.

Spitting out dung, I shouted, "Look to the horses, you fool. Can't you see that we're being raided?"

Nuri whimpered incoherently. So much for the lion he said he'd killed.

I didn't even bother to brush the dung from my beard, and the events that followed smelled of droppings. I reached first for the dagger at my waist, then cursed. The sheath was there, but not the weapon itself. My attacker must have taken it from me in the brief time I was unconscious and was using it even now to run among the herd and cut all their hobbles.

My head throbbing, I scrambled back into the tent. Here I had two spears and, since I'd yet to inherit my father's sword, only an old Roman blade. The sword held a good edge, but was stubby and thick, such as the gladiators used to wield. I took it and the better spear. The other spear I thrust into Nuri's hands, not waiting to calm his protests that he'd never used such a thing.

The raiders had settled for about half the herd, but even in the predawn light I could tell they were the best animals. Fortunately, they'd left the camels. In a moment, I had my mount saddled and on her feet. Shouting her name and the names of the Quraysh and Hubal as a battlecry, I urged her after the herd.

Careening past al-Harith's tent, I saw that he and the slave had both been disarmed and tied up with loose horse hobbles. The slave had managed to work himself free, however, and had begun on the Tamimi herdsman. I left them to catch up with only a shout of encouragement. I galloped on.

The raiders were driving south, toward the wadi I'd had my men abandon the night before. As far as I could tell, there were only three of the enemy. They'd shifted from the camels they'd ridden to horses, which sped their escape. Even riderless, the trio of camels stood higher than the horses, and they weren't nearly so swift-footed. I was gaining on those beasts fast. The raiders seemed content to leave me those while they got away with the more valuable mounts.

I could see the men themselves more clearly now. Black and white headdresses, cloaks, and harness betrayed them as Banu Bakr—same tribe as Hanzala ibn Thalaba who'd visited in all the honor of his armor. One of the men was actually naked. That must have been the man who'd gone to al-Harith's tent to distract the dogs. As everyone in the desert knows, before sunrise, a naked man is invisible with the help of offerings to the jinn.

This one used his knotted headcloth as stirrups on the back of al-Minhal's Little One and struggled to keep a bit of cloak around the rest of him. Escape with the herd was his main purpose, but it was awkward and must certainly have been uncomfortable, bare skin on horse hair. Little One could run much faster than that.

My man, I thought. My first man, the first I shall kill, blood feuds be damned.

This stretch of plain was as flat and barren as a brass tray. The upper curve of the sun had risen now and was blinding to look at. I pulled the red silk down almost into my eyes and a tail of it to cover my nose and mouth. The herd had raised a lot of dust, and skirmishing would raise even more. And, by Hubal, there was going to be a skirmish.

Up ahead coursed the line of dry scrub marking the rim of the wadi. This slowed the raiders. Although they had carefully chosen what I knew to be the shallowest entry into the dry wash, this descent was still steep, and the horses had to be coaxed. I caught up with the naked raider there. I braced my feet and legs all the way up to the knees hard against the saddle. I took care to aim high, not wishing to harm the horse. I called on my tribe and God again, praying the feathers that dangled from my spear's head would lend the flight of the hawks to the Indian shaft. Then I let it fly.

The iron head caught the man in the naked shoulder. Al-Minhal's Little One reared in fright as he fell from her back and she smelled blood. She bounded after the rest of her kind.

And so did I.

The man I'd hit was still alive, groaning with pain and trying, with a hand made slick with his own blood, to pull my spear from his flesh. I helped him as I rode by, catching the shaft on the fly and giving it a vicious twist as I pulled it free. Gouts of red muscle came up on the tangs of the iron head. Without stopping, I followed the churned-up sand and broken brush down into the wadi. My room to maneuver would be hampered there. But so would theirs. And I only had two more to go.

The raiders turned and drove their booty down the wash. They knew enough not to get trapped at the higher end. And the markets of Persia lay at the mouth. But I was closing on them now. Both of the remaining men were bringing up the rear of the herd, their two camels even further behind. I shifted my camel's course to hug one side of the steep, dry wadi walls so as to get a clear shot at another human back. I raised my already smoking spear, braced knees and feet—

And pain jabbed through the robe at my own back.

With a scream of rage, I twisted in the saddle. Just behind me, another son of Bakr reared up on a rock. He must have leapt to that perch from hiding behind it because I'd seen nothing as I passed.

The wicked streak of his sword caught the glint of the sun just hoisting herself above the horizon and onto the rim of the wadi. The blade bore my blood on it.

Under me, the camel lurched and screamed. She had been cut as well. From other rocks appeared more ambushing hands. One grabbed my mount's harness, giving a cruel yank on the nose-ring so she stopped dead in her tracks. My reacting spasm and her thrashing rammed her thick skull into mine. This added to the downward force of a second pair of arms on me.

I hit the ground. Flood-scoured rock met the already tender spot at the back of my head. A dust storm of black whirled before my eyes. The spear clattered from my hand in the fall. Even before I could lift my head, however, I was groping for the scabbard at my side.

An enemy foot kicked my arm from such succor. I heard a hiss as if I'd fallen among snakes. An enemy hand pulled the weapon out of the sheath and out of my reach.

Blood stung in my eyes, rimmed around the already red silk. With three sharp blades at my chest, I struggled to my knees, empty arms outstretched.

"Put your life under our hand, son of Tamimi, and you won't die," the Banu Bakr said.

They thought I was of my milk brothers' tribe, with all the blood feuds they owned. I drew a deep gasp but stifled protest.

Further down the wadi, the indistinct shapes of my horses faded into the pink-gold haze, then vanished altogether. The other half of the herd still stood on the plain—but I couldn't do anything to save them, either, as more sons of Bakr from the ambush backtracked to mop up the rest of the spoils.

Slowly I brought both hands to my dust and dung-caked mouth. I pulled away the red silk as if it were a curse set on me. Slowly, I bit both my own thumbs, hard enough to make tears spring to my eyes for being such a reckless fool. Their taste was bitter with dust and dung. Waggling the empty fingers before my face, I gave the sign of surrender. And to the fearsome black warrior striding toward me, spear aimed at my heart, I prepared to croak out my oath of submission. I had always imagined I'd die before I ever did such a thing.

53

> Time frightened me and was evil to him . . .
> Every man is stoned by time's hearth stones,
> every long, high tent is pulled down.
> Neither their subjects nor kings remain
> of those that the Persian and Rum ruled.
> —Tumadir bint Amr,
> usually called al-Khansa

"Remember the curtains of the qubbah floating over the women of your lineage," Sitt Sameh whispered as she gave one final tug on the faded red silk she knotted around her daughter's waist. How out of place the old cloth was in all of Rayah's borrowed finery, yet she didn't move to take it off.

Her mother pushed her toward the stairs where she could look down into the yard.

For the betrothal meeting, the men had pitched a tent within the court walls. The Muslims had made this practice popular. Fiercely proud of the austerity of their lives and their conquering religion, the Arabs did so for special events in the ruined walls of all the settled lands they overran. The difference, Rayah had learned by listening up in the third-floor room, was that in the desert the women owned and pitched the tents, in places of their choosing. It was different in lands where only men were conquerors and women, without exception, the conquered.

Even with these traditions to fall back on, even with all her family except Sitt Sameh, the meeting with Jaffar's women began awkwardly. Because of the fast, no offerings of food or drink could help ease the tension. Sitt Umm Ali's presence was the most awkward of all. Rayah had been the woman's pupil for several years and had even been to the baths with her, but no words came. Saying nothing seemed the best plan. As soon as possible, Rayah escaped to sit alone under the tent while her kinswomen adjusted their veils and prepared to receive that thing as unusual as a two-headed lamb in their harem: a strange man.

Goat-hair tent breathing over her head, Rayah took courage from the thought that Bint Zura must have done the same in the desert under worsted woven by her own hand. Even in the sacred qubbah itself, although the fabric covering the sacred litter might have been finer.

All too soon, under this same cover, to absolute silence among the women whose harem this was, Sitt Umm Ali and her sister-in-law brought young Jaffar—and he seemed young, even to Rayah. He had, after all, just come from the men's majlis where he'd undergone their inspection. This of the women would, however, be more severe, and completely unlike the masculine scrutiny he underwent every day in the order of living.

The older women then retreated to the northern wall where Auntie Adilah and the rest of the harem waited to force an exchange of small talk. The tent's sides were open, so Rayah and her suitor could never escape keen eyes. But she shifted her cushions close to the fountain, the source of life, and worked at the length of faded red silk tied twice around her own waist. She was prepared.

"The sound of water will cover our voices at least," Rayah said.

She had meant to set Jaffar at ease. Instead, he seemed nervous enough to jump out of his skin at her words. Of course, she should not have spoken first, even as hostess, but rather kept her eyes down and waited for others to act. She knew women who, after their first meeting with their husbands, could still not have been able to pick him out of a crowd; they'd been too shy to actually look at him. Her kinswomen always praised such behavior in their gossip.

Jaffar would not take the cushion across from her but paced anxiously instead. Very well. If they would not talk, at least she could study the figure of the man they meant her to marry. Thin, tall—a flat-chested creature. But he strode like a man, and if he ever had to wrap himself in veils, he'd be in trouble—

Suddenly Rayah understood. She should let him speak. She should not even look at him. But if one of them didn't speak soon, they would get nowhere.

"You've already seen me, haven't you?" she said. "Borrowing the old ladies' veils next door, watching me from their rooftop."

The pacing stopped. He stared at her. She had spoken a point of her strength, and he knew it, although he couldn't guess that was only her first. She hated to do it. The poor fellow was as much a pawn as she, perhaps more so, and she couldn't blame his efforts to discover something about the girl they wanted him to marry. She admired it, in fact. Still, he needed to know she had the power to reveal to others the dishonorable act to which his curiosity had driven him. Now he knew.

He colored like a veil of his own, raised to the roots of his hair. "I beg your pardon," he said. "I did not mean to disturb the sanctity of your harem."

"Did you not?"

"They are my mother's great-aunts, your two old neighbors. I go sometimes to help them out, since they have no man and do not wish to move in with us."

Rayah smiled, though her lips met only veiling. So he was as anxious about this match as she was. Over the burble of the fountain, she couldn't hear, but she knew the watchers had taken note of a change.

"Sit down, please, Abu Gha'ib." She gave him the title of honor due a man who as yet had no son, "Father of the Absent One," realizing only afterward what awkwardness this might entail. Would it make him expect her to become the mother of this absent one? Would it call attention to the fact that he might never become a father at all?

He sat, pulling his cushion closer as he did. The reaction from the watchers was audible. He pushed the cushion back again.

"She is your mother," were his next words.

"Sitt Sameh?"

"No one could see you two together and doubt it."

"Only a few must see it, then."

"Yes." He gave a nod toward the north wall. "I see she isn't here now."

"No. She wouldn't come down."

"Not even to see her daughter's betrothed? Aunt Umm Ali will be disappointed."

He gave another nod, this one just between them. "But Sitt Sameh healed me, may God bless her hands," he went on. "I remember. Not much, I was so fevered. But her hands, I do remember. So gentle. And her eyes. Yours are the same."

Rayah had to look away then. She even pulled her veil up, over her eyes. The watchers made approving noises.

"No, don't."

He reached a hand out toward her. Thankfully, the distance was too far for them to connect. Rayah let her eyes meet his, but she didn't drop the muffle from before her mouth and nose.

"They tell me to beware," Jaffar went on. "We do not know your mother. To heal like this, outside the limits of the gracious Quran—that speaks of cavorting with the jinn."

"There are bad jinn—but there are also good jinn. The Quran tells of the time the Prophet, blessed be he, preached to the Fire Spirits and converted many."

"You have learned much from my aunt."

"I am indebted to her, yes." She plucked an end of the red scarf and twisted it around one finger. She took a breath and added: "The Prophet, blessed be he, died before either you or I were born, Jaffar. We have to make our way on our own."

"With the Quran and Omar the khalifah—may God guide him to righteousness—to show us the way."

"Of course," Rayah said. "And our families."

"Yes. Our families."

Rayah stole a glance toward where the stairs rose up to the third floor.

For his part, Jaffar looked over to the north wall. "Yes. My aunt Umm Ali."

"She is a woman full of learning, God shield her."

He gave a short laugh. "Aunt Umm Ali is quite overbearing."

"She knows the Quran by heart."

"Leaving very little room in that heart for anything else."

Rayah could hardly believe her ears. She dropped her veil from sheer surprise and followed his gaze to stare across the court at Sitt Umm Ali. The large woman seemed to be enduring the fawning of Rayah's kinswomen just barely, with thinned lips and tight brows. Beneath her jeweled cap, hennaed hair bobbed.

"That's the thing, isn't it?" Jaffar went on. "Well as you and I agree, a marriage is not so much between a man and a woman, but between the woman and his harem. My sisters like you well. My mother, she has learned it's best to stay to herself. It's Aunt Umm Ali who rules the roost."

He gave a little laugh as some thought crossed his mind, then he spoke it aloud. "How would you like it, being married not to me but to your teacher, my aunt Umm Ali? She has already driven two husbands into the ground, and I don't know how many young brides of her kinsmen. You, Rayah?"

The worst thing, Rayah decided, is that I should have to take her as my mother before I have heard the end of my own mother's tales. Before I know for certain who I am, which would certainly put me at a disadvantage before Sitt Umm Ali's undeniable force.

"There can be no marriage before the end of Ramadhan." Rayah knew her mouth was moving faster than her mind, with more confusion than could possibly lead to good decisions.

"Of course not, but the Eid is less than two weeks away. Not enough time for Aunt Umm Ali to plan a wedding even at her fastest."

"I . . . I am not a woman yet."

Jaffar's eyes appraised her. "Yes, but it won't be long now. We can make the betrothal public—as if my coming here today doesn't do that already. Or we can marry and you can come to live with us, the bed . . . er . . . to follow later. However you wish, dear Rayah."

But it isn't as I wish, she thought. It never is. Only as God wishes. "Inshallah." She spoke the thought aloud. "What are your wishes in the matter, Abu Gha'ib?" There. She said it again.

"My name is Jaffar," he reminded her.

She smiled under the veil but didn't speak his name. "Your wishes?"

"Mine?" Vitality seemed suddenly to leave his face. "It doesn't matter what my wishes are."

She leaned forward. "Of course it does."

"I've said, it's more my aunt you're marrying."

She narrowed her eyes, conscious of their steely blueness. "But what about you?"

"It's . . . it's time I was married," the young man stumbled. "It's time I was. Your mother saved my life. I will always be grateful to her."

"I am not my mother." Rayah let her voice drop so that even Jaffar could barely hear her above the fountain. And she had only just been thinking that perhaps she and Bint Zura were, indeed, one and the same. If they were all the same, all the women of her lineage, progress was a myth. Progress and new revelation.

"Your mother—my aunt Umm Ali says—must be related to Khalid ibn al-Walīd for her to have attracted the Conqueror's interest so. 'Mark my words, the girl is the very child of the Sword of God,' she said."

The sudden keenness in Jaffar's eyes told her he was trying to read her like the scribe Abd

Allah read his parchments. He wanted to know: What was her reaction to the notion that Khalid ibn al-Walīd Abu Sulaymān had sired her? Rayah rested comfortably in the knowledge that her face betrayed nothing. There was nothing to betray.

"I don't know who my father is—was. I know he is dead, may rain fall softly on his grave."

"Nonsense." Jaffar sniffed at the desert—almost pagan—tone of her wish for the dead. "Every child knows his father."

"Every wise child, the proverb says. I make no claim to wisdom."

"But surely your mother knows."

"She won't say. At least—she tells me stories. I think—I hope—they're leading in that direction. But we aren't there yet. She wants me to . . . to understand things—so many things—first."

"When a woman does not speak the name of her child's father, that seems to cast doubt on the child's legitimacy." It certainly cast doubt on Jaffar; his face clouded.

For her part, Rayah felt her heart lift, although she struggled not to show it. "So I am content to claim Yaqob as my father, the turpentine seller who rescued my mother from the fall of al-Hira and brought her here. Yaqob died fighting Khalid ibn al-Walīd at the battle of Yarmuk and even so, I am not ashamed to say I am his orphan."

Jaffar stammered. "No. No. You are the Conqueror's daughter. Or granddaughter. Or . . . or have some other close connection."

"Does it matter?"

"Of course it matters. I'm thinking of my future."

"Ah—" Rayah said.

Grown red and confused, he cut her off. "I have memorized some poetry at my aunt's bidding, some from the Arabian poets, to woo you." And he began:

> "She won me whenas, shamefaced—no maid to let fall her veil,
> no wanton to glance behind—she walked forth with steady tread—"

"Please, Abu Gha'ib," Rayah begged.

"It doesn't matter, even if you are his bastard. If the Sword of God is willing to claim you, it cannot go ill for my ambitions to trade between his two conquests of Iraq and Syria."

Rayah knew the time had come to draw a sword of her own. "What would you say, then, Abu Gha'ib, if I told you this turban came from the Conqueror's head?" She lifted the end of the faded silk tied around her waist and let it dangle in front of him.

Jaffar stared. "Is it—?" He reached out and fingered the fabric. Then, all at once, he was convinced and pulled it to his lips to kiss. "God's blessing on him and on all Muslims. I knew my aunt Umm Ali could not be wrong."

Even as he spoke, in the dull hot air over the slowly sighing tent, the muezzin began the call to noon prayers.

Sitt Umm Ali may have started to her feet before the call went out, probably the instant her watching eye caught the kiss. In any case, the large woman was full on her feet now, shouting loud enough for Rayah to hear her over the splashing water. "That's enough now, Nephew. Any more and you will fall into sin. Off with you, then, to pray with the men, for men and women should not pray together."

"So we have a match?" Jaffar hissed through the space between him and Rayah. "Say yes."

"No."

"No?"

"I mean, wait a bit."

"Wait? This is my aunt Umm Ali we're talking of."

"There is one more thing I must inquire."

"Ask it."

"Not of you."

"Who? When?" Jaffar mopped his hot face with the end of his own turban.

"Tomorrow," Rayah promised. "No later than noon prayers tomorrow."

"But what am I to tell my aunt Umm Ali in the meantime?"

"Tell her what you wish."

"She will be so insulted. She will never forgive you."

"Well, then say it is your decision. Say that you are a man, old enough to be married and no longer a child to be ruled by women. And that you want to wait, one day, that's all."

A shift in Jaffar's chin showed he was trying that role on. Could he do it? A man? Yes, he would do it.

"Send here . . ." Rayah began, then, "No. Send to my cousin Kefa. You know him?"

"Of course."

"Send to him—at the turpentine shop. Then you shall have your answer."

By this time, Sitt Umm Ali was under the tent with them. She would not touch her nephew, thereby setting her impurity between him and God, but her bulk threatened to bring the tent down on all of them. Like the stubborn camel who tries to get warm with the rest of the family, Rayah thought. Bringing the red silk to her own lips, she fled her kinswomen's questions to quickly climb the stairs, to pray there and then to do what she must do.

54

> And the stars, marching on all night in procession,
> drooping westward as each hies forth to his setting:
> Sure and steadfast their course: the Underworld draws
>   them
> gently downward, as maidens circling the Pillar;
> And we know not, when their luster is vanished,
> whether long be the ropes that bind them, or little.
>   —the Diwan of Labid

"She is a kahinah."

King Iyas ibn Qabissa plucked nervously at the regal gold fringe to his robes as if they didn't really belong to him. Once back within the clay walls of al-Hira, his narrow domain, he suffered second thoughts that he had not felt out in the freedom of the desert. One false step and his new crown might tumble.

"Some call such persons witches, but others say they are to be revered as priestesses," he continued. "She has the name of a kahinah, after all. And though many fear such a name, there is no such fear without true power."

"Still you can't have such a one saying you won't win if you go against the Banu Bakr, or no one will fight for you," countered Zura, for in his right mind he had earned himself the place of wazir to the upstart monarch. "You must deprive her of all power."

Ibn Qabissa agreed with that—to a point. "Stoning, however, is a common death. The sacred, like holy sacrifice, should travel to heaven on smoke. It should be burned, so as not to anger the Gods."

"Are you not a Christian—sire?"

Zura added the title almost as an afterthought, his anger against his lord rising. This new man on the throne of al-Hira had feet of clay. Setting him on that throne seemed the arbitrary decision of a distant and senile empire. The honor might just as easily have gone to a son of Taghlib. It might have gone to *him*. Zura had never quite been able to convince the Persian handlers, however, of his grasp on sanity. That wasn't the fault of the ineffective puppet before him, he told himself. Best to center his vengeance against the woman who truly was to blame, and let the other things follow.

"There are a great number of my people who still hold to the old ways," the king persisted. "And I must ask their support against the fractious tribes of the desert, for they know them best."

Bint Zura, listening from a woman's place in the shadows, behind pillars, was grateful to the monarch for speaking in this fashion. Watching her father the wazir's face, however, she understood that King Iyas was a mere shadow cast against the wall of a tent. In any case, he spoke for her mother's delivery no more than any other.

"And where do you—Your Majesty—propose we get enough fuel to accord the demons such a burnt offering?"

Clearly her father was struggling hard to remember his place as a mere wazir. He trembled beneath his monk's robes, anxious to quit the talk and get to the deed, the most intimate deed those robes allowed him now with his erstwhile wife.

Zura added: "Would you burn her in camel dung, the fuel of the desert? Other climes may burn their kahinahs, we do not. Stones are the weapons for common evils in the desert."

"For shame, Your Highness," agreed Ibn Qabissa's Persian counselor, the Padishah's watchdog sent from Ctesiphon.

This sharp, lean man carefully found the shade of pillars in which to stand like a woman and picked at his teeth with an ivory pick. He had not been in the desert where they'd gone to fight the Tamim and found only the camel and the woman. He'd remained, lounging no doubt in the Encampment's al-Hawarnak Palace, fanned by slaves and cosseted by goblets of wine. He had that sort of oily look about him. Yet even he didn't stop to determine what the accused woman had done.

"How might the great King of Kings, whose slave I have the honor to be, look upon your suggestion that you sully the purity of our divine Lord Ahura Mazda's flame with such evil?" he said. "Isn't it bad enough that all your people blaspheme when they burn camel dung?"

This effectively silenced Ibn Qabissa, an ugly thing in a king, while Zura said: "What, Your Majesty? Would you give the kahinah power in superstitious minds, more than ever she had in life? She is pure evil and must be treated as such, for the betterment of the good on earth."

Then he began a chant, which the crowd gathering in the palace forecourt picked up with relish: "Stone her, stone her!"

Bishop Ahudammah's suggestion was drowned out. "Consider the words of the Gospel, my friends," he urged. "Remember how Christians were stoned, Saint Stephen, the first martyr, and the attempt on Saint Paul? Are Christians, the meek who are to inherit the earth, are they become the hurlers of stones now? Remember our Lord's injunction when a woman taken in adultery was brought to Him. 'Let him without sin cast the first stone.' Who among you will cast the first stone at this woman when our Lord would not?"

A score of voices defiantly claimed the privilege. "We're Christians, after all, not Jews as our Lord's antagonists were."

All this while, the sacrifice they were discussing remained still in the midst of the net of her guard's crossed spears. She had squatted to her heels to rest after the long trek from the desert tied behind a camel. Sometimes she buried her veiled face in her arms crossed over her knees. But this was more from weariness, it seemed to Bint Zura, watching her closely, than from any fear.

For her part, Bint Zura longed to throw her arms around her mother, to comfort her. More, she wanted to comfort herself, the child she still was inside, raised motherless, and who was now fated to lose what she had only just regained. But Bint Zura wasn't sure the old kahinah would accept the gesture, this woman who had lived so alone, so completely without need of any other human. Certainly she never made a sign that she needed the daughter she'd borne.

So Bint Zura hung back with her uncle. Abu Ragheb, fresh from the desert, did not seem confident enough to join in the debate in the al-Hawarnak Palace forecourt other than as one shout among all the crowd. But he had kept the silent boast of his lion-skin standard with him and planted it, as other gathering sharifs theirs, in the dust of the square.

And something had to be done with az-Zuharah. Uncle Abu Ragheb had claimed the honor of leading the white camel all the way back to the Encampment. Bint Zura had walked with them, a calming hand on the white, wooly neck—although whether to calm the beast or her own unsteady feet, she'd be hard pressed to say. Her uncle had kept the honor with him while other beasts were left at the gates. Now Abu Ragheb, wanting to crowd closer to the center of things, held up az-Zuharah's lead in helpless frustration. Any closer was no place for a camel, not even a white one.

"Never mind, Uncle," Bint Zura said. "I'll take care of her."

The girl felt her mother's eyes on her. She tried to send a message to the older woman with her return look: "Don't worry. I will not let them do this to you. Or—or if I can do nothing—the Gods forbid it—I shall be by your side to the very end."

Bint Zura felt as if her mother tried to send her some message in return, some calming negative such as: "No need, my dear." Or "I have seen you once again, grown from the infant born helpless in the holy qubbah to this fine young woman. I don't hope for anything better out of this harsh desert life."

Bint Zura chose to ignore any message those blue eyes might send her if it spoke defeat like that. The crowd was growing so thick that unless she made an effort to push her way to the front, Bint Zura would lose sight of her mother. So she led az-Zuharah out of the forecourt. Plucking a shock of dried grass the goats had miraculously missed, quickly she braided a hobble out of it while az-Zuharah watched with interest, then she bent and knotted the grass around the two rear white legs.

The camel's deep, dark eyes, all the darker in contrast to the white wool, met hers with a glint of humor. "Yes, my treasure, you are to pretend to be fastened," Bint Zura whispered.

She laid a hand once more on her camel's graceful white neck. "The Gods keep you as I go and see what must be done."

"All is in readiness," she heard the king's wazir declare on her return to the shadows of the court. Her father trembled with eagerness. "Bring the whore along."

No one remarked that "whore" might also describe many of the women crowding behind the pillars to watch. Those who made their marriage contracts for only a few hours under their red kerchiefs, too, had been drawn out of their tents. Bint Zura jostled among them, careful only that they were women and not men, as she rejoined the crowd.

The guard around the prisoner came to life and began to move her. Bishop Ahudammah pushed his way through the multitude, many of whom had already weighted their hands with good-sized stones. He tried to speak words to the condemned woman, something about submitting to those God has placed in authority over us. The guard, however, wouldn't let him near, and Bint Zura's mother didn't seem to notice. Her eyes, already haunted in their unusual blue, centered elsewhere on the things in the other world that had been her companions for so long. To which she already mostly belonged.

Dignitaries, soldiers, condemned and executioners, and the mob of men formed themselves into a procession. The last knot in this winding rope were the women, whose mothers or sisters had met such a fate. Women who knew if Umm Taghlib could die thus, how easy it might be for them to meet the same death for similar crimes. Or women who saw, in the murderous anger of their menfolk, how that same anger might so readily fall on them for no reason at all, in the privacy of their homes. For the moment, Umm Taghlib served as a scapegoat for evil that wasn't sin but a common condition of women, falling like rain on the just and the unjust alike. So it was no use, really, trying to find anyone to blame. Women could only weep. They did—and caught Bint Zura up and carried her along with them.

She couldn't see her mother any more.

The procession crossed one branch of the Euphrates canal on a bridge made of two palm trunks that centuries of feet had leveled and dusted together. The company had to pass here single file so that each individual in the mob had, for one moment, to appear reflected alone in the still, jaundiced waters. They passed on quickly, as if their own reflections were jinn. Soon they came to the palm-fringed space beyond al-Hira's walls.

Centuries of feet had been at work here, too, pounding the soil to a fine powder. In the center, around which the faithful wheeled like the stars in their spheres, stood the Two Besmeared, the pair of granite boulders each twice the height of a man. Set on end, they were sacred to as-Sabad. The blood of the sacrifices of that year's pilgrimage stood out still against the generations of other smears: dark streaks reaching halfway up, as high as a man could extend, and running down. Here and there shadowed the memory of an actual handprint, dipped in the blood of a struggling camel or goat as it pooled in the sacred dust. Then the hand pressed fervently to the sacred stone: "God, I was here. God, be mindful of me . . ."

"Goddess, my mother is here. Be mindful of her," Bint Zura prayed.

Between the great standing stones stood other, smaller cairns, perhaps forty altogether. These were the remains of additional sacrifices, more like the one that would be offered today. Perhaps these marked the remains of the nuns of Haleb, the nuns King al-Mundhir was said to have offered to al-Uzza as she rose in the morning horizon. At the site where a new cairn would shortly rise, a deep pit had been dug while the victim's fate was being discussed. In quicklime, a circle had been chalked about twenty-five paces across, with this hole as its core. Men halted at the line and spread around, feeling the power of the Two before them and the many lives the stones had drunk thirstily, like desert sands, to themselves. This new life they would shortly take— Perhaps the Besmeared Ones were too old and steady to tremble, but their smaller kin in human hands did so at the thought.

"Bring the condemned forward," Zura the wazir ordered.

After a moment's hesitation, two of the bravest guards did so. At first, each took Umm Taghlib under an arm, but she shook them off. One pulled a thong from his belt and went to tie her hands, but she shamed him from that, too. She walked to the hole by herself, dragging her veil, ragged though it was, as a freeborn woman, and they trailed after like puppies.

At the hole, she did require assistance. They lifted her between them. She sank in up to her shoulders.

"Remove her veil," the wazir ordered next.

The tone of gloating in his voice betrayed how he felt to have the last shred of his wife's honor taken from her. It must all accrue back to him.

But it didn't. For there was that graying, motherly hair. He liked to think of himself as still in the prime of his life, with many more years of flowering in the light of God's truth. But here was the woman he'd taken as his bride when she'd been no more than a girl, and he nearly twice her age. Here she was, on the edge of eternity. His daughter, hardly a girl herself any longer, read all this confrontation with his own mortality contorting his face.

Those blue eyes gazing steadily back at him— And the cursing of her tongue: "Woe to any Arab who fights on the side of encroaching empire against his own people. Woe to them who go against their coming salvation. Woe—"

With a cry to Isa ibn Maryam, Zura shouted to the shaytan: "Get thee behind me, I say!"

"Cover her up again," the wazir ordered as quickly as he could, but the harm was done. Only the deaf could not have heard her curse. And everyone knew the power of such words spoken just before death—by one with blue eyes. She must be killed, wiped from the memory of the earth, her power snuffed, shown to be no more than the wick of a lamp—and quickly, quickly.

Bint Zura knew she must move quickly, too. She'd been so certain her mother had the power to make her own escape, watching the calm with which the woman faced the whole ordeal. Mothers take care of their children, not the other way around.

But now Bint Zura saw it was not so. No time to make her way to az-Zuharah and all the way back again. Veiled, she realized, she blended like but one indistinguishable thread into the weave of mourning women. With her face completely covered—but not muffled—and with the growing, heckling chants of the men, who could say whence the sharp whistle came? The whistle such as women should never use. The whistle Bint Zura had taught herself during long hours alone in the desert. The whistle she'd taught her camel to break a false hobble and respond to.

55

> The day I leaped onto Unayza's
> howdah, she, fearing, swore: "Damn
> you." But when I leaned forward
> to embrace her, the howdah tipped over,
> and she, turning, cried, "I fear you,
> Imru'l-Qays. If you slew your camel,
> you could slay mine, too—dismount!"
> "Bear up," I said, "Give her the reins
> and do not parry this balmy embrace;
> many pregnant women like you I took before,
> and a mother I wooed away from her babe:
> if he cried, she gave a breast to soothe
> him while I held on to caress the other."
> —The Qasidah of Imru'l-Qays

"So it is not true that the Sword of God has never been defeated in battle?" my scribe exclaims, his eyes wide and black as his ink, his reed forgotten yet again.

I had just finished telling how I had surrendered to the raiding Banu Bakr at dawn in the wadi cracking the face of al-Lussuf Basin.

And I surrender in the present to my scribe. "Now you know. When I was eighteen, I succumbed to a pack of horse raiders and was taken captive. Not only I but my men, three in number, and my childhood friend, al-Harith. Most grievous of all, our beautiful and dearly bought herd of horses, the pride of the eastern tribes, was lost on that day. Do you wonder I never cared to correct popular opinion in the interest of truth?"

The morning after we were carried away with my horses, I awoke in my enemy's encampment. In spite of the sting in what was only a graze to my shoulder, the headache and the bitterness in my mouth, I was convinced I had but dreamed time's passing and the events of the day before.

"Alas, O son of al-Walid, it isn't so," al-Harith assured me. "Just feel your chin."

I did, clumsily lifting hands bound together with thongs to do so. My cheeks and chin were painfully tender, scabbed in spots. It forced me to remember how my young beard, of which I'd been so proud, had been plucked from me by firelight the night before as a mark of shame. I was now as bare-chinned as al-Harith himself was.

As captives, we weren't given the comfort of a tent. A pair of palms shaded the indignity of bare chin and bonds. I turned from my companion as if I could keep even him from too much knowledge of my shame.

Upon our arrival late the previous evening, the two or three campfires shedding dim light had made me take this encampment to be nothing but raiding men. In the night, however, I'd heard the wail of infants, the hushing of women, the jangle of their anklets. I thought I'd dreamed it.

Dawn revealed their howdahs, however, a sea of them on the backs of camels. The beasts raised their dust and dropped their dung where they were hobbled just steps away from the captives'—our—trees.

The howdahs' riders were gone to their harems. These weren't qubbahs, of course, not sacred litters, which were rarer than white camels, as I myself had never seen one. They were just the common winged howdahs of the tribes of the eastern desert. But fine colored silks curtained these mobile tents instead of the usual heavy wool. The silk rippled in and out with a rich sheen in the weight of sunlight like breathing lungs in the merest breath of wind. So these were no ordinary women.

On better ground than where we were bound, beyond the camels, stretched the sharif's tent. Close to this tent, well guarded, were the horses—my horses. The wells were to our right, through a ragged hedge of oleander, surviving near such water and avoided even by starving animals because of its poison. Slaves had been working there since sunrise to bring up all the water necessary for such a spread of men and beasts.

Looking at the howdahs formed the beginning of a plan in my mind. I struggled to my bound feet and leaned for balance against one of the palm trunks, the better to see how the rest of the encampment lay.

As I did so, a group of six or eight sons of Bakr ibn Wa'il broke from the sharif's tent and headed straight for us. Drawn daggers and long knives glinted in their hands. I sank quickly to a squat again; my throat went dry. The Arabs walked up to our trees—then on past.

I let my breath out with a sigh. I understood that they were going out to the sharif's herd to butcher a beast or two. The lately arrived guests, in spite of being mostly women, must be important indeed.

I didn't allow myself to get comfortable but kept the soles of my feet flat on the ground. Tension ran up and down my calves as I watched the Banu Bakr about their business. This took time. The camels selected were two young bulls, even greater honor for the guests. Unlike a dull and worn-out cow with dried-up dugs that lesser men warranted, these animals sensed what was coming. They bolted in opposite directions.

On foot and bareback on other camels, the sons of Bakr set off after them. Once they'd run them down, four or five men led each beast away from the main herd. The rest would also bolt if they saw what was to become of their companions. The men recited a prayer to Bakr's Gods as they turned the camels' braying noses to the sun. One man then found the jugular pulsing in each long, dusty neck and slashed it lengthwise. His companions, having doffed their robes to keep the blood off, hung on. They tried not to get kicked to death themselves as the life thrashed from each animal and into the barren reddish ground.

That could be my blood, I thought, and hesitated. But I must not hesitate too much longer or my chance would pass.

The butchering progressed. The skinning revealed long jaw bones and jutting teeth. The skulls held some resemblance to those posted by graves, but with the bone still white and moist and streaked red with bits of muscle among the tendons. Ribs arced wide like spatulas webbed with thin, desert-honed flesh between.

That's what I'd look like if my plan failed.

The sons of Bakr ibn Wa'il carried out the skinning with greatest care so large water carriers could be made from the main body. Leather thongs—to tie up prisoners—came from the narrower strips, glue from the hooves and bones. Innards were bundled into the flayed skins and men's cloaks for the long trot back to the women, who had fires ready to receive the feast. Little was left, then, to throw to the eagerly waiting dogs.

Finally, my time came. As the wonderful fragrance of searing camel flesh wafted to us on billows of brushwood smoke, I worked my way to my feet once more. An excited sort of fear churned any hunger from my belly.

"There won't even be the scraps of neck meat left for two prisoners," I assured al-Harith—assured myself—and made those my parting words.

"Peace go with you," he told me. I didn't think that was very likely. But maybe peace wasn't what I wanted. I wished peace to stay back with him instead.

Hunching over, I ran with jerky steps the length of my hobbles out of the shade and into the glare. I hoped my turban would not appear too bright over the ranged camel humps, all turned as they were, heads to the sun, to take as little heat as possible on their shaggy backs.

The first saddled camel I came to curved to study me with a distinct sneer. Without hands, I found I couldn't mount a man's saddle.

The creature spat a stream of hot saliva onto my foot where it dried in unpleasant stickiness.

From saddle to saddle I hobbled in a zigzag, keeping camel backs between me and the sharif's tent, until I reached the first of the women's litters, closer in. Now these, I discovered to my great relief, are made for easy mounting, even with hands full of infant or baggage—or bound with camel hide. I shoved the silk curtain aside with the silk on my head and in I tumbled.

I lay panting on the interior cushions for a moment to catch my breath. There is a reason people avoid activity during this heat of the day. But I hadn't dared wait until dark. Sooner or later the howdahs would be unloaded and the camels set out to graze. Besides, I was here now.

No one had seen me—I comforted myself with that thought. No one had seen me and no one would see me now, beneath this frame. The dull gleam of the sun arcing toward its zenith came through the silk pulled taut between the bent hoops of wood over my head. That was the point of howdahs, wasn't it, so women could travel in comfort, unseen? They could remove their veils in here and catch the wind in their loosened locks. They could nurse their infants. They could nap. They could even make love. With a thought for Bint Zura, I recalled the erotic lines of the poet: "The day I leaped onto Unayza's howdah—"

Enough of that, I told myself. I would never see her again.

New sweat on the sweat of my exertions was uncomfortable. It released the smell of the howdah's woman all around me—

Escape first, I told myself sternly, moon about lost love later.

This view of the world as women see it fascinated me. I was surprised to discover some power in this ability to see without being seen, this ability to enjoy free actions. Meanwhile the men, on their exposed saddles, had always to ride well and fearlessly. No wonder there was something of a divine aura about these howdahs when a group of them moved faceless, like the jinn, through the desert haze.

What could be better for escape? Did women realize it? And if they did—?

I had caught my breath now and shifted into a more comfortable position, upright instead of curled into a ball on the floor of the litter. All I had to do was give the verbal command to get this animal to her feet, then the "Woh-ho" to go. I assumed these strangers used the same commands most of the desert shared. In any case, women's camels were always the most tractable. Once moving, no man would bother to stop me, even if the camel was seen. He would assume a woman sat behind these veils, that she knew where she was going, and that it was none of his business.

Again a flash of the power contained in the howdah hit me. The awe.

I decided it didn't much matter which direction the camel took at first. Once she had plodded beyond the encampment, perhaps only as far as the wells, then I would pick up the reins and set a faster pace toward Tamimi lands and freedom.

Looking to that moment, it would be good to have my hands and feet free. Luckily, this howdah's mistress had left a flat, woven bag full of possessions behind her. One of the lumps in it felt very like the knife women use to cut threads at their weaving. I could extract it and cut myself free before I got the camel to her feet and the jarring movement made the activity more difficult.

The camel gave a bellow of protest at my bumping around. The knife slipped deeper into the bag. The camel shifted and complained again. The sharif, I hoped, would ignore even two such protests from a beast who was supposed to be happily at rest, chewing her cud.

Then, for one moment, my heart stood still. I heard somebody outside, close. The woman? I didn't dare move a muscle. I even tried to stop my breath, for it seemed suddenly to pull the howdah's curtains in and out in a telltale manner.

A voice spoke very near me. With a rush of relief, I recognized the particular nasal tones Nuri's noselessness gave him.

For one moment, I flashed on that event from the past: my young self in the saddlebag and Nuri trying to cover for me.

Nuri, how did you manage during the raid? Nuri, come with me. Nuri, at least come and get this cursed knife and cut me free. Nuri—

All these things I wanted to call to him. I stifled them while I cautiously shoved the curtains aside with my head and my red silk turban—on the side of the howdah away from the sharif's tent.

Then, glad as I was to catch a glimpse of my slave, I was glad I'd said nothing. For another man stood with him. The man to whom I'd surrendered, the tall, black, harelipped African.

And Nuri was pointing my howdah out to him.

56

> If any of your women be guilty of whoredom, then . . .
> shut them up within their houses till death release them,
> or God make some way for them . . . For God is He who
> turneth, Merciful!
> —revealed in the Holy Quran, Surah 4,
> after the events told in this chapter about
> Umm Taghlib

Once again, Rayah sat in Ghusoon's darkened room, holding the other girl's hand. There were no words, no flicker of recognition, not even any pressure on the hand this time.

"You see?" the stepmother said. "Hopeless. And the sharif expects a bride at the end of the holy month." With a snort of disgust, the woman turned on her heel and went to see to the evening meal set at a slow simmer over her fire.

The moment she was gone, Rayah spoke in low, calming tones. "Ah, Ghusoon. I know your sorrow. They want to marry me off, too."

If anything, the inert form grew stiffer still.

Rayah let her words wander away from the subject for a bit—"You feel weaker today, my poor girl. May God bless you. You'll see, it will be as He wills, not the others, not your father, your stepmother, not even the sharif with the bad breath"—before coming to what she really wanted to say.

"He seems a nice enough young man they want me to marry, not like yours. Jaffar is his name. I'm just not ready myself and I—"

In the low light, she saw Ghusoon's lips move—a thing she hadn't seen since the beginning of Ramadhan. Rayah pushed on: "I certainly must hear the end of my mother's—"

"Jaffar?" The voice was hoarse and soft, but clear.

"Jaffar ibn Qais, yes. Of a very fine family. Do you know him?"

Ghusoon gave a single shake of her head against the pillow, almost a convulsion, a twitch of the jinni that held her.

Rayah sat there a while longer, talking quietly to no response. When she rose to go, however, she knew she had answers that had not appeared on the surface. The written-down words of the Quran had not brought these answers to her, but something within herself, some power gifted to her alone.

Inshallah, come the morning, she would give her own reply to Jaffar. In the meantime, the night lay before her. Time to break fast, to rest. Time for Sitt Sameh's tale.

The white camel, az-Zuharah, named for the Goddess-star, snorted a greeting as she loped up to where her mistress stood. Bint Zura, who had been shifting from foot to foot, reached out a hand to the animal's flank to steady herself.

The pair of them stood at the outside rim of women all mourning her mother, already planted in the pit to die. From this spot, Bint Zura couldn't see her mother. She didn't think the stones had begun to fly, not yet. The men kept up the rhythmic chant that would drive the strength of their right arms, but roars and cheers didn't yet punctuate it. The hole, the dry well in which her mother stood, had to be filled in first, of course, with rubble up to the sacrifice's shoulders. And there were probably self-congratulatory sermons to be given by those who had caught such a dangerous threat and would now rid the community of it.

When Bint Zura gave the camel the order to kneel, the women nearest her gave up their wailing and breast-beating. They turned to stare.

"A white camel," exclaimed one in an awed whisper, nudging the woman next to her.

"Bearing a holy qubbah on its back." Their veils made each stranger much like the next.

"Wandered into the sacred precinct," said a third.

When this black-shrouded figure saw what Bint Zura was about, her wonder turned to dismay. "Don't you know, blasphemous girl? A camel which a God calls to His precinct may never be milked or slaughtered or ridden by humans again? This camel, obviously a gift of the Gods from birth because of her color, should now have her ears cut as a sign that she belongs to no one but as-Sabad."

More women had turned now, and several took threatening steps to stop the girl. Bint Zura, however, dropped her veil, just to the nose, just so they could see her eyes. After that, no one tried to stop her. It was all wonder again, more wonder than the stoning of an adulteress. A blue-eyed girl stepped up onto the camel's hump, into the qubbah and pulled the gauzy white curtains closed behind her.

Inside, Bint Zura paused to catch her breath. Only then did she think about trying to see. Slowly, she opened her eyes, yes, somewhat surprised that the women's cautions had not come true. The Gods had not struck her dead for her presumption.

Inside the qubbah was blood warm, warmer than the crowded, sun-baked precinct outside. But there were comfortable cushions here, and a soft, golden light. It smelled close, of women's dark mysteries added to the familiar smell of az-Zuharah. The men's threatening chants seemed to belong to a distant valley, where jinn, perhaps, lived. Or mortals, if this were the shadowed place of the jinn to which she'd come.

Bint Zura quickly settled down in the warmth. She gave az-Zuharah the command to rise, then to move forward. The crowd began to look behind itself instead of in front. They parted before the apparition risen from the smoke of Fire Ones: a ghostly camel, the shimmering sail of a qubbah on its back. Bint Zura had known her own reaction to the sight—a fire in the center of her heart—but had thought it might be private, the effect of seeing with blue eyes. Now she understood that she had to see a thing first and then present it so ordinary brown eyes could catch the vision, too.

And the power—

Silence fell as the mob lost the sense of its own strength. It parted in waves until the male voices stopped as one, in the middle of their cry for blood.

Bint Zura urged az-Zuharah forward, but the camel hardly needed to be told what to do. The Goddess moved in her, of course, just as her name said. The padded feet stepped over the quicklime and into the stoning circle. The men at the other rim of the ring fell silent, too. The two guards who'd been raking dirt in over the victim dropped their tools and ran.

The girl made her camel kneel again, right beside the hole, and in such a way that the hole was between the camel and the Two Besmeared Ones where none of the mob stood. This way the camel and its large, curtained litter rested for the moment between most of the mob and their victim, shielding their view.

When Bint Zura threw open the curtains and hissed, "Come," to her mother, the older woman at first shook her head.

"My eyes have seen the salvation," she said. "I need no more . . ."

But Bint Zura insisted and made no move to urge the camel on to safety. The old blue eyes could see the future, at least enough to know that the camel must move on quickly. If she herself were not in awe of the vision, some of the men would lose their own awe. Not only would they put an end to the rescue—with it would fade all future for both her daughter and the Arabs.

So mother caught the daughter's outstretched arms. She worked with the pull, loosening her feet from the rubble, which as yet came only to her knees. Then, bolstering one foot after another on the side of the dry well, she climbed out and into the litter.

Bint Zura called az-Zuharah to her feet. Camel and qubbah sailed on, out of the sacred precinct, out of al-Hira. And though she rose no more gracefully than a camel ever does, to the mob with stones trembling in their hands, their quarry in the pit had simply vanished. By the hand of God, in fact. For although it is easy enough for the will of man to happen in a stoning, should the prisoner escape, it is a sure sign of God's favor—and of her innocence.

Stones dropped from hands turned to water there on the edge of the desert.

57

> If God will, He will vouchsafe relief from the oppression of this strangling rope.
> —a poem of Adi ibn Zaid

I dropped the heavy wool curtain of the strange woman's howdah, holding it closed with one bound finger. Pray al-Uzza, might no movement draw attention!

But Nuri, wandering unbound among our captors as if he owned the place, had already pointed me out. Had my slave truly been such a traitor? He had shielded me when I was a child, hiding in the camel bag. Now . . . I had to hope.

With his long strides, my captor closed quickly. If he could hear my sharp, shallow breaths as clearly as I could hear his free and easy ones—

His shadow loomed on the taunt silk; only a membrane of fabric stood between us.

"Come out, come out, my dove, my sweet one," he whispered through his horrible mouth. "Or let me in to you, love, do."

He knew I was there. Or rather, he knew someone was there. He thought it was his lady love. I confess, I felt a stab of pity for the woman to have such a lover. But I pitied myself more were he to find me tainting his lady's howdah in her stead.

Slowly, straining for quiet so much it made my joints ache, I shoved my hobbled legs together through the curtain on the other side. As soon as they'd found the ground, I slipped the rest of my body onto them. For one awful moment, my robe caught on the howdah's frame. I pulled it away with a jerk that ran throughout the conveyance. I went rigid right where I was, half in, half out. But when no more than another endearment came from the far side of the camel, I went ahead and slipped the rest of the way, my full weight on the ground.

Now, here was a problem: the murmur of many men's voices. I had entered the howdah on the side away from the enemy's tents, the better to shield my actions. I stood now on the side facing them, dangerously exposed. But the stranger was even closer to me than the tents on the other side, and he showed no signs of moving on.

I had to get to the concealment of another camel's back, even of another howdah. I had charted such a course and had taken one hobbled step in that direction when the man behind me suddenly stopped his endearments and gave a shouted command that brought the camel to her feet. My legs stood exposed between her legs on the other side. I might have tried to run, but my hobbles would have made that attempt laughable against the stranger's long, quick stride.

"Wolloo," he shouted.

He gave the camel a fond slap on the rump. That sent her ambling off, but no more than a languid pace or two. At her new site, she merely shifted her angle the better to face her real enemy, the sun. Then she plopped back down, brought up her cud once more with a lazy belch, and began to chew. She had too much dignity to give more attention to the caprices of men.

The stranger's long, quick stride came deliberately around a mound of dung to me. He had his dagger drawn and held just at the level of my rib cage. His eyes were wide in his black African face.

I counted my life in a matter of heartbeats. I prayed only to be granted that I die bravely.

Don't let me soil myself, I quietly begged every God I knew. At least not that. I felt dangerously close to it, however, water rushing through my bowels.

The stranger caught my wrist in one black hand. I pulled back involuntarily, but he pulled with more force until I'd twisted around. Unable to see what he was doing behind me, I could hardly believe it when the next sharp yank on my hands parted their thongs. I brought them around before me and stared at them in wonder.

The stranger slapped the hilt into my right hand. I stood staring at him too stupidly even to grasp the thing. He himself worked my fingers closed around the solid rhinoceros horn within his own elephant-colored, elephant-strong palm.

He jerked his head toward my feet, indicating, I could only imagine—though I couldn't imagine it—that he wanted me to cut the hobble on my own feet.

"Spare me the indignity of bending to you, anyway," I think he said, although the whistles of his mouth made me doubt it. A deformity of my own ears, too, made me question the possibility of such words.

"I do want my dagger back," he said, a twinkle cutting the puffiness at the corner of each black eye. "Your freedom is my gift—if you prove yourself worthy of it as you've begun to by your daring. Yes, I watched it from the moment you pulled yourself to your feet against the palm tree. I do not make a gift of my dagger, however, praise it as any man may."

Then, without another look, he turned his back to me and covered the stride or two necessary to reach where he'd left a heavy pack bundled in exquisite purple brocade in the dust. Doing so, he left his spine exposed.

I made a lunge for that bent, exposed spine. It was a compulsive move. I did not bother to cut my hobbles first. And so I tripped.

With a gazelle's grace and swiftness, the stranger spun to me. He'd pulled the purple fabric back from what it concealed. A glint of steel, the sharpened end of a spear thrust between us. I had to throw myself awkwardly to one side to keep from stumbling onto it, gut first.

"Don't be a damned fool, boy," he hissed. "I don't give freedom to damned fools. They only get themselves killed."

For one moment, our gazes met, held, wrestled. The engagement evoked my youthful fight with Omar to my mind, by glances alone. But this man's leg I wouldn't break. He would break mine. And my neck to follow. I read it plainly in that blackness.

He straightened himself, rethrew the rich fabric over the spearhead once more, and said: "I'll take back my dagger, thank you."

I handed him his dagger, rhinoceros horn first. The harelip stretched in what must have been a grin. He slipped the dagger into its sheath at his waist.

Although he wore a tribal headcloth for his self-respect and against the sun, he wrapped it loosely enough for me to tell a good portion of his skull was shaved. This left a topknot of thick, matted locks, bunched like spikes of peppercorns on the vine. Silver banded the locks, flecked somewhat with gray. The bits of precious metal clinked against one another with his every movement. They clinked now as he tossed his head in the direction of the palm under which al-Harith waited, flinching.

"Back to the tree," my captor said.

Thongs still bound my feet. When I didn't move right away, he caught me by the ear like a naughty child and gave me a sharp kick to the backside to get me moving in the right direction. Walking bound, clumsy, through my captors' camp comprised part of the humility.

Al-Harith had the good grace to look the other way as our captor replaced the bonds he'd cut from my wrists with a new, long leather thong he took from the waistband of his izar. He used it to lash me to the tree.

When, against my will, I gave a childish protest, he made the horrible sound that passed with him for a laugh. Then he said: "You gave me your word when I captured you. If you cannot keep your word like a man, I must bind you like an animal."

58

بســــم الله الرحمــن الرحيــــم

> And before Sulayman were marshalled his hosts, of jinn and men and birds, and they were all kept in order and ranks.
> —The Holy Qur'an, Surah 27:17

"A storm is brewing," the old woman said to her daughter.

They had gained the open desert, an empty place of rocky soil and camel thorn spaced ten paces apart or more between which az-Zuharah strolled, nibbling the tender, salty tips. To the gentle rocking of her movements, mother and daughter lay curtained and in each other's arms, as they had only once before, at the beginning.

This was the mother she had always craved. And yet, perhaps it was too late. There seemed too many others within the qubbah's curtains with them. Her father who had driven her mother first to this place. And, would she or no, the young man, the Qurayshi from Mecca named Khalid. And all the men with stones in their hands, angry, afraid of the wrath of Persia about to descend on them, willing to blame it on witchcraft and so to stone an old woman.

Of course, all these people couldn't really fit in one small litter. Being men, they wouldn't even enter such a place. It must be, Bint Zura realized with a shudder, the jinn who were everywhere in this place. One could only escape such beings by returning to the settled places—which had demons enough of their own.

"A storm brewing?"

Bint Zura thought her mother must still be suffering from the terror of expecting with each breath to feel the stones of her dying with each breath. The sky overhead remained a still and placid blue. No low yellow haze warned of blowing sand. No cloud drifted by, perhaps to start spinning and gathering other tufts to it like tow on a spindle, to grow into a thunderhead.

Bint Zura pointed these signs out to her mother and dared to contradict the prophecies of a known kahinah and seeress. Hadn't she been the one to think of a plan to save her mother's life, after all? "I see no sign of rain. Indeed, it would be strange, at this time of year."

"Do you think storms can brew only in the heavens?" Her mother's reply cut with sharpness.

So that was the end of believing that once she found a mother, unrelieved gentleness would swaddle her.

"I speak of storms in the seasons of men," Umm Taghlib went on.

Bint Zura remembered her father at that moment. And she had imagined, if once she found her mother, the other parent would no longer need to exist. She remembered how he, too, in the jinn-possession this woman had cast upon him, had pointed one twig-like finger at her and, before her, at the stranger from Mecca.

"The coming salvation of the Arabs."

She told her mother of it. Umm Taghlib already seemed to know. The jinn must have come whirling back to her, whispering what they'd told her cursed husband.

"But a storm is not salvation." Bint Zura struggled to understand. "Storms are violent."

"In the desert, you say such a simple thing? When have dark clouds on the horizon not been a sign of hope for thirsty herds, even if their herders know they must move out of the wadis to higher ground or secure the tent stakes more firmly? Do you think salvation is ever gentle?"

Her mother's words were like the hard, prickly thorn amongst which they moved. This was not what Bint Zura had wanted when she'd longed for a mother. This brittle, thin, stony woman was more like camel thorn herself than a soft, forgiving breast to lean upon. Bint Zura, indeed, shifted away, as much as the close litter allowed, hoping this strange woman would not notice.

She hoped a seeress and a kahinah would not notice? A woman who expected, or at least wanted, her daughter to have the same gifts—or curse—as herself along with her same eyes? Having been nowhere near to teach such things earlier in Bint Zura's life, now she wanted to start? A little annoyance bubbled up under the heavy cap of the daughter's fear and awe. She could see things old sunburned eyes, too blue to protect themselves, could not. Was it her own jinni, whispering devilment in her own ear?

"There is someone coming," Bint Zura said, and only after she was certain of the twist of dust rising off the quince-tinted eastern horizon in the direction of al-Hira.

"Ah." Her mother nodded, not without a spiral of triumph. "At last you can see them."

"At last—"

Bint Zura worked to throttle her own shout of exasperation. Just how long had her mother been watching the dust swirl grow without saying a word? Since before it was visible to human eyes? At least Bint Zura could tell why the strangers were following az-Zuharah's prints in the sand.

"They come from al-Hira. They are ignoring the miracle of your escape from the stoning pit. They come to return you there. And to stuff me down there beside you."

Bint Zura reached for the camel's reins. Umm Taghlib stopped her.

"Your az-Zuharah has been drawn by the Gods into the holy precinct. No one may pick up her reins to guide her again, not as long as the Encampment's stones stand."

She is still my camel, Bint Zura wanted to protest. I was there at her birthing, this ghostly white thing. I saved her from the lion's jaws. I have the pelt to prove it—although my uncle-foster-father keeps the skin for his own glory."

The chill across Bint Zura's back told her the Gods would indeed be angry if she voiced such thoughts. Her lips puckered, but the desert air pulled from them the whistle she so often used to urge az-Zuharah to race.

"Stop. Calm." Her mother spoke as if Bint Zura herself were a skittish camel. "Study the heart of the dust."

Even as she wanted to protest more, Bint Zura saw that but a single camel with two riders approached them. It was like theirs but bore only a regular riding saddle, not the qubbah.

The sight did not inspire az-Zuharah to flee, either. She raised her nose and bellowed a greeting to the oncoming camel, who responded in kind and hastened its pace.

Only when she saw that, although there was no qubbah, the camel's driver was a woman did the panic in Bint Zura's chest settle somewhat. That was odd, for the woman to ride in front and rein the beast. When they were a stone's toss apart, the strange camel, a swift, dark, tawny bull, loped to a stop. Of his own accord, he knelt before az-Zuharah and her sacred burden.

The strange woman climbed off, then turned to help the man. This, too, seemed inexplicable. The man was so much younger, well-built and strong. The features they shared made him her son, but he was too old and strong by far to still touch women in public, to be led by the hand.

Then Bint Zura saw that the man was blind, blinking unseeing at the desert's glare around them with milk-filmed eyes. That was when she recognized him as the young Taghlibi poet who had held his own in the battle of words against her tribe's older poet. Some jinni must have gifted this young man, even from the cradle.

Umm Taghlib parted the gauzy curtains of the qubbah and labored off az-Zuharah's back to the ground. The three of them, Umm Taghlib, the blind poet, and his mother, sat down where they were. They took possession of no greater shade than that made by the qubbah and the two camels setting their rumps to the sun side by side. The camels proceeded to chew their cuds in companionable unison.

Bint Zura did not join the unusual majlis. It was not appropriate for her to sit with a strange man, even a blind one, whereas his mother and another older woman, a kahinah indeed, faced no such reservations. Were they at home, Bint Zura would have retreated behind the women's curtain. Where there was no tent, she must draw her veil across her face and find work to take her away from the talk.

She exited the qubbah on the opposite side of the meeting. She must pretend she had no interest in such things, yet perhaps give the man a view of her wifely skills: How she could draw water, perhaps, the curve of her calves showing as she hitched up her gown to do so. Or the mastery of her weaving, her milking, her hand with the churn, any such activity. This man could not see her, no matter how adept she was. And no such activities presented themselves in this deserted corner of the desert.

Only one sad task came to her mind. She didn't want to do it and would have even picked up her hated spinning rather than to undertake it. The Gods, however, gave her no choice of diversion in this place at this time. When az-Zuharah had stepped into the sacred precinct by the standing stones, the white camel had gone from Bint Zura's possession to that of higher powers. She knew she must do it now.

Bint Zura had noticed an aloe plant springing from a nest of purplish rocks as az-Zuharah passed. The Gods had presented that, too, for aloe was not common in this area. Aloe was often hung from the center posts of tents along with skulls and menstrual rags to keep the evil jinn away. It was holy, healing herbage, good for burns from natural fire as well as from fire spirits.

Bint Zura returned to the plant now. Spent blossom stalks forked from its center. Near the base sprang up the old blades that had lost life and their healing sap. They had gone gray and curled in on themselves, leaving only the sharp spikes, even sharper in death, exposed to discourage gnawing desert rats. This is what she stooped for, begging the plant to forgive her for taking but a few of its defenses. Cautiously avoiding the serrated rows of spikes, she took three—one or two for spares, since they were brittle—and carried them back to az-Zuharah.

Her mother and her visitors were still on the formulaic beginnings any conversation must take.

"What is the peace in the desert?"

"It is well. And yours?"

"The peace in your tents?"

"By the grace of the Gods, well." No matter what the truth was.

Bint Zura went and stood at az-Zuharah's head. She embraced the long, soft nose, always haughty with a consciousness of her color and the miracle of her birth. Now that the hand of the Gods had claimed her fully, the droop of the nose was even more imperious.

With a sigh, Bint Zura realized that her darling had never really belonged to her at all, not even when she'd been able to lift her in her arms to carry her to the safety of the Thamudi tomb. She unknotted the bridle and pulled it out through the hole she herself had pierced between the tender nostrils while she'd still clung to that illusion.

"Now no one but the Gods may drive you," Bint Zura whispered into one round, furry ear.

Az-Zuharah flicked that ear and nodded sagely. The damp look in those dark, long-lashed eyes made the tears start in Bint Zura's own. She had to pause in her task and bury her face in the warm, white neck.

From her pillow on that neck, her nostrils full of the smell of warm camel, she heard the talk of her mother and the two guests continuing on. The desert, contrary to the earlier formulas, was far from being at peace.

59

> Devout is he alone who, when he may
> Feast his desires, is found
> With courage to abstain.
> —al-Ma'arri

"You have heard, Grandmother," said the blind poet Mutammim, using a title of respect, "of the death of King an-Numan under the elephant's feet."

That jerked Bint Zura from all thought of the loss of her camel, back to this place in the desert among the camel thorn. For hadn't she once flown as if on the wings of a hawk to the city by the Tigris? Hadn't she seen with her own eyes the thick, gray, iron-spiked ankles crush the once-crowned and still-defiant head like an egg?

"Yes, and how Hanzala of the Banu Bakr has taken an-Numan's armor—may the rains fall soft upon his grave—and his women under his protection," the poet's mother added.

"He stands alone against the Padishah," Mutammim went on, "and all the Persian Empire."

"There will be a great battle. It cannot be avoided."

"Hanzala and his Arabs must lose."

Umm Taghlib the kahinah spoke her first words of this part of the exchange, when all ritual was spent. "Be careful that the Fire Ones do not take away the use of your tongue, poet of the Tamim, as well as your eyes for trying to say what the Gods will and what They will not do."

Mother and son sat in uncomfortable silence for a while.

Then Umm Taghlib said, "We can discuss what men may attempt and what they may not attempt. I myself have but recently escaped, by the grace of the Gods and of my daughter there by the camel's head, from death at the hand of an-Numan's usurper, that slave of Persia. You may imagine what my own will against him is."

Mutammim and his mother nodded solemnly, shifting uneasily on the hot sand.

"So let me ask, then, what the sharif of the Tamim intends to do at this pass. Whom will he support, if the Gods will?"

Umm Mutammim looked at her eldest son, his blind eyes the source of so much of her grief.

"My brother Malik is the sharif of our Arabs. He intends to stay clear of this fray, if the Gods will," Mutammim was careful to add. "His heart is with the Arabs, but he has no desire to risk the men or animals he must surely lose with little hope of winning anything but poet's praise after death."

Umm Mutammim took a breath as if to speak, then stifled it. The look, unnatural in its keenness, with which her mother fixed the other woman made Bint Zura's heart race.

"This is the son who didn't come last time," the kahinah stated.

"You remember all those years ago—?" Umm Mutammim began, then cut it to a simple, "Yes."

"The young boy who gave his eyes to the Ones of this Place in order to bring his playmate back from the dead." The kahinah turned her gaze on the son, pity and, yes, admiration aglow in her blue eyes.

Umm Mutammim went on, uncomfortable haste in her words. "And I cannot agree with my other son's decision not to fight Hanzala of the Banu Bakr."

"Even though he is the son with the honor of sharif?"

"No sharif of the Arabs wields power like a Persian despot." Blind Mutammim silenced his mother with a stroke of his hand. "We are free to think our own minds and to do what we can to sway Malik. We have come to you."

"Why should I try to sway him when the reason of remaining neutral is on his side?"

Umm Mutammim brushed aside her son's stilling hand. "Because my third son has been taken prisoner by that man."

"Your third son? I never heard that an-Nuwaira—may the rains fall soft upon his grave—left a third son."

"His name is Khalid ibn al-Walid."

"Ah. The foster son."

Bint Zura caught her breath and stopped the pretense of fondling her camel's head. There could not be more than one of such a name. Khalid—*her* Qurayshi. No. She must not think of him so, since the wide desert separated them. And who had given them to each other, anyway, in her mind? Her jinn-ridden father. "The coming salvation of the Arabs." Here was her mother, clearly not so pleased.

It cannot be the same Khalid, Bint Zura told herself with her next camel-scented breath. Captured? A prisoner of the man who was bound for honor's sake to be crushed beneath the weight of an entire empire? What must happen to any of such a man's prisoners? Surely, if not killed outright, the empire would suck such prisoners out of the desert to its own dark heart, never to return. No, it could not be the same Khalid.

Although, now that she thought of it, Mutammim had also been in the convent garden. And her Khalid had stood behind his milk brothers at the battle of the poets. It must be the same man. She looked to her mother for a hint as to what to think.

A storm was brewing, if not in the sky, then in her mother's face. Bint Zura could almost see the sand gathering to rise in a stormy twist behind the qubbah.

"Khalid is no less my son than the others," Umm Mutammim insisted.

"Didn't I tell you not to raise that one?"

Bint Zura felt a pain in the pit of her stomach at the thought that her Khalid might have been wiped from the world while just a boy, before she'd ever known him. Worse was the thought that her mother, her own newly discovered mother, wished it so. Her mother, with all her dark powers, willed it so. Was no doubt responsible for Khalid's present condition as the captive of a doomed tribe. With all the effort she could muster, Bint Zura held her tongue.

"You did," Umm Mutammim admitted. "That day in Mecca. But I had already given him suck on that day. You cannot ask a woman to give up a child after that—nor even when, as a man, he gets himself captured."

"He will give you cause to cut off your own breast." The hollow sounds of prophecy rising from her mother's stringy throat shuddered through Bint Zura.

Umm Mutammim stroked the embroidered front of her gown anxiously, but she wasn't dissuaded.

The kahinah threw up her bony hands in helplessness. "And so the jinn find cracks to prey upon the sons of men. Whenever they don't get their due."

"'Don't get their due?'" Umm Mutammim countered. "Look at this eldest son of mine. Those smoky Spirits of Fire took his eyes."

"But gave him a shaytan to touch his tongue in the place of sight." The kahinah snorted at such reasoning in the face of what she knew. "All this while, there's that other one who offered his right arm. He took back his offer, the scrap of cloth he tore from his right sleeve."

"He didn't," Umm Mutammim said.

"Don't let your breast blind you to what the Ones of this Place see very well. The jinn marked that he didn't trust them, that he tried to fool them. The jinn will remember."

Umm Mutammim's face had gone ashen, her tattoos standing out like lines of charcoal on pale sand. "You mean the jinn would have taken Khalid's right arm instead of Mutammim's eyes—?"

A smile played on the kahinah's sun-wrinkled lips. "What the Fire Ones will."

Umm Mutammim was silent but for her breath, coming hard and quick as she considered how the world might have been otherwise. Bint Zura, too, felt her breath coming in ragged gasps. She hated to imagine that man's strong arm— Yet she must—

"We came to ask you what might be done with any of your powers to help that milk brother of mine," Mutammim said. "Now we understand—"

The kahinah nodded with a jingle of cowrie shells on her dusty headdress. "I will not lift a finger or speak one power word to help that man," she confirmed.

"But I—" Bint Zura at her camel's head heard herself say.

She stopped herself before she said more. She wasn't supposed to speak, only to do. She hadn't been at that fateful place where the futures of four young boys were wagered against untrustworthy beings of smoke. She was, however, here now. She was able to wager what was most important to her.

Bint Zura grabbed one round, white camel ear, pulled it taut and, with one quick stab, pierced the aloe blade through the thin center membrane. She yanked. The aloe blade snapped, but not before the skin was cut through, clean through the notch she had made once to mark her own possession. Ownership of the Gods alone was now the only signal the ear gave.

Az-Zuharah moaned with pain, but she didn't lurch to her feet.

Bint Zura took a second blade and cut the other ear. This time the camel made no sound. Her large, moist eyes merely turned to look at her former mistress with understanding and, it seemed, deep sorrow. The white ears flicked, shedding drops of blood over the long, shaggy neck like a string of rubies. And, Bint Zura decided, the camel took the procedure like a woman who ignores the pain of pierced ears for the beauty of new earrings.

Bint Zura tasted blood. At first she thought she must have swallowed some from the divine camel's flicking ears. Then she knew it was not so, but human blood. Her own? Or that of those she may have cursed. For she realized now that she had spoken words as she'd made the cuts, words that had come not from her but from outside. From her wrestle with what she could not see but must call a shaytan. An adversary.

Only then did she hear the skitter of sand as it left her ears open, finally, to normal sound once more. She saw the shift of reddish grains beneath the hem of her skirt as if at a breath of wind—only the air was sun-baked, dry, and still. She smelled a passing whiff of smoke and fire.

Two sets of eyes from a different world, the normal world, were watching her. And the third, in the young man's face, unseeing. They had heard her words brought from the shaytan, although she herself had no memory of them. Her mother had, indeed, abandoned her seat on the ground and stood staring.

Bint Zura spat the blood from her mouth. Then, like a delayed echo, she did hear some of what she herself had said. "The coming salvation of the Arabs." Her own father's mad words tossed back at her. She covered her ears with her hands as if they were wounded as much as az-Zuharah's. Still she heard it. She heard it over whatever Mutammim bent to his mother's veil to whisper to her.

Bint Zura did hear when Umm Mutammim nodded and said, "My son, O kahinah, would like me to speak for your daughter in marriage. He admits he is blind, and so less of a man. He would, however, have been sharif of the Tamim otherwise. Even now he is the brother of the sharif. We can offer not inconsiderable brideprice. My son has, as well, the gift of words. He has just heard that your daughter hears a shaytan herself. He wishes their voices to be combined."

Shyness tied the blind poet's tongue, although his shaytan did gift him with this couplet at least to express his love:

> "What is true religion? A maid kept close that no eye may view her;
> The price of her wedding-gifts and dowry baffles the wooer."

Umm Taghlib gave no indication that she had heard either of these speeches. Her blue eyes only continued to stare at her daughter.

For her part, Bint Zura paid the most attention to communication from az-Zuharah. The Gods' camel gave the delighted groan she always gave whenever Bint Zura offered her a wild, free run across the desert together. The beast tossed her head, ears still bleeding, back toward the qubbah. She wanted her former mistress inside the sacred litter on her back one last time.

Bint Zura felt a stab of regret. This man sitting, one knee up, resting his arm upon that and his head upon that, was a good man. He was a wealthy man, better than she could ever hope for, she the daughter of a banished kahinah and a father, sometimes mad, but at all times siding with the settled Christians. More important, Mutammim ibn an-Nuwaira was kind and gentle. And jinn-touched.

The other one, that Khalid. Hadn't Bint Zura just learned that he had stolen his strong right arm from the jinn? Not an easy man. Never kind—unless, perhaps, it suited his own ambition. As a child, her own mother had seen it would be better never to let him grow to manhood.

It was the jinn, Bint Zura told herself. Her personal passion had nothing to do with anything. And if it did—wasn't passion a well-known sign of possession by the Fire Spirits?

The jinn had a debt with Khalid ibn al-Walid, and they will claim their due. Her—no, the divine—camel knew it. Bint Zura herself must understand it, too.

Bint Zura hesitated no longer. She took her place inside the sun-warmed qubbah. The moment she was settled, az-Zuharah rocked to her feet, back legs first, followed by the front.

Bint Zura took one look back through the litter's curtains toward her mother, the little form of rags standing among the camel thorn alone. Then, without human control, girl and camel set off across the desert to places known only to the Ones of that Place.

60

> Many a young wife's spouse I have cut down,
> his wide gash, like a harelip, hissing:
> my hand beat him to it with a deep thrust,
> and blood red as andami berry gushed in a spray.
> —the Qasidah of Antar ibn Shaddad

I thought our captor would have the grace to leave me to my shame, bound to the palm tree, alone with silent al-Harith who had plenty of shame of his own to stew in. Instead, the African strode just far enough away that no fettered move of mine could harm him. The dust on the hem of his robe swept after him, at a height to fill my throat and make me cough. There he sat, claiming the best shade, and made himself comfortable.

To my further chagrin, Nuri came and sat beside the man. Had my own slave betrayed me because the two of them were Africans? Was it because they shared facial deformities, Nuri his lopped-off nose and our captor the slash from before birth? After all Nuri's time in our family? By the Gods, I'd sell him the minute They ever got us out of here.

I refused to look at my slave and stared steadily at our captor instead. I must confess, that took a muster of courage, not only for the shame he'd put me through, but also because he was the ugliest man I had ever seen. He was huge and black, the harelip opening to the raw pink cavern of his mouth. The battle-hardened muscles of every hand's breadth of dark flesh were like the wild ridges of lava fields, showing the heaved scars of many, many wounds.

"He had much the body then that I have now," I muse to my scribe. "Of which I am now so proud. Had I the skin and the lip to overcome as well, I'd be prouder still."

"You're a God-blessed young man, Khalid ibn al-Walid of the Quraysh of Mecca," the African began by saying to me then.

"God-blessed!" Sarcasm burst from me.

"It seems the young warrior you speared will live, the Gods willing."

I uttered a curse under my breath. I couldn't even kill a man properly.

"But this is a good thing," he assured me with a chuckle. "Had he died, his kinsmen would be clamoring for your blood, and I would turn you over to them. You're my prisoners, not my protected guests."

I spoke as soon as the thought occurred to me. "It would be better to die than to live with this shame."

The dark eyes twinkled. "Then your punishment of continued life is deserved."

"Tell me the price of that man's blood." Yes, let me stand while his strong young son or brother throws his spear at me, I thought. There'd be a chance I'd die. The pain would do something for the shame that threatened to kill me.

"The Gods shield him, he may never throw a spear with that arm again. But I have given the family a horse—a fine white mare—"

"Not al-Minhal's Little One?"

"—A mare and four camels. The family is content."

"My mare. My camels," I blurted.

"No. As of yesterday morning, they are mine by the law of the desert."

"By the law of the desert, you took them during the month of pilgrimage in al-Hira. You broke the law of pilgrimage."

The ravaged lips curled back in a ghastly grin. "What is it the poet Ummayr said?

> "'Are we not the God Ma'add's calendar-makers,
> making profane months sacred, sacred profane?'

"You, a prisoner knotted in thongs? You are to tell me differently? Besides, you were camping in Bakri pastures."

"The basin of al-Lussuf belongs to my milk brothers, the sons of Tamim."

"So they say. We say otherwise." The notion amused my captor. "And we were there at dawn yesterday. Our opinion carries the day."

So it seemed.

What a wide-eyed and uncomprehending stare al-Minhal would fix upon his filly when he saw her being haggled for among the horses in al-Hira! He had thought her well on her way to Rome to win fame among the emperors. As for me—that rude young man who never spoke to take his daughter off his hands—I cannot think what he thought of me.

"May you choke on the gold you trade for those animals," I cried impotently against might's justice.

"Such a curse." The notion made the silver-knotted locks jangle merrily even as he shook his head in feigned sadness. "Then it is good I don't intend to trade—except for blood."

I really didn't care what he did. Yet I couldn't help myself. "You'll keep all my steeds throughout the coming summer?"

"Indeed we will. If needs be."

"In the summer? When your miserable Bakri pastures wither to nothing?"

"We'll feed them on date mash and camel's milk taken from our own children's mouths."

The harelip whistled in a way that disgusted. For one intense moment, all humor was gone from this man facing me. Such a fierce buildup of cavalry in the eastern desert. What could it mean? Did the Banu Bakr intend to raid my milk brothers? The sons of Tamim could never stand the onslaught of such a number of horsemen. I must learn more. I must get word to Malik—

But one thought overrode these concerns. I couldn't think how I'd manage to explain this loss to my father. How he'd ever make it up.

"What has become of my slaves?" I asked numbly. "I mean besides this son-of-a-dog traitor." I would ignore Nuri.

"My slaves now, too. I've put them to work drawing water. So many horses! They need a lot of water. Slaves don't mind, I think. I should know, yes, having been born a slave myself." Of course, the African cast to his skin. "One master is much the same as another, one well the same as the next to them."

How was I going to explain this to my father? To Nuri's young wife and the son she'd borne him? Smuggling me in a saddlebag as a child had failed. Had Nuri always meant it to fail, like he meant my escape in the howdah to fail? By the Gods, I'd lash his skin until it looked like our captors'—

Then there was al-Harith beside me. The herdsman didn't even strain at the leather thongs on his wrists and ankles. He didn't care enough to engage this man in bartering for our lives, wouldn't meet him eye to eye. Had the ladies under their red kerchief in al-Hira left him with nothing to live for at all?

"What ransoms will you ask for us?" I demanded my captor now.

He replied, for the time being, merely "Great ones." Then he said with an open, jovial gesture: "Let your sons of Tamim begin the negotiations whenever they would. Or your Quraysh. I'll deal with either."

My shame at our capture overwhelmed me then. "A sword!" I cried to the world from the shade of the palm where I sat trussed. "A sword, that I may fall upon it! Or but cut my bands, and I shall walk straight out into the desert. I'll avoid all wells and waterholes until I perish of the choking thirst."

The idea made the man laugh right out loud, opening the grotesque cavern of his mouth wide, the sound a nasal whine that made the bile rise in my throat.

"I should introduce myself," he said, as soon as the silver stopped jangling. "I'm not a Bakr at all, but of the tribe of Abs."

"I thought you said you were a slave, not noble."

"Nobility among true, liberal Arabs, my young friend, is the thrust of the spear, the blow of the sword, patience when laboring beneath battle dust. Can you claim such a lineage?"

I couldn't. Not yet. But, by all the Gods, I would. I ran my tongue over the sharpened spikes of my shark's teeth and swore there was no reason why I should not. Except that my hands and feet were bound to the trunk of a palm tree.

"I am a great physician of the tribe of Abs, healing them when they are in the sickness of disgrace."

His phrases were coming out like bursts of poetry—although it was hard to credit this through the ruin of his mouth.

"Although my mother was a bondswoman, my father, may rain soften his grave, was a sharif of the Abs. Shaddad was his name."

"Not . . . not Antar ibn Shaddad?" My scribe stops, his pen poised in the air.

"The same."

"You met Antar ibn Shaddad?"

Even now, if we wanted, I could send out to the nearest corner and find any storyteller. I could set him up here in the garden on cushions and have him recite the exploits of Antar—the bane of cowards and lions alike, his love of the fair Abla—from now until next Friday prayers.

"Yes, I was captured by Antar ibn Shaddad, as it turned out. And your question was my same to him, word for word."

"Not . . . not Antar ibn Shaddad?"

Our captor answered me: "The same."

I flushed hot with shame, shame that I had not recognized the man at once, for his fame filled the desert. Shame that I had tried to hold onto my honor before his face when I might, with more grace, have accepted honor from him. If a man had to be a prisoner, it wasn't so bad, was it, to have fallen to Arabia's greatest hero? The fame of this son of a sharif and an African slave extended far behind the day of my birth, into the realm of fable. Perhaps I had imagined Antar ibn Shaddad not to be real. Or at least, no longer still on earth with the rest of common mortals.

Not only were Antar's deeds of arms renowned, so also were the poetic gifts I'd begun to hear echoing in his every word, once I overcame my horror at his deformity. How the sons of Abs had rejoiced at the discovery of such gifts: "A poet is born to us. See how the Gods favor us, to send their word to earth through the mouth of one of our own." Even if that mouth were a ragged ruin since ignoble birth. I marveled that such hissing sounds as that mouth managed could once have won the poet's contest at the convocation in Ukaz by general acclaim, before I was born. The words, written out on fine parchment, bordered with silk and gold, hung now with six divine others inside the Ka'ba in Mecca. And though we couldn't read, what child could not recite:

> *"But I already fear death might take me*
> *before war's wheel is turned . . ."?*

Would Antar brag that he'd brought Khalid ibn al-Walid down to restraints? Why would he bother? Other exploits were uppermost in his mind.

"We need these horses," he said. "We defend ourselves against the arrogance of Persia. Such arrogance kills the king of al-Hira and puts their own puppet on his throne."

"You mean to support Hanzala ibn Thalaba in that flimsy shell of an-Numan's armor?" I wanted to go on: You, the great hero of Arabia, you should know enough to pick your battles, staying far from ones you cannot hope to win.

"Exactly," he replied. "With the Gods' help."

"There's no honor in sure annihilation," I told him.

The broad black shoulders, wearing their net of pink-white scars, shrugged. "My hairs are going gray now. I do not last so long in the dust of battle as I did in my youth. But one thing all my battles have taught me: While I have breath, I must always fight on the side whose cause has the most honor.

More often than not, that is the side that seems, at the outset, least likely to win."

"Then you, the great hero, come to their aid and all others flee at the sound of your name and the sight of your banner."

"I do not think the Persians will do so."

"Nor do I," I agreed.

"And if the Gods crave my death in this fray—death in a cause truly hopeless—? Why, the poets would know no better end to the life of Arabia's hero."

"I couldn't do it," I confessed. In his presence, the pain of that confession was even sharper. Yet, even suffering now the shame of defeat, I swore I would do everything reason taught me to avoid tasting it ever again in the future.

"I see. You are young." The silver jangled in a nod. "Son of al-Walīd, I have your horses, to divide among my men and the Banu Bakr as I see fit."

"God give you no joy of them." Then curiosity got the better of me. "Do you know where you will meet the Persians and their Arab allies?"

"No, not yet. But it must be soon. The days of great heat are coming."

"Better not to fight then."

"On the contrary, better for us, who are used to it, and fight in hardly more than our shrouds." Antar plucked at the two white strips of cloth he wore, one on the loins, one across the shoulders. "Worse for the Persians, their heavy catafracts of armor, man's head to horse's hoof a plate of iron. Armored men on foot carry the oven of their own baking on their backs."

"You fight over a suit of armor, yet you hope their armor will fight against the other side."

"There is some poetry in that, is there not? The outcome of the battle, yes, only the Gods can say. But it cannot hurt that we ride these fine mounts, not the Persians. You, son of al-Walīd, have no decision to make as far as that goes."

I struggled vainly at my bonds, rasping them on the trunk, as his words seemed to bind me as well. My captor ignored this as he went on with his proposal.

"On the other hand, I like you."

I must have flinched as if from a blow. There came another horrible laugh.

"Prodded by your faithful slave here—" Nuri. He meant Nuri, bitter jest. "I watched your cunning attempt at escape instead of just running you through when first I detected it. Earlier, I watched you fight in defense of your herd."

I stifled the moan in my throat. "I lost." May all the Gods witness that I faced this fact as bravely as any other threat in my life.

"Yes, but you were outnumbered and you fought against Antar ibn Shaddād. That didn't stint your bravery."

Then the clump of thick tresses gave a nod in al-Harith's direction and made this declaration. "Were you and your silent friend there to give me your word you would lend your strong right arms to this fight, I would loose you this moment."

I struggled again, the choice he offered more uncomfortable than the bonds. I ached to be free, *of course. But what would be the point of freedom if I couldn't slip out to the desert with my milk brothers and my horses, to keep that freedom by avoiding the coming storm? To fight beside Antar ibn Shaddad could be glory. But to be freed from his bonds only to have them immediately replaced by Persian chains—I could not see the advantage. Worse, the Persians were unlikely to spare rebels' lives for the ransom they might win, a drop in their vast coffers. Their empire hungered for slaves. I'd be a slave—or dead—before I'd had time to rack up a single deed to echo Antar ibn Shaddad's epic.*

I could always give Antar my word, get freed. Then, the moment battle grew hot, when the old hero was beyond help, I could change sides in time for Persians to reward me for my deeds— And there was my Bint Zura to think of—

But no. The glorious name of Antar made the words to begin such perfidy impossible to form.

Al-Harith beside me started to say something. It held a positive note, submission.

I cut him off. "No, by the Gods. Never. I would rather die." The great day when the Persians annihilated the Arabs over a matter of armor and women would have to be fought without me.

Ibn Shaddad shrugged and got up to leave, shaking more sand from his hem into our faces. "Think on it, Ibn al-Walid. These howdahs you see—in which you tried to escape—they brought King an-Numan's women to these wells last night. Along with Hanzala ibn Thalaba in the dead king's armor. The day of battle comes, quickly as the hawk after sand grouse."

As soon as Antar ibn Shaddad was out of earshot from the tree to which he'd tied me, I said: "Be my witness, O al-Harith."

"By al-Uzza, to what?" The herdsman's son seemed a little sulky. Because I wouldn't let him make a fool of himself and accept that humiliating offer? Simple fellow.

"By Hubal, to this. I, Khalid the son of al-Walid, swear by the God of my fathers, by Hubal, by all three hundred and sixty Gods of the Ka'ba, by any God there may be. By the strength of my right arm—" The muscles of that arm twinged, recalling the last oath I had made by that power—and how I had cheated the jinn with that avowal. "If I am ever set free of Antar ibn Shaddad, I shall never again lose a battle or fall captive to any man. I shall die rather than ever—ever—face the shame of womanish defeat again."

"Such things are best not sworn," al-Harith cautioned. "Such things are in the hands of God."

But I refused his caution. "This is not. Or if it is so, then I defy God. I will not be defeated again, or I am not a man."

Al-Harith touched his amulet against evil, but he witnessed the oath.

And, as God is my witness, I have kept it to this day. In no feat of arms or any other thing that marks a man have I ever been bested. But as evening falls in my garden, it is lines from the tales of Antar I recite, not Quranic verses:

> Did the poets leave no tune to sing of …?
> "O Abla's hearth in Jiwa'i," speak: "Good
> evening, hearth, may you fare in peace …"

61

I was led astray by the stars.
—a saying of the Rwala tribe

"Ya az-Zuharah, not there," Bint Zura pleaded as she rode without control. "This is a mistake."

But the white camel, at a happy trot, had not turned toward the open desert. With all her will, Bint Zura had not been able to steer the halterless animal. The Banu Bakr and their prisoner, that disturbing Khalid of Mecca, would not—not yet—have her help to protect the dead king's armor, women, and honor, either.

Instead, the cushioned feet followed their earlier steps back to the sacred precinct around al-Hira. They skirted the solid green blocks of palm groves, the long, high banks of canals concealing all but their palmed crowns.

Even there, az-Zuharah did not follow tracks familiar to her former mistress, to the convent or church. She did not even go to the Encampment's great stones and the place of sacrifice to which, by her sliced ears, she now belonged. From which she had only just rescued the kahinah.

Az-Zuharah brought her burden to the priestesses of another religion; with a groan, the camel sank to her knees before the tents flying red scarves. Dark with wonder, beautiful kohl-rimmed eyes looked out over their veils at the sight: the filmy curtains of the qubbah and the white camel quietly chewing her cud.

Bint Zura couldn't imagine what the divine camel meant by bringing her to such a place. But she had thrown her lot now to the shaytan of the camel.

Then one of the women raised her voice in the high, sharp trill of triumph. Others echoed around their tents until their air rang. They might not know exactly what the sign meant, but they knew girl and camel were divine; they welcomed the miraculous to them with thanksgiving, ready to answer gift for gift in any way they could.

Drawn by the noise, the crowd grew, drawn from the very edges of the settlement. Were they to witness another miracle, as they had so recently at the stoning pit?

Drawn by the crowd instead of drawing one, Bint Zura's father found her. Before she'd even managed her first words with the women of the scarves, or decided what those words should be.

"This is a mistake," Bint Zura said again into the camel's round ear, crusted now with the new blood of devotion.

But the camel only chewed her cud and seemed to grin and wink at her.

"Indeed, I ought to send you to those women," her father said. "After you escaped with your mother, saved her from a kahinah's justice. I am the king's wazir, after all, and must support the king's law."

Then he raised his voice for the benefit of the shifting crowd. "But I am a man of honor and of mercy."

He returned his daughter to the convent.

"What is the matter with this accursed camel?" he demanded once the nuns had custody of Bint Zura.

Az-Zuharah had placidly followed her former mistress from the whores' tents. But now that the king's wazir was ready to take her into custody, the camel had ideas of her own.

Bint Zura turned. She had been studying by daylight the sematron tower where she'd helped the man of Mecca to escape.

"The bridle slit in the camel's nose has been torn," Zura complained on. "It cannot be led."

"You can't take az-Zuharah where she does not want to go," Bint Zura told her father. "Don't you see the ears? She is dedicated to the Goddess, as she has been, in truth, since birth."

"Pagan blasphemy," the wazir muttered. "One way or another, the beast will come to your uncle. He has unfurled his lion skin and marches with the Persians against the Banu Bakr. The camel, too, should be with him."

"That lion skin is mine. Mine and az-Zuharah's." But she was talking to her father's back as he went to struggle with the camel, who began by spitting at him.

Bint Zura was tempted for one minute to spit at the nuns, who began to use the same force on her.

Then she thought of how her red underdress had fluttered like a harlot's scarf from those tower beams as she'd helped the night invader to escape. How it fluttered now from Khalid the Meccan's head.

Bushra's scream bounced from wall to wall within the courtyard as if in a well. Rayah was the first to reach her and to gather her little cousin in her arms. By then, the girl was trying to laugh through her tears, and Rayah understood what had happened. Kefa and his brother had hidden at the turn in the stairs and then jumped out at their little sister, pretending to be jinn, as she climbed past. They'd done the same thing to Rayah when she was younger and stood now, grinning and slapping their knees at how well their joke had carried off.

Rayah rose, keeping a protective hand on the little head and, although both boys were older than she, righteous fury drove her speech. "Don't you two realize your sister has only just recovered, al-hamdulillah, from a bump to the head that could have killed her? Your childish game might have sent her into a relapse, God forbid, you who are supposed to be the protection of your women."

Most of her indignation flew into the last phrases: "And God forgive you for making a joke of the Ones of this Place, as if Fire Spirits do not exist. You have no fear of them, but I tell you, I do. They must be respected and given their due."

When she finished, Rayah half expected her cousins to be laughing at her as they had done at Bushra. To her surprise, both boys looked away sheepishly as they gathered up the coverlets they'd draped to mimic spirits. As they went ahead up the stairs, the oldest only muttered, "Well, I guess you should know, ya Rayah."

Rayah ignored them. "Come on," she told Bushra then. "Pick up your pillow, and let's go to the roof."

Imperceptibly, the year had turned. Suddenly, though the days were as hot as ever, on the roof the nights became cooler than they were on the bottom floor while the day's heat rose through the air over the court. Rayah, with her frequent hours up there in the third-floor room where Sitt Sameh stayed, summer or winter, had been the first to notice the change. So, having broken their fast with sundown, the turpentine sellers' women went up to the roof to sleep.

That meant no tale of Sitt Sameh winding long into the night. But everyone looked forward to conversing with neighbor women on their roofs hour after hour, a party mood prevailing. Even Bushra quickly forgot her terror of dark corners and climbed to the open air at Rayah's side.

As her head came up out of the stairwell and into the night, Rayah reminded herself that on the morrow, Jaffar would come to the shop. She must find the strength to give him an answer. For his sake. For Ghusoon's. And for her own. A compliant "Yes" seemed best. No one would then require more of her than just a life like any other.

That night, the sky was clear of dust, the stars glinting like sunlight on splashing water. Through their stream soared the Eagle—the constellation Christians called the Cross of Calvary—and through it showered, every half hour or so, a meteor. It was not an Eagle but a Roc, the great bird slain by the prophet Hanzala ibn Safwan, said some. Fire Spirits cast from heaven by the Almighty, said others. Brightest of all, the moon announced just how close to the end of the month it had waned.

And, of course, az-Zuharah. Her grandmother's camel. The evening star. The Goddess. The meanings had become all entwined.

At one point, growing drowsy, Rayah on her mat with a nest of women around looked away from the chatter to the sky again. She saw that Sitt Sameh had come out of her room. The woman hadn't joined the others, however, but stood, tightly wrapped in black, at the southern edge of the roof. Leaning on the plastered wall, blocking the star al-Nair, the Bright One, symbol of undying love and maternal care, she stood listening. To the idle chatter? Or to something beyond? Something beyond the city walls? In the desert? To spirits?

Once again, Rayah wished her mother would do something to help with Ghusoon's cure.

She obviously had much more experience bargaining with jinn. But Rayah didn't dare ask again.

So she would have to undertake it on her own.

Seeing her chance, Rayah slipped out of her place among the other women and crept through the darkness to Sitt Sameh's room. By feel alone—she'd stared so long and so hard at it, she knew right where it would be—she found the ruins of her grandmother's litter. It wasn't difficult to work free one broken arc of acacia wood. Just a little more bending would bring its half circle full. Instead of curtains, as her mothers had done in the desert, Rayah could then stretch something else over its frame—the skin for a drum.

Later than night, after the telltale moon had set, Rayah woke to complete silence. She felt the arc of wood lying hidden beside her. Finding it safe, she realized the day's thirst had returned to her with a vengeance. The jugs the women had brought up with them were empty. At first, she tried to ignore the discomfort. It couldn't be too long now until it would be time to breakfast again and pray against another sunrise. Far below her, though, as if from underground, she could hear the fountain in the court, whispering.

She took a jug and went downstairs toward the sound.

As she approached the turn in the stairs, she remembered her cousins' prank and had the sudden feeling that they were hiding there again. "Kefa, I know you're there," she hissed.

No giggled reply. No reply at all. She was dreaming things.

Rayah took a breath and made the turn. There, to her surprise, she saw a sigh of wind stir what had always before been just solid brick. A cloth—it seemed red silk —hung in front of a door which, never in all her days, had she noticed before. Light burned through the fabric, shimmering, almost as if there were a fire in its heart.

She smelled no smoke, but still she thought she ought to look and be certain no accident threatened her family, trapped up on the roof. She pushed aside the shimmer of silk and stepped within.

A man was there, reclining on cushions, beneath the canopy of a lush garden. Only rather than the clustered, overlapping leaves of usual foliage, these rippled as if painted on silk themselves. The whole room seemed a sheer fabric she could reach out and plunge her hand through, a mirage floating just above the desert horizon.

The glow, she saw, came from the man's face. It was a face made not of clay as are other men's, but of fire. It was so bright she couldn't make out his features, or whether pox had pitted his cheeks. That face sat beneath a telltale turban, however: silk still new red, a woman's underdress.

"Welcome, child," the voice said. It had the sound of smoke. "Please, sit. My home is your home."

Rayah remained standing. She racked her brain for one Quranic verse to say for protection. They had all vanished in such a place.

"I won't," was all she managed.

"Why?"

"You managed to get into our harem, past the blue eye and Sitt Fatima's hand. For all my mother's efforts, you have found a way to worm into our home. Our harem."

"Is it not your mind that has let me in?"

"You have come in on the black magic of parchment and writing."

"Which is also the power of the holy Quran. Surely you know that Islam has come. Our one true God has conquered not only men but shayatan and jinn. The baleful blue eyes of a pagan idol—what power has that for me?"

Rayah still failed to think of a protective verse. "And yet, you're dead."

"Child, I am your grandfather."

"You are not."

"So your mother—whom you call Sitt Sameh—she hasn't had the courage yet to tell you?"

That was the way of Ones of Fire. To tell half-truths like mirages and so lure mortals to death. But what else had her mother been doing? In all that talk, not to come to the point? Still, Rayah had one bit of truth she knew for certain. "A father supports his offspring. Khalid the Conqueror never supported my mother. She lived off the charity of others all the time she raised me."

"Your mother would never accept anything from me." The sound of his white silk robes slipping on cushions was the sound of a snake. "It is a sin to deny and confuse parentage. Bloodlines must be kept pure."

"More destructive is an adulteration of power."

"I am the Conqueror." The voice boomed suddenly, like thunder. "My power cannot be denied."

"No. But you have made others deny theirs."

The echoing rolls of thunder passed. The glow in the face that had burst like lightning dimmed, then worked to make a warmer luster. "I understand you think you can command demons."

"I think . . . I think I must try."

"Don't." The glow grew, hungry, consuming, then tried again for warmth. "You are my child, my dear child. Do you not think I want the best for you? The jinn are chained and converted. Don't you see that fighting with them might serve only to sow doubt instead of conversion in their volatile minds? It might encourage them to strain and perhaps burst from their chains."

Rayah found no answer.

"Sit, child. I will tell you a story of the desert, of the time before the coming of the Prophet, the Time of Ignorance. I will teach you that you don't want to go back."

Rayah sat. She listened. As she listened, however, she couldn't decide if the tale came from her memory of the eunuch reading from his parchment.

Or from the jinni with the face made not of clay, but of fire.

62

> Death overcomes every one of us,
> but it is better to die honored than to swallow humiliation
> or to be subject after one has owned dominion.
> —a poem of Adi ibn Zaid

The men-at-arms mustering around Hanzala ibn Thalaba and an-Numan's armor were of many tribes and greater numbers than I'd ever seen in an encampment before. The tents massed so close together that the next night, from the prisoners' picket, al-Harith and I had no trouble overhearing Hanzala and his men discussing their plans.

"So many horses need much water, much pasture." With every man allowed his say, I didn't recognize the voice of the man who said this.

Antar's replying hiss, however, was unmistakable. "We are all prepared to move further in, to the permanent watering place at Dhu Qar, as is our summer custom. The arrival of your extra animals, while welcome, makes the move all the more urgent."

"But Dhu Qar is eastward." A hint of panic eroded some of the stranger's careful control.

"So it is," Hanzala agreed. "In the direction of al-Hira. Out of the desert, almost. Toward greener pastures."

"Toward the Persians, you mean. Kinsman, you cannot know what Persians are like."

"And you, O kinsman, cannot know what summer in the desert is like."

"I, an Arab, do not know the desert?"

"Then you have forgotten," said the harelipped African. "However, for the sake of argument, tell me. What are Persians like?"

"Since the month of pilgrimage, they have moved into al-Hira in force to support Iyas ibn Qabissa, that puppet, on the throne of an-Numan."

After this speech, several other men spoke up. They described the Great King's despoliation: "Goods and flocks of the Arabs destroyed, stolen. Convents disrupted, honorable women violated."

Convents and women were things of which I wanted more knowledge. I strained at my bonds as if that would help me hear better. If anything had happened to the daughter of Zura— If my captivity had allowed anything—

Sharif Hanzala listened to every man with calm, even the return of some of his eternal humor. He asked: "And what have the other tribes to say of the matter? You are not alone among the tribes to revere al-Hira."

"The Tamim have fled into the desert," said one.

So much for my milk brothers.

"We should follow them," the first voice told Hanzala.

"The Tamim were always rank cowards," Hanzala replied with a dismissive wave of his hand.

This angered me. No cowards had raised me. But then, those who had raised me had not bothered to come to my rescue. I didn't know what to think.

"What of the sons of Taghlib?" Hanzala asked.

I leaned forward again for this answer. What of the daughter of Zura of the Taghlib?

The first voice said: "They support Iyas, the Great King's creature. They take the scraps the Persians leave them."

"They are our kinsmen."

"But without honor," the first man said.

"I say their mothers slept wrong," exclaimed someone from the midst of the crowd.

"That old kahinah speaks long epics about the sort of women the sons of Taghlib breed," said another.

"You mean the one they call Umm Taghlib?"

"The one they wanted to stone, but she escaped."

"She's here?"

The woman who'd first stung me with scorpions and then cured me? I remembered further back and slid a glance at my fellow prisoner. Al-Harith? Did he remember this woman from the spell she had cast to save his life—but to leave him half a man instead? No glimmer of recognition moved across his face. But my right arm began to tingle, remembering my broken vow, and the second vow I'd just made under this very tree. Did fear or interest boil my blood?

"She is even now among the women in our tents," someone else replied. "The Tamimi, her erstwhile protectors, left her behind in their escape."

"Or she stayed of her own will. That is a woman no man tells anything."

"Bring her here," Antar suggested. "She might have wise words to share with us at this time."

A young man from the lesser side of the ring ran into the night to follow the order. He very nearly ran into al-Harith and me in his haste.

When I had ears for the assembly once more, I heard Antar say: "I understand the Taghlib are busy refitting their battle litter."

"They prepare for war." Hanzala nodded.

"They fight at the Persians' command," someone jeered from among the company.

"They are not their own men," said another. There certainly was some fight among these tents.

"But they will have the backing of the entire Persian army to that litter," Hanzala reminded his men. "We cannot stand against such might."

"Death is better than slavery. It is better than the loss of honor we should face if this armor and the women should fall into Persian hands."

"This lot can go to the jinn for all I care," I muttered, putting on a brave face for my fellow prisoner.

Just then, we heard them returning, two sets of feet as one had gone, the young man ushering the heap of rags I knew so well. She hissed something at me as she passed. I recoiled from what sounded like "Better to have cut off a breast—"

Umm Taghlib kept herself completely shrouded not only from me, but to maintain some privacy, some integrity to herself. She stepped into the firelight and a company of all men.

"You are the one they call Umm Taghlib?" Hanzala asked.

No answer. No answer was an affirmative.

"Sit, please, lady," Antar urged. "What say you to all of this? What say you to our fight with the Persians?"

"Remember," Hanzala added, "It is battle against your own tribe of birth, for the Taghlib have thrown their lot with the empire."

They waited. The woman said nothing.

"Sit, lady," Antar repeated.

Umm Taghlib would not. But neither would she flee back into the night, to the safety of women's tents. A single hand came out of her rags. It held a dish of incense. Antar leaned forward and caught a coal on the end of a twig of dried thorn from the fire. Cupping it from the wind in one great black hand, he brought it up to her bowl with a painful tenderness; he only had to rise on his knees. Her incense began to smoke and twist in the dance of the Fire Ones.

Umm Taghlib watched the dance, never flinching if the dish grew hot in her hand. The men watched the dance. Nobody said anything for a long while.

Antar ibn Shaddad was the first to speak. "And yet—" The whistling voice spoke into a pause that seemed created especially for him. "And yet, under his armor, a Persian is just a man after all. They are no Gods. They bleed. They die. And they are not even men with honor, such as flows in the Arab blood."

"That is true," said one and then the next, around the assembly.

"Who says I cannot defeat a Persian?" the African demanded. "I, Antar ibn Shaddad, born a slave, born ugly and deformed. And yet now I am sharif of the Abs in place of my father who at first refused to own me. I would not let slavery or color or harelip defeat me. Why should I let one Persian do so? Persians willingly make themselves slaves. Why should I let three Persians defeat me, four? I have taken on enemies, two or three at once. And these were Arabs, the bravest of brave men. I should not fear to take on Persians—oh, a dozen at least, all at once."

"We cannot go and brazenly tweak the lion's tail," someone protested. They were still speaking in hushed whispers. The burning incense demanded that.

"No," Antar agreed. "But the Banu Bakr can go to Dhu Qar as they have always done at this season. We will go with you. And if the Persians come to us there, by al-Uzza, they are the ones who don't belong at our well. If they try to stop my people there, they have Antar ibn Shaddad to deal with. If they try to gain an-Numan's armor from Dhu Qar, they will have Antar to deal with. If they touch a hair of the black heads of these women behind us—Antar will personally see that they pay. Antar knows what slavery is, and therefore he knows that the Persian, for all his armor, is really the greatest slave of all."

The heap of rags gave a sudden sharp nod, a grunt, and all attention riveted back to her. Her words came in the tight couplets of revelation:

> "Fear not to go to Dhu Qar,
> O sons of the desert.
> It is your right.
> Let the Persians come
> and go as they will.
> I say to you,
> your eyes shall see it,
> the coming salvation of the Arabs."

The singsong stopped abruptly as if a cleaver had dropped on her neck. The heap of rags swung around and looked out into the desert night, directly at where I sat tied to the trunk of a tree. The kahinah knew I was there. I felt my right arm go limp at my side.

In the silence the old woman left him, I heard Hanzala ibn Thalaba say: "We will go east, and let it be as the Gods will."

So, come light, we did move, at the word of a kahinah who could see in the blackest night.

After two stages, Hanzala ibn Thalaba made his camp beside the stream of Dhu Qar. And God set the fate of many a son of woman on that day.

63

> And the stars, marching on all night in procession.
> —the Diwan of Labid

On her seat among the cushions in the room at the bend of the stairs, Rayah shifted uneasily. She felt herself jarred roughly. Then she opened her eyes and saw it was only Auntie Adilah, nudging her awake.

"Time to help serve breakfast before dawn comes and the fast begins," Auntie Adilah told her.

Although it was still dark, hoopoes called to one another from roof to roof. The gentle "Hoop, hoop, hoop" sounded very like what she'd been hearing in her dream. She blessed herself quickly against the visions of the night—

For that's what it had been. There was no secret doorway shimmering with silk at the bend in the stairs. Only, sometimes, her cousins playing pranks.

And yet—there were jinn. The coming of Islam had not put them all to rest. Ghusoon's grief was not the mere imaginings of a storyteller. She must be helped. A girl, Rayah told herself, must do the work that falls to her hands, not sit on comfortable cushions as a father might want for his spoiled daughter. Or hide in safety, as her mother might wish.

Rayah went about her work. She bore trays of yogurt, cucumbers, bread, and olives in to the men, then the special rosewater pastries that augmented the dark hours before the fast. After prayer and sunrise, she helped her aunties with the little ones, finding lost toys as she packed up the night's bedding and stored it for the day. While she did so, she wasn't really in the oasis of Tadmor, however. She lingered in the desert, the desert where the great Antar held a young Khalid ibn al-Walid captive, the Encampment where her grandmother had been stuffed in a pit to be stoned.

Rayah remembered, too, stories of the poets. They swarmed to the recitations of the Quran like bees to honeycomb. They testified how Muhammad, blessed be he, was different from themselves. For example, while walking through the streets of al-Medinah, Hassan ibn Thabit, a close personal companion of the Prophet, was beset upon by his jinni, whom he had thrown over upon hearing his first Surah. The spirit knocked him down into the dust and pummeled him until he recited what she told him to.

And then there was the other poet, whose name Rayah had forgotten, riding alone through the desert. As night fell, he saw a fire in the distance and made for it gratefully, seeking the hospitality that was the law in the wilderness.

"So you are the famous poet," his host, an old graybeard, said after they'd dined on warm camel's milk and dates in the firelight. "So, poet, recite." The same command that had come to the Prophet, blessings on him, in his cave on the mount. "Recite, then, some of this poetry that makes you great."

So the poet chose his most recent creation, brandishing it like a sword new from the forge:

> "Look!
> Crowning that stormcloud.
> Lightning!
> It flashes like a bowman's hand
> flicks arrows from his quiver."

To his surprise, he found the old man reciting along with him into his beard.

The poet stopped. "How is it that you know these verses that I myself was only just perfecting, riding along this day to the rhythm of my camel's gait?"

"Your verses?" The old man seemed close to forgetting the law of hospitality in his sudden anger. "How dare you claim them as yours? They are mine. And to prove it, I will call my daughter."

The girl came out at her father's bidding, a child of no more than ten or twelve and, on command, she recited without a single missed syllable:

> "The mountain peaks minded me of the spindle's
> whirl when the floodtide torrented down its dross
> and dumped the lot on the plain,
> as the merchant dumps his bundle of merchandise
> in the marketplace."

The same song the poet had twisted out of the wind in his empty ears, the shift of sand, his thirst, and his riding camel's heavy lope.

"Those things, too, are gifts of God," the poet mused.

"They are the work of jinn," the old man said into his beard.

"Why, she even repaired a line or two I hadn't quite made to scan right yet."

Even as the poet said it, the old man vanished. His tent, his black-eyed daughter, the fire, gone. The poet found himself alone in the empty desert with only his camel quietly chewing cud beside him. Then the poet blessed himself and knew whose guest he had been.

And hadn't there been that other poet, the woman? People didn't speak of her much. But hadn't Muhammad heard her and afterward recited verses? What had that poetess's name been? Something with an S.

Rayah couldn't remember that tale well enough to dwell on it. What she did know was whose guest she had been that night in the bright room behind the hanging silk. The man on the cushions was neither her father nor her grandfather, although it might well have been the Conqueror Khalid. It was a shaytan, the being against whom she would struggle and, from that struggle, forge her life.

She stroked the arc of acacia wood she'd taken from the battered qubbah before stashing it among her own things along with her baaras root.

The being had been a shaytan, unbound, from the other world, the world of jinn.

There was still time before she had to leave for the turpentine shop in order to answer Jaffar. She could spend an hour or two in Sitt Sameh's room.

Bint Zura leaned over the stone rim of the well and gazed down, down to where the desert's vast arc of sky was caught in such a tiny, flattening space. The water shone silvery-blue, like the silver dirhams with which the Persians sought to tame and purchase the world. Like their highly embossed shields.

Even as she looked, the surface of the water troubled.

"Oh, what are those shining sand dunes, moving?" one of her fellow novices cried.

Those three other girls were avoiding their task of drawing water. Clustered around Hind's grille, they peered outside the convent to the largest stretch of desert near al-Hira. Here, the military might of Persia gathered. Sand dunes moving. Bint Zura remembered the tales of Zarqa, prophetess of Yamamah. Zarqa had seen trees moving with her kohl-rimmed blue eyes. The tribes had not believed her and cut those eyes from her, leaving only blackened sockets.

"Those are elephants," the third novice declared. "The Padishah has sent his very elephants."

"They will never take the elephants into the desert," the first declared. "The beasts need too much water."

"They will go. They will crush the rebels just as they crushed King an-Numan the rebel's head."

"Come, Maryam." They called to Bint Zura by that other, new Goddess, mother of Isa. Maryam, that new name they'd tried to give her with a splash of wasted water. "Come and see. Elephants! You've never seen anything so monstrous."

"I am not Maryam," she murmured to herself. She who had always washed with sand and camel urine. She dropped her bucket into the water. "My mother named me Amat al-Uzza. I was born in the holy qubbah, servant of our Lady, somewhere in the open desert between Nakhlah and Mecca."

But did it serve the Goddess, her Goddess, to do as she was doing? Now that the summer heat was upon them, to take water from earth's heart and give it not to the sturdy lips of camels, but to spill it on the ground? It went to plants that truly didn't belong here without the protection of high walls and shadowy grilles. It went against the will of Her seasons.

In the desert, the camel thorn grew without the sweat of her brow. Camels knew what to do with something no other creature could fathom. Camels nibbled the shoots, chewed the cud, and brought the tangy milk home in their udders to the people of the black hair tents. The camels... az-Zuharah...

Uncle Abu Ragheb had said he would keep the white camel and the qubbah, let them lead the sons of Taghlib to battle. To keep her mother—and her mother's shaytan—from being sealed in a pillar of stone, Bint Zura must let them seal herself with water, a new name, and convent walls. As if she couldn't hear the whistle of the khamsin wind, the voice of al-Uzza. The conspiring whispers of the People of this Place, the jinn. Behind clay walls, they haunted her dreams.

Hand over hand, Bint Zura brought up the bucket. She would not join the others at the grille. That would be like puncturing a swollen water skin with a thorn. She feared she would spill all over the sand.

Above the sound of sloshing of water, she heard the great thump of battle drums strapped to either side of camel backs, the exclamations of the novices.

"Ya Maryam, you must come and see!"

Bint Zura carried the full bucket to the melons, the twining, plate-like leaves that had no business springing from such soil. Such soil grew only narrow, spiny leaves that didn't soak up such quantities of moisture. She scooped water at the roots of each plant—only so much—as the Abbess Hind, Adi's Hind, had shown her.

"Ah, see the fine horses," the novices exclaimed. "See the glint of their fine armor."

The glint of water kept Bint Zura's attention. She hauled up another bucketful. She could bridle her eyes. Her ears, however, obeyed no rein away from the novices' chatter.

"Just see. There are Medes, Persians, Armenians, all in their ranks."

"The entire great army of the empire is here, ya Maryam."

"Those are the faithful Christians, kneeling before the cross in Bishop Ahudemmeh's hand."

"There are the misbelieving magi, purifying their ranks with the fire they hold sacred."

The Arabs? Were the Arabs also there? Az-Zuharah?

"Come and see."

Then, from outside, Bint Zura heard the bellowing of camels. She listened, drinking in the song. She felt muddy water curling about her toes and realized she'd scooped more than its share on this greedy plant. She'd have to haul up yet another bucket.

At the rim of the well, she stopped. One bellow sounded above all the rest.

"Ya Maryam, you must come and look at this wonder."

The novices didn't have to describe it to her. She knew what they saw. Her own eyes could see it, even through the thick clay walls, like a mirage risen from the land of the jinn.

Bint Zura rubbed her eyes, then dropped the bucket into the well—and didn't pull it up again. She made her way to the foot of the convent stairs. She remembered how the young man, that Khalid of the Quraysh, had followed her up these stairs that night, taking them two at a time. Thinking of them as the face of a cliff rather than clay shaped by men's hands, Bint Zura climbed.

"Look," one of the novices said. Not to Maryam now, but concerning her.

"Yes, we could certainly see better up there," agreed the one who was called, at least within these walls, her sister.

"But Mother Hind wouldn't like it," advised the third.

"Mother Hind is at her prayers," considered the first, not to let her turn pass by.

Indeed Bint Zura could see from the sematron tower. Just as in her dream of the death of an-Numan. Only more. And more real. Ranks of horsemen formed of steel, like statues from head to horse's hooves. Men-at-arms, spears at the ready, stood at attention beneath ostrich plumes like the scum on a stagnant pool. Not just one elephant. Scores of them stacked one behind the other, yes, like shifting sand dunes. Just as impossible for men to resist the compulsion of their advance. Instead of a single mahout, a turret full of men—archers, slingers, lancers—atop each animal like a moving fortress.

And the battle camels . . .

Bint Zura reached out and touched the long, swinging block of wood. She remembered the noise it had made that night she'd rung the alarm, loud and deep and rich: A man, a man inside the convent.

Amid the camel troops, she picked out the sons of Taghlib, their feathered spears, the white band woven into their cloaks. She had twisted the white wool for such a weave herself often enough. There—there to the left, her uncle's—*her*—lion-skin standard caught a breeze. Somewhere there, within the dust raised by a thousand thousand massing feet, would be az-Zuharah. The qubbah, Taghlib's empty shell, would crown her sleek, white hump.

Bint Zura whistled. The white camel couldn't hear her over the thud of drums, the shouts of men, the stomp of beasts. The chanted names of Gods.

Bint Zura picked up the stick and struck the sematron. She struck it again.

Had her rhythm matched that of the war drums pounding out the empire's heart, still no one would have heard her. But it was not. It matched instead the rhythm she heard in her head, not the driving charge but the loping swing of the camel across the dunes. The rhythm of the verses jinn whispered into the ears of poets and prophets.

She heard one camel bellow above all the others again. And az-Zuharah materialized out of the dust, striding to that rhythm, her lead rope dragging where she'd broken out of Abu Ragheb's hold. Abu Ragheb had tried to control the camel, when that right belonged only to the Gods now.

In the ringing silence between beats, Bint Zura heard one of the novices ask: "Who's that sounding the sematron?"

"It isn't time for prayer."

"Look, it's Maryam."

"Oh, Mother Hind isn't going to like that."

"Maryam!"

But that wasn't her name. She was the Handmaiden of al-Uzza. She whistled, saw the camel ears twitch. She shouted the name of her camel, of the star as it rises in the evening sky—"Az-Zuharah!" Her voice choked into dust-clogged sobs on the last syllable. But she stood straight and struck the sematron.

Az-Zuharah padded to a stop beneath the tower. She reached up her white neck and bellowed. The camel's neck was long, swaying like a serpent's, but she couldn't reach halfway up the mud-brick wall, and the qubbah remained even lower.

Amat al-Uzza pounded as she remembered her red silk underdress, how it had helped in a similar situation. She pounded—out, swing, back—as she remembered that silk sitting on the scarred brow of Khalid ibn al-Walīd. She remembered she'd yet to replace it.

Swing, pound.

Although her uncle had promised.

Swing, pound.

When the battle was over.

Swing, pound.

Of the enemy's spoils.

Swing, pound.

As a thanksgiving gift to the Virgin Mother of Isa who would be their help in the coming conflict.

That made her lose the rhythm. And then another stretch back made her remember the new tattoos running down her body.

Swing, pound.

Like marks of old campfires in the sand.

Swing, pound.

Her breasts like the swell of the land.

She gave one last swing, pound, then left the sematron ringing while she stripped off her gown. This left her with only a skirt tied about her waist, reaching to just below the knee.

She tied the gown's long arms around the post holding up the palm thatch on the tower roof. She swung a leg over the railing and caught the fabric to test its strength. Then she climbed down hand over hand, as she had always climbed up and down az-Zuharah's haunches without the camel kneeling.

Some of the men-at-arms below her had stopped hearing the drums and turned to look up at the tower. They saw her now and stopped and stared. Mother Hind had appeared, up off her knees and next to the still-swinging sematron. The abbess's face showed above the wall where none had seen it since her Adi had fled in fear of his life before her father.

The abbess opened her mouth. "Maryam!" Then she shut it in silent horror. She tugged at the knot in the overdress, but the tension of her newest novice's weight worked against her. And revulsion froze her fingers. The red silk had torn, but Bint Zura didn't weigh so much. Besides, this fabric was stronger, made by her own hands, and she had only half so far to go. The only thing that tore was her veil with its cowrie shells. It tore away clean away, the leather thongs holding her braids along with it so her hair tumbled thick over her naked torso.

"Maryam!"

Her name wasn't Maryam. And neither was it Bint Zura. Not any longer.

Mother Hind opened her mouth again and said something. Amat al-Uzza couldn't hear her. What she did hear was her own mother as she had walked out into the desert alone.

"Do not ride the camel on the side of Persia. The empire must lose. The empire must fall to the hot wind of the desert."

Perhaps. But who was to say how long is the vision of a seer? The empire must fall, as sand whittled at all things. It need not be at this battle, however, or this year, or even in the next decade. Indeed, looking out over this mass of men, animals, and arms, who could believe it possible?

"The coming salvation of the Arabs," her mother had also prophesied.

"Taking down a mountain with a camel goad . . ." as the proverb said. It was necessary to begin with the first strike.

Kicking one leg free of the skirt, Amat al-Uzza reached out for az-Zuharah's back. Her foot, with its drying melon mud, got tangled in the qubbah's curtain. The camel shifted impatiently.

"Woh-ho, woh-ho, y'az-Zuharah. Hold," she commanded.

She kicked out her foot again and found where the curtain parted. She also felt unexpected heat and realized her uncle must have set a bowl of incense within the sacred enclosure as an offering to the soul of his tribe. She set her foot to one side of the incense and slid her nakedness into the litter's cocoon.

Disappointment murmured through the heat rising off the men who'd been watching her. Amat al-Uzza settled herself on the cushions, then parted the curtains in the front of the litter, hooking them back before her.

Thick incense billowed out of the qubbah, allowing a half-veiled view of the bare-breasted woman inside. It wasn't enough to be lascivious to the men-at-arms, just enough to make them sense the presence of the People of the Place and fight with that power.

A great cheer rose from every armed man's throat, borne like thunder and rain on the heavy clouds of elephants trumpeting the salute and the rolls of kettle drums.

Singing rose over the tears of emotion in the throat of al-Uzza's handmaid:

> "Is there aught good in life? Yea, I—I have seen it. I fight for it.
> And the stars, marching on all night in procession,
> Pre-eminent among them all, az-Zuharah—rise."

The white camel gave a shake of her ears, cut and tasseled for the Gods, and marched forth.

64

> If you cannot shield me from death,
> let me then dare it head on
> with what strength I have.
> —the Qasidah of Antar ibn Shaddad

All at once, dawn came. It threw back night from the sky as the women of Homs throw back the drapes: with blinding light and the clatter of wooden rings against one another and against the resonant rod.

Hanzala's women had pitched their tent on something of a rise. I sat there, on the highest spot in what was otherwise a plain flattened featureless by the periodic flooding of the Euphrates. On that summer's day, however, the river, obscured by haze, was too far away to see. A side branch poured through the space before me like silver wire drawn for chain mail across the rust-colored desert floor. A few clumps of date palms stood more gray than green under the dust.

As if they were a rising seasonal tide, however, black hair tents rose in the plain now. I had given up counting at one thousand dwellings, and I had lots of time, in the thongs of captivity, to count. The black waves spread in front, on all sides of me, set in clan groups with their guy ropes crossing. Laundry hung on the ropes, curd dried on the roofs. Dogs, goats, and children made their morning yawns in the narrow spaces between.

Only in the center of my view did real water, fringed with dry reed, grow shallow and spread to the famous watering hole of Dhu Qar. Here, throughout the previous days, camels, horses, sheep, goats, and women with their water skins waded all together up to their knees to get their share of the life-giving substance. A merciless sun held the pool at blood heat even in the depths. A herd of ibex, too, joined the tame herds at the northeast curve of the pool, unmolested by dogs or hunters as all life bound together in a harmony of need.

And it was there, to the northeast, as the hot and hazy sun rose that morning from almost the same point, I saw the first metallic glint. The peace of this place is a tale only a fool would believe, the sight told me.

"Persian scouts," said a man who stopped in front of my view to observe the same thing.

"Yes," replied his fellow. "Ours have been tailing them for a day as they've slowly made their way here."

"They will see this is just our summer encampment. They will see we have our women and families with us and will go on."

"They will not," retorted the second. And then, with a touch of prophecy: "Generations to come will call this the Day of Dhu Qar, bring with it what the Gods command."

The two men turned to greet the sharif as he came striding up, and then they hurried off to arm.

"Go in with your mother," Sharif Hanzala told a group of children at play outside in the early light.

A protest rose from the oldest boy, a lad not yet ten: "Let me fight, too."

Hanzala laid a hand on the boy's tousled head, then lifted the bundle under his other arm for the lad to see. "Do you know what this is, my son?"

Due reverence filled the young voice. "An-Numan's armor."

"That's right. I've come to give it to your mother. She will sit on this bundle, covering it with her skirts, guarding it with her honor. And you are the one who must stay behind here to guard her honor and that of your sisters. To the death, lad. Do you understand?"

The boy touched his own dagger, too big for him. His eyes wide with seriousness, brimming with tears—of fear, of pride—he didn't dare shed, he nodded earnestly. That would be, perhaps, the most honorably kept station on the plain that day.

Gone to a ten-year-old boy, and not to me.

Having delivered that charge, Hanzala stepped out into the dawn once more and called men to him. He stripped out of his heavier robes to the two simple lengths of white, unseamed cloth that he wrapped around his body like a shroud. Leaving one shoulder bare, this was the izar, such as men wear today in the pilgrimage. Arabs in those days entered battle, as it were, already dressed for the grave.

The sharif did have a belt for his dagger. He buckled a vest sewn with leather scales on under this, lashed a small spur to each bare foot with leather thongs. His untrimmed beard and lovelocks sprung out incongruously from the smooth weight of the nasaled helmet he set on his head: The Roman for whom it had been made would have worn his hair shorter and all hidden beneath the headgear's smooth weight. Most of Hanzala's men would face battle in izar alone.

Hanzala took his sword down from his wife's center pole and strapped it on his back with the hilt jutting over his left shoulder. When the time came, he could sweep it from there into his right hand with but a single, smooth movement. A long bag of camel skin held a sheaf of spears, all double-bound bamboo shafts from India tufted with feathers to teach them swift flight. His bow was not so very large, but compounded mostly of ibex horn, for the spring that material gave. The arrows he shoved into his belt on the left-hand side, where Romans and Persians wear their swords.

The great black Antar strode by, leading his black mare down toward the rising sun. In a full voice, he recited poetry, filling the air and men's souls with its stirring magic:

> *"If You cannot shield me from death,*
> *let me then dare it head on*
> *with what strength I have."*

He would continue to recite—as would every tribe's poet, even those of lesser fame—until death or peace caught up with him. His words were of as much power toward victory as any blow from his arm.

Younger boys and girls and a few old men went by now, driving the tribe's lesser herds of goats and sheep away from the water. They would take them out into the desert to browse on the khimkhim grains that luxuriated there even at this season. Bitter, unsavory fare, but offering greater safety.

Al-Harith and I watched as a man of one tribe or another caught each of the larger animals—fine war mare or dull milk camel, according to his station. He set either a saddle or a rough cloak and his knotted headband for stirrups upon it. Some few, a very few, advanced on foot, armed with tent poles alone. One by one, they proceeded down to the shallows of the stream. And, where women and ibex had watered amicably together so recently, in kindred bands of ten or twelve, the men began to cross to the far side.

Few black tents had pitched on that other, Persian bank. Although herds had been set there to graze, there were none there now, and the tents were abandoned. By this time, the glint of Persian iron on the other side was a snaking line growing out of the haze. The tent where I lay bound faced the battlefield, but that was east-northeast, into the rising sun. As my hands were tied behind my back, I could not even raise them to shield my eyes. Staring at the Persian line for long left a burn of red when I looked away. The Persians had the sun for them; Hanzala's men would be riding into its fierce glare, aiming their blows into armor's dazzle.

So much metal. Not only was each Persian well-equipped with glinting arms and armor, but scales or mail draped his horse as well, to below the knees. A headpiece went to each steed, with half-round baskets of metal over the eyes. Where would arrow or lance find any chink here? Persians even sheathed their war elephants, when they brought them to the field. At least, that's what I'd heard in the assembly. I'd always wanted to see an elephant, but this wasn't to be the day. Rumor had heard of them in al-Hira but no doubt, in the end, the Great King's generals had decided not to venture such valuable creatures. Upon Romans, perhaps, but not upon no more than a wild band of Arabs in the dry desert.

So the Persians carried their fortresses with them, fortresses of steel. Horseman shifted next to horseman. From a distance, the whole waved with fluid movement, like one great scale armor upon the plain. With the Persians were perhaps twice again as many auxiliaries of enemy Arab tribes, but that wild jumble was not what attracted the eye. They seemed no more than additional haze raised up to either side of the solid Persian hooves. Even so must the force of Hanzala appear to the Persians through the slits of their helmets. On this end of the valley stood no sight to gleam and overawe with its rigid and metallic lines.

The Persian cavalry formed up in one long rectangle three or four horses deep and stood in perfect formation as the sun rose higher. A trio broke away from them. Carrying banners that unfurled with their movement—there was no breeze—they rode up to the Arab leaders: Hanzala and Antar I recognized among the rest.

"'By Ahura-Mazda, give us an-Numan's armor,' the Persian satrap is saying."

The quiet, musing voice at my side was al-Harith's. By Hubal, I had forgotten all about him in the face of the forming battle. I had to smile, though, at his condensation of the flowery language that must be passing between the parties.

After a while, Hanzala flung an arm with fury visible all the way to our shady seat.

"By Manat, you may eat my camel's dung." With a timid but sly smile, al-Harith gave his interpretation of what Hanzala's answer must be.

The herdsman can't have been far from the truth. Disgust threatened to disrupt dignity as the Persian leaders reeled their horses' heels with a flip of iron-scale barding and purple banner. They rode back to the formation at a trot and had soon melded with it as one again.

And there they stood for an hour or more while the sun grew higher. The Persians were daring Hanzala's Arabs to batter themselves to pieces against the solid metal wall. And the Persian Arab auxiliaries were going to wait and watch it happen, too, before they swept in to pick up the leftovers.

Hanzala and his seconds understood full well what they were being tempted to. Their men—one can hardly call them rank-and-file, as a Roman might—milled in restless swarms behind them. Somehow rogue parties were kept from setting out on their own forays. That can't have been an easy task, Arabs being Arabs.

Hanzala's force also stood between the Persians and the water. No doubt the invaders had come with their own supplies. But it can't have been any easier to watch Hanzala's men wander off, when the mood suited them, to casually empty a waterskin over their heads or drive their mounts in up to their bellies. Nothing is more cooling than a wet izar.

Nothing hotter than a coat of mail under full sun.

It was Friday, the day to meet Jaffar as Rayah had planned. Another time missed from Sitt Umm Ali's class. Well, it would just have to be.

When young Jaffar called into the darkened turpentine shop, however: "Ya Kefa. Are you here?" Rayah alone stepped out from behind the cooling still.

Jaffar scuttled backward, startled, as if she were a jinni risen from the ashes.

"Where's your cousin?" he asked. "Your uncles?"

"Gone to bathe before going to the mosque for Friday prayers, of course." Rayah had slipped in, just as the last of the uncles had let down the shutters. "They won't be back for hours."

Jaffar backed to the door, ready to bolt.

"Don't worry. Now we can talk."

"I cannot marry a girl who has jeopardized her honor so," he said uncomfortably.

"Good. Because I intend to refuse your suit."

At this, Jaffar clearly didn't know which way to jump.

"Besides, I have my protector." Turning aside, Rayah let Jaffar see who sat at the small table where her uncle of accounts usually had his seat, his abacus, and his tallies.

The eunuch Abd Allah nodded to the young man but said nothing. He turned back to the parchments from which he'd been reading to her while they waited, from which he'd read again when Jaffar was gone, there among the kegs and vials of spirit. In the shop, the smell that had surrounded Rayah in hidden whiffs everywhere since her birth was so strong that it scoured the hollows around her eyes. It made her lightheaded, and she understood very well why some of her younger male cousins suffered such difficulties breathing when they first entered the shop to work. Turpentine could be a curative, as she'd learned, but she'd always have to use it with care, having learned its power. Just as with anything.

As now, with the young man's future she held before her.

And her own.

The sight of Abd Allah seemed to break the invisible shackles that had held Jaffar fast. At least, he found himself able to take a step forward instead of one back that would put him into the street.

"Your answer is 'no' to the marriage?" He seemed truly hurt by the idea, more than she'd prepared herself for. For a moment, she doubted her plan.

"You're a fine young man, Jaffar. My mother healed you with the help of the Almighty so you may lead a fine life."

Jaffar sank helplessly to the low plaster bench reserved for clients, just inside the door. She added: "Your life will be finer, however, if you don't spend it with me."

Jaffar made a sudden move from the bench then, as if forcing a virgin was the only way left to him to get what the powers crushing him left as no alternative. A glance from Abd Allah, however, was enough to teach him otherwise. The young man sank back down on his bench.

"What am I to tell Aunt Umm Ali?" he mourned.

"In order to protect your bride from the difficulties she must surely face in your household, you'll have to stand up for her even before the wedding. Consider her wishes—and yours—even more than your aunt's."

"My wishes don't matter. I can never make trouble for the family concern."

"Not even a bit? Then I can't help you." Rayah threw up her hands and wheeled toward the back of the shop, just as she would have done had she been her uncle and heard a price that insulted the very products she had to offer.

"What I want doesn't matter," Jaffar cried, the desperate buyer who knows he has no more in his wallet. "The girl I want with my own selfish desires is betrothed to another."

There. He'd admitted it. He was ready now to barter in good faith.

"To another—?" Rayah urged.

"An old sharif."

"With rotten teeth that smell, I know." How had she known? In a way beyond herself, yet a way she couldn't deny.

"Yes. Besides, she's gone mad, and I cannot have a jinn-possessed wife."

"Then you certainly don't want me," Rayah assured him. "Yes, Ghusoon is a much better match."

The name proved a conjuring trick. Jaffar stared at her as comprehension dawned on him. "You know Ghusoon?"

"I've spent several days this holy month at her bedside. She is indeed in a bad way."

"Alas, my love. I fear I'm all to blame. But what could I do? What could I do?" The young man buried his face in his hands.

"The question is not what you could have done. The question is, what are you going to do now to remedy a bad situation?"

"The jinni, God shield us, has turned Ghusoon into a girl I do not even recognize any more."

"I agree. But I think the more important part of your statement includes the notion that the jinn are with us still and powerful." Jaffar might not know it, but their bids were close now, very close. Rayah pressed on. "It is wrong to believe that they are chained—or ever could be, leaving us a pure and perfect world in the wake of a desert conquest."

"God have mercy on us helpless mortals, I fear you're right."

"God is merciful. Healing is possible. Some . . . some he presents with the power to speak to the jinn in their language and bargain them to bay."

A new twist of clarity came to Jaffar. "Your mother, Sitt Sameh. Your mother healed me. She can heal, a familiar of spirits, commanding them."

"So she is, just as her mother before her could. The problem is, people call her a kahinah and think they must kill her for it."

"By God, I wouldn't," Jaffar vowed. "If she would heal Ghusoon—"

"Another problem is, in this particular case, my mother won't do it."

"How can we change her—?" Jaffar stopped himself as he realized what Rayah's true asking price was. "But you—you can. And you will."

"Yes. I can."

No need to tell him that she'd never done a cure like this before. That would be like her uncle admitting that some impurities floated in the turpentine yet, that the still hadn't been fired or the mixture proofed. The pivot was: Rayah was willing to face fears even Sitt Sameh didn't dare.

Rayah, now, was willing to try, to act.

"But there are a few things I must ask your help in, Jaffar, to set up this exorcism first."

After Jaffar had scurried away through the Friday-empty streets so as not draw attention to himself by coming to the mosque too late, Rayah took his place on the bench. She let Abd Allah read some to her as she waited to catch her breath from the meeting. As he did, she thought she'd been a little hard on her mother.

For Sitt Sameh, it took all the courage left to her simply, finally to tell the tales, to stand as witness to what had been.

65

> **If you do not protect us, you cannot
> survive, nor live on for anything after us!**
> —the Qasidah of al-Harith ibn Hilza

Eventually, about noon, some order formed itself out of Hanzala's Arabs. And then, at a signal and no doubt a verse from the hero Antar, they expelled against the enemy wall like a heavy sigh of hot air. Like the first explosion, lightning and thunder together, of a thunderstorm, I heard the roar of attack. Battlecries, poetry, the names of Gods, none of these were distinct, and, like distant thunder, I saw the clash heartbeats before I heard it. Then dust rose to cover the sight as well.

Any order the Arabs might have had disintegrated in those first seconds after the sides made contact, before the sound reached me. Each man fought his own little war, fortunate if he had a clansman or two covering his flanks.

Did I say the Persians brought no elephants? It was true, but they might as well have. The dusty swarm of Arabs made no more impression on the Persian force than had they been gnats going against that largest of creatures' hide. If any of the Great King's men fell to well-aimed Arab spears in the center of the formation, I never saw it. The fallen man's neighbors must have shifted over him so swiftly that I never saw the seam.

"By Hubal, what the Arabs could do if they had such discipline," I couldn't help but comment.

Almost before I'd had time to say it, I began to see the first white-wrapped bodies splayed on the ground. In all that dust, they must have been numerous indeed for me to see any. Horses and camels were plainer, riderless, wandering away dazed or wounded and mad with pain. Soon it was as if the Persians were a great iron press, the blood pooling on the desert ground about them like the juice of so many grapes they'd crushed.

And that was when a feeling of black helplessness began to overwhelm me. To this day, I remember the feeling as the Day of Dhu Qar surged forward. I dream of it sometimes at night—not the events, particularly not how things looked—only the feeling. And the feeling is such that, even without sound or light, it is enough to waken me, shaking and sweaty. It is enough to make me sick to my stomach on a placid, peaceful afternoon when no one else is about.

The sun grew hotter. Dust heightened the light until it seemed as if the sun had fallen to earth and set all the valley of Dhu Qar on fire. The heat melted any lump of hope in my heart.

Had I but had a sword in my hand and a good mount beneath me, I would not have cared how many or how well armored the enemy were. I could have seen for myself and done what needed to be done, bolting like an arrow from the bow with the inbred lust for war behind me. I would not have bothered to think until either a blow from the enemy or victory stopped my activity. I should have taken Antar up on his offer to fight— But forbidden activity as I was, the anxiety burst in my mind in a thousand panic-filled notions that were madness itself.

The dust drew thicker. Closer. The sons of Bakr and their allies had broken. The iron Persian mass began to move now, bearing down, flattening the plain before it, toward the water and the tents and women beyond.

Some Arabs actually turned their backs and fled. Fleeing is at least doing something, I thought, yet even that I was denied.

Arabs splashed across the shallows. The Persians followed, pressed close by their auxiliaries who already smelled booty in the air. Here the enemy lingered, the blessing of the water too great a temptation after all those hours. The hub of the battle rotated around the water for a while. This cut the dust. I could see plainly as the Arabs harried their quarry. Heavy armor mired a number of horses in the mud. Some Persians, even only slightly wounded, fell and were unable to lift all their weight out of the water and so drowned. The watering hole bloomed rosy on the top of the stirred-up sludge.

Such an advantage could not last. When the Persian commanders saw the danger, they quickly reshaped their rigid formation beneath the purple banners. Four horsemen wide, in good order, they waded on across and up the near bank. Hanzala's Arabs vanished before them. Another three heartbeats and horses' legs, camels' legs, fleeing, pounded by the tent where I sat.

On this side of the river, tents collapsed—the life leaving them like blood-drained bodies. Persian horsemen slashed the guy ropes on the run to ease their forward progress and to trap their booty— goods, provisions, womenfolk, and children—within. There were women's screams, children's screams. I heard the war songs turn to stifled groans next door as Hanzala's harem prepared for a similar fate.

The Persians' war drums, before just part of the general din, came clearly now. My heart pounded to their driving rhythm. Pressure grew in my chest. I strained at my fetters without even realizing I strained, without even feeling the pain. My being was on the verge of splintering. It would have cracked in pieces, indeed, under the threat and the pressure of forced passivity in its face.

At the very last moment of my endurance, a young girl stepped around the curtain: Hanzala's daughter. She had naught in her hands but a lump of dusty flint such as women use in tanning. Anything sharper had been taken from their kitchen to be used as weapons by the men. At first I despaired, but women work the miraculous without utensils. They think nothing of snapping thread between fingernails, yarn between their teeth. They sever the warm, slippery cord between themselves and their newborn with a thrust of thumb between fingers. Armed with the advanced art of chipped stone, this girl set to work on our leather bands.

She freed al-Harith first. He was first, I supposed, because she realized he was not quite the man

I was. She wished to give him a start that my greater strength and agility could soon catch up with. But he stood foolishly about, humbled to numbness by his gratitude.

"Flee," was the only word she gave him.

The girl turned to me, just as the roof of the tent came billowing down on us. I heard the pole snap at my back. Working blindly, smothering with dust and wool, I pulled my bounds through the broken wood. Al-Harith stood up, giving us space for the girl to finish cutting.

I struggled to my freed feet. They were clumsy and like dead things from little use, but they carried me in one movement, shouldering wool, breathing dust, to light and air. Still al-Harith was not roused to follow me. He followed the girl instead and caught her arm just before she slipped back to help the buried women and weeping children of her harem.

"Come with us," he told her. "Flee with us to the safety of the desert."

"For Hubal's sake!"

My oath drowned out the girl's confused, apologetic, "I . . . I can't."

Like the flight of a swift bird across the open sky, the thought sped through my mind. Would to Hubal the Persians may use her with a bit more gentleness than is their wont with captives. It flew but once and then returned no more.

My body was now free to take the burden of activity from my mind, and it longed to do so.

"We will help you," al-Harith continued to protest to the girl. "I will help you leap over the boulders in our path to safety. I will fend off the enemy's blows."

I cannot believe I stood immobile to hear al-Harith begin reciting heroic poetry at a time when he might have been composing deeds of his own. And yet I am certain of what the girl's final words were because they remained throbbing in my mind in step with my fleeing footfalls.

"We have been charged with an-Numan's armor," she said. "And women do not run off."

What she meant to say, of course, was: "Women cannot run. If their men do not protect them, they are lost indeed." Only time and her concern for my fool of a herdsman made her cut it off abruptly.

Women do not run, my heart said with the half-scorn, half-pity of a superior being.

I—I felt the wonderful pound of long male strides beneath me.

Women do not run.

Then I recalled an-Numan's armor, the cause of this whole bloody day.

I stopped for a moment, looking back at the tent. I heard the words of the poem the women were reciting, one voice above all and the others joining in afterward in a lamented sort of chorus.

> "O men, we lead your horses, saying, 'You aren't
> our husbands if you do not protect us.'
> If you do not protect us, you cannot
> survive, nor live on for anything after us!
> Nothing guards women like a smiting
> that makes play-cocks of strong men's arms."

Humming filled the air. A leaden cloudburst, the pride of the Persian archery, burst on all sides of me. Their slingers were busy, too, and fist-sized stones ripped through those tent roofs still taut or sprang from them in dangerous directions. I left al-Harith to his foolish fate: Here was a man women had no use for, dallying with women.

A son of Bakr brushed my shoulder as he fell from his camel, an arrow piercing his unprotected skull. The camel was struck, too, in the hind thigh. Fear and a lust for life kept her going in spite of it. As God was my Helper, I caught the camel's saddle horn as she passed. After a wrenching jerk upon my numb arms, I threw myself into the vacated seat. Then I took off my headdress (its red made too sharp a target) and used it to whip on my inheritance.

Bravely, the camel struggled on over the dead and wounded, tents, the rubble of flight, while I clung to the horn as if I'd never ridden such a beast before. Then there was the sound of a melon stabbed. An arrow pierced her neck—which she threw flat out and forward in her haste—through the vein. She went down to her knees with a choke-curdled scream. A fountain of blood warmed my bare feet as I moved on.

So did I flee, sometimes riding, sometimes scrambling on my own. Two other mounts were vacated, taken, and then shot from under me. At some point, an arrow grazed my own shoulder, but I hardly noticed it at the time.

Across Dhu Qar's dry expanse of fine, rusty silt I continued to race. The residue of last year's run-off had baked, in the months since, to a salt-like powder. I had to wade through it like mud.

At last the air was clear: the sounds of battle left first the air and then my head. And when my head cleared, it was that sense of shame that struck me most strongly. I had not really gone back on my oath. This had not really been my battle. And yet it was. In the core of my being, in every drop of Arab blood, I felt it.

Into the clearness of my head, the final words of Hanzala's daughter entered, and I realized that they had never left me. Like my exaggerated heartbeat, they had marked time through my brain through the entire escape, even more than the Persian drums.

"Women do not run." They stand their ground, the little bit of shadow cast by their tents pitched. That soul-crushing defenselessness I had found myself unable to bear that morning, they knew every day of their lives. They are bound, not as I had been by thin strips of leather at my wrists and ankles, but by the entire nature of their flesh. And I realized it was with more than sacrificial-camel stupidity that they resigned themselves to their fates. It took active and deliberate courage to stand at the doorway of one's tent, or even crouch in the back among the rugs and pans, and face one's rape and enslavement. All the while, they sing calming lullabies to the infants whom, the very next moment, they may have to endure seeing spitted on an enemy sword. For neither war nor strategy, good or bad, were they responsible. Yet they accept the consequences of both without thought of fleeing.

Then I saw that the walls of the desert were rising around me. This was a defile, dry at this season. The thought occurred to me that fleeing up the dried bed of a river was foolish. You should flee, when you are forced to do so, into the open desert where an ever-increasing number of cut-backs offered themselves. There were only two directions you could go between the high walls of such a gorge, the stone hallway that She'ib Dhu Qar is: up to a dead end or down. And when the enemy has caught the strings at the mouth, you are enclosed indeed.

Every son of Bakr ibn Wa'il had made his escape this way. I did not know this territory, but I could see they were all fools. Exhausted, parched with thirst and footsore, I must die with them for their foolishness.

66

> I see life is a treasure waning every
> night, and what the days and time reduce
> ceases at last—by your life, death may
> spare a youth for a while, but like a
> horseman, keeps the lasso firmly in hand.
> —The Qasidah of Tarafa 'bnu'l-Abd

The wadi walls above Dhu Qar rang with eery ululations. The rolling laughter of jinn, high and piercing, at the Arabs' failure? Then I realized that in every shadow of the carved rocks, a woman crouched. With trilling tongue, she urged her menfolk not to fail. One of these daughters of Bakr stepped forward and held her waterskin up to me.

We were trapped in the She'ib Dhu Qar, Persians tying up the neck of the defile behind us. Nonetheless, I sank gratefully to a stone and let the liquid, warm but wet, flow into my parched throat, and outside as well, down my neck and to my sweat-running chest.

"How is it that you are here, O my aunt?" I asked her once speech returned to me.

"Sharif Hanzala ordered us here last night," she replied. "A good half of the women and children of the Banu Bakr."

"So not all would be lost."

"So we would be waiting here to succor the men after a morning he knew would be full of discouragement."

"You mean to tell me this was part of his strategy?"

She shrugged a pair of fine shoulders up into the string of lapis lazuli and chrysolite at her neck. As if to say she didn't even know what "strategy" meant.

"But tell me—" I insisted.

"Look at you," she said, cutting me off. "You're not a son of Bakr."

"Well, I—" What could I say? Not that I'd fought with them. That I'd run with the rest?

"Your beard is recently plucked—a prisoner! And there's scarcely a scratch on you."

Protesting, I pointed to my shoulder, to the brown blood stiffening.

"That will mend if you never look at it again," she said, not without scorn. Could she even tell the arrow had come at me from my back instead of my face?

"May I have more water, please, my aunt?"

The waterskin hung flaccid as the dugs of a grandmother camel. The daughter of Bakr clutched it protectively against her chest, refusing me. "There are many who bravely took greater wounds. They need it more."

Indeed, scores of bewildered men, blood-spattered, dragging broken spears, wandered about, called for their clansmen, for any other soul with whom to share their woe. There are not enough women to go around, I thought. I felt this acutely, more than the hunger and the thirst.

Before I could find an excuse to win more water from this woman, another crept to the edge of my vision. I turned to smile, to welcome her succor. Then she stepped from shadow to glare of sun. The fog of incense she carried instead of water cleared, and recognition pelted me.

With a cursing finger, the heap of rags pointed me out. "You, O son of al-Walīd. You, look. Look to your honor."

I tried to shrink into the rock against the far side of the wadi but failed.

Step by step, she came at me, still pointing. "You I have known since you were a child at your milk mother's breast. Look to your honor."

I stammered something incoherent. Persians would have more mercy.

Then behind me I heard: "There's that slave of a Qurayshi! Hold him!"

A pair of Antar's strong men had me in a moment. "That's it," one of them hissed so my ear was wet with hot spit. "A man breaks his word to Antar ibn Shaddād twice, he doesn't get another chance."

I actually welcomed them. They were escape from the kahinah. Antar was a man, a fighter, something I understood. It was the heap of rags I could no more get a grasp on in my mind than my hand could grasp her smoke.

"I am not finished with him." The unearthly voice came from those rags.

"Ah, lady, but we are." The man on my left ran one finger along my jugular and went for the dagger in his belt to repeat the gesture.

"Stop," the inhuman voice cried, the screech of a night owl.

And the men of Antar, hero of all the Arabs, stopped at her word.

They stared at her, silent as ibex caught in the lion's gaze. She opened her mouth—and tumbled into poetic prophecy again. Control lay not on her tongue, but in the demon twist of smoke.

> "O Ibn al-Walīd,
> forget your vow to win.
> What is winning
> if you lose honor?
> Go to the enemy's qubbah.
> Cut it low.
> The deed is in your hands.
> You promised your right arm

>   to the Lords of this Place
>   when you were a child.
>   They come now to collect.
>   You cannot turn away,
>   nor can death overtake you."

My right arm burned, and it wasn't just because my captors had gripped it tight enough to put it to sleep.

Now, in fact, the grasp on my arms loosened perceptibly. My captors touched their amulets against unearthly power, the one a cluster of stamped metal at his neck, the other a shriveled root and animal's paw.

"Well, the kahinah has said it," Paw told his fellow.

"You will cut down the qubbah of the enemy?" his companion of the jangling metal spoke directly to me. "That bane of our existence all this morning, rallying the Persians whenever we seemed to make headway?"

"The power is in your right arm?" Paw added. "Then who am I to keep that hand from ever lifting again?"

"We must take him to the sharifs in any case."

A further amulet jangle, and we were moving. Facing the Persians could mean nothing but defeat. And I remembered my vow, to die rather than ever face defeat again. But at least we were moving, away from the blur of frankincense curling like the jinn from the kahinah's bowl. My head cleared.

My captors led me through the defeated troops, around a bend in the wadi to where a stretch of flesh-colored sand pooled out between boulders. I made no resistance. The son of Thalaba and his closest retainers squatted in a circle as if in majlis, as if a welcoming fire crackled at their center.

Antar was there. The great hero had also received an arrow to the shoulder, but this was front to back. You could tell because it had not just nicked but stuck there still. Blood, sweat, and the rust running from his armor streaked his great, black body, the white scarring of previous wounds. Such are the colors women weave into their rugs. Antar sat passively, without even a quiver of his harelip, while a comrade worked to pull the new bolt out.

"Do you feel it here?" the comrade asked.

Antar gave an affirmative grunt.

"Then the arrowhead is close to the surface," the comrade said. "I shall cut in at this point and pull it through this way. The barbs will slide easier."

Antar gave another grunt. It didn't seem to matter to him which way the barbs went. He'd had them both ways.

Having first cut the fletching feathers from the shaft at front, the comrade then cut into the skin at the back. He worked with blood-slick fingers until the bolt came free.

He sniffed at the shaft once it came.

"Poison," the surgeon said grimly.

Antar said nothing, but spat out the wad of clean-smelling hyssop he'd been chewing. This he slapped on the wound himself, then packed it with camel dung from the freshest pile around. Finally he gestured with his good arm for his comrade to bind the whole with a dressing torn from his battle-stained izar. He proceeded to wash himself as best he could with sand scooped from beneath his feet. There was no water. The little grains stuck to the sweat in the swirling patterns left by his hand.

Antar was expected at a gathering of Banu Bakr sharifs. What took me completely by surprise was a man in armor that would have done a Persian proud. He came up to me and grasped me fondly by a shoulder. This was my wounded shoulder, and I flinched as if I had Antar's grief instead of sporting the mere scratch I did.

I saw the face under the conical helmet. Al-Harith?

Then I recognized the armor. The glorious hauberk of King an-Numan.

I felt lightheaded, as if I'd lost more blood than Antar. Surely the assembled sharifs must notice this. They must kill the presumptuous little herdsman first and drag the relics from him afterward before they turned to me. But they didn't. They made room for the two of us around the majlis.

"How—?" I hissed, but got no more as the fellow with the paw amulet fastened new leather bonds on me.

"Your pardon," Paw said. "Sharif Hanzala's orders."

Was it my imagination, or was the knot no tighter than the false hobble a herdsman might set on his most trusted beast? I decided not to test the bond and turned instead to scowl at al-Harith's armor once again.

Hanzala laughed out loud with more than his usual humor. "When I gave the armor to my wife to guard with her honor," he explained, "I knew we'd be hard pressed this morning, and I wouldn't be able to stop and gather the bundle from her. I knew a woman trying to flee with a bundle was bound to be stopped and despoiled before any other. And so I thought, first, that I should tell her to cut your bonds and give the bundle to one of you to run with."

Antar, applying more camel dung to his shoulder, added: "But I told him a man running with a bundle—a purple bundle at that—was even more likely to call attention to the treasure under his arm than a woman. She might at least offer the distraction of her own honor, the Gods forbid."

"I had to agree with the son of Shaddad," Hanzala laughed—at himself now. "So I thought, what sort of person could run among Persians and not call attention to himself? The answer was simple, of course. A man in Persian armor, running among others similarly clad. Sword and spears he could carry, too, without remark. Of course, this armor is finer, even, than most of those we've battered ourselves against to little effect all day. But I hoped, in the dust and confusion, that would go unnoticed."

"It did," al-Harith said.

I looked in wonder from sharif to herdsman and back again.

"The rest was simple. I merely told my daughter to free you should the flight begin and to put the treasures on the back of one of you before you scampered off. How she was to choose between you was up to her."

He didn't offer speculation as to how the girl had made her decision. I could guess. The one who showed the most concern for her, of course, and that had been al-Harith. But for my selfish wish to save my own skin, I might have learned what it felt like to wear such a wonderful hauberk and gained the admiring glance of every man in the company. I tried to console myself by thinking that I had come out alive by personal strength and cunning. Without the armor, al-Harith would not have made it away from the tents at all.

"We left very few women back in the tents, you must know," the sharif explained. "Most of them are here, or with the herds further out in the desert. We left only enough behind to lure the Persians in."

I felt a little frown between my eyes, and Hanzala must have noticed it, for he said: "You seem to be wondering, son of al-Walid, how I knew you could be trusted with the charge of the armor. You have, after all, not been Ibn Shaddad's guests but his prisoners these long days."

Hanzala gave a nod in the direction of the great black hero and said: "The son of Shaddad told us you could be trusted. And I would follow his word to wells across strange desert at the height of summer."

He turned now to the sharifs in the circle. "Come. We have fought. We have tasted the Persians' strength and it is great. Many, too many, of us have died, may their souls not thirst. What think you, my brothers? Where lies our course?"

"The way to peace lies in your hands." A revered old graybeard wrapped in his cloak, for all the heat of the day like Mount Thabira in winter mist, spoke first. Every swing of sword that morning must have made his every joint ache. "Give me the armor and King's harem and let me return to the watering hole alone. I'll surrender them to the Persians. What is it to me if they kill me, an old man like me? I shall ransom your lives, your wives and children. Into your hands, O son of Shaddad, I commit my Umm Subaih and her children. But let me go."

"By God, Abu Hanzala," Antar swore. "You shall not deliver the trust made to you by a man who is now dead and unable to defend himself."

To this speech more of the men were in agreement.

"It would be better—" The man with the stamped metal amulets gave the Arab's usual backup plan. "—To flee further into the desert. Two days' march will bring us to other wells deep in the desert to which the Persians would not dare to follow."

"Many would die on that march, many of the women and children and the weak and wounded," Antar countered. "There is no guarantee that those wells could support such a large number of people and animals in the middle of the summer. They are known to give out in drought."

"But it would be something," those of the middle ground insisted. "And then we would need to face neither the dishonor of giving up the trust nor the deadly rain of Persian arrows once again."

Surely there was no part for me in this discussion. In spite of the armor still shimmering on his unscathed back, there was no part for al-Harith, either.

But the Lord of battle, so they say, often favors the fool. Al-Harith could not control his laughter as he looked at me, with shoulder bleeding on the wrong side, torn and dusty clothes, short lovelocks, and a grimy woman's underdress for a turban. Beneath the sharif's ongoing discussion, al-Harith bent to me and murmured, "O son of al-Walid, was I never witness when you swore you would die rather than face defeat again?"

And then, by the edge of the circle, a whiff of frankincense came to my nostrils. Carrying her smoking incense, Umm Taghlib the kahinah wandered by. I averted my gaze but could not shut my ears.

"Remember, Ibn al-Walid," she whispered—or maybe it was her jinn alone who sent me the words and the tingle to my right arm. "Remember what I have said of the enemy's qubbah."

"The Battle of Dhu Qar," I retorted, anger driving my voice to more volume than was necessary just between the herdsman and me, "may yet see another and concluding encounter. Then Heaven will favor those who ran at this pass. Running is not necessarily defeat."

I spoke in miserable self-defense, never thinking to be overheard, much less what gratitude my words would strike in Hanzala ibn Thalaba.

"Blessed be you, O son of al-Walid," he said. "If you are true in what you say, you are more faithful than these sons of Bakr whom I have nurtured all my life. Those to whom I have divulged my strategy have less faith than you to whom I have not."

"Did Khalid the fight on the Arabs' side?" Rayah asked as Abd Allah packed up his parchments to leave Sitt Sameh's room. "And what of Bint Zura in the litter on az-Zuharah's back?"

"That will have to wait for tomorrow." The eunuch smiled.

Rayah bit her lip. She didn't know if there would be a tomorrow for her to learn more of what had gone before. Tomorrow, or the next day, the holy month would be over. Ghusoon, as her stepmother had threatened, would be carried out to the desert, given over to the jinn completely. And no matter what her ancestors had done, Rayah would have to go on and attempt what she had to for her own life.

Even as she thought it, on the roof outside, the male cousins let out whoops and hollers. Kefa, whom she'd asked to help her stretch goatskin over the frame she'd made of the acacia wood from the litter, tried out the drum—*her* drum—for pure joy. The women trilled their tongues in ululation. Little Bushra, livelier than ever, clapped her hands and skipped for joy in a new dress. It was shortly after sunset, and low in the purple sky westward over the ruins of Zaynab's city hung the merest thread of a new moon. The month of fasting, Ramadhan, was over. Tomorrow—tomorrow Ghusoon must go to her fate. And there were too many parchments left in Abd Allah's heap to possibly finish.

67

**By God, if I remain alive, I will slay thee as no Arab yet
was slain and send thee to thy father.**
—Antar ibn Shaddad

Squatting in the dust of She'ib Dhu Qar, the son of Thalaba proceeded to describe to the company of leaders what strategy he had in mind. "I saw the Persians advancing over the salt desert in their hoards, under their bright banners. I doubted very much, out-numbered almost two to one as we are, that we could defeat them at the first attack, while they were fresh and in the height of discipline. 'Yet give them a night of triumph,' I told myself, 'a little while in which to take their ease and think themselves invincible. Then all that discipline will vanish like a mirage.'"

"But why give them a night?" I blurted out. I had nothing to lose. "A night among your tents, with your women? The Persians have been fighting all day under that massive weight of iron. Persians are neither giants nor jinn. They aren't even men bred to the desert. I watched from your tent and I saw. O sharif, the heat, I believe, will have melted the heart of your enemy. Cut to the core and you will find only a trickle that will pour out on the desert sand and disappear."

"Will you listen to this!" Antar said to the men about him.

"Very well, hear my plan." Hanzala wiped at the sweat and grime on his face with the corner of his headdress and grinned. "I intend to lead the way out of this defile and come at the Persians from the flanks. I thought we should go by night, but if you—"

"How shall we go?" eagerly asked the man of the metal amulet.

Hanzala named a way they all knew to be a narrow and tortuous path, one that only those very familiar with the terrain could guess existed. "These tactics will bolster our cause with surprise, with the higher ground—"

"And—" I was unable to control my excitement as I saw the plan and remembered the blinding morning sun. "If you do not wait, the lowering sun will be at your backs."

"Scenting the water of the stream, our thirsty animals will gallop forward without restraint," Hanzala added.

"For the men, there will also be the sight of the women and children we left behind." The old man of the mountain warmed to the idea.

"Yes. The very thought now makes me want to cut Persian throats," the stamped metal amulet declared, and others agreed.

But some still demurred. "Those goods and dependents we have saved from this dreadful day—we will make good our departure for the inner desert with them." And they got to their feet.

Hanzala waved them down. "There is one more consideration." He exchanged glances with someone behind him. I turned and saw Nuri and another slave. Antar was in on this exchange, too, if the glitter in his eyes was not the poison fever setting in.

Having received the wordless answer he wanted from the bondsmen, Hanzala said, "I do not think you would find much profit in trying to flee further. Nuri, tell the sharifs what you have done."

My great black African stood fingering the golden hilt of a dagger against the blue-black of his naked chest. He spoke with certainty, for all the vanished nose left his language. "Uncle-master tell me cut girth of all pack camel."

"What?"

"He says he's cut the camel girths," I translated, still not understanding the whole myself.

"By the Gods—" Then men swore as the meaning dawned on them.

Some ran out to verify the damage. But most realized that their leader and my—his—slave were in earnest. Nothing could have been easier than for the black man and his partner to go through the gathering under the shadow of the wadi walls to carry out this order.

My slave had been used to cut camel girths, my herdsman to smuggle out the dead king's armor. The sons of Bakr who'd been tricked similarly grinned at their leader with respect. Such is the way of the desert. A man who can plot such a move must win respect—and a following.

Still, Hanzala had to try them. "What you sons of Bakr and of Shayban care to do now is your affair," he said. "I will lead such as want to follow me out of the defile."

Assent was unanimous.

Hanzala turned to al-Harith and me again. "But now, I want to know if this prisoner of ours, this son of Quraysh, thinks this plan may succeed."

"It is a plan as great with wisdom," I said, "as a mare about to deliver twins. But whether it will succeed against these Persians—only the Gods may decide."

My words met with pious and sober assent. Then I added, with no attempt to hide my bitterness, "But I am, as he had said, this great Cutter of Camel Girths' captive. I do not see what this battle has to do with me."

It was I who first gave Hanzala ibn Thalaba that name which he has worn proudly ever since—Mukatti'u'l-Wudhum, Cutter of Camel Girths. And yet he merely grunted at such flattery. Seeming to ignore me, he began instead to divide out commands and posts of honor for the next attack.

"Yezif ibn Shayban, the right wing. Hani, the center. I myself will take the left, for the left must be cautious not to let themselves be driven too near the cliffs of the she'ib. As we saw only too plainly this morning, Harmaz and the Persian regulars like to fight to their right. In the case of a challenge to single combat, let the Yashkori choose a man most suited among them for the honor.

"Finally," he went on, "We will need a few picked men to remain in the defile and return to the field by the same route as our flight. They will serve as cover for the women and the wounded we must leave here. They will make certain the Persians do not take this escape as we have shown them by our example. I had meant to give this command to the Banu Dhohl, but alas, it was God's will to take the best of them from us in brave battle today. Antar ibn Shaddad?"

"Be certain I will fight," the African hero said, "to the last drop of blood." He tentatively worked his wounded shoulder. "But I feel poison fever upon me and should not take a command that might require clear thinking. The qubbah rides in that sector, you know."

"Yes, the qubbah," Hanzala repeated, causing his men to shift uneasily around the circle as if the word were a jinn wind on their drying sweat. The two men with their amulets who'd retaken me looked my way.

Then the sharif made his third choice. "So, Khalid ibn al-Walid, will you lead that guard?"

In that list of great and alien names, my own was a blow to the stomach. I could find no reply.

The Cutter of Camel Girths smiled at this small triumph by ambush as if it were a good omen for the coming enterprise. "Why should you be so amazed?" he asked of me. "Do you doubt you are capable of such honor? Why the silence? Are you now so loath to be a free man?"

My throat was drier than ever and nothing came from it. I stole a glance at Antar. The harelipped warrior grinned.

"We fight the Persians," Hanzala said to his fellow sharifs. "And though Ibn Walid is the enemy of Bakr when we fight in the desert among ourselves, when we fight Persians, men of the desert will band together. I watched you carefully during the retreat today, Qurayshi. I saw what you can do when your bands are cut. By God, you are a jinni when the smell of battle is in your nostrils—only this time, I hope, your action will be to defend rather than flee."

After a general chuckle, Hanzala continued, "If, Manat willing, we should carry the day and it is still mine to give, this evening I shall give you your freedom. You will be free to return to your people with whatever booty your courage may win for you besides. If we should lose—and that may be God's will, too—it is the vast Persian Empire we fight—well, then . . ." He stopped his speech with an open gesture speaking of more generosity than even Heaven might be pleased to show.

From al-Harith, I kept getting signs that I should refuse the offer, gestures at odds with the armor he wore. Indeed, he began to take the armor off to return it to those more willing to defend it. His signals tried to remind me of the vow I had made with his witness never again to see defeat. He knew that if I said "Yes" he would have to be on the front lines with me.

The Persians have a great fondness for eunuchs, you understand.

"If we are found among the baggage cowering with the women and children, do you think our new captors would respect us for our manhood?" I demanded of him. "No, they'll have more if we make ourselves their enemies by facing personal danger."

"Can we trust these strangers to come to our aid if we're surrounded during the fight?" he whispered.

"Then we mustn't fight so as to need any help."

I suspected what al-Harith did not, that if I could not be trusted with a command, we would be found to be useless baggage. Hanzala would not even be bothered to leave us tied up. He would slash our throats as he had slashed the saddle girths. An Arab must travel light, especially when he marches to war.

"The Persian-Arabs," Hanzala reminded his men as they armed, "are led by that pretender to the throne of the sons of Lakhm, Iyas ibn Qabissa—perhaps a thousand of them. He is joined by twelve hundred Persians under Hamarz and eight hundred under Hormus-Kharrad, both Persian generals of note."

I nodded. I had heard both men talked of at al-Hira, and suddenly the leadership of the enemy mattered.

"Intelligent men of the desert on good war mares can outmaneuver discipline made clumsy by a hot day," I suggested.

The sharif answered, "They have won desert Arabs to them as well. There are about a thousand men of the desert led by Qais ibn Mas'ud."

"Isn't the son of Mas'ud a kinsman of yours?" I asked.

"Yes," Hamzala replied with a bitter sarcasm. "And, like the man of honor he is, he has sent word that he will betray the Persians the minute he sees them falter. Even lice leave a dead camel. I do not trust the mother who bore him to be an honest woman—but that will serve our turn."

"That is well," I said. "Such a company would make up for those you have lost so far in the day."

"There are other tribes with him," Hanzala went on, "Tribes with which the sons of Bakr have ancient and bitter feuds that a change of fortune cannot be expected to alter. The Iyad are there," he said, "with al-Minhal in the cavalry. I am sure you know that man's deserved fame with horses."

"Al-Minhal will not come to our side, I think," one of the sharifs said gloomily.

You plundered me of an al-Minhal filly, I wanted to accuse Hanzala, but managed to hold it back. How the fortunes of war and winning had altered my previous associations! The sharif was no doubt right. In a rather horse-like fashion, al-Minhal was not a man with enough subtlety to change loyalties within the span of an afternoon. Perhaps ever.

"I will have the honor of wearing an-Numan's armor." Hanzala picked up the hauberk al-Harith had abandoned. Its links poured like water through his hands. "It will serve as a sort of rallying standard on the field. But here is something for you, Ibn al-Walid, a sword and a mare. From a fallen kinsman of mine, the Gods rest him."

"To his tomb I promise a swift-moving she-camel in sacrifice," I said to express my gratitude. "To carry him over the sword-blade bridge and vast distances in the world to come."

I spoke before I saw the mare. Then I did, Paw having gone to lead her up. She was al-Minhal's Little One.

The irony of the desert is like its sun and shadow, stark and hard in contrasts, strong enough to crack stone. Then, another whiff of burning frankincense twisted its way into my nose. I looked around, but could not see the kahinah.

I turned and confronted Hanzala face on. "God strengthen my right arm, I will fight with you in the next foray—and we will win."

Antar's harelip stretched into a wide grin and Hanzala shoved the dead man's helmet into my hands before I'd had time to work them free of their bonds. The brains that had poured from the dying man into the helmet pan were those of the very one whose kin I had wounded earlier, who had won this horse as blood-price from me. Remnants of gray and pink flesh still stuck to the rivets, and I would have to wear it without any more padding than the red silk.

There was no water. As Antar had done with his body, I tried to do with the helmet. I scoured it with sand. I got rid of visible signs of the death. But I never did get rid of the smell.

As I worked, Antar came and sat by me. "See if I do not take the enemy's sacred litter," *I told him. Antar said:* "The Banu Taghlib will give you trouble on that front."

"The Banu Taghlib?" *My motions froze over the helmet.* "They're fighting for the Persians?"

"Of course, for the Persians."

"I saw them, too," *Hanzala concurred. His busy, nervous preparations carried him first to that side of the wadi, then to ours.* "Their great hero Abu Ragheb fights like seven men. But this is not a problem for you, ibn al-Walid, surely. Your milk family the Tamim has always had bad blood with the Taghlib."

"No, O Cutter of Camel Girths. No problem at all."

By Hubal, I thought, what am I imagining? The child of Zura who owns my interest is not beside her kinsmen near the wells of Dhu Qar today. She can't be. She is in al-Hira, safe behind a convent's walls. There the sandstorm that foolish men cause to fly may not affect the divinity in her spirit.

But there was no more time to consider the matter.

68

> I fell for her by chance as I slew her
> kin—but by your father's life, this
> was never my intent—and you've berthed,
> make no doubt of it, in the core of my
> heart, dearly beloved and honored.
> —the Qasidah of Antar ibn Shaddad

The part I played on the Day of Dhu Qar, holding the mouth of the she'ib, was but a small one, it is true. Still, I remember it before all the blur of countless others that came afterward and earned for me the title of Sword of God.

I dressed for our ride down the defile in borrowed armor. But I dressed with extreme care, as if I thought to gain surrender from the enemy by flashing good looks alone, as if I were going wooing instead of to battle. The armor had been made for a larger man and it sagged a little around my hips where I most wanted to appear trim. But I polished it, and on top of the melon-shaped helmet I wrapped the tails of my red turban. I arranged the headdress in such a manner that it was jaunty enough, yet at the same time hid my locks, still shorn to an ignominious length as a sign of my captivity.

There was no time for rest. We watched Hanzala and the main body of men set off to climb out of the defile on a trail that might have made mountain goats turn back. Then I led the men assigned to me down the churned-up sand of the she'ib.

As we began our march, I found, to my great consternation, every Bakri woman who was able set on following us. I reeled back in the line and tried to impress upon them the danger we would face. I even exaggerated it for my own self-flattery. But they paid no heed. In threes and fours they clung to ragged old mounts without their girths. The walls of the she'ib reverberated with songs of the ancient heroes we were expected to emulate. My plan for deeds of glory did not include maintaining such a harem on this day. I wanted to win a unique one, not be swarmed by a mass of the all-alike.

Unfortunately, a woman has the option to display as much stubbornness as she would toward one not her master. They waved me off with a word, "He is a stranger," pleading that their husbands did not like them to listen to other men. So keeping them quiet turned out to be all I could do, that and herding them up on the safety of the high rocks when, in the lengthening shadows, we reached the end of the defile.

One very old woman persisted in lighting a flicker of fire. I sent a pair of men up to douse it, lest its smoke be seen and give our position away. But the men came back with shrugs and wide eyes saying, "You tell her. She is not of our tribe." My eighteen years and untried leadership thought they were mocking me and I could not endure it. I marched up the hill, planning to take my frustration in the men out on this female.

But when I got close enough to see the shadow of an ancient hand molten with bracelets and charms pass over the flame, the skin on my back tingled and shrank.

"Remember, O son of al-Walid," the heap of rags warned.

"Fire is sacred to the Persians," I told my men when I returned to them. "If they see it, they will fall down and worship it, not take it as a sign of our presence."

A group of thirty or so Persians were there to meet us at the bottom of the defile. One, with drooping mustache and tooled leather gaiters, who seemed to be the leader, gave a shout to his men. In armor, he seemed twice my size and my heart constricted. I wished myself a prisoner, safe once more.

Then the man wheeled his horse. I saw how clumsily it turned, as if its feet were made of lead. This gave me plenty of time to poise my spear. Responding to no more than the tension in my legs as I prepared to throw, Little One firmed up beneath me. My opponent raised his own spear, but the sky seemed to be heavy metal weighing on him. I threw my weapon before his leveled.

The force behind my throw knocked the man from his mount with a loud crash. And suddenly there were screams all around, men, horses—it was hard to tell one from the other. Dust rose nostril high, choking. I threw another spear, brought other limbs flailing heavenward, and then saw that every man of mine was engaged and doing well. I gave them a yell of encouragement.

One of the Persians I'd hit was back on his feet and looming large over the naked back of one of the unhorsed Bakri. I urged Little One at the enemy and caught him by what I thought was the knot of his long hair at the top of his head. The knot, it turned out, was formed of metal and merely painted black. I couldn't sink my fingers in it like hair. The entire helmet slipped up in my hands.

The helmet slid over the Persian's eyes, blinding him. Still he was able to dance out of harm's way, swinging his sword at the fetlocks of a passing Persian horse. That horse whirled up and then over, crushing his rider. But the Persian whose helmet I had in my hand had spun around, sword flashing, sightless but still dangerous. I leapt free of Little One and told her to stay, where she'd be out of harm's way. Then I yanked the helmet off altogether, blinding the man with desert sunlight instead of metal, and went in for the kill.

The instant before my dagger found his throat I had a quelling vision of his face. He was sickly pale beneath a wash of sweat. His skin felt corpse-cool to the touch. His eyes went wide—I saw the shadow of my red turban in them. The blood, when it spurted, seemed as sluggish as his movements.

The core of the Persian force was just as I had told the sharifs. It had melted away here at the edge of the desert.

This was the beginning of the lifelong fulfillment of my vow never to taste defeat. And yet—

The Persians were gone. Except their auxiliaries still came, and these were Arabs. They stepped up to fill the vacancy and soon clear superiority no longer stood with us.

Then the rumor ran through the dust of the valley: "The Taghlib have brought their qubbah to the field. The sacred battle howdah."

In the heat of the battle, Bakri hearts grew cold at this intelligence.

"Hubal protect us, hasn't the thing been in retirement for years?" I heard one man ask his fellow. He had stopped to catch his breath, coughed though his throat was spitless, and touched the feathers and amulets at the end of his spear. "It didn't lead them the last time we skirmished with the sons of Taghlib."

"Yes, since their Sharif Zura became demon-possessed."

They fell silent as we saw it: first, a ragged lion-skin banner. Then a bone-white camel rose from her knees and lifted her God-like burden high above the dust and rubble of the field. My own heart stopped. If this was the effect on us, the enemy, what must its effect be on the sons of Taghlib?

Black tufts of ostrich feathers decorated its sturdy frame. Its sway set the gold and silver amulets, witness to the offered faith of twenty times twenty generations, to chiming in the breeze. Jinn, it seemed, drifted through the haze in a dark shadow about the camel and its burden.

The qubbah bore the very spirit of their tribe, that great force that shadowed a Taghlibi from the cradle to the grave. Should it fall in battle, well then, a son of Taghlib could hardly bear to maintain breath within his lungs. How he would fight!

"Do you think there's someone—do you think there's a woman in it?" al-Harith asked beside me. He had to spit in the middle of the question, to clear his throat of thirst and dust, yes. But against the evil, too.

"I don't know," I said.

Little One, impatient for more action, snorted at me to take her abandoned reins. I did and swung up into the saddle. I felt as impatient as she was, exhilarated by how right I had been about the outcome of the battle, by the killing I'd done with such ease. I gave the men a sign to follow. The auxiliaries had turned to face the threat of Hanzala's men at the flank and rear. The sharif's kinsman Qais ibn Mas'ud had betrayed the empire with all his men. We would miss this action if we didn't hurry.

Little One set off toward the blur at a trot. We passed heaps of metal on our way. Sometimes these heaps moaned to show that what was left of men still lived beneath them. Mostly, they were silent, however, and the shadows—vultures or closing twilight?—slipped silently over us toward them.

We drew closer. On the Day of Dhu Qar, I saw, the men of Taghlib did not have to imagine the spirit of their tribe there riding with them. Even at a distance and through the trelliswork of feathers, we could see that there was something alive within. The pick of Taghlibi youth, battle-worn and disheartened before, now rallied to the standard to defend that spirit inside. That was far more precious than their own. Even a handful of Persian regulars who had fallen back to join what was left of their forces broke their iron discipline to let the qubbah pass.

Like a specter of another world, the white camel and her shadow-black burden made their way to the front lines. Swords went limp in the hands of the sons of Bakr behind me and to the sides. As a man, they drew back from the apparition. And on the rocks behind me, the daughters of Bakr fell silent at the sight of one of their own sex become divine.

I pulled up on my reins.

"By God, we are lost," al-Harith said as he drew beside me. Only a whisper escaped the constriction in his throat.

I was inclined to agree with him. But then I heard a strange, eery song rise from the old women on the cliffs behind me. I remembered my vow—and other things.

"No, by God, I shall never lose," I replied. "God may will that I shall die, but I will hamstring that Taghlibi camel and bring the qubbah crashing to the ground."

With divine compulsion, I pressed my mare with my thighs to urge her forward. "And you, O keeper of my foster father's herds, you will follow and cover me."

Al-Harith whined, al-Harith protested, al-Harith prayed and pleaded. But al-Harith followed in the dust of my charge. Curse the moment that he did.

"O chosen sons of Bakr!" I heard Hanzala call a rally on my left. I could not turn to look at him, nor could I see the multitude that answered him, but I heard the gratitude and relief in his voice. There was in it, too, a chord of self-congratulations for having had the foresight to entrust me with freedom and a sword. "Fight for your wives and children".

And so they did. The Bakri archers and slingers all trained their missiles now at the enemy that stood between me and the qubbah. Cavalry and lancers raced to block any aid the Banu Iyad tried to throw in the direction of the sacred litter. Masses of Bakri foot soldiers could afford no better weapon than a good solid stick if they were fortunate, the inexhaustible supply of desert stones if they were not. They wielded these. On the rocks behind me, the daughters of Bakr remembered the blood in themselves and in their children. They made themselves useful as only women can, with songs, yells, prayers.

"O sons of Bakr," I heard them shout between trilled ululations. "My fine fingers are as soft as sand grubs, my waist like chamois, my thighs like moist papyrus. Thrust your spears, and thrust again, harder. Ah. Ah. Ah. And tonight, when the stars are tethered as with ropes of flax to the peaks of Yathbuli, your shaft may rush to tansy-scented loins, the victor's prize. Ah. Ah. Ah."

And one in particular waved her hand over smoking incense and worked magic in a high, shrill voice.

Persians and their allies fell before me like barley before the scythe. Until the Day of Dhu Qar, I had broken legs but never killed a man. Now I lost count of the number—their blood blooming like anemones in springtime at the touch of my sword. My mare's fine, thick tail blew backward across her flanks in the wind and covered my thighs. I wore no other wrap to protect the gleam of my armor against the heavy rain of other men's blood. It drenched me, seeped in between the links to my skin.

As the Banu Bakr aimed their arrows with ever-greater accuracy toward the litter, I sensed the living thing within growing uneasy. Part of her was not divine. Indeed, one wild arrow had already found its way through the feather-tufted framework. It passed harmlessly out at the other side, as if indeed there were nothing but spirit within. That spirit responded by parting the veiling around her to get a better view of what was before her. Her action gave me, not three ranks of suicidal defenders from my goal, an equally moving sight.

And then it became all too clear why I was so madly drawn toward that litter as toward the destiny of my life. I pulled on Little One's reins. I pulled up hard and screamed as if I'd been dealt a death blow.

Within the Taghlibi's qubbah rode none other than the daughter of Zura. I saw her there, framed by the fluff of black ostrich plumes.

As I did, I became convinced, as she herself was convinced, that riding in her tribe's sacred ark toward victory was the place where she belonged. Only the apostasy of her kin to another God had made her seek a divine carriage elsewhere, among the unrequiting stones of a nunnery.

Within the qubbah, the daughter of Zura had stripped her garments to the waist. I saw her neck and shoulders, supple and white. Her breasts were cupped high and delicately traced with blue-black tattooing. Her only veil was her hair, which she had unbound until it lay thick across her knees. But most fascinating of all I beheld that part of her body in which she was different from all other women—her blue eyes. I saw them lit and transfigured before me.

Did she recognize me as I recognized her? I doubt it.

She was not thinking of Christian festivals in al-Hira just then. Her spirit was open and the jinni had entered; she was possessed as she had been created to be. She yelled to her followers, piercing and otherworldly.

To those watching me—and that was most of the battlefield—my next actions must have caused wonder, totally beyond all explanation. From the straight and deadly path I'd been beating toward the sacred white camel, I suddenly veered. Leaving my back completely exposed to the litter's escort, I— Well, I didn't exactly join the enemy, but there is no doubt that I began very carefully and tenderly to herd the qubbah out of harm's way. My shield left its place before my face and rose instead to deflect any injury to that which floated above the earth in a cloud of ostrich feathers.

Sometimes it seems to me that there was time for all heaven and earth to pass away while I rode thus, protecting the litter, suspending all action about me by sheer amazement. But in the midst of battle, nothing is so amazing that it can dumbfound for more than just a moment or two. If many of the great ones paused to wonder at my actions, there was a single fool who did not. May God char his bones in hell! That fool of a herdsman's son thought I was standing thus to clear the path to the white camel's haunches for his own sword.

"O son of al-Walid, it is done!" I heard his shout of glee. "I am al-Harith the son of Suwaid, and I have brought low the white camel of Taghlib!" He knew the triumph formula well, although he had never before dreamed of using it in his life. The Lord of battle, indeed, loves the fool.

Even as he spoke, and I turned to see, the camel went down with a scream, pitching backward onto her hacked and bleeding hind legs. She threw the rider from her hump. As if in some sort of vicious nightmare—for even true life is rarely so unjust—I saw her, my beloved, fall. She crashed through the feather framework, holding out her smooth, white, naked arms and try to break her fall. I heard her scream, suddenly very human, childlike almost, pained and very afraid.

"Bint Zura!" I called the only name I knew to give her.

I tried to turn my horse, but there was no room in the press of fighting men. I thrashed madly at anything nearby that could feel the vengeance of my sword. Little One gave a squeal. I thought at first it was of fear. Too late I realized it was of recognition—and then horror. My sword had cut down and through.

A nightmare of a face looked up at me, full of reproach for all that it was split in two as neatly as a melon. I have killed, I thought, chuckling madly as at a joke. I have killed my good friend and generous host. I have killed the master of the Arabian horse. Al-Minhal's butchered face stared up at me in the final wonderment of his death. Once he had offered his body between me and harm. But I had no time to suffer that guilt.

"Bint Zura!" I called again.

But she had passed from my view beneath a sudden surge of battle as Taghlib fled and Bakr conquered. As she left, vision passed from me altogether. I was conscious only of a heaviness on my left side. I assumed my heart was breaking.

69

> O al-Uzza! Remove your veil and tuck up your sleeves.
> Summon up all your strength and deal Khalid an
> unmistakable blow
> For unless you kill him this very day,
> You shall be doomed to ignominy and shame.
>> —what Dubayyah the priest of Nakhlah said when
>> he saw Khalid ibn al-Walīd approaching the shrine
>> according to the Hadith of al-Anazi Abu Ali, told
>> him by Ali ibn al-Sabbah told him by Abu'l-Mundhir
>> told him by his father on the authority of Abu Salih,
>> as told him by Ibn Abbas

In the morning, thanksgiving prayers took place at the mosque that was once a church and, before that, a temple. Rayah knotted the faded red silk around her waist and touched the protective lapis lazuli hand over the harem door on her way out.

After that, the family of the turpentine sellers joined much of the community in a celebration of Eid. They paraded out of the mud brick walls of town. Groups of friends set up their rugs and unpacked heavy baskets of food, the men clustered around the great spring called simply "The Source," the women beside "Ladies' Spring," at the edge and under the terebinth orchards. The trees were deliciously fragrant, like the men after a day of making turpentine. The trees' small brown berries filled the day's special cakes so that each mouthful, each breath glowed with a resinous sweetness.

Bright scraps of cloth draped the lowest branches of the largest, oldest tree, the one no one claimed and harvested turpentine from. Women added more cloths as they arrived, and the rags drifted gently in the breeze. The way heat waves rise from the cities of the jinn, Rayah thought as they shifted before her mind. The way Sitt Sameh's tales from the Time of Ignorance had begun to have more reality than the present celebration.

"This in memory of the dead," one woman intoned as she hung her cloth.

Rayah saw it was Ghusoon's stepmother. The sight of her brought a lurch to Rayah's heart, more so the fact that Ghusoon herself did not appear at her side. Did that pale blue cloth the woman offered represent the departed soul? Rayah didn't dare ask. But in a little, she would have to leave to discover for herself. Just not yet, not to draw attention to her going.

Before she could go, Sitt Umm Ali arrived with her entourage at the Ladies' Spring, making a grand entrance jiggling on a donkey. Petitioners crowded about her, kissing her hem. She pushed them aside with a jangle of bracelets and confronted Rayah instead. "My nephew says there may be no marriage," she fumed.

"It will be as God wills," Rayah found tongue to murmur.

"You, orphan of no declared parentage, you would dare refuse him?"

"Sitt, I am only the poor creature of God. I am as He made me."

And, even as she was powerless to fault such an answer, Sitt Umm Ali had to find something else to criticize in Rayah's place. "Believing women shouldn't hang offerings from trees," she announced. "They are emblems left from the Jahiliyya. Didn't Khalid Abu Sulayman the Conqueror chop down the trees in Nakhlah, for the very same reason, the misbelief of the Arabs?"

"I don't know that tale, Sitt Umm Ali," Rayah dared to speak up. "Tell it, please."

Sitt Umm Ali narrowed her eyes and glared at Rayah. Nakhlah, Rayah remembered from Sitt Sameh's tales, was the shrine where her great-grandmother had dug up the images her husband had discarded. Where she had crept into the sacred qubbah when her pains came upon her, riding on her way to Mecca. Clearly, Sitt Sameh hadn't told all there was to tell about the past, not by half. But Rayah declined to flinch, either from this knowledge or from Sitt Umm Ali's scrutiny as the older woman tried to find a way to refuse the girl who dared refuse her family.

"Oh, yes, please, Sitt, tell us," other women took up the chorus as they led Sitt Umm Ali to the softest cushions and plied her with the coolest drinks.

"There were three palms in Nakhlah," Sitt Umm Ali began, "which the people in their ignorance worshipped as signs of a demon Goddess.

"'Go and destroy Nakhlah,' the Prophet—blessings on him—told his greatest general Abu Sulayman, 'so the ignorance may cease.'

"The Conqueror went, but something made him hesitate where he had never hesitated to wield the sword of God before. He chopped down only one of the trees and returned.

"'It is done,' said Abu Sulayman.

"'What did you see?' asked the blessed Messenger of God.

"'Nothing out of the ordinary.'

"'Then go back and destroy the place properly.'

"Khalid returned on the desert way and chopped down the second tree with his divine sword. Then he returned.

"'And what did you see, O Abu Sulayman?' asked the Apostle of God, may his name always be honored.

"'Again, nothing, O God's Prophet.'

"'Then go back and do it right.'

"So the Conqueror returned and once again drew his sword. Now, the priest who stood guardian to the place came out and tried to stop him. 'Two trees have you destroyed,' begged the evil fool. 'From but one tree, I can cut slips and grow other trees. Leave us at least this one.'

"The Conqueror, however, had God Almighty in his right hand and the words of God's Messenger in his ear, and so he cut down first the man, then the tree.

"'What, O Khalid, did you see?'

"'A black smoke, thick, choking of sulfur and the pit.'

"'Seek refuge with the Most Merciful,' replied the Prophet, blessings on him. 'Now, now, O Khalid, you have done well.'"

Rayah felt too much good food burning in her belly. Khalid ibn al-Walīd. The man who called Sitt Sameh his daughter. Whom she refused to see and whom they called the Conqueror but who had been conquered in his turn, leaving only a eunuch to tell his story.

"So what is Nakhlah now, Sitt?" Rayah asked.

"Nothing. It is gone to desert, as such evil deserves."

Nakhlah, the Place of Palms. Her own source. Was it possible? It was dried up so?

Rayah looked at the blue cloth billowing from the terebinth here in Tadmor—Palmyra, another place named for the trees. She, for one, could not begrudge even Ghusoon's cruel stepmother that comfort.

"So, Rayah," Sitt Umm Ali interrupted such thoughts. "Recite for us the Surah of the Unbelievers."

Rayah swallowed and, for a moment, thought she'd never heard of such a thing as a Surah. Then "'In the Name of God, the Compassionate, the Merciful,'" she began.

A shadow drifted overhead. She looked up and saw a hawk flying in very low. She could see each feather in its wing, and it took her breath away.

"Ya Rayah."

"'Say: O unbelievers!'"

A vulture flying north to south and low like that was an omen.

"'I worship not that which you worship.'"

It meant a change.

"'And you do not worship that which I worship.'"

Or a discovery.

"'I shall never worship that which you worship.'"

But how Sitt Umm Ali would disapprove of such soothsaying!

"'Neither will you worship that which I worship.'"

Muhammad, blessed be he, was the Seal of the Prophets, and he had revealed:

"'To you be your religion; to me—'"

To me, what? There was only one thing to do.

"Excuse me."

Rayah got up from the spread blankets. Taking a bag that had still not been opened among the baskets and bundles of food, she moved off, leaving the women to gossip about her. When she was beyond their hearing, she circled the largest terebinth tree until she picked Ghusoon's stepmother's sandal prints out of all the rest. These she followed until she was certain they had come not from town but from the desert. At that point, Rayah dropped her own veil so its end covered her tracks; no one else must use the same means to come looking for her.

70

> Such a camel steers me to an-Numan, a man
> excelling men near and far for charity.
> No one, even among the folk, can equal
> his deeds of virtue toward men, except
> Sulayman to whom the holy spirit said:
> "Rule man and restrain him from evil,
> subdue the jinn that I let rear Tadmor
> with slabs of stone and marble columns."
> —the Qasidah of an-Nabigha Dhubyani

A little farther into the desert, a man's prints ran parallel with the stepmother's. Rayah observed where man and wife had parted: Ghusoon's father going on alone to celebrate with the rest of Palmyra's males, Sherif Diya'l-Din among them. The double trail was easier to follow, and Rayah quickened her pace.

Over the next rise grew a clump of oleander, and out of it stepped Jaffar. He caught up Rayah's bag from her shoulder and urged her to hurry.

"God forbid, Ghusoon may already be dead," he exclaimed. "They may already have killed her."

They didn't have too far to go, and their haste made it pass quickly. They saw the vultures first, the stiff-winged shadows slipping like water over the ground that now barely held a footprint on mostly gravel. Rayah looked up, then looked quickly down again. The sun was too high and powerful to see the birds against the sky; they must remain shadows. She felt her own thirst, panted, then pushed on to keep up with Jaffar's never-flagging strides.

Over a rise, they saw a trio of hyenas. The creatures started, fur raised over heavy shoulders. Rayah saw Jaffar's hand go to his dagger, and she was glad for that. One hyena countered with a growl, but then all ran off, laughing wildly as if they were jinn-possessed.

The next sight to catch the eye in the monotony opening southward to all Arabia was one lone palm tree.

"There." Jaffar started to run.

When she caught up to him, Jaffar had already cut his beloved loose from the base of the tree and was dribbling water from a small skin into her parched and parted lips.

Rayah knelt and reached behind the girl's head to help hold it up. The instant she touched her, Rayah felt it. She recognized the feeling—from Bushra, from her cousin with the wasp-stung face. She recognized it, but she would never grow easy with it. Wonder and fear accompanied the movement—like setting her hand on an auntie's pregnant belly. Otherwise, the only way Rayah could describe it was thus: As if virtue suddenly drained from her like pus from a painful wound, healing both to her and to the one she helped.

Ghusoon's eyes fluttered open. She gave a weak smile. Jaffar beamed and exclaimed: "Ah, my love. You're alive!"

That flicker of life, however, was all the jinni needed to return with vengeance to the body it had abandoned when it had seemed dead. Ghusoon's eyes flew wide with terror as every other limb fled her control. The Fire Spirit was no longer content just to weight her joints with dullness. Ghusoon went rigid. The line from Rayah's hand at the nape of the sufferer's neck to where her heels kicked dents in the gravel snapped stiff as an iron blade.

Jaffar drew back, clutching the water skin to him until fluid gurgled from the unstopped mouth, unnoticed.

Rayah spoke to him sternly. "You see what we're up against? This isn't just a poet's love and joy forever after. Are you certain you want me to try this? Or should we just leave her as we found her, as the poet leaves the abandoned campsite of his beloved and moves on, alone?"

The jinni found his tongue of flame and answered first. He flung back his captive's head and howled. Ghusoon herself surely never had lungs like that. Were any more hyenas creeping up on the scene, this must have sent them scurrying. Something more dreadful than the lion had entered the desert.

Even though she was holding the girl, fused skin to skin, Rayah had not been prepared for the scream. She jumped and continued to tremble as the other body went lax, then began jerking uncontrollably.

Rayah worked to break the seal that had grown between her flesh and the other girl's. She had been wrong, full of pride, just like Khalid the Conqueror on the Day of Dhu Qar. Such pride rarely led to the victory it promised and, when it did, victory came at a price, unforeseen and far beyond what one had bargained for. Rayah realized now that she was too afraid. She hadn't the price demanded of a healer, so much of herself to give to another. She had to flee, too, like a hyena with her tail between her legs.

A second scream lashed her hands to the girl's skull more strongly, however. And Jaffar joined in the sound: a long, low moan beneath what sounded more bestial than human coming from Ghusoon's cracked lips. "O God, save her. Rayah, I beg you. Bring my Ghusoon back to me."

Rayah swallowed with difficulty, her throat drier with fear than from the sun. "And you will take her as your wife if I do?" She hung on, as someone might to a crumbling clay wall, having slipped from the roof.

"Yes," Jaffar sobbed.

"You promise to cherish her, even knowing this is in her past?"

"Oh, yes."

"Not knowing what like trouble the future may hold, putting it only in God's hands?"

Jaffar nodded. "O my love, I am so sorry. I am so sorry I wasn't man enough to stand up to them for you. I am so sorry I let you be promised to that hateful old man to bring you to this."

"Very well." The effort to hang on made Rayah gasp. "You brought kindling, as I asked? Get us a fire going. I need a fire."

Here she was, a girl giving such orders to a boy. How dare she? But Jaffar didn't hesitate to obey.

As soon as he had the first sparks popping in dry camel thorn, Rayah found at last she could free her hands from Ghusoon's head. Quickly, she set her chopped and dried baaras root smoldering in a clay bowl. The bite of the earthy smell reached her nose on the back of the smoke jinni curling upward. As she cupped her hands around the simple censor, she thought of other hands, the gnarled, broken hands of her great-grandmother burning frankincense, stalking the young Conqueror in She'ib Dhu Qar. Even so must Umm Taghlib have held it. Even so must she have waved the twisted jinni to fill the air.

As your hands mold to the bowl, let my hands mold to yours, Rayah thought. And, indeed, it seemed other hands moved within hers, gnarled, dry, broken hands, tattooed blue-black . . .

Except their purposes were different. And there was another presence between them. Hovering just at the edge, waiting, was the man Umm Taghlib had conjured to great deeds at that first defeat of an empire before the desert Arabs.

"Ah!" Ghusoon screamed again, writhing. "The smell of his teeth. The sharif."

Rayah waved the smoking root one more time, then set it down. Reaching into her bag, she brought out the last thing in it: the drum. She swept her hand in a caress around the bent acacia, hearing the first whisper of the instrument like the whisper of wind through the long-dead tree. Wood was so rare in the desert that it was used and reused. Once this wood had sailed on the back of a white camel at the head of an army. Now, it went to something smaller—

Rayah warmed the skin over the fire, testing until it grew tight enough to strike just the right note.

And then it spoke, deep-throated, reverberating, smoky: "I am here. I am everywhere. You cannot escape. Do not even try."

Ghusoon screamed and thrashed. "I smell the smell. Sharif Diya'l-Din. He's here."

Ghusoon gave the demon the name she knew. To one side, Jaffar knelt, reciting prayers, but Rayah hardly spared notice for him.

She smelled the smell, too, but to her, it was not so much of rotting teeth but the fires of a great conflagration, the sulfur of brackish water seeping deep in the desert. She knew the presence had another name, but she didn't speak it aloud. To do so was to give it more strength.

The jinni had no such fear. "What have I to do with you, blue-eyed one? Kahinah, witch?"

The rhythm of his words, coming deep out of Ghusoon's thin lips, was overwhelming. So much so that Rayah's hand moved over the tightened drum skin, wanting to drum to that beat. It was the same rhythm she heard when she imagined Persians moving into battle at Dhu Qar.

With all her strength, she resisted the taunt.

Except she could see him now as she stared at the smoke, the man who'd sat on cushions at the turn of the stairs. The rhythm of blinding features under a red turban.

No. She wore the red silk now, as had a woman in the beginning.

Rayah grasped Ghusoon's hand, fighting for the courage not to look away, not to scream herself. Rayah sensed the pulse of the other girl's life. She realized, weak though it was, it still beat at odds with the jinni's taunt. For a moment, it faltered, then came back differently, sucked up into the controlling force's timing.

"No," Rayah cried. As hard as she could, she thumped out the faint, remembered beat.

"Blue eyes . . . blue eyes . . ."

"No." She thumped harder. Rayah longed to take up Ghusoon's hand again to see if the body remembered as she did, but she didn't dare stop, not for a moment.

"Blue eyes, what have I to do with you?"

"What have *I* to do with *you*? You've invaded our harem, slipped under the door on sheets of parchment, just as you've invaded every other spot on earth."

Rayah felt her veil creep lower with the effort of her drumming. Jaffar would see— Should she stop for a moment, reach up?

"No—" she sang.

"Blue eyes—"

Rayah could hardly feel the skin over bent acacia wood anymore. Below the ache in her wrist, her hand had grown numb with the effort— *Thump-thump, thump-thump*. Ghusoon's pulse and no other.

"Back," she sang. "Back whence you came."

"Blue eyes."

Rayah threw her head. The veil slipped further.

"Blue eyes."

"Yes, I have blue eyes. They are a sign of my power. Yes, I am a kahinah, the daughter of a kahinah, the daughter of those who rode bare-breasted in the desert. I cover myself to protect this power from you. But though you do not look at me, I am still here."

"Witch."

"Yes, yes, I am. You may force me at swordpoint to surrender to you, blaspheme myself when I dip my hand in the water of submission. Cover me so when you look, the world is pure in your image. But I say to you, it is not, nor shall it ever be."

"Kahinah."

"Yes, what have I to do with you, adversary, shaytan, but that your constant presence makes me strong. I am strong in my protected places. In the harem. And at the wells. Without me, still, you die of thirst."

The face below the red turban exploded like lightning on dry camel thorn.

"Listen to me, shaytan," she cried. "I wear the red silk now, as in the beginning—"

Except it was sleight-of-hand, a lie. Like baaras root, Rayah felt herself consumed, her limbs hamstrung like those of the white camel az-Zuharah on the field of Dhu Qar. And black overwhelmed her.

The eunuch's great strong arms carried her up the last few steps to the third floor. The brilliant sunshine on which she'd closed her eyes had given way to twilight. As Sitt Sameh held back the curtain, Abd Allah carried her in and set her down gently on bolsters and rugs.

Incense burned in the little room, not baaras root, something else, sweet and cloying. Against the wall, Sitt Sameh had uncovered her figurines.

"I seek refuge—" Rayah began, and then she was too weak, too calm.

Blue eyes in nets of desert wrinkles searched her keenly, felt her forehead, felt for her pulse.

"How is she?" Abd Allah asked.

"She'll be fine," Sitt Sameh assured him. "She should just rest here with me tonight."

Rayah struggled against the encroaching calmness that wanted to take her to oblivion again. "But I have failed. With Ghusoon I have failed."

"I don't know how you can say that, Little Blue Eyes," the eunuch said in his strange, reedy voice.

Sitt Sameh offered her cool lemon water, but Rayah pushed it aside enough to say: "But I left her, possessed in the desert—"

"And I came upon you under that palm tree just as young Jaffar was trying to pry the drum out of your insensible hands and the girl was struggling to revive you."

"Oh." Rayah welcomed the cool liquid in her throat as she listened to the eunuch's tale.

"'The boy took advantage of your daughter, left alone in the desert,' I told Ghusoon's parents. 'The honored sharif, I think, will want nothing to do with such damaged goods. You'll have to make the boy marry her.'"

"And they agreed?"

"They seemed quite agreeable, yes, once they saw their daughter was herself again." Abd Allah had the ghost of a smile on his lips.

Sitt Sameh shook her head, making the hoop in her nose swing. The hardness in her voice could only be possible in the protection of the harem, not outside where everyone put on a good face. "I doubt that boy will ever really be able to perform such a feat."

Rayah knew the eunuch was conscious of his own state as he shifted on the rug before speaking. "Perhaps the young people don't care. And so it won't matter, as long as he's able to keep the jinn away."

Sitt Sameh shrugged and nodded. She turned to trim the lamp and give the incense a poke.

Abd Allah turned to his parchments and shuffled them. "So, what, my ladies? One more page before bed?"

Rayah started suddenly to her elbows, the seeping calm evaporated. "No, please no."

Sitt Sameh was at her side, offering another drink. "Everyone has a shaytan, child. And you faced yours today. To say you don't have one is to be no better than they are, who claim only purity for themselves."

"You think—you think I should hear this?"

"I think you must. If you fall off a camel, they used to tell us, you must immediately get back on."

"It will make you strong," the eunuch said.

And she believed him.

71

بسم الله الرحيم

In the Name of God, the Compassionate, the Merciful:
They ask you concerning
Things taken as spoils of war.
Say: "Such spoils are
At the disposal of God."
—The Holy Quran, Surah 8

The Prophet, blessed be he, was heard to say: "God is great, God is great! Dhu Qar is the first time that the Arabs got the upper hand of the Persians."

The eunuch Abd Allah read once again from his master's parchments. Around them, night cooled and darkened the town of blue-eyed Zayneb, which fell into its first sleep uninterrupted by the fast in a month.

Dhu Qar was, of course, more than a few years before Muhammad, blessings on him, began his preaching in Mecca. But if the Day touched no one else with faithful thoughts, it did inspire me. The Persians were not just an invincible mountain you had to furtively skirt with your caravan.

I remember the day I shared this inspiration with the Messenger of God, may peace in the life-to-come be his. I remember he smiled and nodded.

I, personally, did not hear any of the sons of Bakr calling the Prophet's name that day. But perhaps it was indeed as is now commonly reported, that they did shout for him whom they had neither seen nor heard of: "Generous Prophet Muhammad, help us."

I do know for a fact that Muhammad, blessed be he, did say: "It is through me that God helped them."

And the next time Arabs met Persians with such success, I was there, too. Only that time, Muhammad's name was on every tongue. By then, Dhu Qar was behind me. I had no doubt it could be done—men of the desert could indeed defeat the Persians with the help of Heaven. And a good, hot sun . . .

Abd Allah's spit finally gave out.

"Was the Conqueror's heart broken on the Day of Dhu Qar?" Rayah had to ask.

"Broken hearts are only for poets," Sitt Sameh declared, although whether with scorn for poets or because she refused the Conqueror the right to such a name, Rayah couldn't tell. "An arrow had found its way in at the gap in his too-big armor, under his left arm. It very nearly found its way out again beneath his collarbone. Abu Ragheb was the author of that shot, vengeance for what the son of al-Walīd had done to his qubbah and to his niece. All those Bakri women who had followed Khalid down the she'ib—they dragged him unconscious from the field and mourned him as dead for the greater part of a week."

Sitt Sameh's fingers had left the spinning of her goat hair. She found instead the ruined pieces of the qubbah—and noticed the arc of missing acacia wood. Then she fished the drum out of Rayah's sack. She looked from girl to qubbah and back again. But she said nothing.

"But he didn't die." Rayah knew she was pressing on the subject of Khalid ibn al-Walīd only because learning about what happened to the woman who'd ridden in the qubbah filled her with more dread. "He went on to submit to God and become the great Conqueror for Islam."

"So he did."

"But then did he tell a lie? Did he try to break into this harem under false pretenses? Is it not true, as he said, that he, God give him rest, was your father, Sitt?"

Now the broken qubbah frame seemed to burn the older woman's fingers. She moved the pieces back to her lap and cradled them there.

Abd Allah found his voice instead and, as if to lend Sitt Sameh a hand, picked up his parchment.

When I gained sense enough to hear human speech again, al-Harith was by my side. He sought to cheer me with these words: "We are free men and as soon as you are well enough to travel, the Gods willing, we may return to the Banu Tamim—loaded with booty. What booty? you ask."

I had not asked, but he told me anyway: "Why, Hanzala ibn Thalaba, our gracious host" (no longer our captor) "has laden us with fourteen mares, fifteen coats of Persian mail, helmets, swords, and rings and broaches from a score of Persian dandies. And to you, O ibn al-Walīd, Hanzala has given Layla bint al-Minhal, beautiful as night, to be your slave. Because you cracked her father's skull—so."

My body surged with pain at his word "so," but he, unfeeling, persisted.

"We may count ourselves most favored for this. Persians do not bring their women into battle with them very often, so there weren't a lot of slaves to be had among the spoils. And do you remember old Umm Taghlib from when we were boys? Probably not, but they say she found me one day, lost in the desert . . . Anyway, she is here, too. She will return with us. It's the most curious thing. Do you remember how they used to say she worked magic all the time to recall her daughter to her? Well, now it seems she has."

"Bint Zura?" I managed to gasp. I had said no other words for a fortnight.

"She in the litter, yes. Hanzala gave her to me. Because it was I who hamstrung the camel. I have taken her to wife. Really, she is a difficult woman and too self-willed to be much of a wife, blue-eyed besides. But such is fortune, praise al-Uzza. She is a rag compared to your Layla, but what can one do when he has no brideprice? One must be satisfied with the spoils of war."

Blessed be God who caused me to faint away again.

One night, during my healing, Bint Zura left her mother's bedside, came and crouched beside Layla, and put an arm about the other girl's shoulders. Layla was weeping because I'd been "beastly" to her again and refused her too-sweet attentions. Bint Zura murmured gently until the other girl sought for her hand, pressed it in gratitude, and tried to dry her eyes and her nose on the sleeve of her dress. Even so affected, I found Layla's features lusterless, lacking in inspiration.

The fire itself, on the other hand, seemed to covet Bint Zura's face. It drew her features to its heart like so much dry kindling, set it ablaze, leaping, and played with limitless joy upon her nose and cheeks and chin. Would that I, jinn-like, could turn to fire, too.

Only then she went away.

Whenever my strength allowed, I called al-Harith to me and tried to barter. My slave for his. His slave for forty camels. Fifty and a mare. Four mares and my sword.

I should have known better than to try and bargain with such a man, who had no more feeling for things of the soul, it seemed to me, than a dry clod of dirt. Perhaps if I'd started my bidding with two camels, he would have taken me seriously. As it was, he could only think that fever and delirium had robbed me of all sense of value, and he would not take dishonorable advantage of a sick man.

Besides, he had tasted the marriage bed with his prize already by now. I preferred delirium to acceptance of the fact, but he did retire to her same bundle of blankets by the chill of night. What the women under the red kerchiefs in al-Hira had failed to do, Bint Zura had done with her magic. How could I bid against that?

And so we returned from our captivity in triumph, loaded with booty, by slow stages because of my wound, to the summer wells of the Banu Yarbu.

"Layla bint al-Minhal, famous throughout the desert for her beauty!" my milk brother Malik said, even his young sharif's pride unable to cover his admiration. "And without a brideprice, too, by al-Uzza. Think of the great horsemen sons she will bear."

"You may take her as your own," I said wearily. "I give her to you as a gift."

The most honored man in the desert is he who walks into the men's tent in tatters. No mount behind him, he is given the seat of honor and the eye of the sacrifice because it is said of him, "Once he was very rich and, in his generosity, he gave it all away." I had no such aspirations in making this gift. I wasn't even trying to be polite.

Malik protested: "I meant no covetousness by my remarks. Don't you know that my very wives are yours if you but ask?"

"Brother," I protested in my turn, "you will be doing me a favor if you unburden me of her, for I am thoroughly tired of Bint al-Minhal."

So it went until the only compromise was to let God's own chance decide the issue. A pair of horses would be raced the distance of four arrow shots and he whose horse won would take the girl. I was very confident of one of the mares I'd been given as booty from Dhu Qar: She could beat anything of Malik's. I therefore suggested the prize should be the simple honor of winning and that the loser be obliged to husband the girl. When Malik insisted we remain within the usual form, there was a to-and-fro as each one tried to outdo the other in the wretchedness of his nag.

The two horses we finally posted were the most ignoble creatures that ever felt a rope about their necks, of lineages so tattered one hardly bothered to mention the dam. Still, I do believe that if I had not paid Nuri, who rode for me, a gold coin to stumble at the turn, I might yet have brought al-Minhal's high-breasted daughter to Mecca with me. Malik did not wish to lose quite as much as I did and remained above bribery.

As she followed my milk brother to his tent, I was certain Layla would call me "beastly" or start to cry again. But she did not. She seemed somehow to be beyond that now. She only stared at me with shallow eyes that allowed no penetration to the thought within. Then she turned without a word into her new home.

72

> **O Believers! . . . As to the month of Ramadhan in which the Quran was sent down to be man's guidance . . . God wishes you ease . . . and that you fulfill the number of days, and that you glorify God for his guidance, and that you be thankful.**
> —The Holy Quran, Surah 2:185

In the lamplight dancing on the walls of the third-floor room, Rayah watched her two companions. Abd Allah held his usual place next to Sitt Sameh, the two like a pair of old cronies as if several lifetimes of secrets lay between them.

Rayah now had secrets of her own. While she was watching the shuffle of parchments, however, Sitt Sameh had helped herself to a rummage through the bag Abd Allah had carried back from the desert along with the girl. A grunt from the woman made Rayah turn in her direction. In her hand, she held what was left of the baaras tuber as if never, in all the generations of which they'd been speaking, such a thing had taken root in the world before. Then Sitt Sameh peered up, cold blue eye to blue eye, at her daughter.

"Where did you get this?" Sitt Sameh asked.

"I found it," Rayah replied.

"By yourself?"

"By the will of God." And the hearing of a stray dog.

Sitt Sameh raised a brow.

"Things—led me to it," Rayah tried again. "Out in the terebinth grove." Then her tongue got away from her. "Where you could have been, if you'd not been hiding up here."

"Child, you do not know the half of it. You do not know how dangerous—" Sitt Sameh stopped herself and remained silent for a long time, her brow furrowed in what looked like fury.

In the end, Rayah decided she had to brave that fury and speak up herself. "It's the herb Bint Zura used to heal her father of his possession. The herb they call baaras. At least—I think it is."

"You think?"

"No. I'm quite certain."

"Because you used it on the possessed girl?" The blue eyes still held her, as if warning her that the wrong herbs can be deadly.

Rayah amended her words to a simple, "Certain."

"I cannot say that casting the demon out of her father Zura had the best of results for my mother—may the rains fall gently upon her cairn," Sitt Sameh mused.

"No, but this one will—inshallah."

"Ghusoon's case will take more than a dirty root."

"And more than the love of a kind young man, yes, I know that."

After a moment, Sitt Sameh set the root down and brushed its dirt off her hand. "I heard little Bushra running and shouting downstairs with the best of them today."

"Yes." Rayah shifted with impatience to have her subject switched like that. "Thank God, she seems quite healed."

"That was your touch, Rayah."

"It was God, praises to Him."

"The girl was dead, Rayah, and you touched her."

Rayah looked away. "I would do better if you left your room and came with me."

"The root, your touch, the Power of God, if you will." Sitt Sameh shrugged. "Child, you must understand. I saved the boy Jaffar's life. But I cannot say he will ever father a child, after what he's been through." Sitt Sameh exchanged a look with Abd Allah. "He may be very like al-Harith of the Conqueror's stories."

"Who took my grandmother captive on the Day of Dhu Qar."

"That's right."

"That cannot be all bad. I mean—look. Here we are, come from that time that seemed so ruinous."

"Some day, Rayah, the lack of a child may grieve Ghusoon so that she may call jinn to her again in order to bear the pain."

"Then, maybe, I shall have to find another cure. At the moment, I simply saved her from Sharif Diya al-Din of the bad breath and the jinn. Mother, don't you think so?"

With a sigh, Sitt Sameh shared another glance with the eunuch as if to say, "Such is the straitened world your Conqueror has left us." Then suddenly, the blue eyes brimmed with tears. It was as if she couldn't look at Rayah any more.

Trying to think what she might have said, Rayah finally decided it might have been that word, "Mother." Although she'd admitted the relationship, she'd never used the title before in direct address. And now it seemed the woman she wanted to give that name was rejecting it.

Sitt Sameh turned fully to Abd Allah instead, his bundle of parchments, the sword, red silk, and broken camel litter he had brought with him from Homs. She said: "What Khalid ibn al-Walīd Abu Sulayman—my father—what he thinks he lost when he conquered the world—"

So they were related. The Conqueror was not Rayah's father, but her grandfather. But suddenly, fatherhood no longer mattered very much. Rayah began desperately: "He thinks he won everything, by the will of God. How could it be otherwise?"

"And yet, it is otherwise." Sitt Sameh wiped her nose and eyes on her sleeve. Then, with the suddenness of a blow, the blue steel of her eyes met Rayah's once more. "His loss has been my gain. It has given me a daughter."

Sitt Sameh opened her arms and Rayah found herself folded in them. Worse, she found herself crying like the baby she'd never allowed herself to be. Only, it wasn't worse. It felt very, very good. As did the childless Abd Allah's hand upon her head.

Presently, when she could, Rayah found voice to say: "Sitt Umm Ali told me a story of Khalid ibn al-Walid, blessings on him."

"Did she now?" asked Sitt Sameh, laughing through her tears and in the midst of her caress.

"She said he destroyed the shrine at Nakhlah, where my grandmother was born. Turned it to desert. Is that so?"

Rayah could tell that, over her head, the two adults had exchanged yet another look.

"Well, yes, Rayah," Adb Allah said. "That is another story the Conqueror had me write down on his parchments."

"Another story to save for another time." Sitt Sameh picked up the goat hair she had been twisting and now knotted its length, blowing upon each as she made it. She added this, too, to the pharmacopeia.

The jinn are always with us, Rayah thought, purify them as Muhammad, precious blessings on him, may have tried.

Outside Sitt Sameh's western window, the new moon for the Eid hung low in a soft purple veil of sky. And beside it, twinkling like a jinn-blue ember—the star of al-Uzza.

Suggestions for Further Reading

I can't begin to list all the sources I have consulted for this work during the thirty years it was my passion. I content myself with listing those that the reader may find the most useful—and only those in English.

Let's begin with the Quran. I own and consulted six different English "Interpretations." Three to begin with may be the Arberry, which many consider to give best the flavor of the original; the Everyman-Rodwell; and the Abdullah Yusuf Ali. In some cases, when quoting, I made choices and translations of my own.

For biographies of the Prophet, you may consider:

Karen Armstrong, *Muhammad: A Biography of the Prophet*

Martin Lings, *Muhammad: His Life Based on the Earliest Sources*

Maxime Rodinson, *Muhammad*

F. E. Peters, *Muhammad and the Origins of Islam*

Betty Kelen, *Muhammad: The Messenger of God*

W. Montgomery Watt, *Muhammad at Mecca, Muhammad at Medina,* and *Muhammad, Prophet and Statesman*

Then there are biographies of Khalid ibn al-Walīd himself. The best of these, *The Sword of God: Khalid bin Waleed*, by the Pakistani general Syed Ameer Ahmed, is now available online, complete with sketches of the battles. Two others are *Khalid bin Walid: The General of Islam* by Major S. K. Malik and *Khalid bin Walid: The Sword of Allah* by Fazl Ahmad.

Of the great number of Arabic historians who've dealt with this matter, one of the ninth Christian century, Jarir al-Tabari, is available in a multivolume set in readable English translation from the State University of New York Press. I also quote the hadith transmitted by A'ishah about her marriage from the 1979 English translation by Dr. Muhammad Muhsin Khan. Permission has been sought from Kazi Publications.

More than anything else, my love for pre-Islamic poetry spurred this work. There simply isn't enough of it to satisfy me, but there are translations and discussions by Christopher Nouryeh, which I quote, and Charles James Lyall, whose translations date to the nineteenth century. Desmond O'Grady's *The Golden Odes of Love* is perhaps the most poetical, modern translation. A slim but very interesting tome is *Religious Trends in Pre-Islamic Arabic Poetry* by Hafiz Ghulam Mustafa. Please note that I have given the proper poets' names with the verses that begin each chapter, but when I have used them in the body of the story, the credit went where the plot demanded.

Besides the time I spent living on the edge of the Arabian desert, which I consider the most formative of my life, modern anthropological studies and earlier travelers to these places helped me to create the world. They make wonderful reading, too, including:

Alois Musil, *The Manners and Customs of the Rwala Bedouin* and *Arabia Deserta*

Carl R. Raswan, *Drinkers of the Wind*

Sir Richard F. Burton, *Personal Narrative of a Pilgrimage to al-Madinah and Meccah*

Lady Anne Blunt, *A Pilgrimage to Nejd*

H. R. P. Dickson, *The Arab of the Desert*

Travels in Arabia Deserta by Charles M. Doughty gave me my description of Meda'in Salih, among other details.

I constantly consulted the articles in the *Encyclopedia of Islam* including those on Khalid b. al-Walid, Tamim, Taghlib, Banu Bakr, Malik and Mutammim b. Nuwayra, Dhu Kar, Kuraish, Lakhmids . . . Well, the list goes on and on.

J. Spencer Trimingham's *Christianity among the Arabs in Pre-Islamic Times* might also be of interest.

I welcome visits to my website annchamberlin.com and my blog at goodreads.com/author/show/180762.Ann_Chamberlin and comments to my email annchamberlin@annchamberlin.com. I am happy to participate in book club meetings.